Another Man's Treasure

S.W. Hubbard

ISBN-13: 978-0-9884055-1-6

For Lily and Noah

ACKNOWLEDGMENTS

No good book is written alone. The following people have earned my deepest gratitude: my fellow authors, Mike Cooper, Hallie Ephron, Pamela Hegarty, and Roberta Isleib for all their love and criticism; Pamela Ahearn for her support and feedback; and Ann Hubbard for her eagle-eyed copy-editing.

Double thanks to Roberta for her boundless cheerleading. Ultimate thanks to Kevin, my husband and personal patron of the arts, without whose love and support no writing would be possible.

Chapter 1

I've done it countless times. Still, this moment makes me feel like I'm pulling the white satin ribbon off a Tiffany's box. I insert the key in the last of three locks and take a final breath of crisp October air. Then I push the door open and inhale.

Dust, overlaid with weak-bladdered kitty. Top notes of sour milk. Undertones of cheap cigar and fried sausage. Eau de Old, Number One.

Oh well.

I've been running estate sales for ten years, so the scent of a house pretty much tells me what I'll find inside. In this case, nothing great. But the sale must go on.

"Ah, shit. That's nasty." Tyshaun, pushing past me, twists his face. Jill, lugging supplies, is right on our heels.

"It's fine," Jill says. "You don't know true nasty."

"Hey, I been places smell a lot worse than *this*," Tyshaun shoots back.

What kind of ridiculous boast is that? I head down the hall to put some space between me and my assistants. The two of them have been squabbling all day. Ever since I hired Tyshaun two months ago, Jill, who's been with me for almost a year, never misses an opportunity to lord her seniority over him. And for Tyshaun, one-upmanship comes as automatically as blinking.

He shrugs off his sweatshirt and flexes his dark, muscular arms. "I'm just sayin', we ain't gonna find anything good here, that's all."

Too true. The furnishings in Agnes Szabo's house are just what my nose told me to expect: beaten down carpeting; lumpy upholstered furniture that wasn't attractive even when new; framed pictures of Jesus, John Kennedy, and four dogs playing poker.

The house, although small, looked fairly ship-shape from the outside. On the front stoop I'd been hoping I might open the door and inhale Eau de Old, Number Two --lemon oil, Windex, Clorox and lavender. Those are the old ladies with bathrooms so clean you could perform brain surgery in the tub. In a Number Two house I might find a Wedgewood service for twelve without a single chip, four hundred Hummel figurines, classic chrome Osterizers that still work. Nice money in a Number Two-- not extravagant, but nice.

But a house doesn't have to smell good to yield treasures. Eau de Old, Number Three proves that: piss, unwashed socks, spilled whiskey, puke. The smell of I-don't-give- a-damn. The smell of I-gave- up- long -ago. Newspapers piled to the ceiling and bulging cans ready to spurt botulism. Those are the houses where you might find anything, from a newly hatched Dodo to the manuscript for *Gone with the Wind, Part II*. If they ever find Jimmy Hoffa, it'll be in a Number Three

I scored my biggest coup in a Number Three. A ten by seven inch watercolor by the American Abstract Expressionist Lee Krasner that I sold to a European collector for $750,000, fifteen percent of which came back to me. My reward for noticing that the only decorative item in the whole house was this little painting hanging over the recliner where an old man sat drinking away the last thirty years of his life.

But Agnes Szabo's house isn't a Two or a Three. It's definitely a One. The most common type of old person's house, filled with the unremarkable possessions of an unremarkable life. I'll make enough to cover my time, plus Tyshaun's and Jill's, but nothing more.

"Let's get to work," I say. "Jill, you take the upstairs. Tyshaun, start in the kitchen. I'll do the basement."

Immediately Tysahun looks suspicious, trying to calculate why the kitchen might be the least desirable assignment. The year he spent in Rahway State Prison on a breaking and entering charge has left him keenly attuned to any sign he's being disrespected.

"How long this old lady been dead?" he asks. "I'm not opening the fridge if there's stuff two months gone in there."

"We're just doing the inventory today," Jill jumps in to answer for me. She tosses her head for added authority, although the gesture is pointless as she's recently buzzed off her long black hair in favor of a post-punk crew cut. When she speaks, the studs in her tongue flash. "Tomorrow we clean. Wear your rubber gloves."

Tyshaun attempts his fierce "you're not the boss of me" glower, but Jill, unintimidated, hands him an inventory list and stomps upstairs. Her Doc Martens raise little tumbleweeds of cat hair on the treads.

I watch her go, then give Tyshaun a "whattya gonna do" shrug. The two of them make me feel like some zany sitcom mom, caring but kick-ass. Not that I'm old enough to be their mother—I only have about ten years on them. And not that I know squat about mothering, having never been on the receiving end of any. At least, none that I remember.

"Mrs. Szabo died a week ago Tuesday," I tell Tyshaun. "The executor wants the estate sale wrapped up this weekend. There won't be a lot of relatives crying and arguing and pulling stuff out of the sale on this job."

"You need rich people for that." Tyshaun looks around the cluttered livingroom. "Ain't nobody want this shit."

"Hey, what's our motto?"

"I know, I know—One man's trash is another man's treasure." Tyshaun slouches toward the kitchen, his jeans drooping below his skinny butt, striped boxers on display. "What're them bowls I'm supposed to look out for?" he calls over his shoulder.

"Fiestaware." I'm crazy pleased that he remembered. I hired Tyshaun for heavy lifting, but unlike the laborers I've had before him, he seems to be taking a genuine interest in the estate sale business. I'm not sure why that matters to me, except that I like being right. When I hired Ty, the howl from my friends, and especially my father, was loud and long. *He'll rip you off...Don't play at being Mother Teresa.* And from dear old dad, always handy with a statistic, *The recidivism rate among convicted felons is 82%.* Ty didn't beg for the job. He didn't want pity. Just a chance to work. All he said was, "I seen some things in prison I don't ever want to see again." What can I say? I believed him. People defy statistics.

Besides, it's not like prime candidates for the job are thick on the ground. Must speak English, must have driver's license, must be able to lift 300 pounds. Can't be allergic to dust, mold or cat hair. Must be willing to work for ten bucks an hour. My applicant pool was Tyshaun and a trembling six-foot-six hulk who assured me he only had trouble following directions when he was off his meds. I hired Ty, and so far, no regrets.

I pause on the threshold of the basement stairs, cooled by mushroom-y subterranean currents. There'll be mice down there, thousand-leggers too. Maybe a garter snake. I should send my staff to the basement, but I prefer the far corners of a house. Bedrooms are too personal. Old age is laid out for you there, in all it's un-glory. Heart medicine, rosary beads, Depends, cents-off coupons, and always, always, a framed photo of a younger self, waist cinched in, hair stiffly curled. I can't help thinking what I'll leave behind fifty years from now when someone comes to clear the remains of my life. Lots of books, lots of dog fur, no family photos whatsoever.

I head down, wielding my flashlight beam like a sword. Skittering sounds indicate wildlife on the move. Not to worry—everything sounds tiny. I prefer not to encounter your larger mammals. Never met a raccoon that didn't have serious anger management issues.

My flashlight beam finds a bench full of tools. So, there is something of value down here after all. I pick up a hammer with a wooden handle smooth as silk from years of use. The tools are old but in perfect condition, everything hanging from hooks or laid out in shallow drawers. Labeled cubbyholes hold carefully sorted bolts and screws and nails. The faded printing is as flawlessly proportioned as typescript. You don't have to be a handwriting analyst to know that Mr. Szabo, long dead, was meticulous, precise, committed to a job well done. He lingers here.

Maybe Mrs. Szabo kept the toolbench like this so she could come down and be near her husband. Or maybe I'm—what's that shrink term?—projecting. As a child I used to crawl into the deep storage closet in the downstairs hall and sit among the boxed holiday decorations using my finger to trace my mother's dramatic, flourishy script. *Tree lights. Window Candles. Centerpiece. Ornaments.* Her presence pulsed in that closet, there among the things she had selected and cared for. Everywhere else in the house she had gradually faded away. Or been cleared away.

Overhead, I hear Tyshaun banging around the kitchen, cabinet doors slamming, drawers rattling as he inventories a lifetime of dented muffin tins and well-scoured frying pans. Maybe a cow creamer or a copper Jell-o mold for the collectibles crowd. Time for me to get to work too. I pull out a clipboard and note the significant tools, then head across the room to check out some lawn furniture.

"Shit! What's up with that?" Tyshaun's voice comes down through the heating vent as clearly as if he were standing beside me. I lose interest in the chaise lounges. What did Tyshaun find? A bundle of twenties in the cookie jar, a diamond ring in the toaster oven? Mrs. Szabo's nephew, the executor of her estate, was supposed to go through the house to check for money and items of sentimental value, but he didn't seem all that interested in his aunt's home. He probably doesn't realize how old people squirrel things away. A knot of tension starts churning this morning's bagel and coffee. If Tyshaun found a wad of cash, will he tell me? Jill is so hyper-scrupulous she won't take aspirin from a client's medicine chest if she gets a headache while we're working. Will Tyshaun be overwhelmed by the temptation of some easy money? This is a test. I realize I'm holding my breath because I really, really want him to pass.

The door to the basement opens. "Yo, Audrey. C'mere. This is wack."

I exhale and trot upstairs. Tyshaun waits for me in the avocado green and harvest gold kitchen. "You know what this is?" He shakes a baggie in front of my face.

I glance at the bright pink pills bouncing inside, each imprinted with a little flower. "E. Ecstasy."

Ty's eyes blink rapidly. He's always amazed when I display knowledge of anything illicit, as if thirty-three year old white women like me live in some sort of Amish bubble.

He drops the pills on the counter. "I don't want no part of this."

A big grin spreads across my face. This is the street equivalent of a sizable wad of cash. Tyshaun passed the test with flying colors. Then my smile fades as I study the hundreds of tabs in this Zip-Loc. "Agnes Szabo was eighty-seven. What would she be doing with club drugs?"

Tyshaun looks at me like I'm a Midwestern tourist trying to navigate the A train. This is the Audrey he wants to believe I am. "Someone using this as a stash house. Maybe her nephew got a little side bizness goin'."

"He's a lawyer. I really don't see him dealing drugs. Where did you find them?"

Tyshaun points to an open drawer. "Right there, next to the egg beater thing."

I stare into the drawer as if the potato masher and spatulas are going to offer some explanation. In the ten years I've been running estate sales I've found guns and porn and tons of prescription drugs hidden away, but this is a first. I reach for my cell phone. "Guess I better call the police."

Tyshaun's hand grips my wrist. His wiry strength always surprises me. "You just askin' for trouble. Best pretend we never saw it. I bet next time we come, it be gone."

"No, that's not right. I have to—"

Above us, a short sharp shriek. Then a thunderous crash shakes the walls. The wagon-wheel ceiling light swings. A china pig tips off a shelf and shatters on the floor.

Jill.

I race for the stairs. "Jill? Jill, are you okay?"

Even with one hand holding up those goofy pants, Tyshaun overtakes me, scaling three steps at a time. A cloud of grayish dust billows from a bedroom into the upstairs hall. Coughing and squinting we make our way into the room, following the sound of Jill's low moans.

She lays spread-eagle on a sagging double bed, in a nest of plaster chunks and splintered lathing. A small trunk pins one leg to the bed. A rotten beam dangles from a five foot wide hole in the ceiling. Her eyes flutter open, two dark holes in her ghastly dust-coated face. At least she's conscious.

"Don't move," I say. "Your neck, your back...we've gotta call an ambulance."

Jill sneezes, then rotates her neck experimentally. "I think I'm okay."

"What happened?" I peer through the hole in the ceiling to see the dusty rafters of the attic far above us.

"I poked my head up into the attic and the only thing up there was that little trunk." Jill points to a rotting leather box down by her legs. "I crossed over to get it and the next thing you know, I fell through the floor. I'm sorry, Audrey."

"Not your fault that termites have been eating up the beams."

Jill tries to squirm into a sitting position. "Ow-- Could you get that box off my leg?"

Tyshaun springs forward and picks up the trunk. As he lifts it, one rotting leather handle rips away, and the trunk tips open.

A shower of gold, diamonds and pearls rains down on Jill.

Tyshaun grabs the trunk from the bottom and sets it on the floor. The three of us gather around and look inside.

"Geez, it's like a buried treasure chest," Jill says.

We forget Jill's trauma as we stare at the tangle of jewelry.

"Why'd she live in this shitty house if she had all that up in the attic?" Tyshaun asks.

Getting down on my knees, I sift through the jewelry. "I've seen it before—rich old people to living like they're poor."

My fingers trace a gaudy garnet and topaz bracelet big enough to encircle a gorilla's wrist and a delicate strand of opals that would barely fit a child. Two men's watches, a strand of pearls, an ornate brooch, some gold door-knocker earrings: Even without a jewelers loupe I can see that much of it is average or low quality. Still, there's too much of value to put out in the general sale. I'll have to get it appraised.

I sit back on my heels. Drugs in the kitchen, jewels in the attic—Mrs. Szabo's house is turning out to be far from the standard Number One. I reach for my cell phone to call my client, Cal Tremaine, when something in the trunk catches my eye.

A ring, pearl and ruby set in a twist of yellow gold.

I pick it up and stare. The ring was designed to twine around a slender finger like a delicate flowering vine. Very unusual. Very familiar.

Jill and Tyshaun and the hole in the ceiling recede to the distance. The entire world rests in my palm.

The ring was made for a hand I know I once held. A hand whose touch I can't recall. A hand that took this ring to the bottom of a cold, cold lake.

Or so I've been told.

Chapter 2

"Audrey? What is it?"

"Yo, Audge—should I sweep this up or what?"

"What should we do with the trunk? "

Their questions bring me back into Agnes Szabo's bedroom. I take a deep breath and start barking out orders. "Sweep up this mess. Make sure all the jewelry goes back in the trunk. Then bring it down and load it in my car." I have my phone pressed to my ear as I listen to the recorded voice of Mrs. Szabo's nephew. "Mr. Tremaine, this is Audrey Nealon. Please call me at your earliest convenience. We've encountered a problem at your aunt's house."

Then I head downstairs with the little ring folded in my fist. I sink into the lumpy depths of the sofa and study the ring some more. There is a framed photo that sat on our piano my whole life. An arty, black and white that shows a child's hand clasped in a woman's hand. No faces, no bodies, just the two hands. The child's hand is mine. The woman's hand is my mother's. And the woman's hand wears this ring, I'm sure of it. The delicate leaf design etched in the gold, the flowers made from tiny rubies and pearls—exactly the same. My work has taught me enough about jewelry to know this piece is no mass-produced shopping mall trinket. What are the chances a ring just like my mother's would be in Mrs. Szabo's attic?

Slim.

I don't know who gave my mother the ring; I never asked. But I always assumed she must have been wearing it thirty years ago on Christmas Eve, when, despite a snowstorm, she went out to buy some last-minute gifts. The next morning, when I came down to see what Santa had brought, I found policemen standing around the tree. I was only three and there's a lot I don't remember. Try as I might, I can't summon up a clear memory of my mother that's mine, and not some lore passed on to me by my grandparents. But one memory is true in my mind: my father's gray face and wild red eyes that Christmas morning as he paced around the house and pleaded with the cops.

They found her car later that day, covered with snow, the driver's door open, twenty feet from Heart Lake. The police speculated that she skidded off the road and slid down a short embankment. Disoriented in the storm, she must've stumbled into the partially frozen lake instead of climbing back up to the road. The snow—the biggest Christmas Eve snowfall on record in New Jersey—obliterated all tracks, so it was impossible to know for sure. In the days following her disappearance, the weather got colder and colder. The lake froze solid. When spring came, they sent a couple of divers in. Her body was never found.

I open my clenched fist. Thirty years without a body, but now her ring. I contemplate what that means. Her flesh rotting away, the ring sliding off the bare bone. Jesus, this is morbid! But I force myself to think it all the way through. The ring somehow washes onto shore, even though nothing else of my mother's—shoes, clothes, bones—has ever made that trip. And Mrs. Szabo, sometime between her fifty-seventh year and her eighty-seventh, finds it. Does that make sense?

No. Back up, Audrey. Apply a little logic here. Maybe my

mother wasn't wearing the ring that day. Maybe she left it behind in her bedroom, from which it was taken, sometime, somehow, by one Agnes Szabo, a woman I've never heard of until I was hired to clean out her home.

I hear Jill and Tyshaun clomping around overhead and I know I'll have some explaining to do if they come down and find I haven't inventoried a thing in the living room and dining room. I slip the ring into my jeans pocket and pick up my clipboard. Moving around the room, I compile a list, but my concentration is shot. I stare at a shelf full of books, but all I see is the rocky, overgrown shores of Heart Lake. And the bare, ascetically tidy top of the dresser in my father's bedroom.

No one found my mother's ring in either place; I'm sure of it.

"Okay, Audrey, we're done upstairs." Jill pops into the living room, still dusty but back to her chipper self. "There are some vintage linen tablecloths in the hall closet. Should I list that in the ad?"

"Huh? Oh, sure, good idea."

"What about the dining room? Anything worthwhile in there?"

"Uh…I'm not sure. I haven't gone through it yet."

Jill tilts her head and furrows her brow. She's not used to me slacking.

I flounder for an explanation, then realize I'm not obliged to offer one. I started Another Man's Treasure so I could work entirely on my own. No boss. No staff. Success forced me to change my ways. Usually I like Jill's company but sometimes I feel crowded by her presence, her questions, her needs. "Go ahead and start loading the van. It'll only take me a few minutes to finish up." When I hear the door shut my mind returns to the idea I was considering when Jill interrupted.

What other path could the ring have traveled from my mother's hand to this attic?

An answer looms in front of me, demanding my consideration, as pushy and hard to dodge as a street-corner prophet passing out tracts. *My mother survived.*

Can that be?

As a child, I daydreamed that my mom would one day walk back in the door, carrying a shopping bag full of those Christmas presents she'd popped out to buy. "Whew, sorry that took so long!"

But as I grew older, that daydream lost its appeal.   If she were alive, why didn't she come back?

So by the time I was ten or twelve, I had firmly rejected the fantasy of the still living mom and replaced her with the frozen mermaid/angel mother dwelling forever at the bottom of Heart Lake. Very occasionally she'd splash up to the surface, visible out of the corner of my eye. When I spun around to catch a glimpse, back to the bottom she'd go.

Eventually, she stopped rising.

Until today.

Chapter 3

Physically and mentally exhausted by my workday at Mrs. Szabo's, I stagger through the door that leads from the garage into the kitchen of my condo, lugging the trunk of jewelry. It's my house all right, but it's never felt like home.

Like so many of my possessions, my condo once belonged to a client, a young school-teacher who died tragically in a skiing accident. I've never handled an estate sale that involved more crying relatives. The sale was postponed three times, then cancelled altogether because her family couldn't bear to part with a single thing that had belonged to her. They cherished her books and clothes and pictures, even her paper towel dispenser and her doormat. Their level of devotion made this condo seem bursting with warmth and energy. If I were to live here I would surely launch my "real" life.

So I bought the walls that surrounded the young schoolteacher, but I didn't buy her life. No cooking. No entertaining. No seasonally adjusted welcome mat. I've never even hung curtains. But life in my condo does offer one big advantage over the shared apartments and group houses of my twenties. Dogs are allowed.

Ethel comes charging out of my bedroom and dances around me on her hind legs. As I move into the livingroom, we fall onto the sofa for a protracted love-fest. She shoves her pointy brown snout under my hand, demanding to be petted, while her brown and white tail rotates around and around in her signature circular wag. Burying my head in her silky fur, I inhale her doggy aroma and thank my lucky stars, as I do every day, that I rescued her from the gas chamber at the shelter.

And that she rescued me with her unconditional love.

I want to believe her affection is completely attributable our all-day separation, but face it—six-thirty is dinner time and Ethel can smell Kung Pao chicken a block away. I sprinkle some Chinese carry-out over the kibble in her dish, but before I eat my share, I cross over to the bookshelf in the living room.

Staring at the framed photo of two entwined hands, I pull the ring out of my pocket. The delicate vine, the flowers crafted of tiny rubies and pearls: identical, as I knew they would be. I swear I feel my mother's cool soft hand on mine.

The ring of my cell phone drives the past away. Mrs. Szabo's nephew, returning my call.

"Cal Tremaine here," the voice on the phone barks. "What's the problem?"

What a pussycat this guy is. "I'm sorry to bother you at work sir, but we encountered some uh…irregularities… at your aunt's house." My account of the pink pills in the kitchen is met with an annoyed grunt and the clatter of rapid-fire keyboarding in the background.

"High blood pressure medication," Tremaine the multi-tasker says.

"I'm afraid not, sir. These are street drugs. Ecstasy."

"But that's absurd. How would my aunt—"

"That's not all." The sound of typing has stopped. I've got his attention now. "We found a chest full of valuable jewelry in the attic."

"Jewelry? My aunt never wore anything more than a wedding band and a Timex watch."

"So you didn't know about the jewelry?" I feel my mother's ring radiating heat in my jeans' pocket. Will Cal Tremaine know how it came to be in his aunt's attic? "I think I should have it appraised so we can get the best price-- "

Tremaine cuts me off.

"Where is this trunk right now?"

"Here in my apartment."

"Give me your address. I'll be right over."

Ethel watches with head cocked and brow furrowed as I race around the condo, pitching shoes and sweaters and junk mail into my bedroom, while spritzing air freshener in a vain attempt to banish the Kung Pao aroma. I'm not sure why I care what impression I make on this guy. I guess I have a need to present myself as a legit grown-up, not some rootless girl living in grad-student squalor. His office is only a few blocks away, so the doorbell is ringing as I yank off my dusty sweatshirt and shrug into a v-neck sweater.

I fling open my door without even looking through the peephole. What I see on the threshold blows me back a few steps.

Michaelangelo's David in a thousand-dollar suit.

I'd been expecting someone like my lawyer—fussy and spongy with a comb-over and horn-rim glasses. The disconnect is so great I lose the power of speech.

"Ms. Nealon?" He smiles with considerable dazzle and extends his hand. "Cal Tremaine." The annoyance he projected on the phone has been replaced with megawatt charm.

Reluctantly I offer my own hand, acutely aware of my ragged cuticles and broken nails. We stand there mutely until Ethel bustles over and plants her paws on his thighs. Sweet Jesus, she's shedding dog-pound fur on his Armani pants.

"Ethel! Off!"

Stunned by my tone, her wagging tail droops and she slinks

away.

"I'm so sorry, Mr. Tremaine. Please come in."

He follows me into the living room, where the chest sits in front of the sofa. Tremaine stares at it. I stare at him. I realize now that he's really not *that* good-looking, just well put-together. On the phone he projected a "when-I-say-jump, you-say-how-high" confidence, but this seems to have abandoned him. Gingerly, he reaches down and lifts the lid as if he's expecting a wild animal to pop out. The glittering snarl of necklaces, watches, rings and brooches winks at him.

A muscle in his jaw begins twitching. "You say you found this in the attic?"

I explain Jill's trip though the attic floor and the scattering of the trunk's contents.

His mouth tightens. "So your assistants know what's in this?"

"Yes."

Tremaine sinks onto my sofa, props his chin in his hands and gazes at the trunk. I want to ask him where the jewelry came from, how my mother's ring happened to be in there, but I keep my mouth shut. The minutes tick by. Even Ethel finds the silence oppressive and lets out a little whimper.

When I can't bear it any longer I say, "Look it's no trouble for me to get this appraised. I work with a very goo—"

"No." The single word is so loud that Ethel counters with a bark.

Cal swivels away from the trunk and meets my eye. "I'm sorry—I didn't mean to sound so harsh." He smiles, and this time it's not the power-broker beam he gave me when he arrived, but a sweet, slightly rueful grin. "I've been under a lot of stress lately. I'm the county chairman of the Democratic Party and I've been working what amounts to a second full time job on Spencer Finneran's campaign for governor. You're probably going to think I'm heartless for saying this, but Agnes's death couldn't have come at a worse time. The election's only a month away."

"In my experience, there's really never a *good* time to die."

He hangs his head, then looks up at me through his now-tousled hair. "Honestly, I'm not a horrible human being. Agnes was my great aunt, my grandmother's sister. I only saw her a few times in my life, at weddings and funerals. Since I'm the family lawyer, I helped her draw up her will and she made me her executor. She never had kids. This jewelry is a little...uh... family complication I wasn't expecting. I'm not sure I'll be selling it, so I don't want to appraise it now. But I can't deal with it until after the election."

In my line of work, I've learned all about family complications. Relatives can come to blows over a hideous cuckoo clock or a chipped turkey platter, never mind a pile of jewelry. Even without knowing the backstory of Agnes Szabo's treasure chest, I can believe that straightening it out might cost Cal Tremaine hours of aggravation that he can't afford right now. And sparing my clients the agita of dealing with their dead relatives' stuff is what my business is all about. "I understand, Mr. Tremaine. Would you like me to hang on to the trunk until after the election? I could have it appraised once you've had time to consider your options."

"That would be ideal, Ms. Nealon." He hesitates on my name. It's pretty ridiculous to keep calling each other Ms. Nealon and Mr. Tremaine when we probably both watched the A-Team and Three's Company growing up.

"I'm Audrey," I say.

"Cal," he answers.

He smiles. His two front teeth have a very slight overlap. "Thanks, Audrey. I really appreciate it."

I feel the ring in my pocket, a tiny little bump that's pressing into me tormentingly, like the Princess and the pea. I should pull it out right now, explain that I think it was my mother's, ask if he has any idea how it came to be in his aunt's house. I glance over at the photo on my bookshelf. The proof of my right to the ring is there, but who is more likely to claim that possession is nine-tenths of the law than a lawyer like Cal Tremaine? I can't risk losing the ring, not before I show it to my father. If Cal's leaving the trunk with me anyway, what difference does it make if the ring is in my pocket or thrown in with the rest of the stuff? When Cal's ready to deal with the jewelry, I'll be ready to ask him about the ring.

In the meantime, I need another answer. "What about the drugs we found in the kitchen? How do you want to handle that?"

The smile disappears like someone pulled a plug and the hard-assed lawyer returns. "You're not suggesting an eighty year old woman was dealing drugs out of her kitchen?"

"Has her house been unoccupied for a while?" I ask.

"About two months. She was in the hospital before she died."

"My assistant thinks a dealer may have been using your aunt's place as a stash house," I explain.

Cal opens his mouth, then shuts it. He sits on my sofa as motionless as a mannequin, but I can practically see the gears spinning beneath his perfectly trimmed brown hair. Something seems to click and he focuses on me again. Now his smile seems a little forced.

"You found the pills today but you haven't called the police yet?"

"I would've called right away, but I got distracted by Jill falling through the ceiling and the discovery of the trunk." *And my mother's ring.*

"So, the drugs are still in the kitchen?"

"They were when we left." I glance over at my phone. "Do you want to call the police right now?"

He holds up a restraining hand. "I can't deal with the police right now--I have plans tonight that can't be cancelled. Tomorrow morning is soon enough, don't you think? I'll take care of it—you've already done so much." He pulls out his Blackberry and sends a text message, his thumbs flying over the tiny keys. A second later the thing beeps and he reads the incoming message. Whatever it says relaxes him because the smile returns. Then he springs up and holds his right hand out to me. "I've been so rude, intruding on your evening like this. Let me take you out for a drink and a bite to eat."

Caught unaware, I immediately start floundering like the fat kid in swim class. "Oh! Oh, I don't know...I'm not dressed. I already had some Chinese—"

"You look fine." He grabs my hand and pulls me to my feet. "We'll just go to Hennessy's. I'm meeting some people there."

"Just Hennessy's" is an oxymoron. Ostensibly an Irish pub, Hennessy's is actually a Manhattan interior designer's fantasy of a place Dubliners might go to drink Guinness and sing weepy songs about the potato famine. A million dollars worth of brass, glass and mahogany transformed an old beer garden into the hot gathering spot for Palmyrton's movers and shakers. I would need to spend a week at the mall, the salon and the manicurist before I would ever dare meet Cal Tremaine and his friends at Hennessy's.

I pull my hand from his firm grasp. "No, seriously—I have a lot to do tonight. Quarterly tax filing due. The IRS waits for no woman."

"If you insist." He flashes that smile again. "I'm not accepting this as a no. I'm simply giving you a rain check."

Chapter 4

Everything about the Manor View Senior Living Center is a lie. There is no manor. There is no view. And believe me, there's precious little living.

The irony that my father now resides in a place that slaps a thin veneer of gilt over reality is not lost on me. Or him.

Armed with the ring, I've come to pry a little truth out of Dad. Armed is the operative word. Conversations with my father have never been easy. Since his stroke, they're exercises in frustration. Always taciturn, he's now angry, uncooperative and willfully obtuse. The stroke felled him in the middle of a lecture on Gauss's Harmonic Function Theorem, leaving him paralyzed on his right side and without the power of speech. His doctors insist his prognosis is quite good, but he stubbornly resists the efforts of the physical and speech therapists, so the hospital banished him to Manor View. At times he lets down his guard and I see that his keen intelligence is intact, but mostly he pretends to blend in with the vacant-eyed Alzheimer's patients who fill half the rooms at the nursing home. Excuse me: Senior Living Center.

I pull into the parking lot and for the first time since my father landed here I am excited to be visiting. Maybe the shock of seeing this ring will jar something loose deep inside him, give him a reason to care, inspire him to try to recover. Maybe it will bridge the gap between us that's grown wider and deeper with every passing year.

A lot to expect from a little gold band.

Getting out of the car, I reach for the leash. "What do you think, Ethel, will he tell me something?"

Ethel fixes her limpid brown eyes on mine and sighs. She's the sighing-est dog I've ever met. My father is crazy about her though, so I always bring her along. When we walk up the Manor View stairs, Ethel's ears perk up and her nose twitches. I'd like to think she's excited because she enjoys bringing joy into the lives of old people, but the truth is, Manor View is nirvana for a chow hound like Ethel. She patrols the floor, snapping up dropped cookies and renegade grapes. Then she jumps up to lick dribbles of gravy off cardigans and afghans. The old folks think she's dispensing kisses, and I don't set them straight.

Ethel waits impatiently at the door while I punch in the security code designed to keep residents in, not strangers out. Then she makes a beeline for the long corridor lined with wheelchairs. The old folks reach for her as she snuffles around. The sharpest ones lure her with treats; the most confused call her by the names of long lost pets. "Here, Trixie. Come, Sheba." I follow in her wake, smiling and waving like Prince Charles trailing Diana.

Finally satisfied that she's scored every available crumb, Ethel heads for my father's room. He's never out in the hall with the others, or in the solarium. She knows she'll find him in his wheelchair wedged in the space between his bed and the bathroom door.

Ethel bounds in and places her paws on Dad's knees. I stand on the threshold and watch. It still stuns me to see my father in a wheelchair. A lifelong runner, his wiry frame was built for movement. At sixty-three, his hair is still more dark than gray. All through my life he's been a superhuman figure, smarter than mere mortals and removed from their petty concerns. And then one day a blood clot breaks loose, jamming an artery in his brain, and he becomes this wreck. Who would've guessed he even had arteries? Or blood, for that matter.

As Dad pets Ethel's silky brown ears, the left corner of his mouth twitches. He's genuinely glad to see the dog. Me, not so much. Every time this touching scene plays out I remember the many childhood hours I spent futilely pleading for a dog. Dad always said he couldn't take care of another living thing. At the time I took that to mean he didn't feel a dog was worth all the effort. Seeing his devotion to Ethel, I realize that if my father had had a dog in the early days of his marriage, I might never have been born.

"Hi, Dad." I drag the hard little visitor chair from the other side of the room and sit down. I make no attempt to kiss him. He's never been big on physical affection and since the stroke he seems to shudder at skin-to-skin contact. Skin to fur is apparently okay, because he continues to stroke Ethel's head. Finally she tires of it and settles at his feet. He has no choice now but to look at me. Our eyes meet briefly, then Dad looks away, scanning his barren surroundings as if anything—the blank TV, the battered chest of drawers, the potted plant that outlived the room's previous resident—holds more interest than his visitor.

I begin my monologue, a filial Conan O'Brien trying to get a rise out of a tough audience. "So, today I'm organizing a sale over on Parkhurst Avenue. The house belonged to Agnes Szabo." I watch him closely for any reaction. A widening of the eyes, an intake of breath—anything that indicates Mrs. Szabo holds some significance in his life.

Nothing. His eyes stare blankly, focused on some point above my left shoulder.

He's letting me know he has no interest in my work, never has. To him, I'm a trash-picker who's squandered her degree in math. He won't respond to guess-what-happened-at- work- today small talk.

"It's a pretty nondescript house. That's why I was so surprised to find this." I pull the ring out of my pocket and extend it toward him on my palm; his gaze stays fixed on the middle distance.

I slide my chair to the left and hold the ring directly before his eyes. "Recognize it?"

He flattens himself against the back of the wheelchair. This is the most reaction I've gotten from him since the stroke. We're getting somewhere.

I lean forward with as much intensity as he used to draw away. "It's Mom's ring, isn't it?"

The right half of his face remains stony and blank. The left half trembles. His gaze stays locked on the ring. He nods.

"Was she wearing it the night she disappeared?"

He hesitates and I sense his mind reeling back thirty years. He has never been willing to talk to me about that night. Ill-timed questions about my mother's last night could send him into weeks-long funks. My maternal grandparents, who helped Dad raise me, always cautioned me to stay away from the topic. What little I know about that night—the snowstorm, the last-minute shopping, my father dozing then awaking to discover my mother still gone—all came from Nana and Pop. They died within months of each other shortly after I graduated college, taking all knowledge of my mother with them. Now, it looks like Dad is actually going to tell me something.

"Was she wearing it the night she disappeared?" I repeat.

His eyes blink rapidly. He can't stop staring at the ring.

I'm encouraged. He may not be conveying any information, but I've got his full attention, that's for sure. "Agnes Szabo would have been fifty-seven when mom disappeared." I keep saying disappeared, not died. I'm not sure he's noticed. "Did my mother have a middle aged friend named Agnes?"

Dad lifts his left shoulder, which passes for a "who knows" shrug.

"Did a woman name Agnes Szabo ever clean for us?"

Again the half-shrug.

Yes, no, maybe—that's all I can get from him these days. Every question has to be posed so he can offer one of those three responses.

"Did she know anyone in that neighborhood, Parkhurst, over near Evergreen Cemetery?" *Nowhere near Heart Lake.*

He stares down at his lap. His sinewy left hand clutches the arm of the wheelchair; his right flops like a dead fish on his pajama-clad legs. But I catch him trying to glance over at the ring, which I've set on the end table beside him.

Even though I know he doesn't like to be touched, I reach out my hand and put my fingertips beneath his chin. The nurses only shave him every other day, so it's covered with coarse gray stubble. I lift his chin up and force him to look at me head on. "Dad, is there any chance that Mom is still alive?"

His eyes widen, the white visible all the way around the gray irises. He pulls back from my touch and for the first time since he's been at Manor View a word croaks out of his throat.

"No."

"Then how did her ring get in Mrs. Szabo's attic?" I swore to myself before I came that I'd stay calm, but that promise is shot to hell. There's a shrill edge in my voice that takes both Dad and me by surprise. He shrinks back in his wheelchair.

I take a deep breath. There's no point in asking open-ended questions. Here's a yes-or-no I've been wanting to ask for years, but never had the courage. "Dad, Mom didn't really go out Christmas shopping that night, did she?"

He places his good hand on the wheel of his chair and tries to roll away from me. The chair backs up crookedly, catching the edge of Ethel's tail. She yelps, scrambling away. Dad uses his left foot to push the chair harder and succeeds in crashing into the bedside table and knocking over the lamp. All the racket brings an aide running.

"What's going on in here? Mr. Nealon, are you all right?" She's a middle-aged Haitian woman with a lilting accent and a nametag that reads, "Desiree."

Dad shakes his head vigorously.

The aide glares at me. "Why do you visit if you're going to upset him?" Her job sucks and I'm making it harder. Desiree pats my father's hand. Her touch doesn't make him cringe. "Do you need to go to the bathroom? Would you like to lie down and take a little nap?"

He nods eagerly. Anything Desiree suggests is fine with him.

Anything to get away from me.

Chapter 5

"Where have you been? Why haven't you answered your cell? Did you forget it again?"

Jill's reproaches begin the moment I set foot in the office. I'm about to provide an explanation but I'm brought up short by her appearance, which is exceptionally bizarre even for Jill. Heavy black liner encircles her eyes, giving her that domestic violence survivor look. Her lips seem to have been painted with Wite-Out, and she's wearing an old Catholic school girl cardigan with the sleeves hacked off, topped by a fringy scarf in baby-poop brown. I'm never sure what kind of response Jill is trying to elicit. She can't possibly expect us to say, "You look lovely today," but Tyshaun can bring her to tears with his, "Girl, that is one butt-ugly outfit," or (my favorite) "You look totally fucked-up."

"I was at a memorial service," I say. I don't like to talk to Jill and Tyshaun about my father, so I report the second half of my morning but not the first. "I had to turn my phone off."

Jill looks chastened. "Who died?"

"Martin Reicker, one of the old fellows at Manor View. He liked

Ethel a lot. His daughter's often there when I visit my dad and we've talked some."

Tyshaun, sprawled across a squishy easy chair that once graced a client's living room, alternates texting and adjusting his iPod. He points at me with the toes of one huge basketball sneaker. "You got a job out of this, didn't you?"

The kid is catching on.

Jill's jaw drops enough that I can see her tongue stud. "You went to a funeral so you could give a sales pitch for Another Man's Treasure. That's awful!"

Jill doesn't care to think of me as a tool of the capitalist machine.

"Mr. Reicker's daughter was very touched that I came to the service." I sidle between Tyshaun's lanky frame and a teetering pile of old computers waiting to go to the electronics recycler, finally reaching my desk. "And yes, it so happens the family needs someone to clear out the house."

"May's well be us," Ty says.

Before I can agree, the phone rings. Jill purrs, "Another Man's Treasure," in her flutiest receptionist voice. "One moment, I'll see if he's available." She puts the call on hold as if she's manning the switchboard at a multinational corporation and turns toward Tyshaun. "You wanna talk to Myesha?"

He shakes his head 'til his earbuds fly out. "No way. That girl thinks I'm her bitch. I had enough o' her shit."

Jill returns to the call. "Tyshaun is out on an all-day job. May I take a message?" She moves the receiver away from her ear as a stream of high-pitched profanity comes through the line, then wraps up with a sweet, "I'll let him know you called."

"Is this the accounting major from Montclair State?" I ask.

"No," Jill explains, "That's Kimberly. Myesha is the x-ray technician. Ty blocked her calls on his cell."

"I had to. She drivin' me crazy."

Ty's love life is a source of never-ending fascination for Jill and me, I guess because neither of us has anything going on in that department ourselves. Much as I'd love to hear more gory details about Myesha, my staff has been idle long enough. "You two get started setting up the sale at Mrs. Szabo's. I'll swing by the Reicker place to see how big a project it'll be." I scan the pink message slips on my desk. "Did Mrs. Szabo's nephew call?"

Cal Tremaine's mention of a rain check for dinner has been replaying in the back of my mind. I tell myself it's the sort of thing guys like him say reflexively, unable to repress their own charm.

Still, I'm hopeful. And that pisses me off.

"No, nothing from him," Jill says. "Did you ever talk to him about the trunk?"

"Yeah—he wants me to hold off on getting an appraisal until after the election. He works for Spencer Finneran and he's too busy to deal with the jewelry right now."

"Whatever." Jill grabs the van keys and heads to the door. "Get some trash bags out of the store room, Ty."

I wait for the expected, "get 'em yourself," but Ty does as he's told. Once Jill is out the door he turns to me.

"What about the pills? What'd the old lady's nephew want to do about that?"

"Cal was supposed to call the police this morning. I don't know if he did."

Ty shakes his head. "I don't like this. Word probably out on the street that we was there messin' around yesterday. The boss sent someone to claim his stash by now."

"The boss? What boss?" I ask.

"Whoever the stuff belongs to," Ty explains patiently. "Then this Tremaine dude going to bring the cops on over with all their sirens and shit and when they get there, he be all, 'never mind, it's gone now.' What you think they gonna say to that? 'No problem, we'll go get some donuts?' They gonna question you. And question Jill. Then they gonna *arrest* me."

"Why would they arrest you?"

" 'Cause I'm the one with the record. I'm the one who's black.

They sure as hell not going to arrest you."

"Ty, relax. Why would they arrest any of us? All we did was find the stuff."

Ty lowers his chin and fixes me with a droopy-eyed, sullen stare that says *you're dumber than dirt*. He cups his hands as if he's gathering up piles to dump in front of me: "Drugs. Brother on probo. Arrest."

I tap my watch. "It's past noon. No one's showed up to arrest you yet. Go over to Mrs. Szabo's house. If the place is crawling with cops, you have my permission to turn around and come back here."

All afternoon while I'm scoping out my new client's house, I keep expecting a call about those pills—either Ty or Cal or the cops. But my phone stays silent. Hours later I pull up behind the Another Man's Treasure van parked in front of Mrs. Szabo's place. Tyshaun and Jill are sitting on the front porch, peaceably drinking cans of Coke and sharing a bag of chips. I expect them to leap up and scurry back to work when they see me, but Ty stretches out his long legs and Jill reaches for another handful of salt and grease.

"We're all done," Jill shouts before stuffing her face.

"Ready for the earlybirds," Tyshaun concurs.

"What about the signs?" I ask.

Ty holds up a stack of estate sale signs with Mrs. Szabo's address and tomorrow's date printed in Jill's perfect block lettering. "I'm'a put 'em up now. I was waitin' to see if you need me to move anything inside."

I walk into the house and stop at the doorway to the living room. Every piece of furniture carries a price tag. The upholstery and rugs bear the marks of vigorous vacuuming. Tables contain artful arrangements of Mrs. Szabo's knick-knacks, books and pictures. It never ceases to amaze me that a woman who goes to such lengths to make herself unattractive can be so talented at making inanimate objects look irresistible. I stare in amazement at a faded sewing basket that Jill has filled with tissue paper and sprinkled with thimbles, pinking shears and darning egg, priced at ten dollars. "I

29

swear to God, Jill, you could sell a hacked up kitty hair ball as long as you had some lace doilies to arrange it on."

She beams. "Gee, thanks."

Not to be outdone, Tyshaun pushes me along. "Wait'll you see the dining room."

Ty has removed the dusty Venetian blinds and hideous maroon draperies from the window and polished the old mahogany table to a high shine. Jill has arranged two place settings of china and some candlesticks, making it possible to imagine a gracious second act for the furniture and dishes.

In the kitchen, everything is clean and shiny and the contents of the cabinets have been laid out on the counters and table. Cautiously I slide open the drawer next to the sink. Empty. Ty gives me a Cheshire cat smile, while Jill bustles around moving a vase from the kitchen into the living room.

"It was gone when you got here?" I ask.

Ty nods and raises the kitchen window. "Lock's broken, screen's gone. He could reach in and grab it without even comin' all the way in the house."

"And the police never showed up here?"

Ty shakes his head. "I bet your guy never called."

I'm puzzled, but in my heart, I'm relieved. I mean, I feel a little guilty for not doing my part to protect the youth of New Jersey from a life of drug-addicted depravity. But let's face it—100 tabs of E isn't exactly the French Connection. Plus, explaining the discovery of the drugs would require mentioning the trunkful of jewelry. And *not* mentioning the ring I took out of it. A challenge, that. I'm not a great liar.

Invigorated, I clap my hands. "C'mon. Let's put up the signs and I'll take you both out for pasta at Tambellini's."

Tyshaun glances at a text on his phone. "Ah, thanks Audge, but I gotta swerve after I hang the signs, know what'm sayin'?"

Jill shifts anxiously. "I'm only eating gluten-free rice noodles these days, Audrey. Some people from my meditation group are going to Vegan Dreams for dinner and we're staying for the performance art." She pauses. "You could come if you want."

"No worries. Some other time." I wave them toward the door. "See you in the morning."

I shuffle around the first floor of the house doing a few things that really don't need to be done. Did my dinner invitation to Jill and Ty sound pathetically needy? I shouldn't be fraternizing with my staff anyway, but the truth is, my social life's been in the crapper lately. I've never been the type to have a huge circle of casual friends. I prefer a tight circle of really close friends. In fact, my circle is really a triangle: Maura, a social butterfly who I rely on to get me out of the house, is off on a six-month work assignment in London; Lydia just gave birth and is caught up in new mommy nirvana; and Eric and Raul are going through one of their periodic break-ups, in which all they want to do is get me to side with one against the other. So my evenings and weekends have been extraordinarily uneventful. I know I need to do something to get out of my rut. I can practically hear *Cosmo* advising me: Go to a gym! Take a class! Volunteer! But the truth is, I've never been much of a joiner. I'm an introvert, more like my dad than I care to admit. I guess I'll order a meatball sub from Tambellini's and take it home to share with Ethel. Again.

"Tambellinis! Hold!" a voice barks in my ear after I speed-dial five times to break through the constant busy signal. I've been ordering from this place since I was old enough to dial a phone and I swear I've never gotten through on the first try. That's what passes for a five star rating in New Jersey. While I'm standing in the sale-ready living room with the phone pressed to my ear, I hear footsteps on the front porch. My empty stomach flip-flops. Did Ty or Jill forget something? Or maybe there are more drugs in here that we didn't uncover. Maybe the boss is coming back again.

I hear a key turn in the lock. My brain tells my feet to run, but they're not listening. I stand rooted to the spot, phone dangling from my fingers, as the Tambellini's man shouts, "what's your order?"

In the dim light, a tall man stands outlined in the living room doorway.

I try to scream, but manage only to squeak.

"I feel I owe you an explanation." The man steps toward me, into the light.

"Cal! Jesus, you scared me!"

"I'm sorry. Didn't you get my message? I texted that I'd be dropping by after work."

"I guess I missed it." My heart rate gradually slows to normal. "An explanation for what?"

"I meant to call the police first thing this morning. But before I even left my house, I got a call from a client with a crisis. I've been tied up in court all day."

"While you were busy, the problem's disappeared."

Cal's eyebrows shoot up. "What do you mean?"

"Whoever put it there came back and claimed his property. It was gone when my staff got here today." I beckon Cal into the kitchen and show him the broken window. "Better get this fixed."

Cal runs his hand through his hair, but somehow that gesture doesn't send one strand out of place. "You probably think I'm not very good at upholding the law."

"No...I don't think... I mean—"

"I really was going to call. I could still call." He reaches for his Blackberry.

"No." My voice comes out sharper than I intended. Cal raises his eyebrows.

"It's just...see, the guy who works for me, Tyshaun, well, he got mixed up with some sketchy guys when he was younger and anyway he got arrested for burglary and served a year in prison and he's worried that the police will think he has something to do with those drugs and it does look kind of bad that I didn't call right away when I found them..."

I realize I'm babbling. "Let's forget about the whole thing."

Cal smiles. "Yeah. Maybe that's easiest. Hey, I'm on my way to meet Spencer and a few of our supporters for drinks. Want to join us?"

I don't say a word. Just extend my sneakered foot and stretch my sweatshirt to display the dirt streak bisecting the front.

"Sorry." Cal smiles and squeezes my shoulder. "I keep forgetting you do real work for a living. Once this campaign is over I'm going to call you up and ask you out. Advance notice and everything. Deal?"

It's just a line. I know my part. "Deal."

Once Cal has driven off I get back on the phone and dial Tambellinis again.

Busy. Busy. Busy.

Chapter 6

I arrive at Mrs. Szabo's house at seven on Saturday morning. Frost coats the grass and the sun has barely struggled above the horizon but there's already a line down the block waiting to get into the sale. The usual suspects are huddled at the head of the queue: Martin Fine and Gerald Lassiter, two dealers who live over their antique shop in Summit and never miss one of my events; Harold Watts, an obsessive/compulsive hoarder who spends hundreds of dollars on things he can't possibly need; and Tamara Simchiss, a middle-aged hippie chick who creates art out of "found objects" and sells it for absurd prices in a Soho gallery. Straggling behind them is a motley crew of adventurous housewives, entrepreneurial immigrants and recent college grads looking to furnish their first home. They're all holding numbers, which means Jill has beaten me here.

The regulars greet me by name.

"Hello, Audrey darling! How have you been?" Martin and Gerald kiss me. "Look what we brought you." Gerald produces three muffins wrapped in blue cellophane and tied with a white grosgrain ribbon. Harold eyes them hungrily, making me worried that he's spent all his food money on garage sales. Tamara strokes my arm and smiles her loopy Zen smile.

"Thanks, guys. I hope you won't be disappointed by this one. I've got a sale coming up over on Beaumont that's going to be a beauty."

Up on the porch, Jill awaits my key. Today she's wearing bright orange leggings and a horizontally striped knit minidress, an ensemble that would make a Chinese gymnast look fat. I pull the key from my fannypack. We enter and firmly close the door on our customers, who crane their necks to catch a glimpse of the treasures within. It's our policy to never start a sale even one minute before eight, for fear of starting a riot among the early birds, whose number gives them the right to leave the line if they return by eight. I hand Jill the cashbox to organize and go upstairs for another quick review before the opening bell.

Tyshaun has tacked a sheet of plastic over the hole in the room with the collapsed ceiling, and placed the two pieces of furniture the room contained out in the hall. I lock the door of the damaged bedroom and move into the other bedroom. Here I find what I'm looking for—a framed photo of a younger Mrs. Szabo. I study the broad square face, the kindly eyes, the stocky figure. Does she look familiar? I stare at the faded photo, willing myself to recognition, but nothing comes.

"Audrey, are you almost ready?" Jill shouts up the stairs to me.

Slipping the photo out of its frame, I put it in my fanny pack. As I slide the pouch around to my back, my hand brushes against my jeans and I check that I still have my mother's ring in my pocket. It's too small to fit on my ring finger, and too big for my pinkie. I should have left it in my bedroom, but I want it with me.

"I'm coming," I shout to Jill. "Go ahead and open the door."

I descend the stairs as Jill admits the ravenous horde. A middle-aged man, eyes burning with fierce determination, feints and dodges his way past the regulars, taking the stairs to the second floor two at a time. I flatten myself against the wall to avoid being trampled. Guess he really needs a bed.

In the living room, Jill presides over the cashbox, while Tyshaun obligingly lifts the sofa so that a couple speaking rapid fire in some Eastern European language—Romanian? Serbian?—can assess the springs. The rest of the assembled customers quickly disperse through the house, picking and poking through Mrs. Szabo's worldly goods. "This is junk," a woman with a Louis Vuitton purse slung over her shoulder says to her friend. "Let's go to the sale on Chestnut." Another woman examines a lamp, raises her eyebrows at the $10 price tag, and walks away. A young couple, hipsters in black, snickers at Mrs. Szabo's vivid, rococo-framed seascape.

This is the sad part of my business—the reason why I advise relatives not to come to the sale of their loved one's belongings. It's too painful to see strangers pawing through your grandmother's china, rejecting it as not good enough. Even if you wouldn't dream of having your mother's pink flowered sofa and chair set in your own home, you don't want to hear other people calling it gaudy. Know this about the end of your own life: your taste will be on trial, your keepsakes up for grabs.

I watch an old woman dragging a wheeled tote bag work her way slowly around the room. Her white hair is pulled back so tightly in a hair-net covered bun that her pink scalp shows through. Very thin but not frail, she studies each item in the sale intently as if she's a one-woman art jury. Right now she's scrutinizing Mrs. Szabo's curio cabinet, carefully turning over each knick-knack, then putting it back on the shelf. After ten minutes, she moves on to the bookcase and begins the same process.

"Are you looking for something in particular?" I ask.

She lifts her steel-gray eyes from the examination of a completely out-of-date world atlas and focuses on me. I haven't felt so pierced by a stare since Mrs. Abernathy halted the fifth grade assembly to wait for me to stop whispering. Then the old woman replaces the book on the shelf, turns her back on me, and marches purposefully into the dining room, pulling her tote bag behind her.

Jill and I exchange a smile and a shrug. As long as no one's actively hallucinating, a little odd behavior doesn't faze us. A moment later, the man in a hurry reappears with a roll of cash and buys Mrs. Szabo's bedroom set. From then on, Jill and I are continuously busy at the check-out table. Estate sales are early morning affairs, and we don't have a lull until noon, when Jill calls out for subs. As we sit eating in the steadily emptying living room, the old lady and her tote bag reappear. Has she been in the house all this time?

She rolls to a stop before me. This time I know better than to speak first.

"Is this everything?" she asks. "The second bedroom is locked. And there's an attic."

"The furniture from the bedroom is in the hall. And the attic is empty." I see no reason to tell her about the hole in the attic floor. Or the trunk that fell through it.

She stands before me, waiting, still and keen-eyed. Suddenly she doesn't seem like a garden-variety crack-pot who might show up at any of our sales. Did this old crone know Mrs. Szabo? Know her better, perhaps, than her nephew Cal Tremaine did?

"Are you a friend of Mrs. Szabo's?"

"I live down the block," she says. "Agnes and I were neighbors for forty-seven years."

That answer sidesteps the issue of whether they were friends. Unsure about offering condolences, I simply say, "Then you must've been in this house many times."

"Not really. We mostly visited out on each other's porches." Her hard, virtually lashless eyes dart around. "She intended to give me something."

Ah, here it comes. With only one living relative, Mrs. Szabo hasn't been troubled by the circling vultures that fly out at most people's death. But in this neighbor, I hear the clack of a vulture beak looking for carrion to pick clean. Then I feel guilty for having such an uncharitable thought. Maybe the old gal simply wants a memento of her long-time neighbor.

"Did you want to take a little something to remember her by?" I ask, glancing over at the last few knick-knacks in the room.

The woman snorts. "Honey, at my age, I don't collect souvenirs. What I meant was, Agnes had something that she wanted me to take care of for her. She'd talk about it when we were together. But then she died."

"So what was it?" I ask.

"She never said. Just insisted she didn't want it to be left here after she was gone."

The bag of drugs? Or the trunk of jewelry? Either would be something Mrs. Szabo wouldn't want her survivors to find. But why give either to her neighbor? How could she explain them to this suspicious old bat?

"Excuse me, would you take fifteen dollars for this end table?" A determined looking housewife waves a ten and a five under my nose. "Something this wobbly isn't worth thirty."

The time has come to start bartering away the last of Mrs. Szabo's wordly goods. I complete the transaction, then turn back to question the old woman further.

She's gone.

Chapter 7

Twelve hours, three hundred buyers, two trips to Salvation Army and three runs to the dump later, Mrs. Szabo's house is empty, broom clean, and ready to be listed for sale. Jill finishes counting the money and writing up the deposit slip. "Five thousand, seven hundred eighty three dollars and ninety-two cents," she announces.

"Ninety-two cents?" I price everything at even dollars.

"Harold was eight cents short for a melon-baller he wanted so I let him have it," Jill looks like she's been caught stealing from the collection plate. "I'm sorry, Audrey. I should have asked you first."

I rub her crew cut. "I don't care about the eight cents, you goof. I just feel bad about enabling Harold's hoarding. Can you imagine what his house must look like? Every melon baller and Chia pet we let him take home feeds his addiction."

"That's right, Jill. Harold's a junkie and you helping him mainline," Ty says. "God got a special place in hell for the likes of you."

Jill grins and prods him with her Doc Marten. "I'll pass you on the way down."

The two of them have been getting along amazingly well today, despite the fact that Tyshaun has been very distracted. He's been checking his cellphone constantly. As we sit here finalizing the deposit, it buzzes again.

Ty flips it open. "I be there. Soon." His voice gets low and velvety as he glances sideways at me. "I promise." He stands up and walks out to the hall, the phone still pressed to his ear.

I can't help smiling. Kimberly? Myesha? Or is some new girl hot for his long, lean body and soulful eyes?

Jill puts the money in the bank night deposit pouch and hands it to me. Because we only accept checks from people we know, over four thousand dollars of our take is in cash. Ty pops his head back into the room, while the rest of his body points toward the door. A horn honks outside. "We done here, Audge? I gotta roll."

"Where do you think you're going?" Jill demands, her earlier good humor gone. "You have to ride with Audrey to the bank while I drive the van back to the office."

Tyshaun looks like Jill told him he has to swim the English Channel. "I can't." His voice has a harsh, don't-mess-with-me edge. The only other time I've heard it is when Ty caught a guy pocketing some silver at a sale and threatened to turn him upside down and shake it out of him.

Jill jumps right in. "It's part of your job to—"

I lay a hand on her arm. Ty usually does escort me to the bank after a sale, but I've done it plenty of times by myself too. He's never asked for time off in all the months he's worked for me. Clearly, he has a date. "Go ahead, Ty. We'll see you on Tuesday," I say. "Have fun."

Jill scowls. "Give me the van—"

The keys are sailing toward her head before she can complete the sentence, and Ty is out the door.

"I'll go to the bank with you, Audrey."

"No, it's out of your way. I'll make the deposit on my way home. You take care of the van." We lock up Mrs. Szabo's house and head toward our vehicles. I toot the Honda's squeaky little horn and wave as I pull out in front of the van and head downtown.

Nearly eight on date night and Main Street in Palmyrton is brightly lit and bustling with people strolling to restaurants and the movie theater. No parking spots near my bank. I circle the block, but even the side streets are parked solid. On my second time around the block, I spy an elderly couple ever so slowly getting ready to vacate their spot. I pull up behind them to wait, but the porky SUV behind me lays on his horn. If he drove a normal sized vehicle he could go around me. I'm tempted to give him the finger, but the old folks are still doddering with their keys and I'm hungry and tired and eager to wash the Eau de Old scent out of my hair. Reluctantly I accept the necessity of parking in the municipal garage at the end of the block. The SUV follows me in.

Even here, the first level is full. Doesn't anyone but me stay home on Saturday night? I go up the ramp to the next level and finally nab a "compact cars only" spot. Score one for Hondas. The SUV keeps lumbering up the ramp.

My car, the rolling estate sale, is full of unsold but too good to throw away left-overs from sales gone by. I pluck a scratched but still chic Coach tote from the back seat to hide the bank deposit bag, stick my keys in my pocket, then head out of the garage. I look around the dim, cavernous space to get my bearings so I can find my car when I return. I head toward the elevator, the Coach tote hitched over my shoulder. Four thousand dollars in small bills is surprisingly heavy.

Pressing the down button, fantasies of food and a hot shower float through my head. My gaze latches on the lights showing the slow progress of the elevator. *Come on.* Slowly the door creaks open.

I see the figure inside but my mind can't quite process the information. Black, all black. A ski mask and gloves, but it's not cold enough for that yet. My right foot is raised to step forward but I don't move.

To scream or not to scream? In the moment I take to consider,

I'm airborne. A hard shove from behind sends me face-first into the elevator. I topple like a tree in a windstorm. The masked man reaches for the tote bag.

Now I realize what's going on, and I hang on tight, curling around the profits of a hard day's work.

A thunderous noise followed by searing pain--the effect of a man's boot connecting with my head. I'm sprawled over the bag, too stunned to move. He rears back to kick me into cooperation. I scuttle away and the edge of his boot catches my forehead. My own blood clouds my vision. The elevator dings incessantly, displeased by the blocked door.

The person behind me reaches down for the tote. Then he yanks up my coat and sweater.

I clench my legs. *Dear lord, not this.*

I feel the fanny pack being ripped off my waist.

The boot pulls back a third time. A wave of strength surges within me, so powerful I feel I can fly. Get through that elevator door, scream for help. I lunge toward the parked cars.

Astonishing how loud my bones crunching sounds from inside my head. The elevator dings grow fainter. I swallow the coppery taste of blood.

The lights go out.

Chapter 8

Meatloaf and canned gravy. Mashed potatoes. Overcooked peas.

My head turns away from the smell. My eyes struggle to open but something holds them shut. I wonder why I'm sleeping in a cafeteria.

"Reduce the morphine. Keep an eye on her vitals."

"And the shunt?"

I want to know who's talking, what they mean. I try raising my eyelids again but it requires too much effort. Maybe later....

A cool dry hand holds mine. "Audrey, Audrey—can you hear me? Wake up, honey."

Slowly, I drag my right eye open. The left stays stubbornly shut. Pain radiates from the spot where someone seems to have hammered a spike into my temple. A woman with short brown hair and a very ugly necklace is hovering right over me. I struggle to bring her into focus.

Her face is friendly but not familiar. The ugly necklace resolves into a stethoscope. I try to speak but my mouth is parched and my lips feel three times their normal size.

"You had an accident, Audrey. You're in the hospital." She swabs my lips with water.

An accident? My mind struggles to process the information. I remember working at a sale. Yes, the sale at Mrs. Szabo's house. Taking the deposit…driving to the bank…looking for a parking spot. What happened after that? I look out the window. The sun is shining brightly. But wait, when I was looking for that parking spot it was dark. How long have I been here? Ethel. My god, Ethel has to be fed, has to go out.

I struggle to sit up. Pain knocks me back.

"Ethel," I croak.

"Ethel? Who's Ethel, honey?" The nurse is taking my blood pressure and writing notes on a chart. "Is she someone you want me to call?"

"My dog. She's all alone. What time is it?"

"You've been here four days, Audrey," the nurse says. "But your friend visits every day. She talks to you and I heard her say she's got the dog and she's taking care of it. Don't you worry."

Four days? I've been in here four days and Jill and Tyshaun have been alone in the office all that time? "I have to make a phone call," I announce, struggling to sit up, ignoring the pain. The room tilts and spins.

"Whoa, whoa." The doctor steps forward, easing me back onto the pillows. "You were brought in with severe head trauma. I had to drill a hole in your skull to relieve the pressure of your brain swelling up against the bone."

"Wait—say again?"

The doctor launches into some long diatribe, of which I understand only every fourth word or so. But I'm getting the picture. I had brain surgery. *Brain surgery.* The urge to struggle ebbs out of me. I want…I want… I want someone here holding my hand. Who wakes up alone after four days in a coma and a drill bit through the skull? A tear slips down my cheek. I want my Nana.

The doctor pauses in his poking and prodding. "Does that hurt?"

I shake my head no, so he shines lights in my eyes, taps me with his little hammer and quizzes me on current events. When I correctly identify the capital of New Jersey and the occupant of the White House, the doctor grudgingly admits my brain seems to be functioning. Impressed, he allows the nurse to disconnect some of the wires and tubes tethering me to the bed.

While they work on me I replay Saturday over and over, but each time

the movie in my head ends with me staring at an elderly couple getting into their car as I wait for their parking spot. It's like I'm watching a scratched DVD that's stuck forever on that scene.

"How did my head get hurt so badly?" I ask. "I was wearing my seatbelt. Didn't my airbag deploy?"

I watch as the doctor and nurse exchange a glance over my bed.

"Severe trauma erases your short-term memory. Sometimes it comes back, usually it doesn't." The pager on his belt goes off and he heads for the door.

The nurse straightens my covers and puts the TV remote within reach. "It's a blessing you can't remember. Nature's way of protecting you."

"Protecting me from what?"

She doesn't answer, just follows the doctor out the door.

Left alone, I go back to piecing together my memories. Since I can't get the tape to move forward, I scroll backward through last Saturday. I replay Mrs. Szabo's estate sale, from end to beginning: counting the profits, cleaning up, haggling, selling, setting up. And that makes me think of what I was doing right before I opened the door to the early birds. I remember putting Mrs. Sazbo's picture in my fannypack. And I remember feeling for my mother's ring in my jeans pocket.

The ring! I look down at my hospital-gowned body. Where are my clothes?

I struggle to sit up and am immediately felled by scorching pain. Breathless, I search out the nurse call button and press frantically.

After an eternity, the same nurse reappears.

"What's the matter, hon?"

"My clothes," I croak. "What happened to my clothes?"

"They were cut off you in the ER."

"But where are they?" I ask again.

She takes my hand and pats it reassuringly. "The staff had to throw them away, hon. They must've been soaked with blood. When you get out of here, go out and treat yourself to a nice new outfit."

"Don't care about the clothes. My pocket. There was something important in my jeans pocket."

"Oh, that's right here." She opens the drawer in my bedside table and holds up a sealed plastic bag. All I can see is loose change. Although I'm not in pain, my eyes well with tears.

"Here you go, hon." She drops the bag on the bed and heads to the door. "Everything they took from your pockets is in there. Except your keys. The police took those."

I snatch up the bag and stare. A hair scrunchie, a linty cough drop, three quarters, two pennies, a dime. And my mother's ring.

Finally able to relax, I fiddle with the buttons on my remote control until I succeed in raising the head of the bed and switching on the TV. Scrolling through the channels, I stop at the local news. Maybe this will help me reclaim the days I lost. A fatal fire in Paterson. A tax protest march in Trenton. Some kids in Summit win a science award.

The anchorwoman lifts a hand and adjusts with the earpiece feeding her instructions from the director. "It appears that we're going live to the courthouse. Perhaps that indictment is about to be handed down."

The camera switches to on- the-scene coverage. A crowd of burly cops surrounds a tall black man who ducks his head to evade the flashing cameras. The cops push the prisoner forward. He looks up, apparently in response to some shout from the crowd.

Tyshaun's eyes meet mine through the TV screen.

Chapter 9

"You begin losing muscle tone within twenty-four hours of becoming bedridden."

I've spent the afternoon pushing an aluminum walker with Larry the physical therapist, an earnest young man with early onset male pattern baldness and a PT aphorism for every occasion. Shaking off his supporting hand as I head to the blessed solitude of my room, I sway and stagger like a drunk on a three-day bender. Larry catches me.

I've taken an irrational dislike to Larry, blaming him for my inability to walk a straight line and for what I saw in the mirror when he took me into the bathroom. I look like the after picture in an exposé on botched plastic surgery. A clump of hair has been shaved off the side of my head, my lips are purple and lumpy—forget bee-stung, they look tarantula-stung. Both eyes are black and a long zipper of stitches runs across my forehead and down my temple.

As Larry and I turn the corner on the final leg of our journey around the fifth floor, I see a familiar black crew cut protruding from a giant, furry purple mohair sweater/sack.

"Jill!"

I shuffle toward her.

"Ohmigod! You look great!" Her purple arms are outstretched and she's jumping up and down in her gladiator sandals. "I mean, you look terrible but great because you're alive. Oh, God I'm so relieved, I thought you were going to die for sure and I didn't know what to do about the office and the customers and the next sale and your dad and Ethel and ..oh thank God!"

Jill is trying to fling her arms around me, a process made difficult by the walker rolling around between us. Tears stream down her face, leaving long tracks of black eyeliner in their wake.

"Okay, okay, don't cry. It's all going to be all right." Abandoning Larry, we make it into my room, and manage to sit down beside each other on the bed. I put my arm around Jill and wait for her to stop sobbing.

"How's Ethel?" I ask to distract her.

The question sets off another torrent. "Ohmigod, it was so sad. She was starving and frantic to go out and so glad to see someone she knew. She drank all the water out of the toilet and knocked over the trash and ate some stuff she found in there and pooped in the laundry room but I cleaned that up. She looked real guilty about it but I said look Ethel it's not your fault you were stuck in here for almost two full days and you did what you had to do, know what I mean? So she's been coming to the office with me every day and I tell her how you're doing and she says hi."

Breathless, Jill scrubs at her teary face with the sleeve of her sweater, spreading eyeliner and purple fuzz from ear to ear. A gush of affection wells up inside me and for the first time since I woke up in this hospital I think everything will be all right. I feel able to tackle the tough question, somehow convinced Jill will be able to explain everything.

"What really happened to me, Jill? Why have the cops arrested Tyshaun?"

"Ooohmyygaawd, I'm sooo sorry. It's all my fault...if only I hadn't said that but I was so mad and I just said to the cop this would never have happened if Tyshaun had gone to the bank with her and the next thing I know they're arresting—"

"Jill. Stop. Right. Now." I take her snotty, smeary face between my hands and turn her head to look at me. "Get a grip. Slow down. Start at the beginning and tell me everything."

So she does. Jill explains it was late Monday afternoon before she connected my failure to show up at work with the nameless beating victim featured on the news. She called the police and they took her to the hospital to identify me. She says my face was so battered she only knew it was me was because she recognized my hair and my hands. Then they questioned her for two hours at the police station. Tyshaun wasn't around for any of this because Monday is his day off.

"They asked me the same questions over and over again," Jill says, cradling her head in her hands. "Who owns the house? How did we arrange the sale? Who bought stuff? How much money was in the deposit? And I was so upset, I could hardly think straight. I kept getting confused and forgetting and repeating. So they told me to walk through the entire day in my mind and tell them every detail. And I did. Because I wanted to help them catch whoever hurt you."

Jill bites her lower lip, her teeth clashing against the silver ring piercing it. "I did something really stupid, Audrey. I got to the part where we were counting the money and getting ready to go to the bank. And I got mad because I thought, if only Ty or I had gone with you, none of this would've happened. So I told them how Ty usually goes with you, but how he was in a rush to go somewhere else on Saturday, and how you let him off early. And they made me say that over, like, three times. And I didn't realize what they were getting at."

Jill's eyes well up with tears. "And then they went to Ty's house and they asked him questions and searched his room and they arrested him and it's all my fault. I didn't say I thought he did it, I just said he should've gone with you to protect you. And I don't know how everything got so messed up. But now that you're better you can tell them what really happened, and they'll let him go, right?"

"I was going to ask *you* to tell *me* what happened. Because no one in this hospital will give me a straight answer."

"You mean you don't remember?"

"The last thing I recall was waiting for a parking spot on Elm Street."

"Elm? No, you parked in the municipal garage. That's where they found you…in the elevator. And your car was on Level 3."

I close my eyes and try to picture myself winding up the ramps in the garage. Nothing. I try to force an image of myself pushing the elevator button. Nada.

"So someone grabbed all the deposit money from me in the garage?"

"And they took your fannypack too," Jill says. "You had no ID on you—that's why they were calling you the Mystery Woman on the news."

And I had no plans for the weekend, so no one missed me until Monday. How sad is that?

Gingerly I touch the long track of my stitches. "What did the mugger do to me, Jill?"

"They didn't tell me anything when I came in to identify you, but the next day, when I was here visiting, a doctor came in with a whole group of medical students, just like on TV. And he told them you were a case of blunt force trauma to the head with multiple lacerations. Those were his exact words. And then he said a lot of medical stuff I didn't understand, but one of the students asked what caused the trauma and the doctor said your injuries were consistent with being kicked in the head. Several times."

Jill pauses and stares at me anxiously. I know she's looking for some sign that all this information has started the projector rolling somewhere in my memory. I'd like to reassure her.

But the screen remains blank.

I feel like I'm riding the waves on a rough surf day at the Jersey shore. Every time I stand on the beach, a wave knocks me flat, turns me upside down and forces me to kick frantically to get my head above water. But even when I'm rightside up, the painkillers I'm on encase my brain in sand. I can't think, can't reason.

Was I the victim of a random mugging, or did someone follow me from Mrs. Szabo's house, intent on stealing the money from the sale? Is that someone Tyshaun? Alone in my hospital room, I see Tyshaun's restlessness on the day of the sale in a whole new light. Rob me…maybe. He is, after all, a convicted thief. Stomp on my head like he's playing Whack-A-Mole on the Boardwalk? I touch the bald spot on my head and lick my swollen lips. No, it can't be. Never. The brutality of the attack simply doesn't jibe with the Tyshaun I know. Funny. Charming. Hard-working. Eager for a new start. And yet…

"Detective Coughlin, ma'am."

A very large man has materialized at my bedside. Hard to believe a person this big could enter my room so silently. "I'm the detective investigating your attack, Ms. Nealon." He extends a spade-sized hand but I have no desire to sustain further injuries and keep my hands under the covers. "Do you feel well enough to answer a few questions?"

The truth is I feel absolutely exhausted. The combination of my fifty-foot stroll with PT Larry and my visit with Jill has left me totally enervated. How will I ever be able to go back to work lifting boxes and moving sofas when I barely have the strength to raise my hand? But I can't send this cop away. I need to know what happened to me.

"Why did you arrest Tyshaun Griggs?" I ask.

Detective Coughlin gives me one long, unblinking look, then pulls out his notebook and begins making name, rank and serial number queries as if I had never spoken.

"Your home address? "

"419 Bishop Street. Did you find the money that was stolen?"

"The location of your business?"

"6312 Aspinwell Avenue. What about my fannypack?"

"Make and model of the car you drive?"

"Green Honda Civic. Who's got my car?"

Coughlin takes notes methodically. His huge hand hides the page as he writes. His face is equally hard to read.

Finally he looks up. "Tell me about Saturday."

"My memory is a little spotty," I explain. "The doctor says that's normal."

"Do your best."

There's something irresistible about this cop, and I don't mean in a sexual way because I've never been attracted to the burly football player type. I mean he exudes a magnetic force that draws out information as if each fact were made of metal. I want information from him, but I find myself talking to him about the sale, the deposit, the drive to the bank, my trouble finding a parking spot.

I leave out Ty's eagerness to be gone at the end of the day.

"Was there anything unusual about this sale?" he asks. "Anyone acting funny, asking a lot of questions?"

Nothing unusual about the sale itself, but plenty of weirdness before the sale. I'd honestly forgotten about the drugs in the kitchen drawer until just now. I should tell this cop about the Ecstasy, no? Maybe my beating has something to do with the drugs. But if I tell him about the drugs, I might have to explain the trunk and the ring I took from it and why that drove every other thought from my head. Shit, this is so confusing! I need to wait until I can think straight before I say anything more.

"Unusual about the sale?" I hear my voice ascending in an Alvin the Chipmunk squeak. "No-o-o, this was one of my smaller sales. Some of the buyers were regulars, some were people I've never seen before. No one dangerous looking."

When I finish, silence descends. Coughlin sits tranquilly, like some meditating yogi.

And even though I know it's a trap, I fall right into it.

"I know Jill told you that Tyshaun didn't want to go to the bank with me. But you're taking that all wrong. Tyshaun had a date, he was eager to get going. I told him I didn't need him to come with me. I've made the deposit by myself many, many times."

Again, that long, unblinking look. "Did he tell you he had a date?"

This is tricky, because Tyshaun didn't tell me anything. I simply assumed sex was the draw pulling him out the door last Saturday.

"He's not in the habit of confiding his personal plans to me," I tell the cop, aware that I sound like some tight-ass librarian. "What makes you think he didn't have a date?"

"He has no alibi for the time of your attack, Ms. Nealon. If he was with a woman, all he needs to do is give us her name so we can establish his whereabouts. Can you think of a reason why he's not willing to do that?"

Coughlin is waiting. Waiting and staring like a cat who's seen a mouse disappear into a crack.

I lean forward and stare back at him. I see a man about my own age, with pale blue eyes and freckles that ought to make him look friendly, but don't. He has a neck as thick as a telephone pole and biceps that warp the pinstripes in his jacket. I'm not afraid of him— why should I be? But I can see he's used to instilling fear in others. I don't like that.

I can think of plenty of reasons why Tyshaun doesn't want to say who he was with on Saturday night. Maybe he was out with a girl whose other boyfriend is even tougher than this cop. Maybe he doesn't want Coughlin hassling his friends. Jail has taught Tyshaun that safety hinges on keeping your mouth shut. He figures I'll wake up and tell the cops who attacked me. I can't do that, but I can do the next best thing.

"Tyshaun doesn't need an alibi, Detective. I don't remember much about the actual attack. But I do remember this: when I was already down on the floor of the elevator and the person was getting ready to kick me again, I saw the skin of his leg." I look boldly into

Coughlin's eyes.

" It was white."

Chapter 10

"Here we are!" Jill sings out gaily as she throws open the door to my condo, sounding like one of the artificially cheery aides at my father's nursing home. "Home again!"

Although I'm profoundly relieved to be out of the hospital, it's hard to feel much joy at being back in this condo. I look around. Same beige carpeting, same unadorned off-white walls, same doggy scent.

I head for the living room, already exhausted by the walk from car. My nose twitches. As I walk into the room I hit a wall of sweet scent. A huge bouquet of flowers sits on the table: lilies, freesia, iris, stock. Not a cheap carnation or mum in sight.

"Wow! Who sent these?" I reach for the little white envelope nestled in the arrangement while Jill watches breathlessly as I read the handwritten note.

Audrey,

I'm so sorry about your terrible injury. Jill tells me you're recovering. Is there any way I can help? Let me know when you're well enough for visitors.

All best,

Cal

I feel myself flushing hotly. "You told Cal Tremaine I was in the hospital?" I didn't intend my voice to sound so accusatory, but I'm humiliated by the thought of Jill calling people, scrounging up pity for me.

"I didn't tell him. It was all over the news. And the police talked to him. He called the office to ask how you were doing. I just told him the truth." Her eyes are wide and shiny, her lower lip slightly tremulous.

Luckily Ethel charges in and dispels the tension. When the fur stops flying I pull myself out of Ethel's embrace and make a casual suggestion.

"How about driving me over to the office?" Although my car is parked outside in its usual spot, I've been forbidden to drive for another week, doctor's orders.

Jill looks at me as if I've suggested an afternoon of kick-boxing. "No, Audrey, you can't! The doctor said you have to take it easy. No stress, no lifting."

"Jill, being away from the office is what I find stressful, not being in it," I plead. "Please, take me over. I won't lift anything heavier than a file folder."

Thrown for a loop by this role reversal, Jill hesitates. I press my advantage. "I just want to check the accounts, look over the mail."

"You can check your email from here. And I brought you all the snail mail." She drops a plastic ShopRite bag bulging with envelopes beside me. "I've paid every bill that's come in since you were hurt."

Shit! Why is she suddenly so efficient? The truth is, I have a caterpillar need for the cocoon of my office. I want to wiggle through the familiar clutter. I want to sit at my desk and gaze at my ever-changing gallery of velvet Elvis paintings. I want to inhale the scent of Jill's aroma therapy candles, and eat wasabi soy nuts from the bag in her drawer. I won't be home until I'm there.

"C'mon, Jill—please? I won't stay long, I promise." I stand up and head for the door, as if going were a foregone conclusion. Unfortunately, I stagger when I reach for my coat. This is the most exercise I've had in a week.

"You see?" Jill accuses, snatching the jacket away. "You're still unsteady on your feet. Sit back down and I'll make you some lunch. And where are those pills the doctor gave you? You're supposed to take your next dose at noon."

"I don't want them."

Jill fishes them out of my coat pocket. "You hafta take 'em."

I've been trying to wean myself off my painkillers. I hate the fog that descends over my brain minutes after I swallow them. But I hate even more the rising tide of pain that thumps against the inside of my skull when I try to do without them.

Sulky at being thwarted, I eat my sandwich but leave the pills like a pile of peas on a toddler's plate. Jill continues to fuss around the apartment, fluffing pillows, cleaning out my fridge, making tea. I feel like I'm being swarmed by a cloud of gnats. A really sweet cloud of gnats, but still.

"Why don't you go back to the office, Jill. I think I'll take a little nap."

She shakes a black nail-polished finger at me. "Take those pills."

I swallow, and in a last flurry of chatter, Jill leaves.

I'm alone for the first time since the attack. It feels good: no nurses, no therapists, no hospital clamor. I begin to sift through the mail.

Ethel's nails click across the kitchen floor. The refrigerator hums. Has this condo always been so creepily quiet in the middle of the day? I glance around for my iPod, then remember it was in my fannypack. Whoever attacked me is listening to my Goo Goo Dolls and Mat Kearney.

I really wish I hadn't thought of that.

Why was I so eager to get rid of Jill? I click on the TV for a little friendly noise. In mid-afternoon, the airwaves are full of *Law and Order* reruns—no thank you. And cooking shows—those will only make the Lean Cuisine that Jill left for my dinner seem even worse. And decorating shows. "When we return, you'll learn how to transform vacation mementos and family snapshots from clutter to *art*," the show's host promises with a wink to the camera.

No need for me to stay tuned for that lesson. I'm woefully short of mementos and snapshots. Except for one. I heave myself off the sofa, a maneuver that leaves me temporarily light-headed. Regaining my equilibrium, I make my way over to the bookshelves under the window.

The picture of my hand clasped in my mother's sits between piles of books. Honestly, I don't look at it that often. But I wanted to have it. So one day, I took it off the piano at Dad's house and brought it over here. I don't know if my father ever noticed the photo was gone. If he did, he didn't care enough to comment.

I study the picture now. Despite the fact that my grandparents poured on stories of my mother's love and devotion, niggling seeds of doubt sprouted as I got older, weeds pushing though a solid slab of concrete.

If she died, why was her body never found? If she didn't die, she must have run away. And what kind of mother abandons her family on Christmas Eve?

What kind of child makes her mother flee?

Now, the ring. The ring is tangible proof that the story of my mother's disappearance cannot be fully explained by the facts on record: the snowy road, the sliding car, the treacherous lake. My fingers tighten on the picture frame as I feel the pill-induced numbness seeping through my body. My fears and doubts are not unfounded. There is more to know.

As the piles of sorted mail grow, my eyelids start to droop. I lean back against the sofa cushions as dreams begin to dance with reality. I'm driving my car around and around. I come to a mountain of flowers and I can't get around it. Soon traffic builds up and horns start blowing. Honk, honk…then the honks turn to bells. A persistent ringing.

My eyes snap open and I jolt upright. That sound is real. Someone's leaning on my doorbell. I stagger to my feet and wipe a trickle of drool from the corner of my mouth. The sun is still brightly shining; I couldn't have been asleep that long, but I feel groggy and stupefied.

"Coming, I'm coming!" I shout as I lumber toward the door. Since no one but Jill knows I'm home, it must be her, returning with more mail. I fling open the door without looking through the peephole.

Tyshaun stands on the threshold.

Delighted, I throw open my arms to welcome him.

He pushes past me and kicks the door shut. Contorted with scorn, his face looks like something you'd see in those violent videos that PTA moms sign petitions against.

I back away. "Look, Ty, I'm sorry they arrested you. But as soon as I woke up and talked to the police I told them—"

"Told them what, Audrey?" Tyshaun fills my tiny foyer. He's never seemed so big before. "When that red-haired cop came to let me outta jail, he told me he still likes me for beating and robbing you. He said he had to let me go for now, but soon as he gets more evidence he's gonna lock my ass back up."

"What do you mean? Why?"

"He thinks you're lying. Thinks I'm threatening you or summin' like that." Tyshaun's fierce glare bores into me. "Why you do me like this Audge? All you had to do is tell him who really hurt you. "

I feel a hot flush surge into my cheeks. "I don't know who attacked me, Tyshaun. The last thing I remember is driving down Elm Street, looking for a parking spot. Everything after that is a blank. When I realized Detective Coughlin had arrested you, I knew he was wrong. So I *did* lie. I told him that I remembered seeing the skin on the mugger's leg, and that it was white."

We stare each other down for a moment. Then Ty hangs his head and scuffs his sneaker on the floor.

"Really? You did that for me?"

My fingers trace the stitches on my forehead. I know Ty didn't do this to me. "I wanted the cops to stop chasing the wrong person.

If you were locked up, then the guy who really attacked me is still out there. But I shouldn't have told Detective Coughlin that the person who kicked me was white. I don't know—he could have been black, white, brown, anything."

Ty peers at me from under his hoodie. "Audge, I been thinking that what happened might be 'cause of the drugs we found. Maybe the dealer thinks you stole his stuff."

"But if he came and took it back, why would he think I stole it?"

Ty scratches his head. "I don't know, man. This is fucked up. I been askin' around on the street and nobody knows nothin' about anyone using that old lady's house as a stash. Maybe we shoulda told the cops about it as soon as we found it."

"I thought about telling Detective Coughlin when he interviewed me in the hospital. But I was so drugged up—I wanted to think about it first before I said anything."

You'd be surprised how little time there is to think in the hospital. Between the steady stream of doctors, nurses, therapists, visitors and meal deliveries, I hardly had a minute to myself. And when I was alone, my brain was either fogged by drugs or wracked by pain. But always back there lurking was the need to grapple with this little lie that seems to be growing bigger and bigger.

"So tell him now," Ty says.

"I have to figure out the right way. I don't want to say anything that might make him suspect you again." I reach out and touch Ty's arm. "I did the best I could to protect you. I guess lying to the police isn't as easy as it looks."

He shifts his weight uneasily. "I couldn't believe I was back in jail again," he says softly. "And this time, I didn't even do nuthin'." He sighs. "Jill was right. If I'd'a went with you to the bank, none of this woulda happened."

"It's okay. But why can't you tell Detective Coughlin who you were with that night? If you're trying to protect the girl, I could talk to Coughlin first. Ask him to meet with her privately. No one else would have to know."

Suddenly the fire is back in Tyshaun's eyes. "Who I was with is my bizness. Don't have nothin' to do with you or with Coughlin. You wanna tell that racist cop something, you tell him to go find the actual goon who robbed you."

Tyshaun pivots and opens the door. "Leave me and mine outta it."

Chapter 11

Day two of my liberation from the hospital. Jill still won't let me come to the office, but she's willing to let me do something much more stressful: visit my dad. Manor View Senior Living hasn't been graced by my presence since the day after I found my mother's ring in Mrs. Szabo's house. Since then I've been beaten, robbed, had brain surgery and lay in a coma for nearly a week. So I guess no one can accuse me of being neglectful—I do have my reasons for not playing the dutiful daughter. But I can't milk my injuries much longer—it's time to make the trip across town to visit my father.

I still haven't been cleared to drive, so Jill is dropping Ethel and me off.

"So, should I come back in an hour, an hour and a half?" Jill asks.

"No!" I realize how frantic my voice sounds at the thought of being left here so long, so I try for a more reasonable tone. "I think half an hour ought to do it. My dad tires easily, you know."

Clearly she thinks there's no point in her leaving if she has to return so soon, but I can't invite her in to meet my father. Even without the power of speech he'll manage to convey his deep disapproval of Jill, with her Chinese calligraphy tattoos, her eyebrow stud and her latest unfortunate coif. I have enough to explain to him without having to defend my choice of employees.

"Okay," Jill says. "I noticed a Dunkin' Donuts not far from here so I'll hang there for a while and you can call me when you're ready to be picked up."

"Perfect." I grab Ethel's leash and prepare myself to be pulled through the front door by a dog ready for a treat-scarfing extravaganza. "See you in a few."

If there are new occupants in the wheelchairs lining the entrance hall, I can't pick them out. Ethel moseys along, licking fingers and snuffling afghans.

"What happened to you, sweetie?" an old lady shouts out. "Ya look like ya got hit by a truck."

There's a perk of old age—you get to blurt out the unfiltered truth wherever you see it. I've stowed my narcotic pain medicine in the bathroom and switched to three ibuprophen every four hours to convince myself that I'm healing nicely and my scars aren't obvious. Clearly I'm delusional. Even my father will probably notice my changed appearance. Pulling Ethel closer for support, I push open the door to his room.

As usual, he's sitting in a chair beside the window, staring blankly at the opposite wall. His slack face lights up as Ethel charges toward him and he keeps his eyes focused on her. The time he spends playing with the dog seems to stretch on interminably. Finally, he can't delay any longer. He raises his eyes and looks at me. I see him recoil.

"Hi, Dad. Sorry I haven't been here for a while." I sink into the other chair. "I don't know if the nurses here told you, but I've been in the hospital."

He shakes his head, his eyes never leaving my face. They move up and down, drinking in every detail, from my patchy hair to my mottled purple-yellow bruises. He opens his mouth and a sound something between a moan and a query comes out.

"I was mugged in a parking garage. I had a lot of cash on me from a house sale. I guess the guy followed me."

He responds with a croak that I'm guessing means "who?"

"The police haven't caught him yet," I say. I wonder if they ever will. Detective Coughlin sent a patrolman to my condo this morning to drop off my keys. Maybe he's lost interest in the case since he had to release Ty.

My father's eyes widen and he gets very agitated. He starts pushing on the arms of his chair as if he's trying to stand up. Then he realizes he can't walk anymore and flings himself backward in frustration. "Bah! Bah!" he shouts at me, all the while waving his right hand in the direction of his nightstand. Ethel slinks under the bed.

On the nightstand I see a small yellow note pad and a pen. I hand it to him and he begins to write.

His brow is furrowed, his breathing labored, his fingers grip the pen fiercely. The nib digs into the paper with every agitated scrawl. Finally, he stops and thrusts the pad toward me.

I have to study the seemingly random lines for a moment before they form into words. JUST MONEY?

He must be worried that I was raped. I reassure him. "Yes, all he did was steal the money from the sale. It was almost $5,000, but I'm insured. I'll get it back eventually."

Dad leans forward and peers at my face. He lifts his hand and gestures toward my scar. "Whuh?"

"Why did he beat me up?"

He nods in agreement. I shrug. I've asked myself that question many times. "Maybe I didn't give it up quickly enough and that made him mad. Maybe he was hopped up on drugs."

He shakes his head furiously, flapping his good hand at me until I return the notepad. More heavy breathing. More illegible writing.

DANGER. WILL TRY AGAIN.

"No, Dad," I reassure him. "I learned my lesson. I'll never carry cash to the bank alone again."

He doesn't try to write any more, but his hands continue to

fidget with the pen and pad. I wouldn't have thought my attack would worry him so much. Well, that's a little harsh. I guess what I mean to say is, I figured he would blame me for what happened. Surely if he still had the power of speech I would have to hear the "this would never have happened if…" lecture. Would never have happened if I'd gone to graduate school in math. Would never have happened if I'd accepted one of the job offers I'd had from Morgan Stanley or the Commerce Department.

So that's the upside of the stroke. He can't say all that. He can only express what he can scratch out on that little pad, so he has to boil it down to the essentials: He's worried about me.

I'm touched.

I reach out to calm his agitated hands. For the first time since he's arrived here, he doesn't pull away. We sit like that for a while, not talking. It's nice.

"Look who's here!" A young woman with a sleek blond ponytail and a tunic printed with dancing cats bounces into the room. "Hi," she says to me. "I'm Ashley, your father's occupational therapist."

She turns to Dad. "I see you're using your note pad to communicate. That's so awesome!" Ashley uses the same high-pitched happy voice I use when congratulating Ethel for sitting still to have her muddy paws wiped. "Do you want to show your daughter how good you're doing with your life skills exercises?"

A scowl darkens my father's face. I can't imagine he wants me to watch him playing games with this chirpy, ungrammatical girl.

"I was just leaving," I tell Ashley. "I won't distract you from your work." I call for Ethel and head to the door. When I turn on the threshold to wave goodbye, my father's eyes lock with mine and I sense an emotion there I've never seen before.

Fear.

Chapter 12

I read the sign in the window of the store on a crooked little block in the West Village: CUSTOM ARTISTRY IN A MASS-PRODUCED WORLD. NO TWO DESIGNS ALIKE. R. ATWELL, PROP. A few clicks of my digital camera, an internet search, and some emails have brought me to the jeweler who designed my mother's ring. I'm carrying the ring in a little silk pouch. I'd like to wear it, but I haven't had it resized yet. The jeweler in Palmyrton said that would take a week, and I was eager to bring it to this little shop in Manhattan to find out the ring's backstory. Because this little piece of gold is starting to feel like the stranger who rides into town in an old-time Western.

I enter the jewelry store.

The man behind the counter has shoulder-length gray hair pulled back in a ponytail, exposing a high forehead and prominent nose. His long fingers open the drawstring pouch and he gently shakes the ring out onto a velvet pad on the countertop. The moment he sees the twisted vine design his eyes light up. Holding the ring inches from his eye, a smile animates his serious face as if he's encountered a long-lost childhood friend.

"You designed the ring?" I ask.

"Yes. It was part of a vine series I did in the seventies." His voice is dreamy. He's speaking to me but his eyes never leave the ring. "This piece was purchased by a math professor as a gift for his wife. He brought her in afterwards to have the ring sized. A lovely woman. Very slender fingers."

He's talking about my parents. He actually remembers them. I try to imagine my father seeking out this off-the-beaten-track store to select the perfect gift for my mother. Spending a significant amount of money. My father, who never picked out a gift for me in my life. For my birthday and Christmas he'd give my grandmother a hundred bucks and tell her to buy me something. By the time I was a teenager, he didn't even bother with that.

"Are you interested in selling this?" Atwell asks.

"No!"

The edge in my voice gets his attention. He stops examining the ring and studies me. "They were your parents," he says finally. "Yes, I see the resemblance. You favor your father."

Unfortunately. My mother was the great beauty: auburn hair, green eyes, delicate features. But I seem to have received more than fifty percent of my genes from my father, from my wiry brown hair and lanky frame to my ability to add columns of figures in my head.

"Yes," I say. "This ring belonged to my mother. It was missing for a long time and I recently found it."

His eyes meet mine and hold for a beat; he seems to intuit that his beautiful creation hasn't spent the past thirty years in happy circumstances. "Losing it must have upset her," Atwell says softly. "She was very pleased with your father's gift."

"I'm amazed that you remember them so clearly," I say. "Do you have such complete recall of all your customers?"

He smiles and shakes his head. "Some I prefer to forget as quickly as possible. Your father was a fri--, not a friend, an adversary of mine." His smile spreads to his eyes. "Roger and I competed against one another in a chess league. He was quite a player. Does he still—."

Atwell's voice trails off. At my age, I assume that people I've lost touch with are still alive, but at his age, that's not a safe bet. I'm not in the mood to explain our sorry family history, so I keep it brief. "My mom has passed away. My dad recently had a stroke and hasn't fully recovered."

"I'm sorry." Atwell has a sort of Buddhist simplicity about him that I really like. No gushing, no pity; accept what is and move on. "Your father wanted a special gift for your mother, so he came to me. They were clearly very much in love. And I was very pleased that particular ring was to be worn by your mother. It suited her perfectly. I remember her holding up her hand to admire it. She said, 'I'll never take this off.'"

But she had. I look over Mr. Atwell's shoulder into a cluttered office behind the shop. Not a computer in sight, but rusty metal file cabinets bulge with orders and receipts. "I wonder if you could tell me when they bought the ring?" I ask.

This is an imposition, I know, but Mr. Atwell is neither impatient nor inquisitive. He ambles back to his office to rummage through the files while I wander around the shop looking in the display cases. I feel like I should buy something to thank him for his trouble, but there are no trinkets here. I can't afford a four-figure thank-you, so I return to look at the ring I already own. I have to admit, I don't for a moment feel that I've stolen it from Cal Tremaine; I've simply repossessed what is rightfully mine.

While Atwell is in the back, I slide the ring onto my little finger. It doesn't look right. I'm definitely taking it to the jewelry store in Palmyrton when I get home.

Atwell comes out of his office and I drop the ring guiltily. I know he won't think it suits me as it suited my mother, won't be happy thinking the ring has found a new home on my hand.

He's holding a yellowed receipt which he places before me. I see my father's name and address, a description of the ring, and the price all printed in Atwell's meticulous script.

And I see the date: seven months before my birth.

I had been along for the ride that day when they visited Atwell's shop. Maybe I was the reason for the gift. I try to imagine my father so excited about my impending arrival that he rushed out to buy my mother this ring. The image isn't coming.

"Is there anything else I can do for you?" the jeweler asks.

There isn't. It's time for me to go, yet I'm strangely reluctant to leave. It's so rare for me to be in the presence of someone who knew both my parents. I realize that since Nana and Pop died, I probably haven't spent time with anyone who knew my mother and father. Mr. Atwell has whetted my appetite. There must be old family friends, neighbors, sorority sisters…someone who can tell me more about my parents, someone else who knew them when they were in love, who can shine some light on what my mother might have been doing that snowy Christmas Eve.

I haven't answered Mr. Atwell so he speaks again. "I'm afraid I haven't been able to offer you what you were looking for." His kind eyes search for reassurance.

I reach across the counter and take his hand in mine. "Oh yes, Mr. Atwell. You've helped me more than you can know."

Chapter 13

Old Spice. Pipe tobacco. Bengay.

It's my first day back at work since the accident and I'm grateful to have this job. Rather than call in another estate sale organizer, Martin Reicker's daughter, Ginny, has waited patiently for my recovery. I'm glad I took the time to go to the old man's memorial service, not only because it brought me this job, but also because the Reickers are truly nice people. Martin Reicker's house exudes a cozy, reassuring smell that makes me want to curl up in his leather club chair with a book from his library and some tea in a mug handmade by one of his granddaughters.

There's good money in this house. The old gent was a collector: shelves of signed first editions, binders full of baseball cards, stamps, coins, civil war artifacts, presidential memorabilia. It'll take me weeks to find the right buyers for all this treasure.

But beyond the valuable items, there's a strong presence here of a life well lived. One wall of the foyer is a shrine to Martin Reicker's family: serious young men in military uniforms, grinning toddlers with Big Bird, hopeful graduates in their motarboards, joyful brides in their finery. There are probably some black sheep in the Reicker flock, but you wouldn't know it from this proud display.

In every room there are little clues to the interest Mr. Reicker took in the world. A pair of binoculars by the window where a birdfeeder is mounted. Post-it notes sticking out of magazines and books. A binder in the kitchen bulging with clipped recipes. A thick address book held together with a rubber band. This is what I love about my work—the chance to press my nose against the glass of another person's life. To see how life is lived in other families. Real families.

The brilliant rays of the morning sun illuminate a display of postcards stuck to Mr. Reicker's fridge. I flip over a picture of the Eiffel Tower and read the message on the back. "Hi Dad! Paris is great. The kids loved Notre Dame. We ate at the café you told us about. Wish you were here, Stephanie"

I run my finger across the faded writing and try to imagine writing a postcard to my father. Then I let my fantasy run wild and picture him wanting to keep something I'd sent him. Too much of a stretch. Back to work.

As I inventory the contents of Mr. Reicker's kitchen, I hear Tyshaun clumping around upstairs. He's been quiet and aloof since spending those three days in jail. Although he works as hard as ever, the jokey camaraderie he shared with me and Jill is gone. Any efforts to jolly him out of his funk are met with a cold stare. He's a black guy with a prison record; I'm a white girl with a BS in math. There's a chasm between us and Ty's not about to let me forget it. At the end of each day he makes a point of asking if there's anything else he needs to do, then he slouches off, hood up, shoulders hunched against the cold.

I'm deeply engrossed in Mr. Reicker's collection of vintage cookbooks when I hear a tapping sound. Spinning around, I see a man's face peering at me through the kitchen window.

I open my mouth, but as in a dream, I can't summon a sound.

The face disappears and I hear footsteps crossing the porch to the back door. The unlocked back door.

I take a deep breath and this time the scream is long and loud.

The noise brings Tyshaun and Jill on the double.

"There's a man outside," I say, pointing at the back porch with a shaking finger.

Tyshaun flings open the door. "Yo! What you doing out here?"

There's the sound of a scuffle as Tyshaun hauls someone from the back porch into the kitchen.

Good lord, it's Cal Tremaine! His tie, which probably cost more than everything I'm wearing, is askew and his perfectly starched shirt has come untucked.

"Let him go, Ty. It's Mr. Tremaine, one of our clients."

Ty releases his grip and Cal brushes the wrinkles out of his Italian wool suit jacket.

"I'm so sorry," I say. "We've been a little jumpy since my attack."

Cal smiles weakly, keeping a wary eye on Tyshaun. "Understandable." Then he switches his focus to me and startles. "My God, Audrey, you look terrible. I didn't understand how badly you were hurt."

"It's not so bad." I turn my head away from his curious stare. "I'm getting better...uh, what *were* you doing out there?"

"I didn't mean to sneak up on you. I stopped by your office to see how you were doing, but there was a note on the door saying you were over here. I was heading this way for an afternoon appointment, so I thought I'd stop by." Cal offers up a rueful smile. "You were supposed to call me when you were up to having visitors. I got tired of waiting."

"Oh...I'm sorry. I meant to... I tried calling you to thank you for the flowers but I got your voicemail. I left a message. They're beautiful. The flowers, I mean." I'm babbling again. Can someone please stuff a sock in my mouth?

At the mention of flowers, a light clicks on in Jill's eyes, as surely as if I'd thrown a switch. "C'mon, Tyshaun. We better get back to work."

He's about to protest but Jill fixes him with a penetrating glare. Christ, could she be any more obvious?

They leave together, but not before Tyshaun tosses one last smoldering stare at Cal.

"Your employees are very protective," Cal says, sitting down at Mr. Reicker's kitchen table.

"Look, I'm really sorry. Ty didn't realize who you were. I hope he didn't hurt you."

"Not at all," Cal smiles and pats the seat next to him, inviting me to sit. "He's loyal to his boss. I can appreciate that."

Cal's remark cheers me. Despite the coolness Ty has been displaying lately, he is loyal, and even someone who barely knows us recognizes it. Once I'm seated, I notice the trembling in my legs. A delayed reaction, I guess, to unaccustomed work, unaccustomed stress, and the unaccustomed presence of a handsome man.

"So how are you, Audrey?" Cal reaches out and gently touches the raw scar on my forehead.

I flinch, not because it hurts but because the gesture seems to cross a boundary. I swivel to present my unscarred side. "I'm fine, honestly. Just fine."

"Have the police made any headway in their investigation? When they talked to me, their focus was on your assistant, but I see he's been released."

I shake my head. "I don't know what's going on. The detective in charge of my case still thinks that Tyshaun's responsible. Ty says the cops are following him, keeping an eye on him. What scares me is that if they're still investigating Ty, maybe they're not even looking for the real mugger. But then, I'm not really helping matters." I screw up my nerve and look straight into Cal's eyes. "You know, I still have never told the cops about the drugs in the kitchen. Maybe whoever owned those drugs attacked me."

Cal meets my gaze, then his mouth tightens and he shakes his head. "God, I've been such an ass. Of course I thought of that. Those drugs would link a criminal with my aunt's house. But when the cop talked to me, he asked general questions and I didn't volunteer anything extra. It's my training as a lawyer, I guess. Never give 'em more than they ask for." He looks down at his hands clasped in the table. "I didn't want those drugs to have anything to do with your attack. The cops were focused on Tyshaun, and I wanted to believe they were right because that would be more convenient for me. I could get the cop out of my office and get back to working on the campaign." He sits silently for a moment, then looks up at me. "I'm so sorry, Audrey. It's like I lost sight of the fact that a real person—someone I know, someone I like—got hurt here. The police need to know about those drugs. You can't keep living in fear."

"But how can I tell them now, after so much time has passed? What can I say? 'Oh, by the way, did I ever mention that Ty found a bag full of Ecstasy in the kitchen two days before the sale, and then it disappeared.' This cop is pretty sharp. He'll ask me a million questions about why I didn't call immediately. Then I'll have to tell him about the trunk of jewelry and that'll look even more suspicious." I bury my head in my hands. "I've been paralyzed by indecision. I don't want to make things worse for Ty, but I can't stand thinking that the guy who came after me is still out there. I don't know what to do."

Cal squeezes my shoulder. "I'll tell them. I'll tell them I found it when I was sorting through my aunt's things, and waited overnight to call the police because I had an important campaign event and didn't have the time to get tied up with filing the report. Then when I came back the next morning intending to call, it was gone. I'll leave you and Ty and the trunk completely out of it."

I lift my head up. "And how will you explain why you're suddenly coming forward now?"

"Guess I'll tell them the truth—that I'm a slimeball lawyer more concerned with my work than with justice." He smiles at me. "Bet they'll have no trouble believing that. Who's the detective I should call?"

"Coughlin."

"*Sean* Coughlin? Big guy with red hair and freckles?"

"Yeah—you know him?"

Cal's mouth twists in distaste. "Oh, I know him all right. My firm represented the city of Palmyrton in a huge police brutality lawsuit a few years back. Coughlin and his partner cost the taxpayers two million bucks. Guy's a real loose cannon. The only reason he's still on the force is his partner took the fall for him on the criminal charges. That and he comes from a long line of cops. One of his uncles used to be chief."

Cal places his hands flat on the table and leans forward urgently. "Listen, Audrey, I know a lot of people in this town. Let me make some calls. I'll get through to the police chief and find out what's really going on. This Coughlin character is the wrong guy for the job. I can get someone top-notch assigned to your case. It's the least I can do after throwing you under the bus."

I have a mini out-of-body experience in which I'm acutely aware of every detail of this scene in Mr. Reicker's kitchen. I'm aware of my breathing, aware that my mouth is slightly open. Aware that Cal's hands are exceptionally nice—manicured, yet strong and masculine. His offer has frozen me. I'm not used to a man wanting to protect me, run interference for me. I'm about to demur, insist there's no need to bother. But I stop myself. Cal Tremaine is willing to push people around on my behalf. It feels good.

I swallow. Pull my gaze away from his hands and look him in the eye. "Thank you. If you'd be willing to do that I'd really appreciate it."

Cal smiles and squeezes my hand. "Consider it done."

Something starts beeping inside his jacket.

"That's the reminder for my two o'clock meeting. I better get going." Cal rises and heads to the door. With his hand on the knob he turns around to look at me. "Are you busy Saturday night?"

I frantically work to keep my face from lighting up like a Christmas tree. I'm pretty sure I fail. "Uh, no—I think I'm free."

"Great! It's Spencer Finneran's sixty-fifth birthday. You can come with me to the party at his house."

Now I probably look like I've been offered anesthesia-free root canal.

Cal doesn't seem to notice. "I really want you to meet him, Audrey. Then you'll understand why this campaign means so much to me. Spencer is all about making New Jersey a great place to live for everybody, not just the rich and the connected."

He smiles that dazzling smile one more time.

"Nothing too fancy. I'll pick you up at seven."

Chapter 14

Shit.

Shit. Shit. Shit.

I'm standing in front of my closet with the kind of curdled feeling you get in your gut when you've eaten three-day-old moo shu pork leftovers. What kind of first date is an invitation to a birthday party for the state's biggest politician? Whatever happened to dinner and a movie? And what does "nothing too fancy" mean? Scotch tape the dog fur off your black pants? Or wear a hot dress from J. Crew instead of a hot dress from Betsey Johnson?

Not that I have hot dresses from either source. The closest I come to glamour is my collection of strapless bridesmaid's dresses. Not only do I have nothing to wear to Spencer Finneran's birthday party, but I also have no clue what I should run out to buy.

Only one person can coach me through this. I press six on my speed dial and wait to be connected to Isabelle Trent. As the owner of Trent Fine Properties, Palmyrton's most exclusive real estate brokerage, Isabelle sends a lot of work my way. She's more than a business contact, but something less than a friend. A pillar of the Junior League, the St Paul's Episcopal Church Vestry, the Bumford-Stanley School Alumni Association and the Westwood Country Club

Greens Committee, Isabelle will most certainly know what to wear to a politician's birthday party.

She answers promptly. The good thing about Isabelle is you can always reach her, day or night.

"Audrey, darling, how are you?"

Before I can answer she continues, "I've got a client on the other line. Let me put you on hold for a sec."

The reason you can always reach Isabelle is because she juggles four or five calls simultaneously. I wait patiently for my turn in the rotation, then I talk fast.

"I've been invited to Spencer Finneran's sixty-fifth birthday party. All I know is it's at his house and it's not too fancy. What should I wear?"

"Spencer's sixty-fifth? Fabulous! How did you— Oh, hang on, I've got to take this."

"I'm going with Cal Tremaine," I tell Isabelle when she returns. Isabelle is listing Mrs. Szabo's house, although it's not the type of property she normally handles. But I imagine Cal Tremaine is the sort of person whose Blackberry Isabelle wants to be in.

"Oh, good show, darling!"

It's taken me years to master Isabelle's own peculiar lexicon. "Good show" is particularly high praise. I guess Isabelle is impressed I landed a date with Cal.

"And I see you've got that precious house all ready for me to sell. Kudos to you!"

"Precious" is Isabelle-ese for ghastly. A precious house is terribly small, poorly located, or atrociously decorated. Or, in Mrs. Szabo's case, all three.

"So the party's on Saturday," I continue quickly. "Can I wear black slacks and my pink cashmere sweater?"

"I'm sure you'd look absolutely precious in that, darling. Another possibility might be— Oh, drat, let me take this. Be right back."

Just as I suspected, the pants and pink sweater are all wrong.

But I dread a shopping excursion to the Short Hills Mall, where I picture myself wandering aimlessly for hours in jeans and clogs, buffeted by crowds of purposeful, stiletto-heeled women.

The phone clicks and Isabelle is back, barking instructions at a brisk clip. "Black sheath. Sleeveless. Nordstrom, second floor. Open-toed pumps."

"Are you sure that's not too fancy?" I protest weakly. I hate wearing dresses.

"Accessories are key here, Audrey. Chunky beads, not pearls or diamonds."

As if had pearls or diamonds. I picture my collection of funky costume jewelry, scavanged from various estate sales. Definitely precious. "I don't have—"

"Lulu's. Tell her I sent you. And Audrey, legs and brows waxed. Mani, Shell Pink. Pedi, Venetian Rose. Must run, darling. But call me on Monday and tell me all about it."

I stare at the dead phone in my hand. Well, at least I have a game plan. Then a new surge of anxiety strikes because I realize I didn't ask Isabelle what to wear over a sleeveless dress in mid-October. My distress telegraphs to Ethel, who lets out a deep sigh from her perch on my bed.

"C'mon baby, let's go see what we can find in the hall closet."

Obligingly, Ethel trails me into the foyer. The closet is stuffed with coats, but each is worse than the next: Patagonia fleece, Lands End down, yellow rain slicker, dirty Sam Spade trench coat. Finally my hand falls on wool and I pull out a full length overcoat.

"Will this work Ethel?"

She cocks her eyebrows and her tail droops.

I haven't worn this coat in years and as I look at myself in the hall mirror, I remember why. A general in the Siege of Leningrad stares back at me from the glass. I go to hang it back up, then stop. This is how the houses I clean out get so stuffed with clutter. Better to pack the coat in a shopping bag and donate it to the homeless. I fully open the louvered folding door on the left side of the closet so I can get a shopping bag from beside the trunk full of Agnes Szabo's jewelry.

The trunk isn't there.

My stomach heaves. I shoved the trunk in the left back corner of this closet, right next to the ironing board. I drop to my knees run my hand along the closet floor—nothing but dust bunnies and a pair of old snow boots.

My heart is hammering now but my brain doesn't want to accept the information being transmitted by my eyes. Ethel feels the need to cram into the closet with me, as if her bloodhound DNA can be of use here. Snuffling around, she knocks the vacuum cleaner over onto both of us.

"Ow!"

Pushing her away, I stand up and wrench open the right-hand closet door.

There, behind the fallen vacuum, sits the trunk.

Thank God! My heart settles down. I'm relieved to see the trunk, but I'm worried now about my short-term memory. I could have sworn that after Cal Tremaine left my condo I shoved the trunk in the left corner of the closet. I can picture myself sliding it past the ironing board. Is that memory false, some kind of hallucination?

I crawl further into the closet. Something else is wrong. The ironing board, which I always keep hanging on a hook, is now propped against the closet wall. I know I didn't move that ironing board. The last time I ironed something, Bill Clinton was in the White House.

I pull the trunk out into the hall. A vague uneasiness has settled over me, the kind of feeling that makes you want to look over your shoulder. Closing my eyes, I picture the jewelry in the trunk as I last saw it. The ugly topaz and garnet brooch was right on top. I lift up the lid and open my eyes.

No brooch.

I dig through the trunk. It's still full of jewelry, but the brooch is now near the bottom.

As if the trunk had been emptied out and repacked.

I rock back on my heels. Someone has been in my apartment, digging through this trunk, pawing through my closet. What else did he touch? The panties in my drawer, the food in my kitchen? Suddenly my home feels dirty.

My fingers run over the scar on my temple. Did the foot that put it there also step into my condo?

S.W. Hubbard

82

Chapter 15

I stand on trembling legs and run for the phone. Punching in three numbers seems to take all my concentration. I keep looking over my shoulder, feeling like the guy who broke into my condo is in here with me still.

"Palmyrton Police. What's your emergen-"

"Listen, I think someone broke into my apartment." My voice sounds high-pitched and shrill as the words tumble out. "This trunk in my closet, it's not where I left it and—"

"Is the intruder still there, ma'am?"

"No, no of course not, but he was here and he got in somehow."

The flat-voiced dispatcher verifies my address and assures me she'll send someone right over. Minutes later, Ethel leaps up from a snooze, puts her paws on the front windowsill and begins barking her crazed "I've got some German Shepherd in me" bark.

Peeking out the window, I see a burly patrolman headed up the walk. I fling open the door before he can knock and Ethel lunges forward.

The cop stops on the sidewalk. "Restrain your dog, ma'am."

I grab Ethel's collar. "Come on in. Put your hand out and let her sniff you. Ethel," I instruct her, "this is a friend."

Ethel stops barking but her ears are still back. Suspiciously she sniffs the cop's hand. Apparently he smells friendly because her ears perk up and her tail begins a slow, circular wag.

"Officer Walsh, ma'am." He pets Ethel's head. "Dog like this is the best burglar alarm you could ever have. But you say someone broke in here?"

"Yes, I—" His comment throws me off balance. I don't think of Ethel as a guard dog; she's a lover, not a fighter. But it's true she defends her turf pretty effectively.

He examines at the front door. "No sign of forcible entry. Good strong deadbolt."

"Yes. That's why I can't understand how he got in here."

"Did you leave the door unlocked?"

"No. He must've picked the lock."

"Only on TV, ma'am." Officer Walsh pulls out a notebook and sizes up the trunk full of jewelry gaping on the hall floor. "What's missing?"

"Uh, I'm not exactly sure." I've never inventoried the jewelry, so I have no idea if the thief took any of the pieces. "This jewelry belongs to a client. I organize estate sales, and I have to have this all appraised, but I haven't gotten around to it yet." As I say the words, I hear how lame they sound. There's something off about this jewelry, some reason why Cal doesn't want me to have it appraised.

Walsh cocks a quizzical eyebrow at me. "Let's start at the beginning ma'am. You noticed signs of a break-in when you came home this afternoon?"

I explain about looking for a coat in the closet and finding things in different places than normal. "This trunk wasn't where I left it."

Writing methodically in his notebook, he continues, "And what else was missing from the closet?"

"I'm not sure. But I do know that the vacuum that was on the left is now on the right, like someone moved everything around.

And the ironing board is off its hook."

Officer Walsh studies me for a long moment. "Your vacuum and your ironing board have been moved. You remember exactly how everything in the closet was arranged?"

I can't blame him for the skepticism in his voice. "Look, I'm sure someone was in here, and searched through the closet."

"And left all this valuable jewelry?"

I can practically hear him thinking, "Watch out for the ones who look normal. They're the craziest of all."

"Thieves like small stuff they can pawn for quick cash. If the thief found this, why would he leave it?"

My mind is racing now. I was so flustered by the trunk being in the wrong spot that I leapt to the conclusion that the person I'm most afraid of had come back for more money. But Walsh's question throws me for a loop. Why wouldn't my attacker take as much jewelry as he could carry? Even a pawn shop would give him at least a thousand bucks for the stuff in the trunk.

"Anything else disturbed in the apartment?" Walsh asks.

"I haven't checked. I called you right away."

"Let's walk through together," he says. He grunts with approval every time he finds another securely locked window, while I relax a little every time I open a cupboard or closet and find everything where it should be. Still, I'm sure that trunk has been moved.

"Place looks clean to me," Walsh says. "Does anyone else have access to your condo? Relative or neighbor with a key?"

"My dad, but he's in a nurs—"

I freeze with my hand on the linen closet door.

Jill.

Jill has the key to my apartment. Jill had the entire week of my hospitalization to go through that trunk. But Jill would never steal anything.

Walsh can see that he's struck a chord. I sense that he's waiting for my explanation, but I'm still trying to work this out in my mind. Maybe Jill just wanted to look at the stuff. She loves campy old jewelry. Maybe she was playing dress-up like a little girl. This idea makes sense. After all, Jill had been taking care of Ethel, and I keep Ethel's leash in the hall closet. Jill must've seen the trunk when she took out the leash, and was tempted to look through the trove of jewelry. I exhale, and all the fear and anxiety leaves my body. That's it. I'm sure that's it.

"I'm so sorry to have over-reacted, officer." I smile at him sheepishly. "You're probably right. My dog-sitter has a key to the apartment. Maybe she knocked some things over when she was getting out Ethel's leash."

"No problem. That's what we're here for." Walsh smiles, but the subtext is, "Dealing with lunatics is part of my job."

Ethel and I watch the patrol car drive off. All's well that ends well.

Chapter 16

For the first time since my attack, I sleep deeply and dreamlessly, waking up nose-to-nose with Ethel, who's been waiting patiently to go out. Bounding out of bed, I pull on sweats and grab the leash. My headache is still with me, but downing three Advil every morning has become as much a part of my morning routine as walking the dog.

Ethel barks steadily while running circles in the front hall. She must really need to pee. I open the door. A strange man stands five feet in front of me.

I scream and slam the door shut.

Heart pounding, I clutch Ethel for courage, too scared to even think what to do next.

The doorbell rings.

Gradually rational thought returns. My attacker would hardly be ringing the bell in broad daylight, now would he? I peer through the peephole. A nondescript, medium built man in gray slacks and a tweed sports coat stands on the stoop. While I watch, he reaches inside his jacket.

"Detective Farrand," he holds up his badge. "I left you a couple of messages yesterday."

Shit! Hours after the patrolman left here yesterday, a call came in from a detective. I intentionally didn't return it because I didn't want to get into a discussion about the trunk. Who knew he'd actually come here in person?

I open the door. "Sorry to react like that. I didn't realize anyone was out here. I opened the door to take my dog out."

"Didn't mean to startle you." He extends his hand. "I'm Detective Elliot Farrand. I'm taking over the investigation of your assault and robbery."

My heart settles down. "Oh, you're replacing Detective Coughlin?"

"Right. I need a moment of your time to go over a few facts."

I feel myself break into a sweat as we sit down at the table. But it turns out there's nothing to be nervous about. Farrand is about as different from Coughlin as two men could be. While Coughlin seemed menacing asking my address, this guy is polite and straightforward. He takes meticulous notes, thanking me when I provide extra information. He doesn't linger on the questions concerning Ty; instead, he seems most interested in who came to Mrs. Szabo's sale and who might have realized how much cash we took in. I try to describe the customers who stick out in my mind: the eastern European couple, the man who charged upstairs to buy the bed, the Hoboken hispters. He writes non-stop.

Then he looks up at me. "When you organized this sale, did you find anything unusual in the house?"

Here it comes. "Unusual? No, Mrs. Szabo didn't have much of great value. Why?"

"Weapons? Drugs? Anything that would lead you to believe there might have been illegal activity going on in the house?"

"No—why?" Playing dumb is not my strong suit, but if Farrand notices I'm nervous he doesn't let on.

"We've recently received some information that this house might have been involved in some drug activity. The executor of Mrs. Szabo's estate, Cal Tremaine—I guess you know him?"

I nod, and Farrand continues. "Mr. Tremaine told us he found some street drugs in his aunt's kitchen when he was going through the house. We don't know if it's related to your attack. We're investigating."

"Great." So, true to his word, Cal did tell the police about the drugs. And Farrand isn't pinning the appearance and disappearance of the Ecstasy on Ty. Imagining Detective Farrand spending the week methodically tracking down anyone ever associated with Mrs. Szabo's house makes me feel better. This guy is on the right track. Cal was right—I don't need a loose cannon like Coughlin on my case. Patient police work will bring in the man who hurt me.

When Farrand stands to go, I shake his hand again. "Thank you, detective. You'll call me as soon as you know something?"

He doesn't smile, just meets my eye steadily. "Absolutely."

By the time we finally get out of the condo, poor Ethel is about to burst. Because the weather is so nice and she's been so patient, I let Ethel drag me on a longer than usual loop around the neighborhood. Although my headaches persist, the dizziness is gone and I feel stronger every day. Rounding a corner onto Birch Street I come upon a yard with a huge pile of leaves raked in front of a plastic climbing structure. I stop and stare.

Melody Olsen.

Looking at the scene takes me back twenty five years. Melody and I used to jump off the ladder of her backyard swing and slide set into a pile of leaves. Over and over we'd jump, until the crackling leaves were down our shirts and inside our ears and between our teeth. Then we'd track the mess into Melody's always chaotic kitchen and drink instant hot chocolate while Mrs. Olsen talked on the phone, cooked dinner and nursed her youngest child.

I haven't thought of Melody for years. Because she lived across town and went to Catholic school, she and I were occasional friends. Every time we met up, I'd be a little shy and stand-offish at first, until Melody would pull me by the hand into whatever outlandish game she and her three brothers had dreamed up for the day. Within minutes, I'd be laughing and screeching with the Olsen kids, all traces of shyness banished.

It was at the Olsen's house that I discovered not everyone ate dinner in total silence with a book beside their plate. That some dads played games other than chess with their kids. That not all mothers were beautiful, ghostly saints.

My mother and Mrs. Olsen met in prenatal exercise class when they were pregnant with us. Apparently we girls played together as toddlers, and after my mother died, Mrs. Olsen would offer to help my father out by watching me on the rare occasions when my grandparents were unavailable. As I got old enough to stay home by myself, I saw Melody and her family less and less. By middle school our paths had diverged. My father, of course, would have had no reason to stay in touch with Mrs. Olsen after her usefulness to him ended.

But looking at the pile of leaves on Birch Street gives me an idea. Mrs. Olsen knew both my mother and my father. The two of them must have met shortly after my mother received the ring from my dad. Mrs. Olsen lived through my mother's disappearance, but she wasn't destroyed by it. I can ask her things that I could never have asked my grandparents or my father.

I hurry Ethel along. "C'mon baby, I have a lot to do today." Put in a full day organizing the Reicker estate sale. Pick up my mother's re-sized ring from the jewelers. Buy a dress for my date with Cal. And pay a visit to the Olsens.

On my way to the Reicker sale I make a quick detour to Parkhurst Avenue. In the disruption following my assault, our ESTATE SALE BY ANOTHER MAN'S TREASURE sign has been left stuck in Mrs. Szabo's yard for two weeks. I need it back for this sale.

I park my van at the curb and survey the house for a moment. Unraked leaves fill the yard. A Chinese food menu, faded and tattered by the weather, peeks out from under the door mat. A rude dog-walker has deposited a blue New York Times home delivery bag full of poop on the driveway. The hole in the attic floor, through which the trunk dropped, must still be there since it doesn't look like anyone's been here since Jill, Ty and I left. How did my mother's ring end up in this forlorn little house, in a part of town where our family knows no one? Who was Mrs. Szabo? Maybe I can find out more from Cal tomorrow tonight.

I cross the yard to retrieve the sign, but it's so firmly anchored in the dry ground of the front yard that I plop on my butt when I finally yank it out.

"Oh, dear! Oh heavens! Are you hurt?"

Heaving myself up, I see a thin woman walking an ancient pug. She and the dog have stopped on the sidewalk to stare at me. I spring up and dust the dry leaves off my jeans.

"Are you all right?" the woman quavers. Her wispy hair whips around in the breeze. The dog strains on his leash, emitting coughing sounds. As small as he is, he looks capable of pulling her over.

"I'm fine." And then, as she shows no inclination to move along, I add, "Just taking my sign back."

"Are you the one who ran the estate sale here?"

A regular Sherlock Holmes, this one. Nevertheless, I smile patiently and extend my hand, "I'm Audrey Nealon. I own Another Man's Treasure." Never know where my next client might come from.

She backs away from my hand. "I can't shake. I have fibromyalgia. And carpal tunnel."

"Sorry." She's really not that old—maybe fifty—but she's what my grandfather used to call "nervous," an all-purpose adjective that covered everything from jumpy to schizophrenic. Still, she seems to want to talk. "Did you know Mrs. Szabo?"

She shakes her head. "Not very well. BoBo and I would say hello when we saw her in the yard. Right BoBo?"

BoBo refuses to confirm or deny. "Did you come to the sale?" I ask.

"No, but Vera told me there were a lot of people."

Vera. "Is Vera Mrs. Szabo's neighbor? The thin lady with the gray bun?"

Her eyes, the pale, pale green of pond water, open wide. "BoBo and I better get on home." She tugs the little dog, and heads down the street, glancing back over her shoulder as if she expects me to follow her waving an ax. I toss the sign in the back of the van and watch as she and BoBo disappear into a house four doors down. Of the three houses between hers and Mrs. Szabo's, only one has a neat garden and a well-swept walk. Not much to go on, but I'll take my chances. If Vera doesn't live there, maybe whoever does will be more willing to talk than BoBo's owner.

I'm knocking on the door before I've given myself time to change my mind, or think of what, exactly, I'm going to ask. The door opens quickly, and the little woman from the sale with the glasses and bun looks me over, almost as if she's been expecting me. Pulling her cardigan around her shoulders, she steps out on the front porch.

"I saw you on the news." Vera squints up at me. "You got robbed of all the money from Agnes's sale. What else did he get?"

This is weird. I came to ask her questions, and she's grilling me. "Nothing. Well, my fannypack, with my keys and my license—that was a hassle. But nothing else of value."

She stares at me long and hard with those lashless gray eyes.

"Look, I know you think your friend left you something in the house, but everything she had was in the sale except this trunk full of old jewelry that we found in the attack. That has to be appraised, so—"

Vera's eyes light up. "Oh, so you found that didya? That was Agnes's retirement fund. She took it from the people she worked for."

Am I hearing right? Did Vera just tell me that the jewelry is stolen? "What do you mean? Who did she work for?"

"All kinds of people. She cleaned houses and watched kids."

My ears perk up. Growing up, my father and I always had household help, a steady stream of women from the Maid for You agency who kept our rugs vacuumed and our clothes laundered. Some lasted for a few years, others stayed only a couple of weeks. My father barely acknowledged their existence. Could Mrs. Szabo have been our housecleaner at some point?

Vera continues, almost chatty. "When Agnes got too worn out to chase after toddlers, she started taking care of old people. She always worked off the books. No benefits, no pension. She didn't even pay into Social Security. She'd always say to me, 'Who's going to look after me when I get too old to work?' She knew her sister's children and grandchildren wouldn't do it."

That would be Cal and his family. This makes sense. Agnes would take a brooch here, a watch there; that's why the stuff was all different sizes and styles. Cal must've guessed that it was stolen when he saw it. No wonder he didn't want to deal with it.

"No one ever suspected her?" I ask.

Vera's crooked brown teeth appear in a satisfied grin. "Nope. She knew how to take things that wouldn't be missed. Those rich people had more than they could keep track of. But in the end, her plan backfired on her."

"How so?"

"She hid the trunk up in the attic while she was taking the stuff, but then when she needed to start using it, she couldn't get to it. She was too old and weak to push herself through that trap door into the attic. She spent all her time worrying about it. 'I need to get it down...how am I going to get it down?'"

"She couldn't find anyone to help her?"

Vera waves a bony hand. "I made suggestions, but she wouldn't listen. To tell the truth, Agnes was starting to get a little strange. When her faucet started leaking, she couldn't decide what plumber to call. When her podiatrist retired, she couldn't figure out how to find a new one. That's what happens when they get old."

They? Vera looks to be pushing a hundred herself. "So, did she really need the money from the jewelry?"

Vera shrugs. "She just kept saying, "I need to get into that trunk. I need something in there." I tell you, I got tired of hearing it."

"Did Agnes ever tell you about the families she worked for? Did she ever mention a Roger and Charlotte Nealon?"

"She'd tell me the things those rich ladies said to her. The way they treated their kids, their parents. But I don't remember those names."

Did my father mistreat Agnes Szabo? Would she have considered a widowed math professor a rich oppressor? Yes, he's aloof, but I don't remember him ever speaking harshly to any of the women who cleaned for us. Would Agnes have felt she "deserved" my mother's ring?

Vera folds her brittle arms across her chest. "I went to visit Agnes in the hospital before she died. All drugged up and stuck full of tubes. I could see in her eyes she had something to tell me, but she couldn't get it out." She shakes her head. "I would've helped her if I could. But Agnes waited too long to tell me what she needed me to do."

"What do you think it was? Was she just worried that she'd need the money from the jewelry to pay her medical bills?"

Vera's hard, little eyes narrow to slits. "She knew she was dying."

Poor Agnes. Dying all alone, worried, and no one but this flinty old gal to offer her comfort. What had she wanted Vera to do? "Could it have something to do with me getting robbed?"

As a cool breeze whips leaves across the porch, Vera turns to go back into her house. With her hand on the doorknob, she shoots me one last keen look. "Maybe what happened to you was just a coincidence."

Chapter 17

In the twenty-odd years since I've last been here, the Olsen's house has shrunk while their trees have grown. The center hall colonial, which I recall as large and rambling compared to our older, quirkier home, now seems like a standard-issue suburban four-bedroom. Meanwhile, the little sapling in the front yard, which we kids did our best to trample, has matured into a 25-foot shade tree. The clutter of bikes and trikes and sports gear is gone, as is the swing set Melody and I used to leap from. But in the large side lawn I can still see the bare patch that served as home base for so many games of kickball and wiffle ball. I can't conjure up many purely joyful moments from my childhood, but swinging the yellow plastic bat and knocking the ball clear out to the curb here is one of them.

A pleasant warm glow fills me up as I ring the doorbell. Even if Mrs. Olsen can't tell me anything about my parents, it will still be nice to see her and find out how Melody and her brothers are doing. Within moments of the chime's sounding, the door flies open and I find myself engulfed in her cushiony bosom.

"Look at you!" Mrs. Olsen squeals. "You're so lovely, all grown up from the shy, skinny little girl I used to know."

"You haven't changed a bit," I answer, and in this case, it's absolutely true. Always a little matronly, Mrs. Olsen never looked young in her mid-thirties and she doesn't look old now that she's over sixty. Her tendency to plumpness and her sunny disposition have kept her face smooth. Her only wrinkles are the laugh-lines crinkling the corners of her blue eyes.

"Come on back to the kitchen. I made oatmeal raisin cookies because they were always your favorites."

I have no recollection of this; as far as I recall, all Mrs. O's cookies were equally good. "That's so sweet. You didn't have to go out of your way like that."

She directs me into a chair at her big kitchen table, then pauses in her bustling for a moment. "It's so good to see you." Her kind eyes search my face. "I've thought of you many times over the years. I really should have gotten in touch. Then, last week, to see you in the news, the victim of a terrible attack—" She shakes her head, her frizzy gray-brown curls bobbing. "I'm so relieved that you're okay. You *are* okay, aren't you?"

Am I? I'm jumpy and suspicious and a little too in touch with the dark side of human nature. But my headaches are mostly gone and my stitches are out. "Yes, I'm fine," I assure my old friend. "Tell me about Melody and the boys."

We spend the next twenty minutes catching up. Melody is a biologist in Montana; her brothers are all in New Jersey, although not in Palmyrton. Mrs. Olsen chats on about their many accomplishments and tells me that she's now taken a part-time job as a social worker at the Midtown Community Center. I tell her about Another Man's Treasure, and about my father's stroke.

"A stroke? Oh, my dear, I'm so sorry." Mrs. Olsen reaches out to pat my hand. As she does, she notices the ring. I only picked it up from being resized a couple of hours ago, and it still feels strange on my finger. Her face lights up. "You're wearing your mother's ring—how nice! She loved that ring."

I straighten up in my chair. All the family chat has been nice, but this is what I came here for. Suddenly the ring feels like a heavy weight. I need Mrs. Olsen to help me carry it.

"Did she always wear this ring?" I ask.

"Oh yes. Her wedding band was on her left hand and that ring was always on her right."

I look Mrs. Olsen straight in the eye. "Then why wasn't she wearing it the night she disappeared? I found it recently, not at my father's house, but in a trunk of jewelry in the attic of an old woman whose house I was clearing out."

"Really? How odd." Mrs. O looks genuinely perplexed. "What was the woman's name?"

"Agnes Szabo." I say the name slowly and clearly, hoping for some start of recognition.

"Never heard of her."

"She worked as a housekeeper and a nanny. She stole this jewelry—one or two pieces from each employer—as a kind of nest egg for her retirement. So I was thinking she might have worked for us at some point. But our family always used an agency, Maid for You. I checked, and they have no record of an Agnes Szabo in their files. Yet somehow this woman stole the ring. From my father...or from my mother."

Mrs. Olsen starts fussing around, straining and pouring the tea. "Maybe your mother took it off in a restroom, and this woman found it. Or maybe it slipped off her finger. What does your father have to say about it?" She gasps and covers her mouth. "I'm so sorry. I forgot you said he's not able to speak."

"He couldn't tell me anything about the ring. But it upset him, Mrs. Olsen. You'd think he'd be happy that I found it, but seeing it made him angry."

Her gaze is focused on the green pottery sugar bowl on the table but I can tell she's looking far back in time.

"Why is my dad so cold?" I ask her softly. "Why is he angry at me? Was he ever happy?"

Her thick, strong fingers interlace with mine. "Oh my dear, yes. He adored you. When you were born he was brimming with wonder and joy. You were fussy at first and I remember your mother used to tell me that you'd cry all day until your Daddy came home, then you'd settle right down as soon as he took you in his arms."

It's as if I'm listening to her recite a fairy tale. This can't be my father she's talking about. "He held me?" I ask. I don't remember ever sitting in my father's lap.

"Oh yes, he was willing to sit with you for hours. In fact, he was good with all babies. I think it was because he had such deep inner reserves. Your mom and I would talk about how lonely it could get being home with a baby all day, but your dad never felt that way. He was content with his own company. I envied him that."

"You make it seem like a positive thing. But to me, he's always seemed like a recluse, walled off from the world."

Mrs. Olsen nods. "All he ever truly needed was Charlotte and you, but he still enjoyed other people's company. That's what changed when your mother died. Once she was gone, not only did he not need anyone else, he couldn't even tolerate anyone else."

I take a deep breath and squeeze her hands in mine. "What do you know about the night she disappeared, Mrs. O? Do you really think her car slid into that lake while she was out Christmas shopping?"

Mrs. Olsen squirms in her seat, the way Melody and I used to squirm when she interrogated us about large quantities of missing cookies. Finally she speaks, looking past my right shoulder.

"Well, it must've happened that way. That's what the police said."

"I know the official story. But what do you think? If she ran out to go shopping, why wasn't she wearing the ring she never took off?" My eyes lock with Mrs. Olsen's and she's the first to look away. She knows something; I'm sure of it.

I force her to look at me. "Tell me. Please."

She sighs. "I don't know, Audrey. It's probably nothing. But, well, your mom didn't seem herself for a few months before...before Christmas. We weren't spending as much time together--she was busy with her work and I had my hands full because the twins had just been born. But when we would see each other she seemed—" Mrs. Olsen searches for a word. "...keyed up. Like she was about to burst."

"And you didn't ask her what was going on?"

"Oh, I did. She'd laugh it off. Say life was good and she was happy, that's all."

"But you didn't believe her?"

"At the time I did. I figured I was a little envious of Charlotte, which isn't a nice feeling to have for a friend. I was feeling fat and exhausted and zoned out on Sesame Street and your mom was getting her life back together. She had this great new job that she loved at a small PR firm, and a husband who was willing and able to help out with child care. Not like me. My poor George would catch the 6:16 train into the city and not make it home again 'til eight at night." She shudders as she glances around her cheerful kitchen. "Sometimes I wonder how we ever made it through those years."

Maybe she's seeing herself trapped in here from sun-up to sundown every day of her kids' toddlerhood. It's hard to connect this tale of maternal discontent to the jolly, loving uber-Mom of my childhood memories. And it's hard to figure out where she's going with this story. It seems like yet another page in the "Charlotte Perry had a perfect life" book. But Mrs. O. must have a reason, so I sit quietly and wait. It worked for detective Coughlin; why not for me?

After a protracted silence, Mrs. Olsen starts talking again. "Your mother and I were from the generation of women who were taught we could have it all: career, kids, marriage of equals. We started our careers and married our true loves and had a baby and then we hit the wall. We found out it wasn't so simple. Bosses were demanding, childcare was unreliable, husbands only supported equality if there were clean socks in their drawer. So we made sacrifices. I gave up my career when I realized I couldn't do a good job at work and at home with three kids under the age of three." She pauses and strokes my arm. "Your mom made a different sacrifice."

"What?"

"She decided she was only going to have one child. She loved you dearly, but she knew she wouldn't be a good mother to a bigger family. She worried that she'd be resentful if she had to give up working to take care of another child. Plus, she was sick as a dog when she was pregnant with you, and I don't think she could've faced going through that again. We used to joke about 'the final solution'—making our husbands get vasectomies."

This is new. The first indication I've ever had that my mother wasn't a cross between the Virgin Mary and Princess Diana. And Nana never mentioned that my mother had a difficult pregnancy. But then, she wouldn't have. She only talked about things Charlotte did well. But I still don't see where Mrs. O's going with this and I guess it shows on my face.

"After that Christmas Eve, I kept thinking….." Another inhalation, as if she's trying to find the oxygen to swim across the deep end of the pool. "…kept thinking about the last time we were together. It was the second weekend in December. I had a fancy Christmas party to go to, and your mom agreed to take me shopping. In Bloomingdales, one of those perfume sampler ladies squirted a big blast on Charlotte. All the color rushed out of her face, she broke out in a sweat and doubled over. I thought she was going to heave right there in Cosmetics. She ended up buying a new blouse to change into because she couldn't bear the scent on the one she had been wearing."

"Did she always have such a dramatic reaction to perfume?" I ask.

She shakes her head. "Never. And it was a nice scent. Chanel Cristalle. I can never smell it without thinking of Charlotte." Mrs. O. isn't looking at me as she says this. Her eyes are focused on the tangle of snapshots and children's drawings stuck to her refrigerator. With some effort, she drags her attention back to me. I see a glimmer of tears in her eyes.

"What?" I ask. "What is it about the perfume that bothers you?"

"Sometimes strong smells can make you queasy if you're... if you're pregnant."

I feel like she's thrown hot tea in my face. My mother was pregnant when she died? I didn't just lose a parent that night; I lost the thing I've always wanted more than anything else—a sibling.

Mrs. Olsen sees that she's upset me. She comes around to my side of the table to give me a hug. "I'm probably wrong. I should never have mentioned it."

"But that would explain why she seemed excited. Maybe it was so early she didn't want to tell anyone yet. Not even her mom. Maybe not even my dad."

Mrs. Olsen nods. "Yes, I suppose. It's just, well—"

"Did you ever ask him about it?" I demand.

"No, I didn't want to upset him." She picks up my empty teacup and bustles over to the sink. "Like I said, I'm probably way off base."

I can't figure her out. She's the one who brought up the idea that my mom was pregnant, and now she's backpedaling. "But what do you really think, was she or wasn't she?"

When there's a safe distance between us, Mrs. Olsen speaks. "I think she might have been pregnant. What I can't figure out is why being pregnant again would've made her that happy."

Chapter 18

I look good. I look *damn* good.

I think.

"What's your opinion, Ethel?" I spin around in front of the full-length mirror so Ethel can get the full effect of my new black dress and heels.

She buries her snout between her paws and sneezes.

"What's the matter? Did I go too heavy on the perfume?"

Perfume. I stop in mid-pirouette. My giddy excitement over my date with Cal dissipates as the memory of my conversation with Mrs. Olsen crowds its way back into my consciousness.

Ethel scootches away from me on her belly, not sure I'm really me. The salesladies at Nordstrom knocked themselves out getting me outfitted (it was a slow day), and Trevor, the stylist at Isabelle Trent's salon, cut me these punky, fringy bangs that hide the shaved spot on my head. I've been pretty successful at keeping the whole scene with Mrs. O. boxed up in a corner of my mind while I shopped and fussed and primped for Cal. But the box pops open at unlikely moments. There's something alive in there, eager to escape.

For about the thousandth time since leaving the Olsen's yesterday, I look at the ring on my finger and think about

Charlotte—who's now not just my mother but the mother of my incipient baby brother or sister—and I wonder about that Christmas Eve expedition. Wouldn't being pregnant make a woman more cautious? Wouldn't she have been less likely to go out into that storm if she knew she was risking another life? And if my father knew she was pregnant, wouldn't he have stopped her from leaving on her crazy mission? And how did Mrs. Szabo steal her ring? Somehow I have to tell Cal that I know how his aunt got the jewelry...don't I? Won't that make it okay that I stole from him what was already stolen? The more I poke and prod at these ideas, the further I sink into a funk.

The ring of the doorbell knocks me out of my trance.

Ethel shoots out of my bedroom and flings herself at the front door, baying at the top of her voice. Out in the hall I clip on Ethel's leash and loop it around the newel post. Then I take a deep breath and open the front door.

A slow grin spreads over Cal's face. "Hey, you look great! I like the new do." Casually, he reaches out and touches my hair.

A hot current races to my core. "Thanks," I say, trying not to gasp.

Cal steps into the foyer and sees Ethel straining to get to him. "Hi, girl." He moves toward her with his hand outstretched. She licks Cal as if he's a soft-serve cone on the Boardwalk. As I pull her away, Ethel points her nose toward the ceiling and lets out a long, mournful howl.

"Oh, for God's sake. You can't come with us. Get over it." I grab my snappy little black clutch and turn Cal around. In the soft light of the hall lamp, my mother's ring glints on my finger. I take a second to admire how nice it looks on my manicured right hand. Then I release Ethel and slip out the door. The sound of her scratching paws follows us down the walk.

Spencer Finneran lives in a beautifully restored Victorian a few blocks from the center of Palmyrton. There are bigger, fancier houses on the outskirts of town, but these few blocks of graceful Queen Annes and Gothic Revivals have always been my favorites. By the time we arrive, cars are already parked up and down the street. It's clear which house is the Finneran's—every light's ablaze and men are smoking cigars on the big wrap-around porch despite the cold weather. Cal pulls his BMW into the driveway of the house next door.

"Spencer's neighbors won't mind if we park here," Cal says. "They're invited to the party."

The ride from my house to the party has gone rather well. I've walked without tripping, talked without stammering, even managed a little joke. And steered clear of the stolen jewelry. But Cal's parking maneuver unnerves me. It reminds me that my date is an insider here. Cal knows the senator well enough to know his neighbors; knows the neighbors well enough to park in their drive with confidence. When Cal opens the car door for me I feel as I did the summer after third grade, standing on the edge of the pool, waiting to take the test that would give me unlimited access to the deep end.

Cal puts his hand on the small of my back and guides me toward the stately green and cream painted house. As we draw closer to the porch, men begin calling out to him.

"Hey, Cal—nice work on the Henderson deal."

"Saw you on Channel 4. You gave as good as you got."

"C'mere and tell me about this golf outing you roped me into."

Cal leads me through the crush of men, introducing me left and right. Bob, Bill, Dave, Steve, Stan, Marty—the names whiz by like bullets in a shoot out. They smile and nod and crush my hand in theirs as they look right through me. I'm sure they've met—and forgotten—scores of women who've shown up on Cal's arm. They slap him on the back and tell him hilarious anecdotes about people I don't know. They make him promises and beg him to call and murmur advice in his ear.

I feel my dream date unraveling. This is going to be a helluva a long night, and, unlike these guys, I don't even have a drink in hand to numb the pain. I look out over the crowd and see a teenage boy in skinny jeans and black Chuck Taylors sitting on the porch swing gazing morosely into the night. A cigarette glows in his right hand. I'd like to join him.

Then there's a warm breath in my ear and a strong, smooth hand holding mine. "Sorry about this crew. Let's get inside the house. There's someone I want you to meet."

Once we're in the foyer, the frat party atmosphere dissipates. The house is lovely: A Federal highboy, a grandfather clock, a Persian carpet, its blues and roses mellow with age. I could have a field day in here, but Cal is urging me forward. We pass the formal living room, filled with a buzzing group of men in blue blazers and women all wearing some version of my outfit. Score one for Isabelle. A tall man with a mane of silver hair is moving among the groups, smiling and chatting. That's Spencer Finneran—I recognize him from TV— but Cal keeps directing me down a hall toward a large gourmet kitchen that's been added on to the rear of the house. There, a flock of white-aproned caterers flaps back and forth refilling trays. A huge cake with sixty-five red, white and blue candles rests on the granite countertop. In the midst of all the activity stands a short, plumpish woman in a beige and maroon flowered dress, a strand of pearls, and sensible low heels. Isabelle would find her just this side of precious.

"Anne!" Cal holds out his arms.

"Cal, my dear—there you are!" The woman allows herself to be hugged. "Now the party can start." She turns to me and takes my hand in both of hers. "And you must be Audrey. I've heard so much about you."

She has?

"This is Spencer's wife, Anne Finneran," Cal completes the introduction. "She's the great woman behind the man."

Anne snorts, the laugh lines at the corners of her eyes crinkling. "No need for the PR nonsense back here in the kitchen, Cal. Why doesn't this poor girl have a drink?" She shoots a look at one of the food service minions and a glass of wine materializes. "Cal told me how you met. What a fascinating job you have. Tell me, what's the most interesting thing you've ever found in someone's house?"

I twist my mother's ring on my finger. But of course, I don't mention that. Anne is looking me straight in the eye. She genuinely wants to know. So I tell her about the abstract impressionist painting, and she knows all about the artist's work. Soon she's taking me to see a portrait hanging in their dining room, which leads me to ask about the vintage Noritake china I see there, which gets us onto the soaring value of Rookwood and the impossibility of finding nice Fenton glass. Another woman chimes in, and half an hour goes by before I realize that neither Anne nor Cal is anywhere nearby, but I'm having a fine old time talking art and antiques and historic preservation with some very nice people. It dawns on me then that Anne is an outstanding hostess. She's taken the new kid under her wing and found her some friends to play with.

My chat with an art history professor is interrupted by the sound of a loud gong. The door from the kitchen opens and the cake is wheeled in. At the same time, party guests from every other room in the house start cramming into the dining room. Cal appears at my side just as Spencer and Anne Finneran arrive. To make more room, he steps behind me and puts his hands on my shoulders. I can't help but lean back into him a bit.

I like it.

Anne and Spencer stand behind the candle-encrusted cake, flanked by their four children, two boys and two girls, and the kids' spouses. Ten grandchildren complete the tableau. Spencer, despite his shock of silver hair, looks far younger than sixty-five, while Anne looks older. She's chosen to let her brown hair fade to nondescript gray, and she hasn't fought against wrinkles or a spreading waistline. She wears the scars of raising four kids and living in the political spotlight like a badge of honor. I like her for that.

The Finneran children are easy to distinguish from the in-laws, all sharing their father's strong jaw and high cheekbones. They're the kind of siblings about whom strangers say, "…and this is obviously your sister." I wonder what it would be like to be part of a family like this—more than a family: a clan, a dynasty.

The grandchildren range in age from an infant in arms to a stunning young woman who, according to an overheard conversation, just started Harvard. The little girls wear party dresses, the older ones slightly hipper versions of the dress I've got on. The boys all sport khakis and blue blazers. Except for one. The sullen teenager from the porch is among them, looking like he wants to dump a bowl of punch on his cousins and run.

Spencer begins to speak. He starts with a charming little story about his sixth birthday that captures the attention of everyone in the room, even the little kids. Once he has his audience in his hands, he calls out various people for bringing him safely to this point in his life: his golf buddies, his priest, his law partners, Cal. With obvious pride, he thanks all of his children individually for inspiring him with their courage and their accomplishments. A daughter who survived leukemia, a son who served in the Peace Corps—each tribute comes straight from his heart. Then he turns to Anne.

I've been watching her throughout Spencer's speech. It's hard to describe the expression on her face. Devotion implies subservience and she's clearly not anyone's slave. Love is there, certainly, but her look is more complex than that.

Satisfaction. That's what I see. Satisfaction with the man she married and the life she's created with him.

Spencer raises a glass in a toast. "To my bride, my anchor in rough seas, my muse."

If there's a dry eye in the house, I don't know who it belongs to.

Then the caterer steps in to light the candles on the cake and the moment dissolves into singing happy birthday and joking about the need for a fire truck. I notice the sullen teen edging toward the door. His mother, a Finneran daughter-in-law, stops him with a fierce glare. Then Anne looks his way. Her left eyebrow goes up. A silent message passes between them and I see the corner of his mouth twitch in a repressed smile.

Grandma understands. I like her even more.

Chapter 19

After the cake, I spy some lovely Delft on the mantle in the living room that I'd like to check out, but Cal steers me across the room directly toward Spencer. Lifting his head from a conversation with a much shorter man, Spencer looks straight at me as I approach. It seems to me that his eyes widen, like he's amazed to see Cal with the likes of me. Standing right before the senator, I can feel his vitality. What a difference between him and my father, who will also be turning sixty-five in a few months.

Spencer smiles broadly at Cal, covering his moment of surprise. "Finally getting around to introducing me to your lovely friend?"

"Audrey Nealon, Spencer Finneran," Cal says.

I shake his hand. "Happy birthday. This is a lovely party."

"Thank you." He leans in, still holding my hand, and says sotto voce, "Because it's my birthday, Anne insisted we only invite people we actually like. That's why Cal brought you, instead of some dreadful lobbyist. Right, Cal?"

"Absolutely. Tonight I'm off duty."

I smile, even though I know Cal and Spencer are always at work. The glad handers on the front porch are evidence of that. Still, Spencer's comment reassures me. I come with absolutely no political benefits, so Cal must have brought me for purely social reasons.

I only have a chance to say a few more words to Spencer before some other friend pulls him away. Then Cal and I make the rounds of the party together, Cal whispering sly commentaries about the guests in my ear. Eventually, one of the thick-necked, ruddy-faced blowhards from the front porch corners Cal, and I excuse myself to use the ladies room. A line has formed outside the powder room in the hall, and a woman descending the stairs urges me to use the upstairs bathroom. "Second door on the left," she directs.

Once upstairs, I'm distracted by the oil portraits hanging at regular intervals in the hall. Stern-faced, barrel-chested men; dour women in mob caps. These are what I call ancestor paintings, and these ancestors look to go way back to Revolutionary times. Old family, old money—nothing like my roots. I'm curious if these are Spencer's forebears or Anne's until I come to a painting of newer vintage, showing a not quite beautiful woman in an evening gown of a style popular in the 1930s or 40s. She has Anne's laughing eyes and high forehead. It must be her mother.

As I stand admiring it, my nose begins to twitch. A distinctive aroma, but not one I smell all that often anymore. I inhale deeply, then cough.

Weed.

Someone in one of these bedrooms is getting high while the senator's birthday rocks on below.

My first impulse is to giggle and slip away to the bathroom. Clearly the poor kid in the black tee shirt and jeans needs a little something to help him get through this family get-together.

But the Finnerans are no ordinary family. The governor's election is a couple weeks away. Cal has been working so hard, and any taint of scandal could tilt the tight race. Despite what Spencer said, the people downstairs are not just friends and family; Cal introduced me to a woman who's a reporter for the Style section of the New York Times. A woman who very well might wander up here to use the bathroom, just as I did.

I'll go down and get Cal—he'll know how to deal with the problem. But when I look over the banister, I know it will take me ten minutes to find him and pry him away from whomever he's talking to. Meanwhile, the aroma of burning weed grows stronger.

It's coming from the bedroom across the hall from Anne's mother's painting. Glancing over my shoulder, I step up to the door and tap softly. There's a clatter within, then dead silence.

I try the door: locked.

I tap again. "Listen," I stage-whisper into the crack between the door and the frame. "I can smell that here in the hall. You'd better put it out before there's trouble. I'm saying this as a friend, okay?"

No response. Now what do I do?

I have no way of knowing that it's the kid in black who's in there smoking. In fact, I'm annoyed with myself for playing to stereotypes. Maybe it's one of the aging frat boys from the porch. Or maybe it's one of the botoxed, highlighted matrons fluttering around Spencer. But deep inside I'm sure it's the kid. I haven't seen him since the cake-cutting, since he shared that glance with Anne.

I decide to play the guilt card. "I know this party's a drag for you, but it's important to your grandmother. Don't wreck it for her."

The door flies open.

"Who the fuck are you?"

The kid is two feet away from me, wreathed in a cloud of smoke. I step into the room and quickly shut the door.

He backs away from me, his eyes big black pools of confusion. "Who…"

"I'm a friend of a friend of your grandfather's. Cal Tremaine's date."

"Asshole," he murmurs under his breath.

I'm not sure if that's directed at me, Cal, or Spencer. Maybe all three.

He seems stupefied, either by what he's been smoking or by my appearance. I figure this is no time for lengthy discussions. I pluck the remains of the smoldering joint from between his fingers, march it over to the attached bathroom, and flush.

"I hate to be a tool," I say when I'm back in the bedroom, "but if you were to get caught tonight, the result would be worse than a little argument with your parents. It could cost your grandfather the election."

"Like I give a shit." He's sprawled across the pretty lavender and white bedspread in this guestroom, his face arranged in perfectly cultivated teenage disdain.

I don't need to keep talking to him but I feel a surge of sympathy. I've been envying the Finneran solidarity, but maybe he hates growing up in the glare of politics. He didn't choose to be born into this family.

Well, none of us chooses our family, do we?

I extend my hand. "I'm Audrey Nealon. What's your name?"

He ignores the hand, but answers. "Dylan."

"Well, Dylan, no matter how bad it might be to have a grandfather who's the governor of New Jersey, it'll be even worse to be the reason why your grandfather's *not* the governor of New Jersey. It might be best for you to chill up here—smoke free—until the party's over."

"Whatever." His eyelids droop as if he might doze off while he's talking to me.

I cross the room and listen for any sounds in the hall before opening the door. "Thanks, Dylan. Stay out of trouble for your grandma's sake."

My words ignite Dylan. He springs off the bed and shouts after me, "Lady, you don't know anything about what would make my grandma happy."

Chapter 20

By the time I get back downstairs, the atmosphere in the house has shifted subtly. The party has peaked; people are starting to say their good-byes and head home. Anne stands in the hallway, thanking a steady stream of guests for coming. The caterers load their van.

Cal emerges from the living room and holds out his hand to me. "There you are." He takes my hand and leads me over to Spencer. "Look at Audrey, Spence. She's survived her first Finneran party and she's still on her feet. A real trouper, wouldn't you say?"

Spencer beams at me. "She's a keeper, Cal. Now Audrey, tell this cheap bastard to take you somewhere fancy for your next date."

For some reason I'm absurdly pleased by Spencer's approval. At the same time, I'm embarrassed by his assumption that Cal and I are headed for a second date. I cast about for some lighthearted response but come up short.

"Cheap! I'm not cheap!" Cal pulls me closer. "Tell Spencer to give me one day off from his campaign, and I'll gladly take you to the fanciest restaurant in New York."

"Don't be drawn in by his promises, Audrey." Now Anne is in on the banter. "Our lives won't be our own until after Election Day.

In the meantime, he'll expect you to make all sorts of absurd accommodations to meet his needs." She wags her index finger at me, but her face lights up with an indulgent smile. "Don't do it. You give an inch and they take a mile."

I feel myself blushing but I sense it's a nice rosy glow, not my usual crimson blotches of humiliation. I'm not used to being the center of attention, but this is quite pleasant. For once, I'm not the girl on the outside looking in.

"I had a wonderful time tonight," I say. "This was more fun than going to a fancy restaurant. Honestly."

"I'm delighted to have met you, dear." Anne takes my hand in hers. "And I don't say this to all the girls Cal brings around, do I Spencer?"

"Whew, that's for sure!"

"Let's not go any further down that path," Cal says. "Time for me to take Audrey home." Cal wraps me in the shawl the Nordstrom salesladies picked out for me. The appearance of one accessory makes me realize I'm missing another. Where's my little evening clutch? Shit! I must've set it down somewhere when I was trying to balance a glass of wine and an hors d'oeuvre. I look around anxiously. I should have known I couldn't pull off this fancy cocktail party thing.

"What's wrong?" Cal asks.

"I seem to have left my purse somewhere."

Am I paranoid or do I see a flicker of irritation pass across Anne's face as she imagines a half-hour hunt for my bag when all she wants is to get everyone out the door. She draws the catering crew boss to her side with nothing more than a raised eyebrow and murmurs in his ear.

"Black with sequins? It's in the kitchen." He returns momentarily with the silly little satin envelope. I must've set it down when Cal introduced me to Anne.

"Aren't these things a nuisance?" Anne says with a heavenward glance. I think now I must've imagined her impatience. "When

Spencer and I go out, I make him carry my lipstick in his jacket."

"I keep telling her if a reporter ever sees me pull a tube of Revlon out of my pocket, my career's over."

We say our good-byes in a cloud of laughter and make our way out to the car. As we're buckling our seat belts, Cal reaches over and pats my knee. "You've cleared a really high bar, Audrey. Anne likes you."

Does she?

"She's a very gracious lady. I'm sure she's nice to everyone who comes to her home."

"Oh, she is, she is. A politician's wife can't afford not to be. But believe me, I know her well enough to recognize when she's being politically correct and when she's genuine. You, she truly likes."

I feel a warm glow inside me. I don't know why it should matter, but I want Anne Finneran's approval.

On the drive home, I tell Cal about my encounter with Dylan. I watch as his hands tighten on the steering wheel, then relax when I get to the part where I flush the joint down the toilet. He turns to look at me while we're stopped at a light.

"That was brilliant, Audrey. You did exactly the right thing. That damn kid's always in trouble. Wait until I tell Spencer about this."

I reach out and touch Cal's arm. "Don't tell Spencer, please. Tell Anne. She'll know how to handle it. Dylan's an unhappy kid. It can't always be easy to be a Finneran."

Two vertical lines appear on Cal's brow. "This isn't the first time he's fucked up. Dylan's a scandal waiting to happen. He has to be reined in before he jeopardizes Spencer's election."

"The race really is that tight that something like this could tip it?"

Cal looks away from the road for a second to catch my eye. "It's not just about winning, Audrey. It's about the future of this state. Do you realize that you and I have never had the opportunity to vote for a principled, honorable person for the governor of New Jersey? Since we've been old enough to vote, every candidate of either party has been a buffoon or a crook."

"Sometimes both."

Cal smiles, but I can see he's not really amused. This means too much to him.

"Spencer Finneran is different, Audrey. He's the real deal. He has a solid plan to make life better for the people of New Jersey. All the people, not just the special interests. So, yeah, I don't want that brat Dylan to undermine it all."

"I understand. But he's a kid, Cal. Didn't you ever do anything reckless when you were sixteen?"

He takes a quick sidelong glance at me, but the worry lines don't disappear.

"C'mon…I can't believe you were a choirboy all through high school."

Cal starts to laugh. "I ran track in high school. Several colleges had their scouts out looking at me. I really needed the scholarship money. So, what do I do? The night before the big all-county meet I go to a big beer blast at the house of some kid whose parents were out of town. Of course the party got busted by the police. I knew if they caught me I wouldn't be able to run in the meet. So as the cops were coming through the front door, I took off out the back. One cop saw me and gave chase. He followed me up hills and through back yards. I was a sprinter, but he clearly was a distance runner. He was gaining on me when I came to a little backyard goldfish pond. I leaped over it, but when he tried, he fell about a foot short. Landed in water up to his thighs. I dashed through a hedge and got away."

"So, how did you do in the big meet?"

"Broke a record for the 100 meter sprint. Won a full ride to Brown."

Maybe it's the wine I drank, or maybe I'm a little high on the praise I've won from Spencer and Anne. I reach over and lightly stroke Cal's cheek. "So maybe Dylan will turn out to be as successful as you. Cut the kid a break."

Cal smiles. "You're really a champion of the underdog, aren't you Audrey?"

"Let's just say I can identify."

Cal glides into a parking spot in front of my condo. Somehow the whole evening has gone by without my finding a chance to ask him about Agnes's stolen jewelry. He kills the ignition and slides his arm across the back of my seat. Now is definitely not the time. A surge of heat from my core makes my own perfume smell stronger. It mixes with the clean leathery smell of the BMW and the subtle scent of Cal's aftershave. I can only detect it when he's very close, as he is right now.

"I didn't really know what to expect tonight, Audrey." He runs his thumb lightly along my jaw. He might as well have touched me with a live wire. "But I found I enjoyed your company very much. Can I see you again? And I mean soon, not after the election."

I try to play it cool, but I know I'm pathetically incapable of nonchalance. "Yes. I'd like that," I manage to choke out.

He pulls me closer and kisses me. It's a wonderful kiss. Lingering, not demanding. This man knows what he's doing.

He can sense my eagerness; I know he can. I haven't had sex for over a year, since I broke up with Gavin, a chronically despondent unpublished novelist and paralegal. I haven't been kissed by anyone since except for a slobberingly inept software engineer I met at a St. Patrick's Day party.

Then Cal draws back. He knows I'm his for the asking, but he opens the driver's side door and walks around to hold my door for me. He leads me up the walk, then smoothes the hair back from my face. I realize I've forgotten all about Agnes's stolen jewelry. Well, too late now. Cal kisses the top of my head and whispers in my ear. "Good night, Audrey. I'll call you tomorrow."

Shakily, I pull the keys from my bag and let myself into the condo. Ethel bounds up to greet me, then skids to a stop. She seems to know that if she jumps up on me now she'll knock me flat on my ass.

Chapter 21

I'm so wound up after my date with Cal that it takes until two AM for me to fall asleep. Consequently I don't arise on Sunday until nearly ten, when a frantic Ethel leaps onto the bed and walks across my kidneys. Staggering into the bathroom, I look in the mirror. My hip new haircut is flat on one side, cow-licky on the other. My eyes are ringed with black mascara. A pillowcase wrinkle imprints my cheek. Princess Audrey has disappeared; scullery-maid Audrey is back.

"C'mon Ethel. We'll take our walk, swing by Sol's Bagels, then head out to visit Dad, okay?" I haven't been to the nursing home all week, and the information Mrs. Olsen gave me about the possibility that my mother was pregnant when she disappeared has been floating around me, like something I glimpse from the corner of my eye but can't quite bring into focus. I want to find out things only my father can tell me, although I dread asking.

Ethel embraces my plan wholeheartedly, as I knew she would. I take a quick shower, mindful of poor Ethel's urgent biological needs, then we head down to the bagel shop. A Palmyrton landmark, Sol's sells the best bagels south of Fort Lee and west of Newark. The place is always hopping, and Sunday mornings are busiest of all. I invariably run into someone I know there, but I'm praying today it won't be Cal. I'm not yet ready to see him again; I know I'll have to work too hard to pull off a "fancy meeting you here." Besides, my jeans and UVA sweatshirt are a far cry from the slinky little black dress of last night. Seductress is not a role I can maintain 24/7.

Ethel strains on her leash as we walk the three blocks to Sol's. She knows when we head off in this direction she's about to get her favorite treat, a salt bagel stick. "What do you think, Ethel, should we get a bagel for Dad too?" Pre-stroke my father disdained bagels as carbohydrate bombs, but he looks terribly frail now and given the slop they serve him at Manor View, I think he might appreciate seven hundred kosher calories. Ethel whines and pulls harder.

When we arrive at Sol's the line spills out the door. The five or six sidewalk tables are all occupied and I can't bring Ethel inside, so I tie her leash to a lamppost and get in the queue. Used to total freedom, Ethel can be a little testy when restrained, but she clearly knows what's coming her way so she lies down patiently to wait. It shouldn't take long—Sol's countermen are famously efficient, and they don't encourage idle chit-chat on Sundays.

I make it up to the bagel bin and practice my order: two everything bagels with cream cheese, two coffees and a salt bagel stick. The counterman hands over one order, then makes eye contact with the woman ahead of me on the line. This is her cue to speak, but she hesitates.

"Next!" he barks at her.

"Do the everything bagels have garlic?" she asks. "I don't like garlic."

"Everything is everything!" the counterman shouts.

"Didn't Nietzsche say that?" the guy behind me mutters. "Or maybe it was Kurt Cobain."

"They have garlic," I tell her, thinking to move things along. Big mistake. Now she's agonizing between sesame and poppy. I shift restlessly and crane my neck to look at Ethel. I can only see part of her tail. It's not moving, so she must be fine.

Finally it's my turn and I place my order. While I'm paying, I hear a crescendo of furious barking. "Shit! That's my dog," I say as I slap ten bucks in the counterman's hand, grab my order, and rush for the door.

"Hey, lady—your change," he calls but I'm already darting through the crowd. Ethel's quite the libertarian canine—you do your thing and let me do mine—but when someone pushes her buttons she can turn fierce. The tone of her barking worries me. I have visions of bratty kids poking their fingers in her ears and getting bitten for their efforts.

When I finally make my way onto the sidewalk, I see a crowd forming around the lamppost where I left Ethel tied. A skinny woman in black leggings that accentuate her bow-legs is screeching while trying to pull a big bearded collie away from Ethel. Ethel lunges at the hairball on four legs and succeeds in pulling out a good mouthful of gray and white fur. Maybe the big oaf tossed some doggy insult in Ethel's direction. She's not one to turn the other whisker. Before I can reach Ethel, a powerfully built man in basketball shorts and a T-shirt grabs each dog by its collar and separates them by the span of his long arms. Now the bearded collie owner is able to drag her dog away, so by the time I reach Ethel she has given one last "get lost, fatso" yelp and is wagging her tail sweetly at the towering referee.

"Thank you so much," I say, taking Ethel's leash. "Ethel, what's gotten into you?" I'm so busy scolding Ethel I barely glance at the man who broke up the fight.

"Trouble seems to follow you around, Ms. Nealon," he says.

I stop fussing with Ethel to really look at him. Short red hair, bright blue eyes, a neck as thick as my thigh. I definitely know this guy, but from where? Customer? Neighbor? And what did he mean by that crack about trouble?

He unties Ethel from the lamppost and hands me the leash. "There's an ordinance against this, you know."

Now it clicks. Detective Coughlin. I haven't seen him since I was in the hospital, addled on painkillers. Looking at him in the cold light of sobriety isn't making him any more appealing. I remember what Cal said about police brutality. Yeah, I can picture this cop knocking people around.

"I hear you called 911. Someone broke into your condo?"

Crap—does he know everything? "A misunderstanding. No one broke in. My assistant, Jill, has a key. She moved some things without telling me."

"Does Griggs have a key to your place?"

"No! Why are you asking me all this? I thought you were off my case."

"Oh, yeah--how's your string-pulling friend over at Democratic Headquarters?"

"What charm school did you graduate from, Detective?"

"It lost its accreditation."

I hand Ethel her bagel stick, effectively rewarding her for her bad behavior. She settles down on the sidewalk with the chewy bread between her front paws and starts working it over. What was I thinking? Now I'm stuck here with Coughlin. We both stare at the dog.

"You been okay?" Coughlin asks. "Nobody hassling you?"

"I'm fine. Detective Farrand told me I can call to request a patrol car to escort me to the bank after my sale this week."

"Good. I told him to do that."

Good grief, how childish men are. Coughlin's like the star quarterback who pouts when the promising sophomore gets put in the game.

"When's the sale? Where?" he asks. His eyes, startlingly blue, lock with mine. I hold the stare for a moment, until a strange uptick in my heart rate makes me look away.

Annoyed, I consider telling him it's none of his business. But Tyshaun will put up signs advertising the sale all around town and the ad will run in the paper and online, so Coughlin can certainly figure it out. After all, he is a detective. So I tell him about the Reicker sale.

While I'm talking, my gaze strays from Ethel to Coughlin's gigantic basketball shoes. I don't think I've ever known a man with feet that size. It's hard to imagine how he can maneuver with those things. The very act of walking must be like steering twin ocean liners.

"You expecting a big crowd?" he asks. He stands with his hands clasped behind his back, his legs slightly spread, like an at-ease soldier. But his voice never loses that interrogator's intensity.

"Yes. Mr. Reicker had some nice antiques. This will be a bigger sale than Mrs. Szabo's."

"That punk still working for you?"

I stare him down. "I don't have any punks on my payroll. I'm lucky—if it hadn't been for Tyshaun and Jill, I wouldn't have been able to get my business back up to speed so soon after the accident."

"Accident? What happened to you was no ordinary push, grab and run. Someone's angry at you. Someone wants you dead. You got any psycho boyfriends?"

"I went over this with Detective Farrand," I say. "Believe me, I'm not the type to inspire insane jealousy."

Coughlin snorts. "I saw a guy beat the crap outta someone over a three hundred pound chick with a mustache thicker than mine. You never know."

"Gee, thanks for sharing. I guess there's still hope for me."

Coughlin actually blushes. "C'mon—you know what I mean."

Ethel is busy licking the last crumbs of her bagel stick off the sidewalk. Coughlin reaches down to scratch behind her ears. Immediately she puts her paws on his waist to make his job easier.

"This is a good dog," Coughlin says. Then he looks at me. "Keep her with you all the time."

I can only imagine that, once inside a dog's stomach, a bagel stick must inflate to monstrous proportions because Ethel is quite subdued on the ride to Manor View. We arrive to eerily empty halls and a deserted rec room. Most of the inmates are down at the chapel for the weekly non-denominational service. I guess having one foot in the grave must make everyone more religious. Not my father, though. He's never embraced what he calls "spiritual claptrap" and his stroke hasn't changed that. I'm sure we'll find him in his room, staring at the wall. Ethel charges ahead of me, but before I get to the door of Dad's room, she has already popped back out again. That's odd.

I step into his room and find it empty, the bed made, the lights all extinguished. Where could he be? I'm pierced by a shaft of panic. Could he be...dead? Surely someone would have called me? I scramble for my cell phone. Maybe it's out of juice. Maybe I didn't hear it ringing during the Ethel confrontation. But it's on and shows no messages or missed calls.

Just then an aide passes by.

"Excuse me—where's my father?"

She looks left and right as if she expects him to be running laps around the nurse's station. Then she snaps her fingers. "Oh, that's right. He's out."

"Out? Out where?"

"He had a visitor who took him out for brunch."

"Visitor? Brunch?" I couldn't be more incredulous if she'd told me Dad had hopped in his car and driven to Atlantic City for an afternoon of blackjack.

"He's allowed to leave," the aide says. Her tone implies she thinks it's nice someone has taken him somewhere, since I never do. Frankly, an outing has never occurred to me. Why go to all the trouble of hauling him to a restaurant to sit in stony silence? We can do that right here.

"Who took him out?" I ask. So far as I know, no one visits him but me. The aide points me to a visitor's log book at the nurse's station. Someone named Brian Bascomb signed my father out at 11:00 AM and has indicated 12:30 as his estimated time of return. That's only half an hour from now. Ethel and I sit down in dad's room to wait.

Brian Bascomb? Is that name familiar? In the weeks after his stroke, Dad received a few get well cards from colleagues at the university, but the trickle of mail has stopped. Seems strange that one of his co-workers would show up to take him out to lunch now that so many months have passed by. Maybe Brian Bascomb is a long-lost friend from the early days of my parents' marriage, back when Dad was some other man, brimming with sunshine and charm. I hope Brian, whoever he is, is prepared for the Roger Nealon of today.

I eat my bagel and drink my tepid coffee and think about my father and mother. According to Mrs. Olsen, my mother had a job she loved. This is the first I've ever heard that my mom was at all career-driven. To hear Nana and Pop talk, my mother was one hundred percent devoted to me. June Cleaver, Princess Diana and the Virgin Mary rolled into one—that was the family party line. Dad had never contradicted their portrayal. But now that I really think about it, he never talked their talk either. In fact, he was always stubbornly silent on the subject of my mother. Pop said it was because talking about her was too painful for Dad. And answering my questions about her was too painful for Nana. And my being too curious "stirred things up."

Pop was adamantly "anti-stir." I adored my grandfather. As the family's tidal wave of love, he compensated for my mother's absence, my father's coldness and Nana's bouts of despair. All he asked in return was that I not stir things up. How could I refuse?

I glance heavenward. Pop wouldn't like what I'm about to do today. Stick a giant spoon in the pot and stir, stir, stir.

"Look who's here!"

I jump at the sound of a high-pitched voice fluting in from the hallway. Dad is being pushed in his wheelchair by another of Manor View's fleet of aides. No Brian Bascomb to be seen.

"Two visitors in one day! Aren't you *lucky?*"

Judging from the expression on his face, Dad doesn't feel he's hit the jackpot. With a little effort, I can convince myself his wooden demeanor is due to the stroke.

Ethel trots over and gets as much of herself into the wheelchair as caninely possible. Dad's features soften as he strokes her velvety brown ears.

"So," I begin once the aide has left us, "you had a brunch date. Did you have a nice time? Who's Brian Bascomb?"

Dad shoots me a stealthy glance, but of course he can't answer. I retrieve the pen and pad from beside his bed and hand them to him. He keeps his hands sunk into Ethel's fur so I have no choice but to dump the pen and pad into his lap.

When he makes no effort to use the pen and paper, I press on. "Is Brian Bascomb someone you worked with?" The minute the words are out of my mouth I could kick myself. You better believe Detective Coughlin would never make such a stupid blunder—offer up a ready-made lie. Sure enough, Dad looks up and nods eagerly.

I decide to come back to Brian Bascomb later. I have more important matters to tackle.

"Guess who I saw this week? Melody Olsen's mother, Lisa. Remember her?"

Dad's hand freezes on Ethel's head.

"She and mom were good friends. You must remember her."

He nods warily.

"She's such a kind person. Generous, you know? I'd forgotten that."

I can see his sunken chest rising and falling under the gray shroud of a cardigan he wears every day.

"She was willing to sit and talk to me about Mom. Really talk, I mean. Answer questions, reminisce." I let this information hang there for a moment. No one moves.

After the silence has dragged on long enough, I continue. "Mrs. Olsen told me Mom had gone back to work a year after I was born. I never knew that. Said she worked for a small PR firm—really loved it."

Dad nods while keeping his eyes focused on Ethel.

"What was the firm called?" This could be valuable information. Maybe I can find other people who knew my mother well at the time of her disappearance.

Dad shakes his head.

"You won't tell me?"

Finally he picks up the pen and pad. He writes and holds it up. *Don't remember.*

This may or may not be true. Dad has never had a good memory for mundane details, like when the garbage men pick up or how to change the ink in the printer. But maybe he doesn't want me to know. Why?

"Mrs. Olsen said mom quit her job in the city when I was born, but then didn't like not working so she found a job closer to home." I try to arrange my features to look nothing more than mildly curious. "How close was her office to our house? I think I remember going there with her."

In the harsh fluorescent light of the nursing home, my father looks exceptionally pale and frail. But his bright blue eyes haven't dimmed. Despite his refusal to work on his recovery, despite his inability to speak, my father—sharp, shrewd, analytical--is in there. He knows I'm after something although he's not sure what it might be. We play a non-verbal game of cat and mouse. Me, smiling benignly as I take a little stroll down memory lane. Him, gauging whether I'll drop the subject faster if he answers or he refuses.

Finally, he drops his gaze to the notepad, and gripping the pen in his left hand, awkwardly scratches out a few words. When he's done I squint to read what he's written: *Reston Ave. She took you in stroller.*

Whattaya know? The bit about remembering going there with her was total fabrication on my part, but apparently true. "She didn't take me every day? Sometimes you watched me, right?"

Dad nods, a faraway look in his eyes.

"Didn't you ever have a nanny, even a part-time babysitter?" I ask. "It must've been hard for you to get your work done with a crying baby to deal with." He shakes his head and croaks out a word

I can't understand.

"What?"

Dad picks up the pen again. *Good baby.*

Ridiculously, I feel a lump form in my throat. Imagine--I was a good baby. That's the most complimentary thing my father has said to me in years.

We're quiet for a moment, but it's not the usual excruciating silence of seconds counted until we can be released from each other's company. Instead we're sort of basking in the glow of a happier time, a time I don't truly remember.

And then, to paraphrase Frank Sinatra, I go and spoil it all by saying something stupid. "Dad, Mrs. Olsen said she thought Mom might have been pregnant when she disappeared. Is that true?"

I see his hands tighten on the arms of his wheelchair. His eyes widen and he shakes his head furiously, as if I'm the knife-wielding maniac and he's the cornered babysitter. Then he lurches forward and pounds the call button beside his bed. Of course I shouldn't have blurted out the question so brutally. It's just that I'm not used to protecting his feelings. I'm not used to him having feelings.

Out in the hall I hear the squeak of the aide's approaching feet. I need to recoup. "Dad? Mrs. O. said Mom was excited about something in the weeks before she…, before Christmas. Was it a baby? Do you know?"

But there's no time to say more. Desiree the aide has arrived and Dad thrusts his chin toward the bathroom. As she wheels him in, the light reflects something shiny.

His cheeks are wet with tears.

Chapter 22

I try to ride out my father's retreat into the bathroom, but after twenty minutes Desiree comes back in, fixes me with a withering glare, and tells me Dad is having trouble "moving things along" and my continuing presence must be "constricting." Her dark eyes lock with mine, her broad, brown face frozen with disdain. I know in that moment that if Desiree's father ever had a stroke she would not put him in a place like Manor View. She'd bring him to her house, carry him in her strong arms, feed him, wipe him, bathe him, all without complaint. She doesn't understand us Americans, doesn't like us much either, although it's our strange ways that create a job for her. She'd like to tell me what a sorry excuse I am for a daughter that I don't take my father out myself. That I don't, apparently, even know who his one friend is. But honesty is not one of the perks of her job.

Invalids trump healthy people every time—I have no choice but to leave. But I know damn well it's not an intestinal crisis keeping him holed up in the loo. I want to shout "we're not done with this conversation" through the bathroom door as I leave his room, but the aide's tapping foot and crossed arms silence me, and I slink out with Ethel.

Now she and I are home, grappling with the saddest stretch of the week: Sunday afternoon. This is the time when lovers lounge in bed, trading sections of the New York Times; when families go bike-riding or apple-picking or some other hyphenated activity; when old married couples take long hand-in-hand walks. Ethel and I are none of those things, so we struggle to find ways to fill the long hours between sleeping in and going to bed early. Ethel alternates restless pacing with heavy sighing. I mostly brood.

The Sundays of my childhood were spent with Nana and Pop. They'd pick me up at eight for Sunday school, an activity my father only tolerated because it got me out of the house early and motivated my grandparents to keep me all day. How I loved Sunday school! Making the Popsicle stick manger with the clothespin baby Jesus. Eating the wholesome graham cracker and apple juice snack. Memorizing the 23rd Psalm. *Yea, though I walk through the valley of the shadow of death, I will fear no evil....Thy rod and thy staff they comfort me.... Thou preparest a table before me in the presence of mine enemies....* I had no idea what it meant but I loved the sound of the words as they rolled off my tongue.

After church, we'd go out to lunch at the Afton Restaurant and I'd get a Shirley Temple with my grilled cheese sandwich. At the table Nana would pull out the neatly clipped THINGS TO DO column from the Palmyrton *Daily Record* and suggest outings. Petting Zoo? Hay ride? Gingerbread house competition? As I look back on those Sundays, I marvel at my optimism. Every week, brimming with anticipation, I'd choose an excursion. Every week I was just slightly let down. I could never lose the feeling that the other kids—the ones who were there with their screaming little brothers and bored older sisters and piggy-back ride giving fathers—were having more fun than I was. Most of all, I couldn't shake the sense that if my mom had been there to shoo away the aggressive goose at the farm or take my picture in the funny colonial hat, my Sunday afternoon would have been pure bliss. Instead, on the way home I often wept quietly in the back seat, overcome by waves of sadness, while my grandparents chatted away in the front of the big Buick, pleased with the success of their entertainment.

Sundays haven't improved much in the past twenty-five years. I still feel pulled toward tears, and it doesn't take much to set me off. A guy puts his hand on his wife's shoulder as they're crossing the street and I start scrabbling through my pockets looking for a balled up napkin to mop up my over-reaction.

Sometimes I surrender to the sadness and wallow. Make like a pig and wade right into the mire. That's when the scrap book comes out.

I slide my feet out from under Ethel's sprawl at the end of the sofa and pad over to the bookcase. The scrapbook resides on the top shelf, holding the only remnants of family I possess. Nana assembled it, and every page is a testament to her resolute cheerfulness and her despair.

The book begins with my mother's birth. A velum card, only slightly yellow around the edges, trumpets the arrival of Charlotte Elizabeth Perry, 6 pounds, 7 ounces. Proud parents: William and Elinor. The next few pages chronicle my mother's meteoric rise: star of the ballet recital, champion of the summer swim league, top seller of Girl Scout cookies. Nana has saved every ribbon and award, carefully mounting and labeling them. Nestled between the mementoes are faded snapshots of a smiling Charlotte in a number of different get-ups, even then projecting an astonishing grace.

I study the pictures as I always have, searching for some similarity between us. Where in that beautiful, confident, athletic girl is the seed that would one day become me?

I turn two pages and we are into the high school years. Cheerleader, prom queen, school musical soloist, field hockey star. Face it—if I had met my mother at my high school, I would've been scared to death of her. Wouldn't any mere mortal? I know Nana assembled this scrapbook with the best of intentions. She wanted me to know my mother, to love her as she and Pop did. But the scrapbook has always backfired.

If you asked the average person to conjure up the sensation of dread what would they imagine? A trip to the dentist, maybe, or a phone ringing in the middle of the night. For me, it would be the sight of Nana advancing on me with that scrapbook in her hands. I knew I should have enjoyed snuggling on the sofa with Nana, breathing in her familiar combination of peppermint Lifesavers, Estee Lauder and Aqua Net, leafing through the pages of my mother's life. The fact that I hated it scared me, and instinctively I knew I could never tell Nana how I really felt. I needed Nana, needed her desperately, so I couldn't afford to do anything that might make her stop loving me. That's why I endured those sessions, endured them right up until the day before she died.

I still hate the scrapbook, but with Nana gone at least I don't have to pretend to like it. Now when I get it out it's because I want the perverse pleasure of picking at a scab. Today I flip past the early years and cut to the chase: Charlotte as wife and mother. I study the wedding pictures with an interest I've never felt before. Naturally, my mother was a stunning bride. But today I don't focus on her elegant gown or the flowing illusion veil. I scrutinize my father. He appears in only two photos, as if he were a bit player on this big day. But in both pictures he looks like he's just won the Nobel Prize, basking in the glow of knowing the world finally recognizes his true genius. Dad was never conventionally handsome, but in these pictures he radiates an energy that makes him attractive. It's not a stretch to understand why my mother married him.

My hand hesitates on the scrapbook page. These final photos have always been the hardest for me to look at. Charlotte as Madonna. Nana has selected only those photos that portray my mother with one foot in Heaven. Exhausted but proud Charlotte in her hospital bed. Doting Charlotte nursing. Laughing Charlotte spooning in the baby food. Energetic Charlotte pushing the stroller. I'm in the pictures, but just like my father at the wedding, I seem like nothing more than a prop.

There are three empty pages at the end of the scrapbook. Of course Nana didn't include the obituary or the newspaper article entitled, "Young Mother Apparent Drowning Victim." I slap the book shut. There's nothing I don't already know here. Time to move on to something more productive.

On a lark I go to the Rutgers website and search the faculty list. No Brian Bascomb there. Then I Google the name and get several hits. One is an obituary of a 103- year-old Brian in Plano, Texas. Another is a plastic surgeon in Palo Alto. The third is a Brian Bascomb with a Facebook page. The Info page says he's from Somerville, NJ. I can't view the rest unless I become Brian's friend. Now I'm getting somewhere. I try finding a phone listing in Somerville but come up empty.

I guess Facebook is my best bet. I put in a friend request with a message: "Hi, I'm Audrey Nealon, Roger's daughter. Thanks for taking him out to lunch." As I hit send, my phone rings: Cal.

"Hi." I strive for blasé but fall significantly short.

"Hi, yourself. Busy?"

Busy working myself into a twist. "No, just relaxing with Ethel. You?"

Cal sighs. "I'm at the office, trying to get a jump on this week's campaign events. That's why I called. What works better for you, Tuesday or Wednesday?"

I feel a prickle of fear. Surely he doesn't expect me to host some rubber chicken dinner or give a speech for Spencer in front of the Montclair Rotary Club? "Works for what?" I can hear the wariness in my voice.

"To have dinner with me." For the first time since I met him, Cal sounds uncertain. "I mean...I guess I thought you, you know, might want to, but..."

Stupid, stupid Audrey! "I do! I definitely do. But the way you said 'planning campaign events' and 'what works for you' I thought you meant you wanted me to campaign for Spencer." I prattle on until Cal's laughter cuts me off.

"Poor Audrey—I expect you to read my mind. What I was trying to express was I can leave one night this week free of campaign events so I can see you. Which would you prefer? I promise I won't put you to work ringing doorbells."

Now my heart is pounding. I'm about to say either night is fine, but I catch myself. No need for him to know I'm sitting home alone every night. "Tuesday," I say with conviction. "Tuesday works best for me."

"Tuesday it is. Oh, hell—there's Spencer on my call waiting. See you at seven, baby."

I stare at the dead phone in my hand. Baby?

Preparations for the Reicker sale are in full swing when I get to the office on Monday morning. I can hear the phone ringing and the sound of packing tape zipping off the roll even before I open the door. The tower of packages waiting for the UPS man, the spicy aroma of Jill's chai latte, the tinny, insistent beat emanating from Ty's iPod—I embrace the reassuring familiarity of my office. What a relief it is to be away from home, where I've spent the last eighteen hours obsessing about my father's reaction to my question about my mother's pregnancy.

"Audrey, have you seen your picture in the Sunday *Star Ledger*?" Jill squeals the moment I walk through the door. "It's from that party you went to."

"What picture?" I hold out my hand for the paper. There on the Style page is a big picture of two people in profile: Spencer shaking the hand of a slender, long-legged woman in a black dress. "Are you nuts? That's not me!"

"It is too," Jill insists. "The caption says, 'Audrey Nealon helps Spencer Finneran celebrate his birthday.' And that's your new haircut. *Love* your dress. You look fabulous."

I squint at the photo. That is my haircut. And my new ridiculously high pumps. "Geez, I didn't even recognize myself."

Ty crowds over my shoulder. "Dress is hot." He taps the page. "You got great legs, Audge. Why you always wear those baggy sweats?"

I pull the paper away from them and toss it face-down on the desk. I'm not comfortable with this Audrey- as-Angelina-Jolie schtick. "Let's get to work. Any messages?"

"The Chamber of Commerce called twice," Jill says. "They want to know if you're going to the Meet and Greet next Wednesday at five."

I wrinkle my nose. Guys whose guts are ready to pop out of their button down shirts talking to my boobs. Women with frosted hair and color coordinated handbags tossing around terms like loyalty index and cycle time. At the Chamber Meet and Greet, I always feel like the only kid at the grown-up's table. "Do I have to go? God, I hate those things."

"We got three new customers the last time you networked there," Jill reminds me. "You told me then it was my job to force you to go every time."

"It's your job to reconcile the checkbook every month and you never do that. And don't use network as a verb in a sentence where I'm the subject. What I do at these functions is hover pathetically near the cheese and crackers until Isabelle arrives, then trail around in her shadow, handing out my card to everyone she hands hers to."

"Seems to be working. Should I call and say you'll be there?"

"Whatever." I sit at my desk and start going through the mail. Seconds later, Jill is motioning for me to pick up the phone.

"Louise, the assistant director, wants to talk to you."

I roll my eyes and pick up. Turns out Louise wants to know if I'll serve on the table decorations committee for the Chamber's annual fundraising dinner dance. Gee, poke a sharp stick in my eye/serve on the decorations committee. It's a toss-up. "Honestly Louise, I'm honored to be asked, but you know, I haven't fully recovered from being in the hospital. Maybe next year, when I've got all my energy back." Was that brilliant, or what? I have twelve months to figure out an excuse for next year.

"Oh, Audrey, I totally understand!" Louise's voice drips remorse. "I shouldn't have asked—I don't know what I was thinking. Is there anything we here at the Chamber can do for you?"

I'm about to gracefully decline and make my escape when an idea pops into my head. "Actually, Louise, there is something I could use your help with. I'm looking for a PR firm—do you maintain a list of Chamber members sorted by business type?"

"Absolutely—I can call it right up on my computer. You're probably looking for a small, boutique firm, right?"

"Uh…actually, I'm doing a little research for a friend. I think she wants a firm with a lot of experience. Can you tell how long each one's been in business?"

"No, but I can see how long they've been members of the Chamber. Let's see…Burke and Fein, thirty-five years; Media Solutions, thirty years…" Louise keeps going until I cut her off at twenty-five years and say my good-byes. Now I have a place to start my search.

"I'm not driving old books to Oscar's," Tyshaun warns Jill as I tune back in to what's going on around me. "Last time I was in his shop I seen a rat as big as my arm."

"I thought you weren't afraid of anything," Jill says.

"I'm afraid of rats. Rats and snakes, man. That shit freaks me out." Tyshaun's broad shoulders tremble in disgust.

"How about bears?" I ask. It feels good to be teasing Ty again, instead of tip-toeing around on eggshells.

"Aw, Audge, don't get me started on bears. D'jou see that story in the paper last week? Big ass bear comes right into this guy's kitchen. Opens up the fridge. Guy comes down for breakfast and there's this bear sitting on the kitchen floor eating baloney and yogurt. Knew how to open the packages and everything. That's messed up."

"Yeah, there was a bear over by Lawnwood Elementary school the other day," Jill says. "They had to call all the kids in from recess."

"See—that's what I'm sayin'. This is New Jersey, man, not Alaska. Shouldn't have to worry about that. They oughta shoot them mothers. I see any bears around here, I'm'a get me a gun."

"Don't you dare," I say, suddenly serious. "If you see a bear, you call the police and they'll come shoot it with a tranquilizer dart."

Ty scowls. "I don't call the cops for nuthin'. I take my chances with the damn bear." His phone rings and as he holds it to his ear, his face grows even fiercer. "A'right, a'right." Ty puts his phone in his pocket and snatches up the van keys. "I'm going to Home Depot before it gets too busy. Gimme the list."

Jill hands it over silently. Our giddy mood has evaporated. How did we manage to go from rare books to Oscar to rats to bears to the unhappy topic of the police? Ty stomps off, leaving an awkward silence in his wake.

"Those are cute earrings," I tell Jill, just to say something.

Normally she wears ten or twelve silver studs and hoops in each ear, but today she's sporting bulbous orange and green clip-ons that look like rhinestone encrusted gum drops. Jill brightens.

"Aren't they amazing? They remind me of something Bette Davis wore in *Now, Voyager.*"

"Before my time." There's no doubt the earrings Jill's wearing now are costume jewelry, but their campy, retro style reminds me of the jewelry in Mrs. Szabo's trunk. "Where'd you get those?" I ask lightly.

"I dunno." Jill fingers the earrings. "The flea market, maybe...No wait, I remember. It was a sidewalk vendor in the city. Oh my God, Audrey, you should have seen this guy--he had *so* much sick stuff!" Jill's hands are waving and she's bouncing in her seat like the old people at Manor View doing their chair aerobics. "There was this awesome snake bracelet with rubies for eyes and these metal fringe-y things on the tail end that rattled. I wanted it *so* bad but he was asking fifty bucks and he wouldn't come down." Jill sighs. "I wish I wasn't always so broke."

"Sorry I can't pay you better." I say it with a smile but there's an unsettling thought in the back of my mind. What if Jill feels she deserves a little bonus? What if that trunk full of jewelry has been tempting her? I'm casting about for a way to ask if she's ever looked through it, when she turns her big, super-mascara-ed eyes on me.

"Oh, I didn't mean it *that* way, Audge." Her face is as sweet and yearning as the faces in those adopt-a South-American-orphan photos you get at Christmastime. "This is the best job I ever had." Then her gaze shifts from my face to my hands. "Say, that's a cool new ring you've got on, too. Where'd you get yours?"

Stole it back from someone who stole it from who....my mom or my dad?

"It's old." I shove my hands in my sweatshirt pockets. "I had misplaced it and then I found it again."

Jill spins around on her desk chair and goes back to her typing. "I love when that happens, don't you? It's like getting something brand new without spending any money."

Chapter 23

Six-thirty on Tuesday has rolled around a lot faster than I would have thought possible. I'm in my bedroom confronting the reality that it's too late to go shopping for a whole new wardrobe before Cal arrives. Somehow I have to find something to wear right here in my closet. Why don't I own anything else that makes me look as amazing as the dress I wore to Spencer's party? I've gotten as far as putting on my best bra and panties. Hey, good undergarments are the secret to well-fitting clothes, right? Except that doesn't explain why I've also shaved my legs right up to the bikini line.

The black pants are my only option; the remaining variable is the cream silk blouse or the rose cashmere sweater. I reach for the blouse, and as I'm buttoning it notice a tiny splash of red wine on the cuff. Ethel leaps off my bed and charges to the foyer, barking like a maniac.

Shit! So it's got to be the cashmere sweater. I liked this a lot when I bought it—classy yet bold. Now, with Cal coming up the walk, it seems prim yet loud.

I pull the sweater on with no time to study my reflection before the doorbell chimes. Better not to know, I figure as I go to let Cal in.

I open the door and Cal takes a step forward, but Ethel, in her frenzy to greet our guest, lunges forward and slams the door in Cal's face. Restraining Ethel with one hand and yanking the doorknob with the other, I manage to create a footwide opening, and Cal sidles in. Ethel breaks free and runs frenetic circles around the foyer. Her paw snags the lamp cord, sending the light pitching into Cal, who catches it neatly. Ethel sits down, throws back her head, and howls.

"Ethel stop! This isn't an audition for *Call of the Wild*."

My hair is disheveled, my sweater twisted. A clump of Ethel's white fur sticks to my pants and a clump of her brown fur drifts through the air and lands on Cal's crisp white shirt. Gingerly, I pluck it off. "Sorry for all the commotion."

Cal sets the lamp back on the table, puts his hands on my shoulders, and turns me to face him. "I get a kick out of you, Audrey. You're so...unaffected. That's refreshing."

Unaffected? I feel the way I used to when I won the coach's "best team spirit" award every year at the field hockey banquet. "Yeah, I pull this social grace off with no forethought whatsoever."

Cal pulls me closer, tips my chin up, and kisses me. It takes a while. The room tilts as if I've been chugging vodka and Sunny D at a frat party.

"We better go," Cal whispers in my ear, "or I won't feel like eating at all."

At Hennessy's Cal is greeted like rock star. The maître d' calls him by name, the bartender waves, the chef pokes his head out of the kitchen and recommends the best specials. They've probably seen Cal come through here with scores of different women. I sense they're sizing me up. *Where did he find this one? Not his usual type.*

When he's here with his political cronies they probably sit in the more boisterous Grill Room, but tonight we're shown to a cozy booth in the back of the formal dining room. This must be his "date" table. As I sink into the plush banquette, the flickering candles and muted hunting prints suck every possible conversational gambit out of my brain. Staring across the table at Cal, mute as my poor stroked-out father, I long for a carry-out tin of Thai basil chicken and the weight of Ethel's head on my knee.

If Cal senses my frantic desire to cut and run, he doesn't let it show. His moving lips and smiling eyes indicate he's talking to me, but I'm too gripped with anxiety to understand what he's saying. All I can think about is that we're on a date, a real date, a date that's going to end…and then what? Freshly shaven legs notwithstanding, I'm not ready for this.

"So did you?" Cal's apparently repeating a question that I totally missed.

I lean forward. "I'm sorry—did I what?"

"Grow up in Palmyrton."

"Yes, my dad and I lived on Skytop Drive. Then I went away to UVA for college, but I came back."

"To take over the family business?"

I choke back a snort. "My father was a math professor at Rutgers. Believe me, he wanted me to go into his line of work, but instead, as he puts it, I 'set up garage sales of other people's crap'."

Cal lightly strokes the inside of my wrist. "You own your own successful business. He's not proud of you for that?"

This is *not* what I want to be talking about, but I'm powerless to steer the conversation elsewhere. I shake my head. "He thinks I'm squandering my abilities. I had a summer job in college working for an estate sale firm. I liked it, but I saw how my boss sold things for less than they were worth because he couldn't be bothered to learn about art and antiques and collectibles. So I started selling things for people…this was pre- eBay…and the rest is, well, history." I shrug. "It's a weird business, but I like it. I like poking around in other people's lives. Nosy, I guess."

Before Cal can ask me another question, I shift the spotlight to him. "What about you? You couldn't have gone to Palmyrton High or I would remember you."

"I grew up in Summit, in the smallest house of the nicest neighborhood. My family was all about keeping up with the

Joneses." He smiles, but he doesn't look particularly amused. "Running was the perfect sport for me. I was always eating the dust of someone who was just a little bit taller, stronger, faster. Until I finally worked out my own strategy for getting to the head of the pack."

"Which is?"

"Focus on the three feet of road ahead of you, and the finish line will take care of itself."

He says this with great conviction. Maybe that pragmatic philosophy is what accounts for his supreme self-confidence. It wouldn't hurt me to borrow a page from Cal's playbook.

"Me, I'm always looking ahead, seeing all the possible twists and turns and pitfalls that lie down the road. Guess that's what comes of being captain of the chess team, not the track team."

Cal chokes on his drink. "You were captain of the chess team?"

"Until senior year, when it finally dawned on me how uber-geeky it was. Boy, was my dad pissed when I quit."

"He taught you to play?"

"Yeah, that was his great gift to me. Chess, and an ability to multiply large numbers in my head. Forms quite an emotional bond."

"You know what my mother gave to me?" Cal rips a dinner roll in half. "Impeccable table manners and good fashion sense. And my father taught me how to slip a maître d' a twenty to get a good table without a reservation. Quite a legacy, huh?"

I recognize the disappointment in his voice. I've heard it often enough in my own. Guess Cal and I share some common ground after all. "I take it you're not close to your parents?"

"They divorced when I was a sophomore. Got bored and decided they could each do better. They could've waited 'til my sister and I were in college, but they weren't ones for delaying gratification. Still aren't."

Cal's hand rests on the table—no doubt his mother wouldn't approve. I'm tempted to touch it, but I'm not quite bold enough.

"Still, you turned out okay."

"I guess. For a long time I was pretty committed to using their divorce as an excuse to do whatever I damn pleased. Or do nothing at all."

Cal props his chin on his hand and gazes at me for a long moment. "I admire you, Audrey, I really do. It takes guts to start your own business without any family support. I graduated from college with an English degree and no earthly idea what I wanted to do. My mother was nagging me, my friends all seemed to have a plan. So I took the coward's way out and went to law school." He rolls his eyes. "Just what the world needs—another paper-pushing, nit-picking asshole billing five hundred bucks an hour to add layers of complexity to every business transaction."

I smile as some of my tension dissolves. I've never heard Cal express the slightest self-doubt before. "I thought you loved being a lawyer. You're certainly successful at it."

He pushes aside the bread basket, clearing the space between us. "What I love is politics, Audrey. That's my passion, but I didn't realize it when I was twenty-two. I should have gone to Capitol Hill and worked as a gofer for some Congressman, shared a ratty house with five other guys doing the same thing. It's too late for me to live that life now, but I can run Spencer's campaign in Palmer County. And if he wins the election—*when* he wins—I'm going to be his chief of staff in Trenton."

Cal's eyes reflect the flickering candlelight. The worldly self-confidence he always projects—that thing about him that both attracts me and terrifies me—has slipped away. Suddenly he's a little boy on Christmas morning, thrilled to have received the race car set of his dreams. "That's great, Cal. You're going to quit the law firm?"

"Taking a leave of absence," he explains. "In the long run, I'm worth more to them in Trenton than Palmyrton. And I can take a break from contract law." He shivers and leans closer to me. "I hate preparing cases, hate filing briefs. I'm a horse-trader, Audrey. Spencer likes to keep himself above the fray, but I tell you, I love rolling around in the dirt, hashing out the deals."

The waiter chooses this moment to materialize, demanding our order. Cal selects steak; I foolishly order the entrée that sounds most appealing: grilled sesame tuna. The moment the waiter retreats I'm filled with diner's remorse. Garlic/soy/ginger marinade—my mouth will reek for days. What was I thinking?

I give up on flagging the waiter down so I can switch to baked filet of sole, and turn my attention back to Cal. "How did you first meet Spencer?"

"It was five years ago. I wanted to score points with this girl who was working at Spencer's Senate campaign headquarters, so I volunteered to stuff envelopes. Spencer was in the office that day and he started talking about what he hoped to accomplish in Washington. He talked about how the chasm between rich and poor in New Jersey was bad for everyone. He said he wanted to be the first senator who'd represent Paterson *and* Peapack; Camden *and* Upper Saddle River; Newark *and* Princeton. He was ahead of the curve, talking about public-private initiatives, getting corporations to understand it was in their best interest to improve inner city schools." Cal pauses, breathless. "The next thing you know, I was offering to make phone calls and give speeches. Meeting Spencer—and Anne— changed my life."

I've never been the slightest bit interested in politics, but I find myself experiencing a pang of envy. It must be nice to feel committed to a higher purpose than getting the very best price for a vintage Jetsons lunchbox. Plus, Cal has managed to do what I've always longed to: trade in the defective family he was born into for a fully functioning, deluxe model. But I can't tell him all that. So I say, "Anne seems very fond of you."

"She is. None of their kids has been bitten by the politics bug. So I've become the son who wants to follow dad into the family business." Cal leans forward and drops his voice. "By the way, Anne really likes *you*. She was very pleased when I told her I was seeing you tonight. She thinks I have awful taste in women, so she warned me not to mess this up."

Cal mess up? I'm the one who needs advice on how not to blow this. Luckily, the waiter arrives bearing our appetizers, sparing me the need to come up with a coolly witty response. Before leaving our table, he refills our wineglasses. Mine was far emptier than Cal's. Nevertheless, I take another big gulp.

Gradually, the conversation comes a little easier. I find myself telling funny stories about Ty and Jill and my regular customers, like Howard the Hoarder. At least, I guess they're funny because Cal is laughing. He tells me about life on the campaign trail with Spencer—the reporters, the gadflies who come to every event to ask annoying questions, the crooks who try to slip him wads of cash.

"Is he ever tempted?" Of course I know what Cal will say, but it's kind of sweet to see the intense sincerity in his eyes when he says it.

"Spencer wouldn't take a stick of gum from a constituent." Then Cal laughs. "Of course, he always leaves it to me to get rid of these people. Once I had to tell some Mafioso from Atlantic City no thanks for the foot high stack of chips, the suite, and the call girl."

The waiter shows up on "call girl" and we both giggle like middle-schoolers.

"This cake is delicious," Cal says. "Try it." Aiming a loaded fork at my mouth like a mother robin with a worm, he steadies my chin with his other hand, an oddly tender gesture that makes my spine dissolve.

Even after he's fed me, Cal continues to lean across the table, stroking my right hand with his fingertips. "Pretty ring—unique."

I feel a hot flush rising. This is it. Tell him now, or never.

"It was my mother's. My father had it specially made for her."

"Sweet."

"I found it in the trunk in your aunt's attic."

Cal aspirates the coffee he's sipping and starts to cough.

Nice one, Audrey—I have all the tact of a chainsaw. "Sorry. Look, Cal, I kinda figured out what the deal was with your aunt and the jewelry. Her neighbor told me that Agnes was a housekeeper and a nanny...the jewelry is all different sizes and styles..."

Cal holds his hand up and glances around the restaurant.

Right. Not the best place to be discussing Agnes's larcenous habits. I think I'm blowing my beautiful evening out, but my need to know how Agnes got my mother's ring is greater than my need to charm Cal. "Can we talk about it later?"

Cal nods, but then he can't let the matter drop. "She worked hard all her life, Audrey. Her husband was sick for years. She never had two cents to call her own. When I saw the stuff, I knew."

Now I'm the one who reaches for his hand. "I understand. It's not so terrible—seems like none of it was ever missed."

Cal touches my ring. "Your mom never wondered what happened to this?"

"My mom disappeared on Christmas Eve when I was three years old."

Cal signals the waiter. "Let's get out of here."

Back at my place, several glasses of cognac later, I've told Cal the entire story of my life—my mother's disappearance, my father's estrangement, my suspicions that my mother might have been pregnant, my determination to know the entire truth.

"Finding the ring after thirty years, and then nearly dying two days later—what can I say? All that stuff you hear about near-death experiences is true. I feel liberated, like I'm finally free to do exactly what I want to do." All the booze has loosened my tongue. I'm saying things that I never realized I felt. "All my life I tried to keep my grandparents happy, and my father—he's impossible to make happy, but I tried not to make him more unhappy. But this I'm doing for me. I deserve to know what happened to my mother."

"Of course you do." Cal pulls me close to him on the sofa and studies the ring on my finger. "I don't know when my Aunt Agnes crossed your mother's path. She didn't keep records of the families she worked for, and she was always paid off the books."

"I'm pretty sure she never worked for us—my father always used an agency. But there has to be some link between our families. Do you remember her talking about the people she worked for? Any names at all?"

Cal shakes his head. "I really didn't spend much time with her, Audrey. She wasn't our most fun-loving relative."

"Who would know? Your mom?"

"Maybe. I'll ask." Cal massages his temples. "When I ask her what the hell I should do about all that stolen jewelry. That should be a great conversation. My mother's policy is to ignore all unpleasantness and shoot any messenger who brings it to her door. Thanks for keeping the trunk for me, by the way. I'll take it off your hands after the election, I promise."

"If your mom can't tell you who Agnes worked for, you're not going to be able to return the stuff to the rightful owners."

"I know. I'd like to toss it in the Passaic River, but in politics you can always be sure a reporter will pop up at the worst possible time."

"I have an idea. Whenever we have stuff left over from a sale that's too good to throw away, we ask the estate if they'd like to donate it to this community group in Newark run by Sister Alice. She always finds a way to sell it or use it."

Cal raises his eyebrows. "I don't know—how are you going to explain a trunk full of jewelry to a nun? I don't want it traced back to me."

"She won't ask questions. Sister Alice is a great believer in the hand of God. She'll see that jewelry as the divine intervention she needs to get her furnace repaired."

"Okay, I like the Robin Hood angle. Just to be on the safe side, can we wait 'til after the election to give it to her? "

"Sure."

"Thank you." Cal brushes his lips across my forehead.

Oh, God—here it comes! Can I do this?

"You're so tense, Audrey. Relax."

He runs his hands along my back and pulls me close to him. I let out a little moan.

Ethel comes over and tries to insinuate herself between us. I nudge her away with my knee.

I can definitely do this.

Chapter 24

I don't cross the threshold of the office until nearly eleven, and before I can stagger to my desk someone starts pounding on the door. Each knock is like a jackhammer to my aching head, so I rush back to the door to shut the insistent fool up. I'm greeted by a delivery man with a monumental bouquet of flowers, which is why Jill is now kvelling.

"Ooo, Audge! Who sent them?"

Of course it has to be Cal, but he left my bed only three hours ago, after which I fell back into a fitful doze. How could he have managed to get these flowers here so quickly, when I'm still too exhausted and hung over to even contemplate a bowl of Cheerios?

I stagger slightly as I read the card tucked among the lilies and iris. Maybe it's the cognac still circulating in my bloodstream, or maybe it's the message: "You're on my mind, Cal."

"Who sent them?" Jill continues to demand. She's as puzzled by my stunned response as she is by the lavish arrangement.

"Cal Tremaine."

Jill cocks her head, bearing an uncanny resemblance to Ethel when she's trying to discern the source of distant barking. "Wow, Audge—this is the second time he's sent you flowers. What's going

149

on?"

"Nothing, nothing. That's the kind of guy he is."

A player.

I know that. This thing with Cal is nothing serious, but I can still enjoy it, right? I'm finally doing what my friend Maura is always encouraging me to do: change up my game. Maura accuses me of always dating what she refers to so charmingly as "pencil dicks"— thin, mournful intellectuals. Why not try a fireman, a lacrosse coach, a bond trader? You might be surprised how much you like it, she tells me. Oh, yes, Maura would approve of Cal. The attention, the flowers, the sex: all good, as long as I accept it for what it is.

A hook-up.

Having escaped Jill's prying eyes by inventing errands to run, I now stand in the lobby of a big boxy office building staring at the board listing the tenants. Burke and Fein, the first PR firm on my Chamber of Commerce list, is on the third floor. Will they know anything about my mother? Will I even be able to talk my way in to find out? My work has made me adept at persuading people to do what they secretly long to do. (I'm sure your grandmother would *want* you to sell her mink coat if you'll never wear it. That sterling flatware could pay off your student loans—why not let me find a buyer?) But I'm less confident in my powers of persuasion when it comes to convincing people to do what I want. I take a steadying breath and press the button for the elevator. The doors slide open before I have the chance to cut and run.

The minute I step into the Burke and Fein reception area I'm filled with doubt. The vibe is all wrong here: utilitarian office furniture, factory-produced "art," a honeycomb of cubicles stretching out from either side of a long hallway. Surely my mother never worked here. Of course, the Burke and Fein of thirty years ago might have been less antiseptic. But still...

"May I help you?" the efficient looking woman at the front desk asks.

I stammer out my request. My fears that my cover story would sound implausible were groundless. This woman wants nothing more than to process me out of her reception area—either back into the maze or out the door, it matters not to her. With a few clicks of her computer and buzzes of her intercom she has my answer. This firm was never located on Reston Ave; Charlotte Perry never worked here.

Out the door I go.

The reaction at the second PR firm on my list is much the same: no Reston Ave, no Charlotte Perry. I get back in the car to drive to the third address. Traffic is stop and go, and as I glance in the rearview mirror before changing lanes, I notice a small gray car with the dinged front bumper. Wasn't that car parked across the street from Burke and Fein when I left? I watch it behind me for three blocks. Then I turn right and it keeps going straight. I realize I've been gripping the steering wheel awfully tightly, and peel my fingers back. Paranoia really isn't my style—I've got to relax.

As soon as I pull up in front of The Van Houten Group, I feel a tingle of anticipation. The red brick building looks as if it started life as a standard issue suburban bank, and somewhere along the way encountered a post-modern architecture fairy. Two wings cantilever out of the building's sides at improbable angles. The front wall is solid glass. The Van Houten Group is etched on a slab of granite by the curb. This is the kind of firm that could have started out in a Victorian on Reston Ave.; I'm sure of it.

Two steps into the foyer and I'm overcome with wardrobe anxiety. Everything is smoky gray and stainless steel. I should be wearing black, as I'm sure all the employees here are required to do. Certainly the receptionist, with her long raven hair, short black dress and high black boots, blends in chameleon-like with her surroundings. Her black mascaraed eyes scan me from top to bottom. She pauses a beat, then speaks. "And you have an appointment with…?"

All right, obviously I don't look like one of their regular clients, but does she have to treat me like a Jehovah's Witness? As I stammer out an explanation, a young man in big rectangular glasses (black, natch) glides up to her desk and adds his curious stare.

"We've been in this space for seven years," he says with authority. "Before that we were somewhere on the west side of Palmyrton, I believe."

"Reston Avenue," a deep voice says from behind me.

I see Black Glasses exchange a glance with Black Boots.

"Good afternoon, Mr. Van Houten." The receptionist strides out from behind her desk, skates around me, and holds her arms out to the old man who's just entered. "Let me take your coat."

"Who are you?" he asks me. His voice is imperious but not insulting. Sharp blue eyes stare at me from under a crest of pure white hair. I feel compelled to tell the absolute truth.

"Audrey Nealon, Charlotte Perry's daughter. Did she used to work here?"

"Charlotte Perry!" His whole face lights up. "You're her daughter? My God, the last time I saw you, you were wearing a pink hat with bunny ears." His eyes narrow to a squint. "You don't look much like her."

"So I've been told. Did you know her well?"

"Oh, my yes. I hired her."

Now I'm the one whose face lights up. "Look, I understand if this is not a good time, but could I talk to you for a few minutes about my mother? I mean, I can make an appointment and come back..."

"Tamberlynn." Mr. Van Houten's voice is as sharp as a finger snap. "Bring Miss Nealon and me some coffee in my office. And take her coat."

As Tamberlynn scrambles to do his bidding, Mr. Van Houten smiles at me and extends his arm. "Right this way my dear."

Van Houten's office is a shrine to Mid-century modern. There's a Milo Baughman chrome sofa and a Morris Lapidus coffee table.

Gingerly, I sit in an Eames chair opposite his desk. I'm sure this is the real deal and it takes every ounce of self-control I possess not to flip the chair over and check for the trademark underneath. I should be thinking about what I want to ask the man, but my eyes keep darting around, lighting on the kinds of things I'd kill to find in the homes of aging baby boomers being shipped off to assisted living: Eero Saarinen stools, Heathware pottery, a chrome cigarette lighter, even though no one can smoke in offices. Finally, I bring my attention back to Mr. Van Houten. That's when I notice the framed painting above his desk. I'm out of my chair in a flash.

"My God! Is that a David Salle?"

He swivels in his chair to watch me studying his artwork. "Yes, one of his early pieces. You know his work?"

I tell him the story of the Lee Krasner I found in the home of an old drunk. Van Houten looks pleased.

"You have a keen eye for quality. So did your mother. She was with me when I acquired that painting at a gallery in Soho." He chuckles. "That was when Soho was quite disreputable."

"Really?" I have an intense desire to touch the painting, or even the simple black frame. I clasp my hands behind my back and turn to face him. Van Houten looks to be about ten years older than my father. What was he doing taking my mother to Soho art shows in the seventies?

He seems to pluck the question right out of my mind. "In those days, this firm had all sorts of dodgy clients who couldn't afford to pay their bills. The gallery owner went to art school with someone who worked here. He hired us to get publicity for his shows, and then couldn't come up with any cash. So I agreed to take a painting instead. Your mother chose that one. It's valued at two hundred thousand today. Not bad for getting *New York* and the *Village Voice* to write a few lines about the show, eh?"

I feel a slow smile spread across my face. Maybe I did inherit some traits from my mother after all. "Thanks for telling me that. I was only three when she disappeared, and I've always felt I wasn't much like her.'"

"No one was like Charlotte. She was one of a kind."

Oh cripes—here it comes. The Charlotte Perry was an angel come to earth routine. Somehow I'd expected better than that from Mr. Van Houten.

"Hell to work with, of course. Demanding, temperamental, volatile. Couldn't keep a secretary. Alienated a few clients who had the nerve to disagree with her. But when she had one of her strokes of insight—look out." The old man shakes his head. "She would've been one of the PR greats. Such a shame she didn't live to see the 21st century. The internet, blogs, YouTube—she could have done so much with today's media."

There's a timid knock on the door and Tamberlynn enters with the coffee. The break gives me a chance to collect my thoughts. So, my mother wasn't a saint. Secretaries hated her. She ticked people off. I feel an uneasy trembling in my jaw. Christ, I can't cry here! But Van Houten has opened up a new view of my mother, as if he chopped down a tree to reveal a panorama that's always been there. I like this new, flawed mother. I miss her.

As the door closes behind Tamberlynn, Van Houten leans back in his chair and spends an inordinate amount of time doctoring his coffee. Then he fixes his bright blue stare on me. "Your mother's been dead for thirty years, Miss Nealon. Why are you inquiring about her now?"

The old man sure doesn't pull any punches. Completely direct, says what he means, leaves no room for misinterpretation. What a welcome change of pace from my father. Or Cal, for that matter. I find myself twisting the pearl ring on my finger. When I realize what I'm doing, I force myself to stop, but the impulse remains like an unscratched itch.

"That was your mother's ring, no?" Mr. Van Houten asks.

"Yes." I can admit that without saying how I got it. Why would I tell him about Mrs. Szabo's attic when I've told no one else? But his directness seems to demand honesty in return. I extend my hand.

"Supposedly my mother never took this ring off. So, she should have been wearing it the night she…disappeared." I've stopped saying died. "But I found it a few weeks ago. Found it in the attic of an old lady's house. Her name was Agnes Szabo—does that name mean anything to you?"

Mr. Van Houten arches his bushy white eyebrows. After a lifetime in PR, his mental address book must hold thousands of names. He's processing Mrs. Szabo. I wait anxiously.

Ultimately he shakes his head. "Szabo—an unusual name. It doesn't ring a bell. Where was this house?"

When I tell him the address his eyebrows tick up another quarter inch, as if to say, "What would Charlotte have been doing *there*?" He continues to gaze at me appraisingly. "So finding this ring has caused you to….?"

Turn into an obsessed lunatic. Question my sanity . "Well, it made me wonder, wonder what really happened that night. You know, the last minute gifts on Christmas Eve, the car accident." I'm rambling now. "I mean, you knew her. Does that seem plausible to you?"

Van Houten sits without speaking. His eyebrows have descended to their rightful place.

I keep blathering. "I've started wondering if my father…and my grandparents…if they were entirely truthful with me, about, you know, my mother. I mean, they always portrayed her as this, this saint. And you're the first person to say she wasn't and, well, I wonder if the whole last minute Christmas gifts, drowning in the lake story makes sense to you?" My ramble ends on a high-pitched, inquisitive note.

The eyebrows are creeping up again. "And the alternative would be…what?"

That she ran away. I can't speak those words aloud, so I change tacks. "Do you remember the weeks before that Christmas? Did my mother seem different to you? Excited? Keyed-up?"

Van Houten smiles. "Charlotte was always keyed up. And impulsive, so I accepted that she might have run out for Christmas gifts in a snow storm." He leans back in his chair and makes a steeple of his long, gnarled fingers. "But yes, now that you mention it, I recall she did seem rather more excitable than usual in those weeks before she died. As if she were about to burst."

This is it—I lean forward eagerly. "Burst about what? Did she tell you what was going on?"

He doesn't answer immediately, so I leap in with more questions. "Could she have just found out she was pregnant?"

Now Mr. Van Houten has the decency to blush, which I find charming in an old-world way. "My dear, we were colleagues. That's not the kind of news she would have shared with me. But it wasn't—"

"Wasn't what?"

Smooth as he is, Mr. Van Houten seems a little flustered, like he's wishing he'd never gotten into this discussion. This lead had seemed so promising, but I feel the possibility of learning something significant slipping away. I scramble to keep the door open. "Did she have a friend here at the office?"

"At the time, Charlotte was the only woman on the professional staff. The other female employees were secretaries—she wouldn't have confided something personal to any of them, I'm sure." Mr. Van Houten glances at his watch.

"Did you know my father?" I ask quickly.

"I met him at a few office parties. As I recall, he had a very droll sense of humor. I always felt he kept Charlotte balanced."

His Blackberry begins tinkling a tinny rendition of Bach's cantata in F.

"Did they seem happy to you?" I toss this out desperately, knowing it will be my last question.

Mr. Van Houten rises. He looks truly uncomfortable now, like he regrets ever having invited me in. "I have a meeting to attend. But yes, your parents struck me as happily married. I'm sorry I couldn't have been of more help."

"Oh, no—you were very helpful," I assure him, even as I

desperately fight the urge to shove him back in his chair. "Thank you so much for your time."

He walks with me toward to door, but his phone rings and he pauses to answer it. While I'm waiting to say good-bye, I get a chance to look at the wall of photographs that I've had my back to throughout my visit. They depict Mr. Van Houten through the years with all sorts of famous people. The most recent photos are nearest to the door. A silver-haired Van Houten with Derek Jeter, Oprah Winfrey, Katie Couric, Michelle Obama. Further to the right, a salt and pepper Van Houten with Bill Clinton, Tom Kean, Robert Redford. All the way in the corner a smooth faced, dark-haired but still easily recognizable Van Houten shakes hands with Jimmy Carter. Some of the other celebrities in that corner I'm having a hard time identifying—this era is before my time. Maybe that glamorous-looking woman is Elizabeth Taylor. The golfer might be Arnold Palmer. Finally, my eye rests on a photo of Van Houten with a young, attractive couple. The man looks very familiar; the smiling woman even more so, like someone I know personally. I take a step closer and squint.

"I know those people." I say, pointing.

Van Houten pockets his phone and follows the direction of my finger. "Anne and Spencer Finneran. This firm handled his first three campaigns."

My heels dig into the carpet although Van Houten is gently urging me toward the door. "Did my mother know Anne and Spencer? Did she work on those campaigns? "

"She may have." Van Houten holds the door for me. "Everyone here had a hand in them."

Chapter 25

Lying in my bed, I stare at the patterns on the ceiling made by the beams of the rising run. Ethel has tried a few times to come up to the head of the bed to cuddle with me, but I push her away. Miffed, she retreats to the foot of the bed. Why am I so harsh? Because I don't want Ethel's doggy smell to obliterate the delicious aroma of Cal that still lingers on the pillow next to mine. Smelling him is the next best thing to lying in his arms, which is the next best thing to feeling his weight on top of me, inside of me.

My heart rate kicks up and I hear the sound of my own breathing. I'm horny. Intensely, squirmingly, itchingly horny. I went without sex for a year and barely missed it. Now, I've been celibate for three days and I can hardly contain my need to make love to Cal again. Unfortunately he has campaign events all week and he told me we can't go out again until Sunday. I wanted to say, "To hell with going out. Just come here after you're done with your fundraising dinner. I don't care how late it is." But I didn't want to sound desperate, so I kept my mouth shut. Now I'm regretting that restraint. I feel like I'm about to jump out of my skin, like I'm about to—

I sit bolt upright.

To burst.

Jesus, this is what Mrs. Olsen and Mr. Van Houten were trying to tell me about my mother. She was excited…keyed up…ready to burst. A woman doesn't get that way because she's pregnant with her second child.

She was in love.

Newly in love. The kind of in love that makes you do stupid things, like go out in the middle of a snow storm. The kind of love that makes you take off the ring your husband gave you. The kind of love that makes your husband cry thirty years later. I fling the covers off, burying Ethel. There's no point in even trying to fall back asleep now. I head for the kitchen.

I had read the newspaper accounts of my mother's accident years ago as soon as I was old enough to go to the public library alone. Those stories all supported the image of Charlotte as loving wife and mother, come to a tragic end. But surely the police must have considered the possibility that there was more to her accident than met the eye. Wouldn't they have looked into the possibility that there was another man involved in her disappearance? I want to see the official police report on the accident investigation. Sitting down at my computer, I fire off an email to Detective Farrand asking if he'll pull the file on my mother's accident. The clock on the microwave reads 6:35 A.M.

Ethel sits expectantly by her dish, nudging it occasionally to emphasize its emptiness. Absently, I go to fetch her kibble, all the while thinking of my poor father. No wonder he barricaded himself in the bathroom at my last visit. He knows—he's always known—that his wife ran off with another man. Yet he covered for her. Why? To protect his own pride? Or to shield me from the awful truth that my mother loved some man more than she loved me? I feel a sudden overwhelming tenderness for him.

But that doesn't explain everything, does it? If Dad was so hellbent on preserving the image of a loving mother for me, why did he turn into such a cold father? Why did he take his rage at Charlotte out on me? Maybe I remind him of her, in a way only he can see.

I sigh. If he had told me the truth, we could have been allies, united in our anger against her. Maybe it's not too late.

Across the kitchen I hear the ping of an email landing in my inbox. Someone else is up as early as I am. Maybe it's Brian Bascomb. He still hasn't answered my Facebook request.

I pad over to look. Farrand. Excitedly, I open the message.

Ms. Nealon:

I am currently pursuing several active leads pursuant to your assault. If you have an interest in a closed case, you must put in a request to the police records department by completing form Q1324. Non-urgent requests are processed at the discretion of the records department and may take up to a week to fulfill.

Detective Elliot Farrand

He sure blew me off. But if he's working on my case at 6:30 in the morning, I guess I can't complain. Still, a week to pull my mother's file? That's bullshit. As Ethel methodically crunches though her breakfast, I stare at my email. I do know another cop in the Palmyrton police department, one who's probably less concerned with playing by the rules. I'll have to come up with a plausible reason for why I'm suddenly interested…one that doesn't involve the ring and Cal's trunkful of stolen jewelry. I think a while longer. When I'm sure I can explain my reasons, I send Coughlin the same email I sent Farrand. Then I take Ethel for her walk.

By the time I'm back, I have my answer.

.Meet me at the bagel shop at noon. I'll have what you want.

Chapter 26

Running an estate sale on three hours' sleep is sub-optimal, to say the least. When I stagger up the walk to Mr. Reicker's house at 7:30 AM, Jill already has her hands full managing an unruly crowd of early-birds, and she's managed to tick off Tyshaun by ordering him to do things two seconds before he intended to do them anyway.

"Can you tell me if there's any china? Limoges, Spode, Royal Doulton?" a fat lady in rhinestone glasses whines. "I don't want to wait if there's no china."

"I already told you ma'am, I really can't—"

"Ain't none of that shit," Tyshaun overrules Jill as he walks past the line hauling a heavy table saw.

"Ty!"

Our rule is not to answer these kinds of questions because you never know what people might end up buying if they don't find the thing they came for. But Ty's clearly had enough of this woman and her bitching, and he may be right. Some customers aren't worth the hassle. Before Jill can light into Ty and put him in a worse mood, I send her inside with the cash box to set up the check-out desk. Together, Ty and I put the finishing touches on the garage, which contains a good assortment of tools, garden supplies, patio furniture

161

and even some sports equipment that Mr. Reicker must have kept around for visiting grandchildren.

"You work out here, Ty," I say. "Keep an eye on the stuff in the garage, manage the line and help people load their cars. I think we're going to be really busy."

"No problem, Audge. Just keep Jill in the house, wouldja? I don't need her up in my face."

I pat Ty on the shoulder. "I'm going inside to work with her. I'll start the sale in about ten minutes. You're on your own out here."

I see the mantle of resentment slip off him. He nods his head curtly. "'K, Audge. I got it covered."

I head inside, where Mr. Reicker's life has been laid out for the vultures. His spirit, which was so strongly present when I first walked through this house, has been stripped right out of it by my efforts. His hobbies: boxed up to be sold to other collectors; his personal mementos: dispersed among his children and grandchildren. What remains is the skeleton of his life, with a few pieces of flesh still stuck to it. His furniture, some artifacts from his travels, a few of his less valuable collectibles, and his household items are all priced, displayed, and ready to be sold. His daughter wanted to come to the sale, but I advised against it. I like Ginny too much to let her watch strangers pawing through her Dad's possessions.

I take one final look around as Jill watches me expectantly.

"Looks great. Another outstanding job, Boo."

Jill beams. "Thanks, Audrey. Do you need to fix anything, or should I open the doors."

Through the living room window I can see the line snaking down the driveway. "The natives are getting restless. Let the first twenty-five in."

The earliest early-birds rush in with the frantic desperation of starving refugees at a U.N. feeding center. Some head for the tools, others the china, others the books. Within a few minutes, the expert shoppers have found what they were looking for, and Jill and I begin processing sales. The morning passes quickly—ten satisfied shoppers out, ten new eager buyers in every fifteen minutes. I'm keeping an eye on the clock, mindful of my appointment with Coughlin at the bagel shop. At 11:45, I'll volunteer to run over there and bring back lunch for Jill and Ty.

Jill gets up to let in the next group of buyers. Through the open front door comes the sound of voices raised in anger.

"Yo! Where you going with that?'

"I bought it. It's mine."

"You did not. Let's see your receipt."

Suddenly there's a yell and the sound of sneakers pounding on pavement, followed by a loud howl.

"Ow! Stoppit! Put me down!"

I push through the crowd on the front porch to see Ty at the foot of the driveway with a skinny teenager tucked under his arm like a football. The kid's legs, arms and head are all flailing, but he's no match for Ty's lean power.

I trot down to the curb. Looking like he just nabbed a terrorist in the boarding line at the airport, Ty sets the kid upright on the sidewalk while keeping his arms pinned. I notice an odd protrusion in the kid's torso. Sticking my hand inside the kangaroo pocket of his baggy hoodie, I pull out a ceramic flower pot with a pretty green glaze. Kind of an odd item for a teenage boy to shoplift.

"He stole that outta the garage. I watched him put it right into his sweatshirt." The price tag on the pot reads three dollars, but Ty couldn't be more outraged if the kid had robbed him of his life's savings at knifepoint.

Futilely, the boy tries to shake himself free of Ty's grasp. Something about the way his stringy black hair flies back from his forehead is vaguely familiar. I take a step closer and tilt his chin up, forcing him to look me in the eye.

It's Anne and Spencer's pot-smoking grandson, Dylan.

He recognizes me at the same moment I recognize him. Now he's frantic to get away. Twisting and kicking, he manages to free one arm from Ty's grip. Then he slides out of his sweatshirt and takes off running. Flinging the sweatshirt down in disgust, Ty sprints after him.

"Let him go, Ty—it doesn't matter!" I shout after them. But Ty's long legs are pumping and he's gaining on Dylan. At the end of the block, he brings the kid down in a full body tackle. Why Ty is so determined to seek justice for a three dollar flower pot, I can't imagine. I only hope he hasn't broken any bones—either his or Dylan's.

Ty hauls Dylan back to me and gives him a shake. "You know what we do with thieves? We turn 'em in to the cops."

Now I get it. Ty's bound and determined not to let a white kid get away with something he and his friends would be arrested for. I'm between a rock and a hard place. If I tell Dylan it's no big deal and let him go, I'll destroy the fragile peace I've found with Tyshaun. On the other hand, if I call the cops on Spencer Finneran's grandson, there'll be hell to pay with Spencer, Anne, and most importantly, Cal. I suddenly realize every customer at the Reicker estate sale has gathered around to watch this drama unfold.

"Let's go in the house, okay?"

I shepherd Dylan into the kitchen. Picked clean of all but a few mismatched coffee mugs, the room has lost all its cozy charm. Perfect for an interrogation. I order him into a wobbly chair and stand looking down at him.

"What's going on?" I ask. "What made you steal that flower pot?"

He declines to meet my eye. Suddenly linoleum holds a powerful fascination for him.

"What brought you here?"

He shrugs. "My house is right around the corner. I saw all the people and thought I'd see what was going on."

"Thought you'd see what you could steal?"

He jumps up. "What's the big fuckin' deal? It's a crummy flower pot. You can have it back. I'm outta here."

I step in front of him to block his path. He's a little taller than I am, but no heavier. "Stealing things is a kick, isn't it?"

He tosses his hair back. "It brightens up my day."

"That and smoking dope. What else do you do to promote the bad-boy pose—a little graffiti, some vandalism?"

He tries to stare me down, but I don't blink. Finally he starts to laugh. "You think you're some kinda hard-ass, huh? I gotta say, you're not much like the chicks that suck-up Tremaine usually brings around." He tosses the hair again. "I know you won't call the cops. You gonna to call your boyfriend, or what?"

I think Dylan means that "not like the other chicks" remark as a compliment, although I suspect any other woman would take it as an insult. The kid's a pain in the ass, but there's something about his cocky nonchalance that I can't help but like. Still, I don't want him to think he's got me in his back pocket.

"No, I'm not calling Cal. I was thinking maybe calling your grandmother would be a better plan."

Instantly his face darkens. "You leave her out of this."

"Your grandma's very special to you, isn't she? I'm sure she wouldn't be happy to hear you've been out on a shoplifting expedition." I decide to push the envelope. "Again."

"Shut up!"

Dylan tries to dodge around me, but I grab his arm. "Look, your grandmother's got a lot on her plate right now with this election. Can't you do her a favor and lay low until it's over?"

Dylan wrenches his arm out of my grasp. The cockiness has dissolved into anger and hurt with the breathtaking speed only teenagers can summon. "Why would she care about the stupid little crap that I do? Why doesn't she—why doesn't anyone—care about the shit that *he* does?"

"Who?"

"My grandfather! He's been screwing around for years. He's always got some piece of ass on the side. And my old man is a chip off the old block. They think I don't see, but I do. You wonder why

I had to get stoned at my grandfather's birthday party? Because there's nothing worse than having to smile through all that Finneran family togetherness BS."

Dylan's words hit me harder than they should. Spencer cheats on Anne? Surely not. I saw they way they looked at each other at the party. That kind of happiness can't be fake. Can it?

Dylan jabs his index finger at me. "You think I'm a poser? They're the ones who put on a show."

The kid pivots and heads for the door. It closes behind him with a wall-shaking slam. The stolen flowerpot, perched on the edge of the counter, crashes to the floor. I expect it to shatter, but it bounces and rolls to my feet, intact.

But when I pick it up, a sharp wedge breaks loose in my hand.

Chapter 27

I'm still mulling over what Dylan told me about his grandparents when I catch sight of the clock on Mr. Reicker's stove. 11:57! Shit, I'm going to be late for my appointment with Coughlin. I shout to Jill to hold down the fort, and peel down the driveway, telling Ty I'll be back with lunch soon.

I charge into Sol's ten minutes later and spot Coughlin instantly. He's sitting with his back to the wall, eyes scanning the room as if he expects Mafia hit men to knock over the bagel bins and shoot up the deli case at any minute. His impassive face shows only a flicker of interest when I drop into the other chair at his table. There's a file folder in front on him on the table.

"Sorry I'm late. I got a little held up at the sale I'm running."

He nods. "I hear your man Griggs was tackling the customers. Whatever happened to service with a smile?"

My stomach clenches. "How do you know about that?"

"There's a car keeping an eye on the place. The officer was about to break it up, but he said you had the situation under control. Said the perp was a kid. A kid you seemed to know."

Coughlin looks at me expectantly but I'm not going there. "Just a kid from the neighborhood. He took a flowerpot on a dare. A prank—nothing to worry about." I squint at him. "Detective Farrand said he'd have someone swing by the sale, but I didn't notice a patrol car on the street."

"You ready to order?" The waitress arrives and I know if we send her away she won't return for a good fifteen minutes. A guy digging into a hot pastrami sandwich at the next table inspires me to get the same, and I put in an order for two take-out sandwiches for Jill and Ty. Coughlin asks for the Veggie Volcano.

When the waitress dashes off, I arch my eyebrows and smirk. "Veggie Volcano?"

Coughlin runs a giant paw over his cropped red hair. "Hey, growing up, the only vegetable my mother ever served was boiled potatoes. And that was only to stretch the pot roast and the corn beef to feed seven. I'm trying to make up for thirty vitamin-free years, know what I'm saying?" He rolls his massive shoulders. "You ever read that book, *The Omnivore's Dilemma*? All those antibiotics in factory-farmed meat'll kill ya."

There's more to Coughlin than I give him credit for, although I can't help but smile at the vision of him reading that organic eating manifesto while on a break with the other cops at Dunkin' Donuts. "There were five kids in your family?" I ask.

"Yeah. My mom had five babies in seven years. Then she put her foot down and said unless the Pope was coming over to help her with the laundry and dishes, she was going on the Pill. Good thing she wised up when she did, or one of us woulda gotten killed. Every day it was fight for the bathroom, fight for the last bowl of Cheerios, fight for the TV. Our house was a freakin' zoo."

I laugh, but inside I feel the old familiar longing. The Coughlin's house sounds nice to me. "I can't relate. I was an only child."

Coughlin looks at me. Right through me. "Yeah, I know."

I drop my gaze to the file folder. "What do you have for me there?"

He folds his hands on top of the folder. "Let's talk a little. My guys tell me Griggs comes and goes from your office...often works on his own."

"What guys? You have my office under *surveillance?*" I feel like I'm in some cheesy made-for-TV movie.

"Not your office. Griggs."

"You're off my case. Detective Farrand is investigating my assault. What does it take to get you to leave Tyshaun alone?"

"I'm not working your case. I'm on something else. And interestingly enough, it's leading me right back to Griggs."

I feel a flicker of uneasiness. "What are you talking about?"

"Griggs occasionally takes your van on little road trips—south to New Brunswick, east to Paterson. You got any business there?"

I know I don't have to speak for Coughlin to understand there's no legit reason for Ty to be driving the van to those towns. "What does he do there?"

"Talks to some guys and leaves."

" That's not a crime. All right—he shouldn't be driving there without my permission, but he can't afford a car of his own yet. So he takes a little joyride on company time—no big deal."

Coughlin leans forward, his voice low and intense. "You don't know who you're dealing with here, Audrey. This kid grew up on the streets. His father is serving a life term in Trenton for murder. His mother was a crack addict. His grandmother's not a bad woman, but she can't handle what life's handed her. At any given moment she's got five or six grandkids and great-grandkids living with her. She can't keep tabs on them all."

I'm stunned. Ty's father is a murderer? I knew that his grandmother had raised him, but I didn't know why. "You know Ty's family?"

Coughlins snorts. "Every cop in Palmyrton knows the Griggs clan. We've all arrested one or the other of them. Most more than once. They're bad news."

Our food arrives with a crash, giving me a moment to regroup. Uneasiness has turned to dread. Why is Coughlin watching Ty? Is it really another case, or is he still trying to pin my assault on Ty? Why is Ty driving all over New Jersey in my van? Why did Coughlin jump so eagerly to help me get my mother's case file?

I look at the file folder sitting tantalizingly on the table between us and wish I could grab it and run. I've never felt less like eating a pastrami sandwich.

Coughlin picks up the folder. "The detective who handled your mother's disappearance was one of the best: Stan Arteglier. He covered every angle."

I'd like to believe Coughlin has said all he intends to about Ty, but I know I'm deluding myself. "Is he retired now? Can I talk to him?"

"He died three, four years ago."

Coughlin must have noticed my face fall. His fierce gaze softens a little. "Stan's notes are very thorough. We can go over them."

I lean forward, but he doesn't open the folder. He's giving me that look again. I swear this guy could crack an egg with his stare.

"What are you looking for, Audrey? Why are you suddenly interested in this now?"

Here it comes, as I knew it would. I roll out the story I've prepared: the publicity around my attack put me back in touch with Mrs. Olsen, an old family friend. I tell him Mrs. O. led me to believe my mother had been acting excited in the weeks before her disappearance. I tell him about my father's tears.

"So you think there was another man." Coughlin says it flatly— no shock, no curiosity. It sounds worse spoken aloud. I can barely bring myself to nod.

He flips open the folder. "Well, Audrey, as you can probably imagine, when a woman goes missing, that's the first thing we look at: the husband, the boyfriend. In your mother's case, Stan Arteglier questioned your father several times. The notes say he was upset but never changed his story. Your grandparents backed him up. Stan talked to neighbors, friends, colleagues—no one mentioned any strain in the marriage, no hint of another man."

I lean across the table squinting at that folder, trying to read upside down. "Did he talk to Lisa Olsen or Reid Van Houten?"

Coughlin's thick, blunt index finger runs down the page and stops near the bottom. "Yep, talked to both. They didn't report anything unusual."

"Then why did they both tell me she was acting different...keyed-up?"

"Not unusual. People are maybe a little uneasy, but they don't want to cause trouble. They figured if she wanted to run away, that was her business. Or maybe the doubts nagged at them over the years. Either way, they were more likely to be truthful talking to her daughter than talking to the police. They could see you have a real stake in knowing the truth."

"What about the car at the lake?" I ask. "What does your detective's report say about that? Did he believe she could've fallen into that lake and never been found?"

"It's possible, Audrey." Coughlin pulls a diagram out of the folder and slides it between us. "If she left the mall at closing time, she would've been passing by the lake between 9:30 and 10:00. Her car went off the road here and slid down the embankment, turning ninety degrees and coming to a stop against a tree about three feet from the shore. According to the weather reports, the snow was falling at a rate of three inches per hour at that point—complete white-out conditions. She wouldn't have been able to see the road from where she was. She was scared and disoriented—didn't realize she was walking away from the road and toward the water. The spot where she went in has a steep drop off. Her heavy coat would've weighed her down."

I shiver. I've never contemplated the moment of my mother's death. Did she struggle? Did she cry for help?

"So you're telling me it *is* plausible that she drowned?"

"Oh, it's plausible—she may well have drowned. But if she used this set-up to cover her disappearance, she chose very well."

"She couldn't have planned it," I object. "No one could have been certain that it would snow that hard on Christmas Eve. The weatherman always predicts big blizzards for New Jersey and half the time they fizzle out."

Coughlin cocks his strawberry blond eyebrows. "Sometimes circumstances come together in just the right way. Everything falls into place. The perfect storm, so to speak. You jump to take advantage of what fate has handed you."

The vision of my poor mother flailing in the water dissolves. A cold stone of suspicion displaces my compassion. "So you think she and her lover might have been talking about running away together, and the perfect opportunity presented itself on Christmas Eve?"

Coughlin looks me in the eye and nods.

"Why are you so sure that's what happened?" I demand. "Was there activity on her credit cards after Christmas?"

"Nah, they checked for that." Coughlin takes another bite of Veggie Volcano, chews thoroughly and swallows. "Let's talk about Griggs."

What a prick! Coughlin has played me like a fish on a line. Given me enough slack to think I was free, then reeled me up tight. I look at the folder longingly. I don't have to play Coughlin's game. I could get what's in there—if there even is something worthwhile in there—by going through the channels Farrand outlined. But I want it now. Coughlin knows that. What terrible thing do I have to do to get it?

I cover my sandwich with my napkin and push my plate away. "What?"

"Keep an eye on Griggs. Tell me how he's acting, who he talks to on his cell."

"How would I know who he's talking to? Why do you need me to spy—can't you just tap his phone?"

"Not enough evidence for that. I'm building my case."

"Evidence of what?"

"Drugs. He's dealing, low-level. I want the big guys. So be aware, and listen. Call me if you hear anything, all right?"

Coughlin's eyes bore into me. I want to howl in protest. Why has he zeroed in on Ty? Why is he so determined to send the poor kid back to jail? But something holds me back. I feel like Coughlin's drilled a hole and drained me of all my free will.

"Yeah, fine." I look over Coughlin's head to focus on the deli counter. "If I hear anything strange, I'll call. Now tell me why you're so sure my mother staged her disappearance."

"The gifts."

I shift my gaze back to Coughlin's face. "What about them? They found them in the car, right? That proved she really had been to the mall."

"In the trunk of the car was a bag from Snapdragons and Fireflies, the upscale toy store at the mall. It contained three items, but no receipt."

"She might have stuck it in her pocket." Suddenly I realize I'm picking holes in Coughlin's arguments, looking for a way to defend my mother. "Sorry. Go on."

"This was thirty years ago, so not everyone had computerized cash registers and bar code scanning. This little store had the kind of register that you just ring up the amounts. Arteglier found this particular sequence of prices appeared three times on the cash register tape from Christmas Eve."

"So there's no conclusive proof that the gifts in the car were bought on Christmas Eve," I say. "But they could've been."

"Right."

"But didn't they show my mother's picture to the store clerks?"

"Not until the day after Christmas. By that time, her picture had appeared on the news as an accident victim. All the clerks picked her picture out of the array, even the ones who worked the morning shift, at a time when we know for a fact she wasn't at the mall." Coughlin smiles ruefully. "Eyewitnesses. Ya gotta love 'em."

"Okay, so the gifts are a wash. They don't prove or disprove anything."

"That's what Arteglier thought. I think that's why he closed out the case as an accidental death. But smart as Arteglier was, I think he missed something. Not that I blame him—he was a bachelor. He didn't know about toys."

I look at Coughlin's naked left hand. "I thought you were too."

"I'm a bachelor with twelve nieces and nephews. These are the toys they found in the car, Audrey: a doll, a puzzle and a bead kit."

I look at him blankly. I guess I'm not any more knowledgeable about toys than Arteglier.

"A bead kit," Coughlin repeats. "You were three years old. A mother doesn't give tiny beads to a toddler. They're a choking hazard."

"Oh. Oh, right." My brain feels like it's wading through a swamp, trying to find solid ground. "That means—"

"Those toys weren't bought for you."

Chapter 28

When I get back to the Reicker sale, it's time to dig in and work. I have no time to think about what Detective Coughlin has told me, but the information about Ty and those gifts lurks at the back of my mind like an uninvited guest at a wedding. I find myself compartmentalizing. With one part of my mind I slash prices, strike deals, add columns of numbers. With the other part I watch Ty, eavesdrop on his phone calls, speculate on my mother's ability to concoct her own disappearance while planning for Santa's arrival. By five-thirty when the last customer leaves, I feel edgy and dirty, like a spy who's sold out his country for a sports car and a wide screen TV.

Because I've already sold many of Mr. Reicker's more valuable pieces to dealers, the public sale has netted only a little more than Mrs. Szabo's sale: $6,215. This is far from the largest deposit we've ever made, but we're all eyeing the money as if it were an unpredictable wild animal.

"I think all three of us should go to the bank together," Jill says.

"Yeah, I'm cool with that," Ty says too quickly. It's clear he doesn't want all the responsibility for protecting me and that money to fall on his shoulders. And I realize, with a horrible twist in my gut, that I'm not entirely comfortable with Ty as my only bodyguard.

Just as I'm about to agree that we should all go, we hear a loud knock at the door. Jill jumps and lets out a little yelp; Ty's powerful arms tense. I stand behind the livingroom curtains and peek out. Two uniformed cops stand on the front porch. When I open the door, they announce that Detective Farrand has sent them to escort me to the bank. I accept the offer and five of us make the trip to the bank. I want to ask Ty about the unauthorized trips in the van, but clearly we won't be alone together tonight. Our talk will have to wait.

With the money safely deposited, I return home to a starving and restless Ethel. She makes quick work of her kibble, and we head out for our evening walk. As Ethel sniffs every tree, manhole and trash can on our block, I review the events of the day. The incident with Dylan Finneran was strange, but lunch with Detective Coughlin was even stranger. Is he really on a new case that involves Ty, or is he pissed about being removed from my assault investigation and looking for a way to pin something, anything, on Ty? I get such mixed signals from Coughlin; he's certainly not stupid, but he's stubborn, relentless, always convinced he's right.

Like my father.

My feet stop moving. Ethel looks back impatiently over her shoulder and drags me onward. According to Cal, Coughlin's police brutality case was big news when it happened seven years ago, but I can only vaguely remember the uproar. At the time, I was launching my business and every day was taken up with work…and arguing with my father about my work. When Ethel and I get back home, I'm going to look up the news articles on Coughlin's case.

It seems we've made it all the way around the block without my noticing. Ethel picks up her pace as the lights of my condo development come into view, forcing me into a trot. As we zip into my cul de sac, a blue car—or is it gray—pulls away from the curb. Was it in front of my place? As the car passes under a streetlight, I notice a dinged front right bumper. Then it's gone.

My hand tightens on the leash as I look up and down the row of condos. There are lights on in almost every one. I can see one neighbor watching TV, and another serving wine and cheese to some friends. An average Saturday night in suburban New Jersey. Nothing to worry about.

I go inside and lock my front door. Then, to be on the safe side, I double-check the door that leads to my garage.

"Okay, Ethel—looks like we're safe. Let's do a little research, shall we?"

Ethel settles herself under my desk as I pull up the on-line archives of the Palmyrton Daily Record. A few keystrokes and I'm reading the headlines of Coughlin's police brutality case: YOUTHFUL OFFENDER ALLEGES POLICE BRUTALITY, "HE DIDN'T HAVE TO BEAT ME" PETTY THIEF SAYS, RACE A FACTOR IN POLICE BEATING CASE, BRUTALITY LAWSUIT TO COST TAXPAYERS $2 MIL.

It doesn't surprise me that the headlines are so sensational. Bad news sells papers. Not for nothing that Palmyrtonians call their rag the Daily Wretched. I try to keep an open mind as I digest what I read.

Jason Powell was a 17-year-old high school drop-out who got it in his head to steal a canister on the counter of the 7-11 that had been placed there by the Policemen's Benevolent Association to collect change for a little girl who needed a heart transplant. A little girl who happened to be the daughter of a cop. That summer night, the manager of the 7-11 turned around in time to see Jason sprint out the door with the jar of money in his hands. He pursued Jason into the parking lot, just as two cops pulled in to buy coffee. They gave chase and caught Jason within a block of the store. One of the cops was Sean Coughlin.

Despite the amazingly fast response of the police, Jason was empty-handed when Coughlin and his partner put him in the back of the patrol car. Down at the station, they demanded to know what the kid had done with the money. Jason insisted he had panicked and thrown the plastic jar as the cops chased him. Despite an extensive search of the block, the cops couldn't find the money.

They accused Jason of having passed the jar off to an accomplice. That's when matters got ugly.

The more Jason insisted he didn't know where the jar was, the more infuriated the cops became that they were being stonewalled by a lying punk. A lying punk who stole money donated by the generous patrons of the 7-11. A lying punk who stole a little girl's chance for a new heart. A lying black punk who, when it came right down to it, as good as killed a white cop's daughter.

The door to the interrogation room was locked, with Jason, Coughlin , and Coughlin's partner inside. Three hours later, Jason left the police station in an ambulance. Ten hours of surgery and two years of rehab later, Jason went home with a permanent limp, a metal plate in his head, and short-term memory loss that made it impossible for him to hold a job.

Three months after the robbery, when all the leaves had fallen from the trees, a homeowner down the street from the 7-11 raked the jar out from under his viburnum bush. It contained twenty-three dollars and seventy-two cents.

I log off the newspaper's website with trembling hands. Is Ty in danger of becoming the next Jason Powell, forever marked by the cops because he once did something irresponsible? I think of Dylan Finneran. If I had called the police today because of Dylan's shoplifting stunt, would they have locked him in a room and knocked him around?

Not likely. I know that, and so does Ty. No wonder he doesn't trust the police. And now Coughlin wants me to spy on Ty, report anything I find suspicious. Anything I, white thirty-three year old woman with a math degree from UVA, find suspicious about a twenty year old black guy with a prison record.

I can't do this. I won't.

I log off my computer and realize that I never checked my home phone for messages. There's one from the caseworker at Manor View. "Please stop in to see me on Sunday, Monday or Tuesday. We need to discuss your father's prognosis." Sounds ominous. I was planning on visiting dad tomorrow anyway. I'm determined to ask him about the gifts in the car, the possibility that my mother ran away from him and me, the likelihood that I could have a half-sibling. If I'm tackling all that, can a conversation with Martha the caseworker really add much more anxiety?

I lie on the sofa with Ethel curled at my feet and turn over in my mind all that I know. Taken all together, the evidence seems to point in one direction: my mother was in love with another man, maybe pregnant by him, and ran off to start a new life, a new family, using the Christmas Eve snowstorm as a convenient cover-up. But when I examine each fact individually, I can come up with a plausible explanation for every one. Her excitement could have been due to some surprise she was planning for the holidays; her nausea when she was shopping with Mrs. Olsen might have been sparked by the flu; the bead kit in her car might have been a gift for the older child of a friend.

But always I come back to the ring. If she never took it off, why wasn't she wearing it the night she disappeared? What if Mrs. Szabo stole the ring from my mother at some point after she started her new life? Nannies sometimes go along on family vacations—maybe Mrs. Szabo encountered my mother in some place far away from Palmyrton. Maybe my mother is still there, unconcerned about the loss of a ring given to her by the man she abandoned.

My cell phone chirps the arrival of a text. I glance down. Cal. He's at some fundraising dinner tonight.

Miss u. Will b @ ur place by 3 Sunday.

A nice glow of contentment replaces the stress of the day. I don't mind spending Saturday night with Ethel if the wretched expanse of Sunday afternoon will be filled by Cal.

Chapter 29

Ethel's got her head out the window, her ears blowing back in the breeze. Any car trip is a good trip as far as she's concerned. I wish I could say the same. I've got a knot in my stomach that feels like a living, breathing entity. This is how the character in *Alien* must have felt right before the parasite snake thing burst out of his gut.

Somehow I've got to get my father to tell me what he knows. And I can only do that if I can find a way to keep from antagonizing him. I'm no Daddy's Little Girl. I've never known how to manipulate him, guilt him, cajole him. Disappoint him, that I've got covered. The others, not so much.

But before I talk to Dad, I have to deal with this Martha caseworker person. "We need to discuss your father's prognosis," is what her message had said. Were they thinking of kicking him out of Manor View for underachieving? Christ, were there places even more awful where a man could be sent to die?

I park the car at Manor View and head inside, Ethel trotting at my side. But once we're in the foyer, I have to pull Ethel left toward the staff offices when she wants to go right towards Dad's room. "Ethel, c'mon," I cajole. "We'll see him a little later, I promise." Never one to embrace change, Ethel locks all four legs and I have to drag her, stiff and stubborn, toward Martha the caseworker.

A perfectly agreeable middle-aged woman, Martha greets us both warmly. But once Ethel determines that the caseworker doesn't have any part of her lunch adhering to her clothes, she settles down to sulk under my chair. I'm not any more enthusiastic than my dog, but I try harder to feign cordiality.

"I've called you in to plan for your father's release," Martha says. "If his recovery continues at this pace, he should be ready to leave in about a month." She looks up from the folder containing my father's paperwork and smiles brightly. "Will he be moving in with you?"

I can feel my mouth hanging open. I must look like a soap opera actress emoting surprise. "He's progressing rapidly? Since when?"

"Every person reacts differently to a stroke," Martha says. Some are determined to recover right from the get-go, rarin' to start on their therapy from the moment they get out of ICU. Others go through a period of mourning their loss. Then something happens to inspire them—the birth of a grandchild, maybe, or a visit from someone who's bounced back from a stroke-- and they kick into gear and start improving rapidly. That seems to be what happened to your father."

"Really?" I know my obvious surprise leads her to conclude that I'm one of those horrible, neglectful children who abandons her parent to rot in a nursing home. But I can't pull off pretending that I'm aware my father's had a breakthrough and that I know the reason why. And I can't very well tell her the truth: The last time I saw him, he was locked in the bathroom, refusing to come out until I was gone.

"Well," I start off with a tentative smile. "He sure hasn't had a new grandchild. I'm trying to think what could have inspired him. I don't know what's changed."

Martha glances at the file. "His therapy team agrees that his motivation changed about three weeks ago. Wasn't that about the time you got out of the hospital after your attack?"

I nod dumbly.

"Maybe seeing how quickly you bounced back has inspired him," Martha says.

I've only seen Dad twice in those three weeks, and the second visit didn't go too well. It's hard for me to imagine that I've had an inspirational effect on him. In fact, it seems quite the reverse.

"So, will he be moving in with you?" the caseworker repeats.

"I don't see how he could. I only have a one-bedroom condo."

"His own house...?"

I imagine the house I grew up in. It's full of steps, narrow hallways, and cramped bathrooms. "It's not exactly barrier-free."

"Well, that's why I called you in. You should start looking for something all on one level. He's been walking, but he's still unsteady on his feet. His right side may always have residual weakness." Martha rises and hands me some brochures. "These are over-55 communities. Some provide independent living and graduated care. Talk over the options with him today."

"Talk?"

"We've been weaning him off some of his meds. That's really helped his speech." Martha glances out into the hallway. "There goes Megan, his speech therapist. She can walk over to your father's room with you."

"I just love working with your dad," Megan confides as she walks with me from the therapy area to the residential wing. "He was a little reserved as first, but now he's always got a joke and smile for me. And so sweet—he even bought me a little African violet when he was out with his friend Brian because he knows how much I love flowers."

I stretch my lips over my teeth in what passes for a smile, but jealous rage corrodes me from the inside out. So my dad bought his therapist a little potted plant—big deal. So he jokes with her—that's nice. I guess he speaks for the therapists, speaks for the aides, and only retreats into silence for me.

I blink once, twice, three times. I can't cry here. I can't.

"You know, I've never met this friend Brian," I manage to say. "Apparently he's one of my dad's old work colleagues."

Megan cocks her head, looking as puzzled as Ethel when she sees me wearing a coat but not holding her leash.

"Oh, Brian Bascomb's not old--he's closer to your age." Megan scans me appraisingly. "Maybe a few years younger. So cute."

Brian Bascomb is young and handsome, so the guy I contacted through Facebook must be him. Why won't he answer me?

. "I'd really like to get in touch with this guy—you know, to thank him for taking my dad out. Would they have his phone number in the main office?"

"No. We don't monitor our patients' visitors."

"You mean, anyone could come and take him out? Is that safe?"

Megan stops in the middle of the hall. "Ms. Nealon, there's nothing wrong with your father's cognitive function. The stroke simply affected his speech and his balance. He's free to visit with anyone he wants to."

Guess she set me straight. I nod sheepishly and start walking again.

As we get close to Dad's room, Ethel starts straining at her leash. When I'm sure she can run straight in without bowling over any tottering old folks, I let her go. I hear a voice say, "Ed-dell!" and I pick up my pace. Who's in there with Dad? Could it be the mysterious Brian Bascomb?

But when I step across the threshold, Dad is sitting alone, his face buried in Ethel's fur. Megan catches up to me as Dad lifts his head. I see his face light up, then immediately darken. Delight for Megan. Disgust for me.

"Hi, Mr. Nealon!" Megan speaks before I can summon any words. "I thought we'd show your daughter how much progress you've made. Won't that be great?"

Dad eyes me warily, looking distinctly unenthused.

"Now, don't be shy," Megan says. "Audrey will be very proud

of you." She turns to me, "Right?"

"Oh, absolutely." I paste a smile on my face and sink into a chair.

Megan begins taking Dad through his paces, doing exercises for his tongue, making him repeat sounds, holding up a mirror so he can see if he's got his lips in the right position. At every juncture she encourages him, cheering, patting his arm, clapping her hands in delight. I can hardly bear to watch—it's like spying on sex, the kind of thing a child doesn't want to see her parent do. Finally Megan takes a deep breath and says, "Okay, are you ready to deliver your message?"

Dad's eyes squint half shut, the way he used to when he was solving a functional derivative in his head. Eventually he nods. Then he turns to face me. "Tans or vis-uh. Id nye to eee ooo."

It's like listening to a broadcast with a three second tape delay. I see his lips move, hear the sounds, then process the meaning: Thanks for the visit. It's nice to see you.

Ducking my head, I rub my eyes with the back of my hand. "It's nice to see you too, Dad," I finally choke out.

"Yay! Good job!" Megan jumps up. "I'll leave you two alone. Go ahead and practice a little, Mr. Nealon, but don't get worn out. I'll see you tomorrow."

Megan's departure leaves a void in the room that Dad and I both are desperate to fill. Luckily, there's Ethel.

"Goo duh," Dad tells her, rubbing her ears. "Ooo wanna tree?" He rolls over to his nightstand.

Even without the final consonant, Ethel knows the word treat when she hears it. Her ears stand straight up and she starts licking her chops. I figure Dad has something from breakfast stashed, but he opens the drawer and pulls out a small box of freeze-dried liver snaps, a doggy snack that can only be purchased in high-end pet stores.

Ethel goes ballistic.

Dad holds the treat over his head and makes Ethel dance on her hind legs.

"Those are her favorites, Dad. Where did you get them?"

Dad doesn't answer. An idea pops into my head. "Did Brian take you shopping?"

Dad's having too much fun with Ethel to be suspicious of my question. "Yah."

"Brian's been taking you out a lot."

Dad darts a furtive glance in my direction, but I'm determined not to repeat the mistakes of my last visit. I say nothing more, and meet his glance with a pleasant smile. I'm also not ready to bring up the business of where he's going to live after they let him out of Manor View.

I notice his shoulders ease out of their hunch. He goes back to playing with the dog, while I make idle chit-chat about Ethel, the Reicker sale, Ty's encounter with the shoplifter. Dad answers as best he can, alternating grunts and nods with actual sentences. As my ear adjusts, I'm able to understand him more and more.

A rambling conversation about nothing in particular. Families do that a lot, I imagine, but it's a new experience for me and my father. Maybe this is the upside of stroke—he's lost the need for every dialogue to be significant, purposeful.

Maintaining the same aimless tone, I say, "So, guess who I met the other day—Reid van Houten."

Dad looks puzzled. "Ooo?"

"The man who was mom's boss at the PR firm where she used to work, The Van Houten Group. He said he remembered you."

Dad smiles and nods. "Ood man. Ike him."

Okay, so there's nothing suspicious about Van Houten. Dad apparently liked him.

Then Dad tips his head and peers at me. "Ow you know him?"

"Chamber of Commerce," I lie blithely. "I go to the meetings to drum up business."

"I have a job for you." Dad is looking at Ethel when he speaks but he says this sentence more clearly than any other words he's uttered.

"You do? What's that?"

"Sell 'ouse. Not go back 'ere."

Again I feel myself displaying mindless surprise. I never thought he'd be willing to give up the house so easily. Ever since I went off to college, people have been suggesting that he move. Although the house isn't huge, it's more than a man like him needs. Why have a yard when you don't garden? Why have a dining room if you don't entertain? Why have three bedrooms when you never have houseguests? But Dad has always clung to the house tenaciously. Nana and Pop said the house represented the happy times he shared with my mother. You might think I would represent that, but apparently not.

"You want to sell our house?"

He nods. "I ge' apar-men."

"You want to move to an apartment after you get out of here?"

He nods eagerly. For the first time in months I see him smile at something other than Ethel.

"Okay, Dad, I'll talk to my friend Isabelle Trent. She's a great real estate agent." I show dad some of the brochures Martha gave me for over-55 communities. "Do you want me to look for an apartment for you in one of these places? That one in Basking Ridge looks nice."

He shakes his head. "Too far away. Someplace near you."

I'm stunned into speechlessness. Maybe Dad's newfound commitment to his stroke therapy really has been inspired by my recovery from the attack. Does this mean we're going to launch into a new life of father/daughter togetherness once he's out of here? Dad makes a great show of playing with Ethel, but I sense he's tense, waiting to hear how this suggestion goes over.

"Okay," I say slowly. "There's that brand new apartment building on Sycamore. It's really nice, but kind of pricey." The place has elevators, a doorman and a health club. I doubt my thrifty father will spring for that, but he smiles brightly.

"Goo'. Close to downtown. I can walk ever' where."

I've never known him to spend much time in downtown Palmyrton before, but clearly his worldview has changed. If he's interested in Palmer Centre, why should I argue? Settling him there will be easy for me.

Disoriented by how well the visit is going, I can't bring myself to ask him about the police report on my mother's disappearance and the gifts they found in the trunk of the car. We chat instead about how he can take Ethel out in the middle of the day for me once he's living right around the corner. His voice, which had reached a peak of clarity, is now starting to slur from the unaccustomed effort of so much talking. I can see him searching for words, struggling to form them. My window of opportunity is closing. I have to ask him at least one of my questions. I try a roundabout approach.

"Maybe you can get a dog of your own once you move into your apartment," I suggest.

Dad shakes his head and smiles. "Ethel wou' na lie tha'."

"Sure she would," I contradict. "Ethel would like a sibling, right girl?"

Ethel wags her tail obligingly, and I press on. "I've always wished I had a brother or sister. Did you and mom plan on having more kids?"

Dad's smile evaporates. He slumps in his chair. "I wanna. Har' for her."

"She was sick a lot when she was pregnant with me?" I know this from Mrs. Olsen. I want to see what Dad will say. He nods, but his eyes don't meet mine. He's a million miles away.

"She was pregnant that Christmas, wasn't she Dad?" I ask softly. "Nana and Pop didn't know."

He says nothing. I see his Adam's apple move jerkily in his throat as he swallows hard.

I reach over and take his hand in mine. "She left us, didn't she Dad? She's still alive. I don't want her back, but I need to know--do I have a brother or sister somewhere?"

He squeezes my hand tight. "Lon' time, Audrey. Le' ih' go. Le' ih go."

"I can't let it go!" Despite my vows to be calm and encouraging, there's a sharp edge in my voice. I take a deep breath and try to dial my emotions down a notch. "She didn't go out shopping that night, did she? At least tell me that much."

"No," Dad whispers.

I drop to my knees in front of his chair so that even with his eyes downcast he's forced to look at my face. "Tell me what happened, Dad. I nearly died in that parking garage. I need to know the truth. I can handle it."

He doesn't try to avoid my gaze. His eyes meet mine boldly. "You thin' you wanna know, bu' you don'."

"Yes!" My voice is too loud. If the aides hear me yelling at him they'll come running. "Yes I do," I hiss.

He shakes his head. Then he closes his eyes and folds his hands. He's done.

Chapter 30

"You're mad at me."

Cal has arrived at my condo at three, as promised. He swept me into his arms as soon as I opened the door. But I guess I didn't return his kiss as enthusiastically as he expected because he's taken a step back and is smoothing the hair away from my face as he talks. "Look, baby, I'm sorry I haven't been able to see you since Tuesday. I swear things will be better after the election. Bear with me."

"No, I'm not mad at you. I'm a little distracted." I sigh deeply. "I just got back from visiting my father at the nursing home."

Cal slaps his forehead. "You mean everything's not about me? I must come across as the most self-centered clod on the planet." He leads me to the sofa and pulls me down beside him. "What happened? You dad's taken a turn for the worse?"

I give a bitter little laugh. "Actually, he's taken a turn for the better. He used to not be able to talk to me. Now he *can* talk, but he refuses to tell me the truth about anything." Quickly, I recap the scene at the nursing home for Cal. He turns me around and massages my shoulders as I talk.

When I finish he kisses the top of my head. "I can see why you're frustrated."

I crumple into his arms. "I keep turning everything over in my head. You want to hear what I've come up with?" The offer is out of my mouth without my giving any thought to whether I really want to share this with him.

"Sure I do." He takes my hands in his, straightening my mother's ring on my finger.

"I think my mom was pregnant with another man's child and she ran off with him and abandoned Dad and me. I think she might still be alive. I think I might have a half-sibling somewhere."

"Whoa, baby—slow down."

"It makes sense." I turn to face Cal. "Agnes only took jewelry that people didn't wear anymore—stuff she knew they wouldn't miss. Once my mother left us, she probably took this ring off and tossed it in a drawer. Maybe Agnes left Palmyrton for a time…or maybe she went along on vacation with one of her families to take care of the kids. And that's where she crossed paths with my mother. And stole the ring."

Cal opens his mouth, then shuts it. He takes a deep breath and reaches for my hand. "Audrey, baby, don't take this wrong, but you kind of sound like a desperate defense attorney who's spinning a tale for the jury of an alternate scenario for the crime that he knows damn well his client committed. You have no evidence that your mother is alive. You just want her to be."

"I don't! I don't care about her. But she had another baby, and that baby is my half-brother."

The words hang there, surprising me as much as Cal.

"Brother? If she was pregnant, what makes you think the baby was a boy?"

"I don't know." I pull my knees up and curl into a ball. "There's this guy who's been visiting my father. He's young and good looking. My father lied and said he was a colleague from work, but he's not. I found the guy on Facebook and sent him a message, but he won't answer me. If he were simply a nice person who likes my dad, why wouldn't he answer?"

"Audrey, I ignore Facebook messages all the time. I'm too busy for that crap."

"Yeah, but this is a guy who takes elderly stroke victims out to lunch. He's clearly not as overworked as you."

"So if he's the baby your mother had with another man, why in God's name would he be visiting your father?"

"Okay, I admit I haven't thought it all the way through. All I know is there's something about this guy my father doesn't want me to know...and there's a lot about my mother he doesn't want me to know. So maybe my mother sent Brian to talk to my dad. Maybe because of the attack she saw my name and my picture in the paper, and she wants to—" My eyes fill with tears. Oh, crap! This isn't what I wanted my evening with Cal to be.

Cal pulls me into a hug. "Wants to what?"

"Go back on her deal," I whisper. "She left, knowing she was going to have another baby. I figure she gave me to Dad because I was just like him, not beautiful like her."

Cal pulls me up and forces me to look in the mirror over the fireplace. "Why do you keep saying you're not beautiful? You've got lovely skin, high cheekbones, perfect teeth." His hand slides lower. "A great ass."

I see a wiry, tough brunette in a lint-y sweater who can't maintain her hip haircut because she doesn't know how to apply "product." Her eyes are red, her nose is swollen and her lips are chapped. I twist out of Cal's grip and plop onto the sofa. Every fear, every doubt, every heartbreak I've ever known seems to lie scattered on the ground, available to anyone who passes by. I can't bear being this vulnerable. I want Cal gone.

"I'm sorry, I can't talk about this. I can't-- You'd better go home. Just leave."

He doesn't try to touch me, but he sinks to his knees so I'm forced to look him in the eye. "Don't make me go home. You don't have to talk about anything. Let me stay. Let me hold you."

I turn my head away from him. "What do you see in me? Why

do you keep coming around? I'm nothing like the women you usually date."

Cal grabs my hand. "That's right. You're nothing like the self-absorbed, status-seeking, demanding bitches I usually chase. The ones who make me miserable. The ones I lose interest in after I-- Never mind."

He walks away from me and perches on the arm of the sofa, staring down at his perfectly shined tassel loafers as he speaks.

"I'm insanely competitive, Audrey. I had to run the fastest, get into the best law school, make the most money, drive the hottest car, walk into the party with the skinniest, blondest babe. It's all a way of telling other men my dick is bigger than yours." He shoots me a quick glance. "That's why Anne was so happy when I brought you around. She sees you as a positive sign that I'm capable of an emotion other than aggression."

I always think of Cal as being more grown-up than I am, but he looks oddly boyish right now, like a gawky teenager in need of a hug. "I don't think you're aggressive."

He smiles a little. "Maybe I'm not around you. Maybe you bring out a better side of me, a side I forgot I had."

Ethel comes over and forces her snout under my hand so I have to pet her.

"Will that work with me?" Cal asks.

"Try and see."

It doesn't take long for Cal to drive away all thoughts of my father, my mother, my putative brother, my attacker and every other worry lurking in my brain. Cal is as single-minded about sex as he is about Spencer's campaign. For half an hour, I'm lost in physical pleasure and sweet release. Afterwards, as I lie next to him waiting for my heart to slow down, the real world comes creeping back, one thought at a time. Images surface of my mother having sex with her faceless lover. I push them away. My mind hopscotches to another act of infidelity: Dylan's accusation that Spencer has cheated on

Anne. I realize that in my preoccupation with my father, I've forgotten to tell Cal about Dylan's larcenous appearance at the Reicker sale. Beside me I hear Cal's breathing become slow and regular. The poor guy's drifting off to sleep, but now that Dylan's popped into my mind, I have to talk to Cal about him.

"Cal?"

"Mmph." His hand strokes my arm but his eyes don't open. The tense energy that normally courses through him has dissipated. On the verge of sleep he looks childlike, innocent. As much as I'd like to savor the sweetness of this moment, I can't seem to restrain myself.

"Cal, I need to tell you this. Spencer's grandson Dylan showed up at my estate sale yesterday. He tried to shoplift a vase, but Ty caught him."

Cal bolts upright, the covers dropping away from his wonderfully sexy chest. "Dylan did what?"

I stay reclined, with the covers pulled up to my chin. "No big deal, but I did think it was kind of odd for a teenage boy to come to an estate sale. And then for him to take a ceramic pot—well, I guess he stole it just for the thrill. I'm not mad or anything—but I thought you should know."

Cal thumps the pillow with his fist. "Dammit! What are we going to do with this kid? He's hellbent on getting himself arrested before the election."

"I did mention that he should behave himself for Spencer and Anne's sake. He...uh...had kind of a strange reaction."

Cal watches uneasily, waiting for me to continue.

"He said he didn't see why Anne would care what he does when Spencer does much worse things. He claims he grandfather has been cheating on Anne for years. Is that true, Cal?"

Call rolls his eyes. "Of course not. Spencer is devoted to Anne—anyone can see that. And Anne's certainly not the kind of woman who would put up with a philandering husband."

"But why would Dyl—"

"Dylan's not happy unless he's the center of attention. Spencer's campaign has been keeping Anne too busy to dote on Dylan. You'd think he would've outgrown his need for Grandma's undivided devotion, but apparently not."

"They do seem to be quite close."

"Apparently Dylan was a sickly baby," Cal explains. "Was born with some kind of heart condition, spent months at a time in the hospital as a little kid. He's perfectly fine now, but Anne has a blind spot a mile wide when it comes to that particular grandchild."

Cal springs out of bed, completely unselfconscious of his nakedness. "You handled it just right Audrey. Thanks for telling me. I'll tell Anne and let her deal with Dylan." He holds out his hand. "Let's take a shower and go out for some dinner, hmm?"

A hot shower, a big dinner, a few glasses of wine. By ten Cal has brought me back to the condo and gone home (big early-morning meeting) and I'm in bed as spent and satisfied as Ethel after a long run in the park and a big bowl of kibble. Too drowsy to read, I turn on the TV for a little mindless entertainment. I toggle back and forth between Friends and Seinfeld reruns, switching every time a commercial comes on. Jerry delivers a quip to Kramer, and the screen dissolves to a big image of Spencer Finneran. I pause with my finger on the remote and watch as the camera tracks Spencer eating at a diner with truck drivers, sitting in a classroom with teachers, walking on the street with cops. Then the announcer intones: "Spencer Finneran: the honest choice for the hardworking people of New Jersey."

Nice ad. Then I remember—I never did ask Cal about my mother working on Spencer's first campaign.

Chapter 31

I'm bracing myself but it hasn't happened yet. Isabelle Trent and I are touring my father's house—my childhood home—so Isabelle can tell me what it's worth and what I have to do to get it ready to be listed. I'm waiting for her to utter the "P" word, but we're halfway through the first floor and Isabelle still hasn't deemed the house "precious."

"Why those gloomy drapes?" Isabelle strides across the living room in her five-inch heels and gives the cord a yank. Sunlight floods the room. "Look at that view! That's what we're selling here on Skytop Drive." I go to stand beside her and together we look out the window. The leaves have all fallen from the trees so we can see downtown Palmyrton nestled below and the rolling hills of Palmer County on the horizon. Did my mother like this view? Did she ever miss it after she left?

"Fabulous!" Isabelle says. "When I bring buyers up here I tell them you're paying for the view, and we throw the house in for free."

The houses on Skytop follow a ridge. Built in the '40s, they're not that far apart, but each one inhabits its own little world, surrounded by tall oaks, maples and evergreens.

I look straight down to the driveway which slopes steeply to the street after a small level area in front of the garage. "I imagine some buyers would object to the driveway. I can't tell you how many balls I chased down that thing."

Isabelle waves this problem off as too minor to worry about. "Real estate is all about putting a positive spin on every negative feature. I tell them when you're on a hill, you never have to worry about water in the basement."

"And what do you tell people in the flatlands?"

"That they'll never have to worry about not being able to get up their driveway in a snowstorm."

Right.

Isabelle keeps yakking, completely unaware that she's touched a nerve. "The décor is a little dated, darling. Very common with the old gentlemen living alone. This house would be a perfect starter home for a young family, but they need to be able to picture themselves in it." Isabelle points one perfectly manicured finger like a magician casting a spell. "So get rid of that sagging brocade easy chair, and replace it with something contemporary in a nice neutral color."

The chair in question has the impression of my dad's butt in it. He's sat there every day for the past thirty-three years, when he first moved his young family into this starter home. I wonder if he'll want to take it with him to the apartment in Palmer Towers—his end-er home--or whether he'll be willing to let it go.

I trail Isabelle upstairs, taking notes as she fires off her commentary. "Bathroom needs a facelift, but no need to remodel-- get a new light fixture and lose that sea-shell shower curtain." We pass my childhood bedroom, which has all the charm of a nun's cell, then head into the master bedroom. "Nice size." Isabelle yanks open a closet door. My father's meager wardrobe hangs forlornly. "Impressively uncluttered," Isabelle says. "Your father's not a hoarder, is he?"

"Just the opposite," I say. "He tosses everything." Including every construction paper father's day card I ever made for him.

"Our goal is to sell this right after the holidays," Isabelle says. "So take a few days to freshen the place up, then let's get it listed." Isabelle gives me her trademark double air kiss and flies off to her next appointment, leaving a lingering whiff of Diorisimo in her wake.

A second later the front door pops back open. "And darling, do something about these monstrous holly bushes. Zero curb appeal."

All alone in the house, I wander from room to room trying to imagine a time when my parents and I were happy here. I end up in the small third bedroom, the room that might have been a nursery if my mother had been willing to have a second child with Dad. Instead, it's always been used as a home office. There's a computer, a filing cabinet and a bookcase, all neatly arranged. When Dad had his stroke I had no trouble paying his bills because everything was filed meticulously. I took the folders I needed and never looked any further. Now, my hand slides across the dusty surface of the desk. Could there be some information about my mother in here? Maybe he's always known where she is.

Dusk is settling over Skytop Drive. Even though Isabelle has snapped open the window shade, there's not enough natural light for me to see clearly. I turn on the desk lamp and begin my search.

Each drawer in the file cabinet contains folders labeled in my father's precise mathematician's printing: insurance policies, appliance manuals, warranties, tax records. What did I expect-- folders labeled "Letters from Charlotte" or "True Whereabouts of Missing Wife"? Of course, if he's got something about my mother hidden in here, wouldn't it make sense to slip it in with the banal warranties and policies? So, I search through the contents of every folder. All contain just what they say they do and nothing more. The desk drawers are equally unrevealing, but still I can't give up.

I turn to the bookcase. A few mathematics textbooks. Some nonfiction books on the history of science. And a larger book with a faded orange cover. I pull it out: the Princeton yearbook, 1969. I'm surprised that Dad kept it. I've never known him to be sentimental about his alma mater. It might be fun to look through, but not now.

I've got more important things to do. I bring the yearbook over to the desk and sit down.

One thing remains: the computer. As a mathematician Dad has always had the latest, most powerful computer available. While it boots up, I search the room's small closet. Five empty shelves march up one side. Above my head, on the top shelf, a tattered edge of paper peeps out. I reach up and pull it off the shelf. MY FAMILY BY AUDREY N. GRADE 2 is crayoned across the top. Even then I had neat handwriting. The picture below shows a fairly accurate representation of our house. Next to the house stand a large stick figure with white hair wearing a dress and a large stick figure with no hair wearing pants holding the hands of a small stick figure with long dark hair and a big red smile. NANA. ME. POP. read the captions. On the other side of the house stands a much smaller solitary stick figure with spiky black hair and a straight line mouth wearing pants. DAD. Jesus, a shrink would have a field day with this! I wonder what Miss Davidson, my second grade teacher thought? I slide the picture into an empty file folder and put it on top of the yearbook.

Back in front of the computer, I scan the list of folders in My Documents. Most are labeled with mathematical formulae. I call up the Search function and type in Charlotte Perry. Nothing. Then I try Brian Bascomb. Impatiently I watch as the computer sifts through its own memory. I'm about the give up when a file pops up on the screen. It's a spreadsheet labeled Spring 07 Advanced Number Theory. My father's grade roster for that class. I click and it opens. The second entry on the roster is Bascomb, Brian: A.

Brian Bascomb was my father's student, and apparently a very smart one. I lean back in the desk chair to think. Did Dad intentionally try to mislead me about Brian's identity or did I simply misunderstand my father's grunts and nods? Why would a student he taught years ago come to visit him now in a nursing home? Would my father inspire that kind of devotion? I don't recall my father ever talking about his students. Is this another facet of him I know nothing about? Is he some revered Mr. Chips-like figure at Rutgers?

I hit PRINT so I have tangible evidence that Brian is Dad's student.

A noise knocks me out of my reverie. Was that downstairs or outside? I listen, every nerve alert. Mostly what I hear is my blood pounding through my veins. I glance at the window. Although it's only six, night has completely fallen. I'll have to turn out all the lights and walk through a dark house, out to a dark driveway to get into my car, which I'm sure I left unlocked. Shit! I wish Ethel were with me.

Suddenly, this two story colonial that I grew up in, as familiar to me as my own body, feels like an amusement park haunted house. Grabbing the yearbook and the file folder with the picture and grade roster, I power down the computer, then go out in the hall to turn on the overhead light before I turn off the desk lamp. Looking both ways as if I expect a skeleton to jump out of the linen closet or a tiger to chase me from the other end of the hall, I scamper down the stairs. As my feet pound on the treads, I think I hear another noise. Is it the old house creaking in the wind, or has someone come in through the back door? Did I lock it after Isabelle left?

Heart racing, I reach the foyer and pause to listen again. All quiet. Once in the foyer, I'm able to turn off the upstairs hall light from below, while turning on the downstairs light. Now, I'll turn on the kitchen light, come back and turn off the foyer light, and exit the back door right next to my car. In the kitchen, I peer out the window at the pitch black driveway. Skytop Drive seems as foreboding as the moors in a Bronte novel. Unraked leaves spin in whirlwinds. The two untrimmed holly bushes loom. Naked tree branches sway and dip. The house next door broods, silent and dark, behind the tall hedge dividing the properties. If I had to scream for help, would anyone hear me? I decide to turn on the light over the back door. I'll have to leave it on all night, but I can come back tomorrow in the daylight to turn it off. Wasting energy seems preferable to venturing out into the void.

I set the book, file folder and my purse on the counter while I put on my coat and get my car keys ready in my hand. Then I switch on the outside light and bolt for the car. Once inside I switch on the dome light and check the back seat. Empty. Of course. How ridiculous am I?

As I drive east on Skytop Drive toward home, I hear the squeal of tires as a car pulls out behind me. What driveway did it come from? In my rearview mirror I see the tail lights of a car disappear in the opposite direction.

Chapter 32

I'm going to have a hard time explaining to Jill how it is that I'm getting absolutely nothing accomplished while she and Ty are doing the preliminaries for the sale at the Siverson house. Instead of working, I'm obsessively checking Facebook, wondering how I can pry my way into Brian Bascomb's full profile. Can I set up a new email account and send a friend request under a fake name? Tell him I went to Rutgers with him? Would he respond then?

Geez, this is how stalkers and pedophiles must think. I'm scaring myself. I close out of Facebook and open up my accounting software.

I have plenty of bookkeeping work to attend to, but without Jill here to handle the basic hustle and flow of the office, I find I'm not making much headway. Pick-ups, deliveries, phone calls, more pick-ups—how did I ever manage all this by myself? When the phone rings for the fourth time in five minutes, I snatch it up and bark, "Another Man's Treasure," with all the warmth of an IRS agent.

"May I speak to Audrey Nealon, please." The woman's voice, low and soothing, is vaguely familiar.

"This is she."

"Audrey, this is Anne Finneran. I'm sorry to bother you at

work. You must be terribly busy."

Shit! Anne Finneran? Why is she calling me? "Oh, hi Anne. No, I'm not busy. I mean, I am a little busy because my assistant isn't here. I didn't mean to sound so crabby when I answered the phone, I just—" Oh, crap—I'm babbling like a moron. I take a deep breath and start again. "I'm sorry. How are you? Can I help you with something?"

"I'm calling to apologize to *you*. I feel terrible that Spencer has been commandeering all of Cal's time so that he doesn't have a spare minute to take you out on a proper date. I said to Spencer last night, 'Cal's finally met a wonderful woman and you're going to ruin this romance for him. We've got to do something to make it up to Audrey.' "

I'm flabbergasted. Anne and Spencer spend their time talking about me? Has Cal been telling them that I complain about his schedule? That's a little irritating—I've never uttered a peep about his work hours. "Not a problem, Anne," I say with more ice than I'm normally capable of. "Cal is free to work as hard as he wants to on this campaign."

"Oh, I know there's no slowing him down." If Anne noticed my tone, she doesn't let on. She continues full of cheer. "I thought if we had dinner here at the house we could let those two talk shop for an hour, then grab the reins and make them behave like civilized creatures for the rest of the evening. What do you think? Are you willing to collaborate with me?"

Dinner? At their house? Collaborate? Where is this concern for my love life coming from? "Uh...What day?...I haven't talked to Cal recently. I don't know his plans."

"That's my point, dear. We have to ambush them so they can't make excuses. Let's say Friday, seven-ish here at the house. You come a little early. I'll take care of rounding up the boys."

Friday at seven? I can't imagine anything more inconvenient with the Siverson sale coming up on Saturday. "Gee, Anne, I really think I'm going to have to take a rain check. I'll be setting up a sale all day and who knows when we'll—"

"Nonsense. That's what staff is for, Audrey." Anne's voice has lost its flutey tone and she's scolding me like a nun. I can practically feel the crack of her ruler on my knuckles. " As I always say to Spencer, what's the point of having people work for you if you can't trust them to execute anything without your constant supervision?"

Gee, tell me what you really think. "True, but after a long day...and I have to be up early on Satur—."

"Oh, Audrey! Forgive me, dear." In a quick one-eighty, Anne now sounds plaintive and yearning. "It's just that over the years I've learned that if I want to have any time at all with my family and friends I simply have to stand my ground and demand that they show up for dinner. Life is so short, and there really never is a convenient time for anything, don't you agree? I won't keep you out late. Please come."

When's the last time anyone's begged me to do anything? I'm powerless to resist. "Okay, Friday at seven. I'll see you then."

I hang up the phone. What just happened to me? Talk about ambushed!

Outside I hear the familiar cough and sputter of the AMT van, followed by Jill's, "Get it yourself. I'm not your bitch."

The temperature in the office seems to drop fifty degrees as Ty and Jill blow in, engulfed in their own personal snowstorm. Frosty doesn't begin to describe the atmosphere between them. Jill flings herself into her desk chair and begins hammering her computer keys like a blacksmith forging a horseshoe. If she keeps this up I'll be upgrading our office systems a little sooner than anticipated. Meanwhile, Ty does his best to impersonate a raccoon in a Dumpster, crashing through stacked boxes, tossing paper, kicking chairs.

"What's wrong with you two?" I ask. More pounding. More crashing. No words.

Ty lives by the "no snitching" credo of the streets. Dick Cheney himself couldn't get him to rat out Jill to me. Jill, on the other hand, will crumple into a weeping mound the minute I get her alone.

"Jill, I need to go over to my Dad's house to turn off that light. Why don't you come with me and tell me what you think I need to buy to do a good job with the staging."

Jill brightens, clearly pleased to be the chosen one.

"I'll come and help you move stuff," Ty immediately volunteers.

"Not yet, Ty. Once I figure out what I'm getting rid of, I'll definitely need all the help you can give."

Ty gives his funny reverse nod, an upward jerk of the head that means *I'm just as important as you.* "You got it, Audge." Then he fixes Jill with a piercing glare.

Jill stalks out to the van without looking at him. I smile sweetly. "Hold down the fort, Ty. We'll be back in an hour."

We ride in silence to the stop sign at the end of the block. Then the dam breaks.

"I did all the work at the Siversons'. We got there and Ty helped me move the sofa and take down the drapes and then he said he had to go out for a minute and did I want anything so I said yeah a Diet Snapple and he said okay be right back and then I NEVER SAW HIM AGAIN until three o'clock and by that time I had all the stuff sorted and priced and there was nothing left to do and when I said where the hell have you been he told me shut up you fat skank and that is just not right when all I wanted was—"

"Jill—"

"to know why he went off and left me with all the—"

"Jill—"

"work and then to come back and not even say sorry and call me a bad—"

"Jill! Take a breath!"

"Sorry, Audrey." Her lower lip juts out in a trembling pout and the tears begin to flow. "It's just not fair, is all. And he knows I'm sensitive about my weight. And I am not a skank."

"Of course you're not. I'm sure he didn't mean it."

Shit! This is exactly the kind of sketchy behavior Coughlin warned me to look out for. I've got to get to the bottom of this. But first I have to calm Jill down. "Probably he was feeling guilty and lashed out to cover up for that," I tell her. "I'll talk to him about it."

"No!" Jill twists in the passenger seat to face me. "You can't do that. Then he'll know I told you."

"Ummm—I'm pretty sure he's already figured that out."

"No, you saw how he looked at me when we were leaving. He'll kill me for telling you."

"Jill, we're not in middle school. I'm trying to run a business here. Ty needs to work when I send him on a job. And it's not appropriate for him to insult his colleagues." Wow, that sounds like I got it out of some kind of human resources textbook. I feel very authoritative.

Jill launches herself across the front seat and wraps her arms around me. "No-o-o-o!"

Her jangly earrings catch in the loose weave of my sweater, linking us like Siamese twins. Luckily, we're stuck in traffic.

"You can't say anything to him! Please, please promise me you won't. He's still mad at me about the whole thing with the police when you were mugged. He blames me that they arrested him."

I disentangle myself as horns begin blowing behind me. "If Ty blames you, then it's time for him to let it go. You did nothing wrong. Now, I will handle this as I see fit."

Jill shrinks down in her seat, as unaccustomed to sternness from me as Ethel is. I reach over and crank up the radio to drown out the oppressive silence of her sulking. A couple of Green Day tunes later, we're at the house and Jill has perked up. She jumps out of the car and starts looking around the exterior of the house. "Cool! This is where you grew up? This is such a cute house. And look at that great view, and all those trees. Did you have a tree fort out here?"

I gaze up at the wide bare braches of the oaks and maples in the back yard. How I used to daydream about climbing up into their leafy branches and watching the world from a secret aerie. To see everyone without being seen. "I always wanted one. I had my grandpa convinced to build it, but my grandmother thought I'd fall and kill myself. She was a little overprotective after my mother...died."

Jill rams her hands in the pockets of her shapeless Chairman Mao jacket. "Oh."

Her innocent question brings back the strain between us. I've never told Jill the story of my childhood, other than to say my mom died when I was little and my grandparents helped raise me. Jill and her mom are as close as sisters, calling and texting each other all day long. The story of my mother's demise would overload Jill's compassion circuits. With her penchant for melodrama, I know I'd never hear the end of her consolation and mourning for my tragic loss. I don't need her sympathy. I don't want her pity.

I want to return us to our comfort zone. "C'mon, let me show you the inside and you can tell me what we can do to make it look like a house a young family would want to buy."

We enter through the back door. After the crisp, cold air of the back yard, the kitchen seems oppressively hot and musty. "The place really needs to be aired out. It's been shut up for months." I go to open the window over the kitchen sink, then think better of it. I don't want to walk out and remember later that I've left a window open.

Jill prowls around, inquisitive as a cat. "It's not bad. Just a little...bare. We could get some of those really realistic looking fake apples and pears and put a fruit bowl on the table, then burn some scented candles. My new favorite is this one called Cinnamon Cookie. It makes the house smell like you've been baking all day." She pivots and takes in the blank expanse of the wall in the breakfast nook, scene of so many silent meals. "Remember those Portuguese pottery plates that didn't sell at the Reicker sale? Wouldn't those look really cute hanging there?"

Jill's enthusiasm is contagious. I start to see the house as it might be if "regular" people lived here. Cheery. Cozy. "Come in the living room," I say. "Isabelle insists this chair has to go. What can I get to replace it?"

Jill studies the room; moves a lamp, angles a table. "I saw the most awesome chairs at Ikea the other day. Sort of a mushroom color with a hint of plum. We could get two of them and put them right under that window. Then, when the house sells, you could put them in your living room. You know, you really don't have enough furniture at your place."

No sooner are the words out of her mouth than Jill turns beet red. "I'm sorry Audrey. I didn't mean your condo isn't nice the way it is. I like it. I do."

I put my arm around her shoulders and pull her in for a hug. "It sucks, Jill. I know it. You know it. When we get my dad's house sold, you can work on redecorating my place. Make it look less like a Holiday Inn suite occupied by a traveling salesman, and more like the bachelorette pad of my dreams."

Jill giggles. "Really? You'd let me do that? Because I'd love to and I wouldn't do anything crazy just warm it up a little, you know, and maybe introduce some color...sage?....or plum and gold? I love that combo..and then--"

"You can have free reign, but let's tackle this first, okay?"

"Oh, right!" Jill spins around. "Candles. Let's get one of those big candelabra things and put it in the hearth, just to suggest the possibility of a fire, know what I mean?"

"Candles are your solution to everything," I mutter as I follow her upstairs. There, Jill diagnoses new bedspreads, area rugs and lampshades.

"You think you can bring this in for under a thousands bucks?" I ask.

"Absolutely. They do it on those decorating shows all the time."

I pull out the AMT company credit card and hand it over. "Get what you need tomorrow and come over here and work your magic. Move everything we're getting rid of into the front hall, okay?"

Jill gets her saucer-eyed, Little Orphan Annie look. "You mean you trust me to do it all by myself?"

"Of course I do." I head for the kitchen. "Now, let's get out of here. Don't let me forget to turn off that back porch light."

By the back door we double-check everything. With my hand on the doorknob, I'm swept by a sensation of déjà vu. I went through these exact motions yesterday when I was here alone. Except then I was scared shitless and today I'm perfectly calm. And there's one other difference. Yesterday I had something in my hand as I was locking the door. What was it? Oh, Dad's yearbook and that folder with my little art project and Dad's grade roster in it. I put them right on the counter while I got my keys out. And then I must've left them there when I went out the door, because they're not in my car or my house. I look around. So where are they?

"Jill, did you see a file folder and a book on the counter here when we came in?"

"No, the counter was empty. I remember thinking how neat your dad is."

I glance around the kitchen. Nothing. But I know I brought those things down here from upstairs. I can see myself putting them on the counter. Where is the stuff? My heart starts to beat a little faster. I flip open cabinet doors and pull out drawers.

"What is it, Audrey? What are you looking for?"

Ignoring Jill, I pace around the kitchen. Why does it matter? It was only a kid's drawing and Dad's old book. But where did it go? Why can't I find it? A cool breeze sends a shiver through me. I'm near the short hall leading to the powder room. I step in there and see the window wide open. I feel my own nails sinking into my palms. Isabelle and I didn't open any windows yesterday.

I think about the car with the dented bumper. Is that the car that pulled out last night when I left here? It's not my imagination. Someone is following me, watching me. Someone broke into this house. Someone was down here last night when I was upstairs. Someone took that folder and that book.

Chapter 33

"Audrey?"

I'm aware of Jill's voice in the way I might be conscious of a foreign language radio station—meaningless background chatter. My whole focus is on that window, on the sickening sensation that someone really has been following me. That the noises I heard here last night weren't random bumps in the night. That maybe all my crazy little suspicions aren't so crazy. It's not paranoia if someone really is out to get you.

"Audrey? Are you ready to leave, or what? I have to be back downtown for my yoga class by six."

"Hmm?" I'm staring at the wide-open powder room window, its curtain rippling slightly in the breeze. Could a skinny man fit through there? It would be tight, but I think he could. No more burying my head in the sand--I need to tell the police about this. I'll call detective Farrand as soon as I get back to the office.

"Yeah—let's go." I lock the door, then toss the car keys to Jill. I don't want her to see my hands trembling on the steering wheel. "Do you mind driving? I'm kind of tired." She looks at me strangely, but does as she's told.

As we wind down the hill toward downtown, I blurt out what's

209

on my mind. "Jill, there's something I have to ask you. The trunk of jewelry that we found in Mrs. Szabo's house—did you ever…I mean, when I was in the hospital and you were taking care of Ethel…did you happen to look through that trunk?"

Jill's hands tighten on the steering wheel. "What do you mean?"

"I went in the closet last week and the trunk was in a different spot. The brooch that had been on the top was on the bottom, like someone dumped it out and put it all back in again."

Jill's gaze darts from the road to me and back again. "What are you saying? You think I stole stuff from that trunk?"

"No, no, no. I need to know if you looked at it, because first I thought someone broke in, but there was no sign of that. And then I realized you have the key, so maybe you might have—."

"You think I'm a thief." Jill's voice keeps climbing up the scale. "That's basically what you're saying. A thief!"

This isn't going the way I hoped. "Jill, listen. I'm not mad if you looked at the stuff. It would be better if you did, because if you didn't that means some stranger really did break in. I just need to know the truth: did you move that trunk?"

We're in front of the office by now and Jill throws the car into reverse. With a few vicious cranks of the wheel, she parallel parks. "When you were in the hospital I came to your condo every day to take care of Ethel. I fed her and walked her and cleaned up after her and that's all I did. I didn't snoop through your closets or steal your stuff or touch anything and I can't believe you think I'm—."

"Jill, stop—"

"a thief and a liar and I thought you trusted me but apparently not and—"

"Jill I do, I—"

She tosses the car keys in my lap. "I'm going to yoga. Have a nice night."

Watching Jill stomp off, I'm not sure what to think. Can I attribute her over-reaction to just plain Jill-yness, which means she didn't look through the trunk and I do have to worry that someone...Brian?....was in my apartment? Or did she freak because she really did go through the trunk and help herself to something? I'm not quite sure which possibility I prefer.

When I walk into the office, the place has been transformed. The usual chaos of boxes, packing material and stacks of unsold junk has been cleared away. Ty, a slight sheen of sweat highlighting his rippling biceps, stands watchfully by the window.

"Wow, this place looks great," I say, happy to latch onto anything that will distract me from what just happened.

"I packed up the van with the stuff goin' to Sister Alice," Ty says. "Then I cleaned up this whole corner here. There was boxes and bubble wrap and tape and shit everywhere. No wonder Jill can't never find what she's looking for."

I give him a long, silent stare. His gaze drops to the floor.

"Look, Audrey—about this afternoon. I didn't mean to leave Jill with all the work. I thought I'd jus' be out for fifteen minutes or somethin'. ."

"Sounds like the 'or something' turned into the entire afternoon. What's up with that?"

Ty rolls his powerful shoulders. "It's complicated, Audge. I got some shit I'm dealin' with."

"What kind of shit? Where did you go?"

Ty shakes his head. I know that stubborn, hard-eyed look. He's not talking.

I've been thinking over the past two days how I'm going to ask Ty about the other trips in the van without revealing that it was Coughlin who told me. Now's the time to roll out my plan.

"There's something else I have to ask you about. My friend Lydia's husband is a salesman—he's on the road all the time. He told me he passed the AMT van on the Turnpike north of New Brunswick. I thought he must've been mistaken, but now I think he was right. What do you say?"

Ty looks like I kicked him in the balls. His skin actually changes color—I didn't think African Americans could blush. "My cousin Marcus," he stammers. "He graduated from Rutgers last spring. He asked me to help him move some stuff he left in his old apartment. That's why I took the van to New Brunswick. It was the day I delivered that table to Somerville, so I figured it wasn't much further."

Sounds plausible. I want to believe him, but what about Paterson, what about today?

"Look, Ty, I've been very happy with your work. If you need a day off to take care of personal business, all you have to do is ask. But it's not okay to drive my van without permission. It's not okay to just head out without telling anyone and stick Jill with all your work. And it's definitely not okay to insult her when she objects."

Ty's head droops lower. "I'm sorry about that. I didn't mean nothin'. It's just, sometimes when I'm worried, stuff don't come out right, know what I'm sayin'?"

Boy, do I ever. I reach out and put my hand on Ty's forearm. It looks very small and white there. "Ty, if you've got problems, why don't you tell me about it. Maybe I can help."

My fingers scald him—he flinches away from my touch. "I can handle it. Just some drama with this girl I'm talkin' to. Her parents don't like me."

Before I can plead any further, Ty lopes to the door. "Tell Jill I said sorry and shit. I make it up to her." And he's gone.

Sorry and shit. An eloquent apology, if ever there was one. Uneasily, I look around the ship-shape office. What kind of problems is Ty up against? Would standard-issue girlfriend drama have produced this reaction? Or is he feeling guilty about something, guilty and in over his head? Guilty and exposing me to dangerous people, just as Coughlin said? Am I being willfully obtuse, unable to admit I was wrong about Ty all along? Or is Coughlin manipulating me, playing on my fears so I'll give him something he can use against Ty?

If I tell Coughlin Ty's been acting sketchy because of a girl, he'll want to know the name of the girl, and I know damn well Ty won't give that up. I decide to bide my time and keep an eye on Ty. In the meantime, I need to call Farrand and tell him about the break-in at my father's house. He answers on the first ring.

I explain about the open window at my father's house and the missing items. As I hear my words tumbling out, I start to squirm. Spoken aloud my concerns sound so paltry and insignificant. I feel I'm bothering him, distracting him from important work.

"Anything else missing?" he inquires blandly. "Jewelry, electronics, cash?"

"No, but—"

"But what?"

"Last night, when I was there alone, I heard noises downstairs when I was upstairs. I think whoever broke in was there when I was. He was, he was…watching me."

"Watching you do what?"

What indeed? Wander aimlessly around the house…dig through every file folder in the desk…scroll through the computer…find a drawing and a yearbook. Put some papers in a folder. Leave said folder behind.

"Well," I begin. "I just…since the attack, I've kinda felt like—."

I pause. I picture him on the other end of the line rolling his eyes. But I'm wrong.

"It's perfectly normal for the victim of a violent crime to feel nervous and stressed, Ms. Nealon. I can give you a contact at the County Victim Services department—they offer free counseling. Do you have a pen?"

Dutifully, I write down the number, although I know I'll never call. I look at my right hand as it forms the number. Is the ring what the watcher wants? At the time the trunk was searched, the only person who knew I had this ring was my father. He certainly didn't break into my condo. But he does have my keys, just as I have his. He could have sent someone to search my place. Someone like Brian Bascomb. How can I explain this to the uber-logical Farrand?

He's put on that bland, noncommittal tone cops use when they ask for your license and registration. They must practice it at the police academy. "Possibly some kids noticed that your father's house has been unoccupied for a while and they decided to use it for a little recreation. Did you find any cigarette butts, beer bottles, condoms?"

Eeew, teenagers having a tryst in my father's bed—could that explain the open window? "I went all through the house and didn't see any signs that anyone had been there," I say. "None of the beds had been messed up."

"They may not have bothered going all the way upstairs," Farrand says. I blush hotly at the memory of Cal's and my antics on my sofa.

Farrand has succeeded in sowing the seeds of doubt in my mind. Maybe I was imagining the sounds I heard last night. Maybe that window had been open for a while and Isabelle and I didn't notice it. But what about the folder and the book? They've definitely disappeared.

"Why would teenagers take a file folder and a yearbook that I left on the counter, and not take anything else?" I ask him.

"Why would anyone take it, Ms. Nealon? What was in it?"

"Just—" Suddenly I don't want to be talking to this guy anymore. I definitely don't want to tell him about my sentimental need for my childhood artwork, or about Brian Bascomb. "Just some personal papers," I finish lamely.

"Maybe the intruder needed a piece of paper and grabbed the first thing he saw. If the folder was important to you, you might look around outside. He may have dropped it. If you'd like, I can send someone from community policing over to look around with you and make sure the house is secure."

Farrand is so attentive, so prepared with a police service for every occasion. Why not take him up on it? Put my tax dollars to work and all that. But I can't bring myself to come across as whiny and demanding. I'm low-maintenance Audrey—isn't that what Cal likes about me? "Thanks for the offer, Detective. I don't think that'll be necessary."

After I hang up with Farrand, I feel my fingers itching, creeping toward the computer keyboard. Like so many other things, e-commerce has made the marketplace for old yearbooks much more efficient. Want to relive your high school or college days but can't find your yearbook? No problem—all the old yearbooks ever given to Goodwill or the church bazaar or used book shops have been consolidated on a few websites. Request the year and school you want and see what happens. I've sold plenty of yearbooks on FINDYOURYEARBOOK.com. Now it's time to buy one— Princeton, Class of 69, In Stock. I buy it and choose regular shipping. It'll be in my hands in under a week. Maybe I've wasted my money, but there has to be some reason the thief took my folder and that yearbook. There's nothing I can do about the drawing, but I can try to see what was so interesting about that yearbook.

Chapter 34

At 6:30 I'm dressed and waiting for Cal to pick me up for dinner at the Finneran's. At 6:32, my phone chirps the arrival of a text message: *Held up @ office. Head over to Anne's. I'll meet u there.*

Great. Walking into Anne and Spencer's house solo is right up there with root canal on my things-I'm-eager-to-do-list.

Driving over, I realize the steering wheel is slippery with sweat from my palms and I'm not sure why. This is not a big party. Anne has been unfailingly nice to me. I don't even have to worry about what I'm wearing because Anne has that Barbara Bush-like frumpiness that I find so reassuring. And yet…. And yet…

I turn a corner onto the Finneran's street. Almost all the leaves have fallen from the trees now, and huge piles line the curbs waiting to be scooped up by the public works department. Plowing directly into one of those leaf mountains, I park the car and study the Finneran's big Victorian. Lights glow in all the downstairs windows; pumpkins and mums line the wrap-around porch. I let the sharp breeze push me up the walk into that Hallmark card. I want to be in there, yet my finger hesitates on the doorbell. I feel a little bead of sweat forming between my breasts, despite the nippy night air. Why am I so nervous? I press and hear the chime echo on the other side of the door. A dog starts barking and a calming voice reassures him.

"Now, now Bix, that's enough."

It's Anne. I run my fingers through my hair and lick my parched lips. Maybe, just maybe, I can smile without my face cracking in half.

The door swings open.

"Audrey, dear!" Anne flings wide her arms and herds me into the house. "That dreadful Cal called and told me he'd be late. I said, 'I'm already having a glass of wine and it doesn't look good for a woman my age to drink alone, so you send Audrey over to keep me company.' I'm so glad you listened."

Frankly, it never dawned on me not to listen. My self-will seems to evaporate in the presence of Cal, Anne and Spencer.

"We have to stay back here in the kitchen," Anne says, taking my coat and tossing it heedlessly onto a Hepplewhite settee in the corner of the huge foyer. "I'm making risotto and I have to keep an eye on it. You know how temperamental risotto can be."

"Actually, I have no clue," I say. "I'm more of a Minute Rice kind of girl."

Anne throws her head back and laughs. It's a nice reassuring sound, the kind of laugh that makes you feel like you're the most entertaining person on the planet. I watch as she bends over to check something in the oven.

"I couldn't boil water when I married Spencer. We always had a cook when I was growing up. Can you imagine!" Anne rolls her eyes. "Those days are gone forever. Anyway, I soon discovered my husband expected a hot meal on the table every night."

Bustling around her gleaming granite and stainless steel fiefdom as she talks, Anne stirs a pot bubbling on the stove, pours me a glass of wine, and causes some marvelous looking cheese puff thingies to materialize. Despite the high-end design, the kitchen would never make it into a decorating magazine. Piles of mail teeter on one end of the counter. A slightly cock-eyed bulletin board bristles with invitations and appointment cards; snapshots of Anne and Spencer and various combinations of children and grandchildren peep through the tangle. Post-it note reminders screaming "Leila B-day card!" and "artichoke hearts!" are stuck to the microwave and coffee pot. The combination of the wine and the clutter works on me. I begin to relax.

"So Spencer expected you to learn to cook?" I ask. It's hard for me to imagine Anne as a compliant, eager-to-please bride. Wouldn't she and Spencer have been married around the same time as my parents? And Roger and Charlotte were apparently the model of equality.

"Spencer and I met through his sister. She and I were both Alpha Chi Omega at Bucknell," Anne says. "A very smart family, the Finnerans. All three children won full academic scholarships."

On the face of it, her words conveyed pride, but something clicks for me. The money was all on Anne's side of the family. Spencer Finneran was a poor boy who made good.

"I learned to cook for myself as much as him. With Spencer in law school, we were poor as church mice. We couldn't afford to eat out. And I've never been one to subsist on celery and seltzer water," she says, patting herself on her ample hips.

I grin and pop another cheese puff in my mouth. It's so refreshing to be around a woman—thin or fat—who's not talking about dieting. And, one who's not concerned with fashion. Anne's droopy khaki slacks and navy cardigan make me look positively glamorous. I'm starting to have fun.

"Your mother never taught you to cook?" Anne asks.

"My mother died when I was just three."

Anne's hands stop their deft chopping and she looks deeply into my eyes. "Oh my dear, how tactless of me. Cal did mention that. I'm sorry."

"That's okay. My grandmother was a good cook, but a fussy housekeeper. She never really liked having me in the kitchen. Too afraid I'd make a mess."

"Well, as you can see, neatness has never been a concern of mine." Anne waves her right hand, which happens to hold a large chef's knife. A slice of avocado sails across the kitchen. The dog nails it. As Anne returns to chopping, the phone rings. She glances at the caller ID, looks apologetically at me. "My daughter, Ginny. She's stuck at home with a sick baby. I'd better answer."

Trying not to eavesdrop, I cross the kitchen to study some Italian pottery displayed on a shelf. Still, I can hear Anne emphatically dispensing advice.

"Good grief, Ginny, she's been crying for three hours. Just give her a little Benadryl. You both need to get some sleep." There's a silence, then Anne continues. "It's Benadryl, honey, not arsenic. I used to give it to you all the time, and you ended up magna cum laude at Yale." Another silence, then a final snap, "Well, if you don't want to listen to me, I don't know why you called." The receiver hits the cradle sharply.

Flustered by having overheard this less than idyllic mother/daughter exchange, I keep my back turned even after the steady thwack of Anne's chef's knife resumes.

"Come back, Audrey," she calls. "I promise I won't yell at you too."

I return to the stool at the island where I had been perched.

"Grandchildren," Anne sighs, "a constant source of joy and conflict. Speaking of which, I understand my grandson Dylan paid a visit to your last estate sale." She brushes her gray bangs off her forehead with the back of her hand. A "V" of worry is etched between her brows. "Thank you for your patience."

"Oh, no big deal," I say, focusing my attention on folding my cocktail napkin into a fan. Patience? Has Anne talked to Dylan about what happened at the Reicker sale? If so, apparently Dylan left out the part about Ty bringing him down in a full body tackle.

Anne pauses in her meal preparations. Suddenly her face shows every one of her sixty-five years. "Dylan's been going through a tough stretch. My son's marriage has been a little rocky."

So, that much of what Dylan told me was true. I wonder about the rest of his accusation—'my grandpa's always got some piece of ass on the side.' Can that be accurate, or was Dylan making another play for attention, as Cal insists? I'm dying to know, but I can't very well ask.

Before I can say anything, Anne continues with a sigh. "Dylan takes everything so personally. He seems to think everyone else's family is perfect. That the Finnerans are the only people with any problems."

Hmmm—I can relate to that. Except the Finneran's brand of family dysfunction—big, messy, exuberant—seems a lot more appealing than the cold, constipated secret-keeping of mine. "He doesn't seem to be looking forward to being the grandson of the next governor of New Jersey," I say.

Anne rolls her eyes. "He makes that clear to everyone, usually within the first minute of meeting them. Dylan thinks his grandfather conceived this run for office as a personal vendetta against him."

I laugh. "That's exactly the impression he gives. You really seem to understand him."

Anne decapitates some broccoli florets with one sure blow. "It's taken me years to learn to cope with being caught in the spotlight of Spencer's career. Dylan's not used to the glare." Then she grins at me and grabs the wine bottle. "Tuesday. We all just need to make it through Tuesday."

For some unaccountable reason I feel a lump forming in my throat. I want to know how to chop like that. I want my picture up on the kitchen bulletin board. I want "Audrey—lunch!" scrawled on Post-it note. I even want to be scolded when I'm ornery. I want to belong here. Here in the middle of this big topsy-turvy family so different from my own.

Then my brain makes a leap. I visualize the picture of the young Spencer and Anne hanging on Reid VanHouten's office wall. "Did you know my mother?" I ask.

Anne's knife pauses over some scallions. "I don't think I know any Nealons. Why do you ask?"

"Perry. Charlotte Perry—she kept her maiden name. She worked for the Van Houten Group. I was in Reid Van Houten's office the other day. I saw a photo of you and Spencer on his wall."

The knife resumes its rapid-fire assault on the vegetables. "Must've been some fundraising event. Our paths cross all the time."

"No, this was an old photo. Mr. Van Houten said it was taken during Spencer's first political campaign. I understand the Van Houten Group handled the PR."

"Did they?" Anne's back is to me as she fills a pot with water. "I suppose it's possible—until Spencer got Cal to manage all that for him, there always seemed to be a revolving door of PR firms, hired guns and freelancers pulling Spencer in every direction.

"Mr. Van Houten said my mother might have worked on one of Spencer's campaigns."

"Did she?" Anne smiles and sweeps the broccoli into a steamer. "What a small world! You'll have to ask Spencer. I was pregnant and coping with two toddlers at the time—I didn't have much interaction with Spencer's staff."

Suddenly the dog, who's been sprawled in front of the kitchen island waiting for another random scrap of food to fly off Anne's chopping block, stands up and trots to the back door.

"Ah, that must be Spencer and Cal now. About time."

Chapter 35

A cool breeze dissipates some of the kitchen's heat as Spencer and Cal come through the back door.

"If the polls in South Jersey can be trusted——." Cal, his face etched with urgency, is fully focused on Spencer. But Spencer has shrugged off his overcoat and Cal with the same gesture, and he's heading across the kitchen with his arms outstretched.

"Hello, darling! Aren't you a sight for sore eyes!"

Anne drops her risotto-stirring spoon and offers herself up to her husband's embrace. For a moment, they stand entwined, swaying, oblivious to their surroundings. Then the oven timer beeps and Anne breaks away, but not before brushing Spencer's cheek with her fingertips. The gesture is so intimate I look away, flustered.

Cal has slipped up behind me and places his hands on my shoulders. "Hey beautiful—how are you?"

I smile up at him, wondering if he can feel my accelerated heartbeat. As always, when I haven't seen him for a few days, I'm as giddy as a schoolgirl. I should tell him about the break-in, but I don't want to do it here and draw unwanted attention to myself. Finally, I get my brain and mouth working in synch. "Fine. I'm sitting here watching Anne cook, being no help whatsoever."

"Ah, that's the story of all of our lives, Audrey," Spencer says from across the room. "Anne has never needed any help with anything."

Anne snorts, but the little smile on her face shows that Spencer's remark is quite true. In a few easy moves she's placed cocktails and a plate of hors d'oeuvres in front of her husband and Cal. "There you go, boys. I suppose you haven't eaten a thing all day?"

"Not so," Cal says. "I distinctly remember some sort of chicken and pasta product at a rally in Edison this afternoon."

"And half a knish at a retirement community in Fort Lee," Spencer adds.

"And a bag of Doritos in the car," Cal confesses.

Anne shudders. "Cal, can't you plan a campaign event for organic farmers, or nouvelle cuisine restaurateurs?"

"He's already sewn up the liberal vote, Anne. Unfortunately, swing voters eat foot-long hot dogs and calzones."

"Once I'm governor, I promise I'll eat nothing but yogurt and salad," Spencer says, winking at me over Anne's head.

I must say, for two people surviving on rubber chicken and junk food, both Cal and Spencer are in great shape. Spencer is lean and paunch-free, still a very attractive man. I wonder how Anne feels about that. Is she intimidated by her husband's good looks? Concerned by her own dowdiness? Does she ever wonder, as I wonder about Cal, what her man sees in her? But I detect no lack of confidence in Anne. She's the queen of all she surveys, and the connection between her and Spencer is visceral, vital.

I think about Dylan's accusation. *Does* Spencer fool around with other women? Is Anne another in a long line of clueless, used and abused politician's wives? No, surely Anne is too sharp for that. Still, you don't have to be dumb to be a dupe, as so many smart, cheated upon women have proved.

While I've been daydreaming, the conversation has moved on. I tune back in to find both Cal and Spencer listening raptly to Anne.

"...and Jerry Berlinski knows that," she's saying, as she ladles risotto into a serving bowl. "He's got his own agenda, which is why I think you'll regret striking a deal with him." She raps the spoon sharply on the edge of the pot, dislodging the last grains of rice.

There's a moment of silence.

Cal breaks it. "Anne's right. Too risky."

Spencer looks back and forth between his wife and his aide. Then he throws his hands up in defeat. "Okay, wiser heads prevail. I'm just the front man of this operation." Spencer picks up a platter of grilled salmon and moves toward the dining room. "Come on, Audrey. Let Cal and Anne talk politics. You and I will talk collectibles. Did you know I have a 1963 Yogi Berra rookie card?"

In the soft glow of candlelight and Anne's twinkling crystal chandelier, the dinner unwinds. True to his word, Spencer has declined to talk shop. He quizzes me on my work, and proves to be surprisingly knowledgeable on the subject of American antiques, 20th century art, and sports memorabilia. Most of all, he listens. Spencer has the knack of making the person he's talking to feel like she's the only one in the room. Handy trait for a politician. On some level, I know I'm not really as special as he makes me feel. Still, the experience is very pleasant. As I talk, my wine glass refills magically.

The conversation ranges from antique furniture to baseball memorabilia to contemporary painting. For once, it's Cal who's a bit out of his depth. From the corner of my eye I see him sprawled back in his chair with a pleased half-smile on his face as he watches me banter with his mentor. Once, I catch him exchanging a glance with Anne, and she nods approvingly.

"David Salle has gotten hot in the past few years," I tell Spencer while we're on the topic of underappreciated contemporary artists. "I used to find paintings of his that people were ready to toss out on the curb. Not anymore. In fact, you know who has one hanging on his wall? Reid Van Houten."

Anne pushes away from the table. "Let me bring in the dessert. Spencer, can you help me?"

"I'll help," Cal says.

My mind, dulled from too much rich food and too many glasses of wine, lurches clumsily from our original topic to a new one that blossoms before me like an insanely prolific jungle plant.

"Did you know my mother?" I ask Spencer. "Charlotte Perry. She worked for Reid Van Houten."

I'm drunk, but not too drunk to notice Spencer looking as if he's opened the shower curtain to a big, hairy thousand-legger.

Startled, I twist in my chair. My leg pulls on the tablecloth, which in turn knocks over my nearly empty wine glass. A deep red stain spreads across the pristine linen tablecloth.

"Oh, God! I'm sorry!" I reach for my napkin to try to blot up the mess.

Anne appears at my side and slides the napkin smoothly from my hand before I compound the problem. "I think Audrey's tired, Cal. Perhaps it's time for us all to call it a night."

"That's not the first wine spilled on this tablecloth and it won't be the last," Spencer says. "I thought there was dessert? Bring it on, Anne."

The awkward moment dissolves. Did it even happen? Did I imagine Spencer's reaction at the mention of my mother?

"Now let's see….Charlotte Perry," Spencer says. "I think I do remember a young woman named Charlotte who worked for Reid. Very pretty, as I recall." He grins at Cal. "But it's so long ago. The late seventies are a blur to me now. Making partner…running for office…becoming a father. I think there were entire years that got lost. Right Anne?"

Anne has reappeared bearing a magnificent chocolate cake. "You were lost," she says wryly. "I was right here."

Spencer pulls her into a hug. "She's a trouper. Always was, always will be."

Anne's lips assume the smile position, but her eyes don't look amused. In fact, I think she seems downright pained.

Spencer represents a link to my mother that I'm not ready to let go. I keep talking, even though it no longer seems he's hanging on my every word, as he was earlier. "I asked whether you knew my mom because, well, I've been trying lately to figure her out." Without waiting for encouragement, I plow on. "You see, my father was never willing to tell me much about her, and to my grandparents she was this saint, completely perfect. I wish I knew what she was *really* like, you know?"

Spencer leans across the table and pats my hand. "Perfectly understandable, Audrey. Maybe I saw her in the halls at Reid's office, but—" he shrugs. "I wish I'd known her well enough to share a memory with you."

Spencer pops a bite of cake in his mouth, chews, and turns to Anne. "This cake is fabulous, honey."

The cake is delicious, but too rich to finish. I leave half of it on my plate. Soon, Cal is helping Anne clear the dishes and we all head for the foyer.

Spencer helps me on with my coat, then caresses my shoulder. "So glad you could make it tonight, Audrey. It's a rare treat for me to talk about something other than politics. You bring out the best in us."

Cal takes me by the hand. "Indeed she does."

"You know," Spencer says, putting his arm around Anne, "As I was leaving a meeting the other day I noticed a poster one of the secretaries had hung in her cubicle. It said, 'Marry well. Your spouse accounts for 75% of your happiness.'" His arm tightens around Anne's waist. "So true. Marry well."

Chapter 36

Because I drove to the Finnerans' and Cal came with Spencer, I've got to drive Cal home. He lives in a fancy new condo in downtown Palmyrton that I'm dying to see, but when we pull into the drive, Cal is full of apologies about a 5AM wake-up for a 6AM breakfast meeting. His goodbye kiss leaves me molten as a puddle of candle wax. Drunk and horny, I wend my way home, slither into my living room and collapse on the sofa. Did Cal really have an early morning meeting, or was he repulsed by my behavior at Spencer's dinner table? Did I make a fool of myself, asking Spencer so many questions about my mother? Or maybe Cal was turned off by Anne's heavy-handed matchmaking. God, I hate this!

A firm knock at my door is as effective as AED paddles at jump-starting my heart. Maybe Cal changed his mind and came back. Ridiculously hopeful, I follow a barking Ethel to the door and press my eye against the peephole. The man on my porch is so big and so close to the door that I can't see his face.

"Who is it?"

"Sean Coughlin."

Sean, not detective? Is he my new best friend? I take a deep breath to settle my heart and open the door. We stare at each other for a moment.

"Kind of late for a social call," I say.

"I need to talk to you." He strides right into the foyer, not waiting for an invitation and I melt back out of his way. The unstoppable force meets a very movable object.

"I want to talk to you about your man, Griggs."

Annoyance fights a losing battle with anxiety, as I trail Coughlin into my living room. "What about him?"

"He was spotted at two this afternoon getting out of a car on Ditmars Avenue."

I keep my face impassive. That was the time Ty was missing in action from the Siverson job. Ditmars Avenue is about as far away from the Siversons' neighborhood as you can get and still be in Palmyrton. "And is that a crime?"

"It is when you're on probation and the car belongs to Mondel Johnson."

It's a safe bet Mondel Johnson is not the pastor of the Baptist church or the coach of the Rec Department basketball league, but I won't give Coughlin the satisfaction of asking, 'who's that?' I sit quietly staring at him. Two can play at this game.

"Street name: Trigger," Coughlin finally continues. "He's an enforcer for a guy named Nichols, who runs a major drug operation out of Newark."

I feel a bead of sweat break out along my hairline. This can't be. Not Ty. Not now. Then I get suspicious. Why is Coughlin telling me this? If it truly is a crime for Ty to be associating with this Mondel character, why didn't the cops arrest him?

Coughlin's tough guy pose makes me feel equally belligerent. I start talking as if the creators of *Women Behind Bars* are writing my lines. "So you barge into my house at ten at night to tell me about it? What's up with that?"

Coughlin leans forward, resting his hamhock arms on his tree trunk thighs. The easy chair he's chosen to sit in sags under his weight. His pale blue eyes drill right into me. "I'm worried about you,

Audrey. You're protecting a guy who's a known associate of some very dangerous people. Your kindness could get you killed."

I feel the defiance draining out of me. Coughlin is serious. He thinks I'm in danger. The anxiety I've been feeling lately, the sensation that someone's watching me, looking for something they think I have—maybe it's not all in my head. I haven't said a word yet, but Coughlin, with his eerie sixth sense, picks up on my uneasiness.

"You lied to me when you told me the man who beat you was white, didn't you?" he asks. Those pale blue eyes seem to rake through my brain, separating truth from falsehood. I'm powerless.

"I did lie. I didn't see who attacked me. I don't know what race he was, what he looked like. But I'm sure—I'm positive—that it wasn't Ty."

A muscle begins to twitch in Coughlin's jaw. "Maybe it wasn't Griggs himself who attacked you, but he was behind it. He set you up."

"I don't believe that!" Ethel's ears perk up at the high-pitched anxiety in my voice. "Ty has worked hard to turn his life around. I gave him a break when he needed one—he likes me. He would never hurt me. Or let someone else hurt me."

"Let me tell you something about criminals, Audrey. The most successful ones are friendly, charming, likeable. They're able to separate their criminal behavior from their day-to-day life. I knew a hit man for the mob who was a freakin' Little League coach. They lie. They lie so well, they believe their own lies. They're sociopaths."

A sociopath? Charles Manson was a sociopath; Ty is just a recovering juvenile delinquent. This is my problem with Coughlin— he starts out reasonable, but he always ends up going too far, saying something outrageous that makes me doubt everything that comes out of his mouth.

"Look, all Ty did was drive the getaway car when his friends broke into a house. He served his time. He's been working hard since he got out of jail. Just because he's from a troubled family, does that mean he's condemned forever? That he never gets a second chance?"

Coughlin pounds his fist into the palm of his other hand. "You people make me nuts!"

"You people? Exactly what kind of 'you people' am I?"

"Freakin' bleeding heart liberal Pollyana!"

I jump up. "Yeah, that's me. Maybe the world needs a few more Pollyanas to stand up against racist police brutality." Ethel echoes my sentiments with a few high, sharp, don't-mess-with-me barks.

Coughlin springs to his feet and wags a massive index finger at me. "Don't play the race card with me. I go after crooks—white, black, Spanish, Chinese, Indian—they're all the same to me."

"Oh, big-time crooks, like the kid who stole a cup of change from the 7-11?"

"Don't throw that up to me! I was cleared!"

"Covered up is more like it. Your partner took the rap, then agreed to retire early. Problem solved."

"That's not what happened." Coughlin thrusts his index finger at me, his voice loud and harsh.

Ethel growls low in her throat.

Immediately Coughlin drops the aggressive pose and extends an open hand for Ethel to sniff. She approaches warily, no longer growling but not wagging her tail either.

"My partner was the one who beat Jason Powell. But I did nothing to stop him. I was young, didn't think it was my place to challenge an older cop." Coughlin looks up and holds my gaze. "I learned that day to be my own man. You have such a great belief that people can change—why doesn't that apply to me?"

His jab makes me flinch and I lash out. "So I'm supposed to feel sorry for the poor, misunderstood six-foot-five bully who thinks he's always right?"

"You're a hypocrite, Audrey." He says it without the slightest heat, very matter-of-fact. "Once you make up your mind about someone, that's it; that person's cast in stone for you. But let me tell you—people are unpredictable. They're pushed against a wall, they'll do whatever it takes to survive. Fifteen years on the job, I've lost my ability to be surprised."

"Or to trust."

He touches the top of my head: "Pot." Then he touches his: "Kettle."

Touché.

I take what Jill's yoga teacher calls a cleansing breath and try to ratchet down the anger in the room. "If you saw Ty with this Mondel Johnson character, and that's a violation of his parole, then why didn't you arrest him?"

"We're watching him. You're right about one thing. He's just a low-level punk. We're after bigger fish."

"Why are you telling me about it? Aren't you afraid I'll tell Ty?"

"It's no secret we're watching him. I want you to tell him I've been here. Tell him if he doesn't want to join his old man down in Trenton, he better tell us what he knows. About what happened to you. About Nichols's operation."

I look at Coughlin's stony face. What does he know about the Ecstasy in Mrs. Szabo's kitchen? He's as good at hiding what he knows as he is at ferreting out what others know. But if Coughlin is investigating this big drug gang, wouldn't Farrand have told him about the pills? How they were there and then disappeared? Of course, Farrand thinks Cal found them. If Coughlin knows about that, he may think Ty hid the drugs in Mrs. Szabo's house, then took them away again. But if I tell Coughlin it was Ty who found them and willingly told me about them, wouldn't that dispel Coughlin's suspicions? Should I tell Coughlin this? But what if he doesn't know anything about the pills… Shit, I'm so confused!

To buy time, I ask a question. "When you say Mondel Johnson is an enforcer for Nichols, what does that mean?"

"He collects the money. Makes sure no one's ripping off the boss."

"So you think Ty owes the big guy money for drugs that he's

sold, and now he can't pay?"

"Probably. That would explain why he had Mondel and his crew rob you."

"But you don't know for sure? You've never seen Ty make a sale?"

"No." Coughlin admits.

"Even though you've been watching him?" Coughlin's answers are giving me hope. There's got to be some simple explanation for Ty's behavior. Some reason for my attack that doesn't involve Ty setting me up.

"All that means is he's not selling on the street corner. He's selling to people he knows."

"Then why did—" the information about the pills in the kitchen starts bubbling up.

"Why what?" Coughlin asks.

"Nothing," I mutter.

Too late. Three little words, and Coughlin knows I'm withholding something. He leans back in his chair, crosses his arms across his massive chest, and stares at me.

This is ridiculous. I'm not in some windowless interrogation room on Riker's Island. This is my home. I can kick Coughlin out any time.

"It's way past my bedtime. I think you'd better leave."

Coughlin crosses his legs without ever breaking eye contact.

I stare back.

My bravado lasts for about thirty seconds. I'm not quite sure how Coughlin manages to project such relentlessness, but whatever it is, it works. I feel my resolve weakening. Maybe Ty's problems and my own fear will be resolved if I tell Coughlin the truth about the pills in the kitchen drawer. Maybe I should trust him. But how do I explain why we lied in the first place without opening up the Pandora's box of the trunkful of jewelry? The election is less than a week away. I can't ruin all that Cal and Spencer have worked for, especially when I'm not even positive that the information will help

Ty. I can't confess now. I have to talk to Ty, talk to Cal, then decide.

I take a deep breath and stand up. Ethel trots to my side, imparting courage. Since lying to Coughlin is pointless, I settle on offering him a limited truth. "Look, detective, I appreciate your concern; I really do. And you're right, there is some information I haven't told you. But that information affects people other than just me. I need to discuss it with them first. After I do, I'll give you a call."

Before he can utter a word, I pivot and walk to the front door. A moment or two later, I hear Coughlin's footsteps behind me. I open the door and Ethel races out to pee on the little patch of grass in front of the condo. The commotion provides me with some cover so I don't have to look at my uninvited guest.

As I keep an eye on Ethel, Coughlin follows me onto the front porch and places his hand, large as a dinner plate, on my shoulder. It feels oddly light. The domineering, I-call-the-shots-here expression that I've grown used to from him has been replaced by something softer, almost quizzical. Like he's a scientist and I'm an experiment that's produced totally unexpected results.

Finished with her business, Ethel charges onto the porch and shoots into the house. As I turn to follow, Coughlin speaks. "Do what you have to do, Audrey. Just remember this: I'm not the enemy." His hand tightens ever so slightly on my shoulder. "Call me anytime."

A wave of heat passes through me as Coughlin's hand lifts from my shoulder and I watch him disappear down the front walk.

Now what the hell is that about?

Chapter 37

"Oh, God, Audrey—I think I've made it worse."

I come out of my father's house and move into the center of the yard to assess the effect of Jill's work. She and Ty are helping me get the house ready for listing, and following Isabelle's instructions, Jill has taken the hedge trimmers to the holly bushes. With a vengeance. Now, instead of huge overgrown shrubs threatening to consume anyone who ventures onto the front porch, we have two clumps of bare sticks surrounded by a pile of holly leaves and berries.

"They look like post-modernist sculptures," I say.

"I'm so sorry, Audrey! I didn't mean to strip them naked. But when I pruned them back so they wouldn't touch the porch, I cut off all their leaves. Underneath, there's nothing but bare branches. Isabelle will have a fit—there's no curb appeal in stumps!"

The gardening debacle has set Jill's lower lip trembling, something that seems to happen with increasing frequency these days. The three of us have been treating one another with elaborate politeness, a symptom, I guess, of our mutual suspicion and hurt feelings. I'm still not sure if Jill searched the trunk of jewelry or not, still not sure what Ty is up to. I could draw a line in the sand and demand absolute honesty from both of them, or else. But what if my ultimatum backfires? I can't run the business without them right now, not with Dad being sprung from the nursing home and my mind preoccupied with my attacker, my mother, and the sibling I may or may not have. It's easier to muddle along, one day at a time, hoping that one of these problems will resolve itself and provide me with some slack to work on the others.

"Don't worry about the bushes, Jill." I pat her on the back. "We'll dig them out and plant something new. Ty can help." I find a shovel in the garage and set Ty to work digging.

I hear the steady chink, chink, chink of the shovel as I work in the living room. Through the window I can see that Ty has peeled off his sweatshirt and his tee shirt is stuck to his back with sweat. This is a bigger job than I realized. I go outside with a glass of water for him.

"Man, these bushes have some kind of root system, huh?" I look into the huge hole Ty has created. "They've been here as long as I can remember."

"Thirty years of roots," Ty says, slashing at a thick tendon with the sharp edge of the shovel. He severs it, and yanks it out, tugging with both hands. Looking down, I see something pink poking up out of the soil. It's plastic, the color faded and dirty, but somewhere deep in my mind it triggers a memory. As I excavate around it a bit with my sneaker, a wheel emerges. An old toy of mine, buried under the earth.

I crouch down to examine it more closely. Brushing the clods of damp earth aside, I see a flat piece of pink plastic, some rusty metal, and the edge of a tattered, decomposing scrap of bunny-printed fabric. The bunnies do it; suddenly I see two little hands on a handle and a baby doll staring up at me from under that blanket. The vision is as crisp and detailed as a movie playing in my mind. This was my doll carriage and I remember pushing it around and around a few feet from here on the flat part of the driveway. And I hear my mother's voice calling me, "Let's go in sweetie—it's getting late." Try as I might, I can only hear her, not see her. But the memory is mine, wholly mine, not placed there by my grandparents as all the other memories of my mother have been.

Suddenly, I've got to have this doll carriage. I start clawing at the dirt with my bare hands.

"Audge, what you doin'? I'll finish that—just let me drink my water."

Ignoring Ty's words, I grab his shovel. The carriage isn't buried very deep. A few good thrusts with the shovel untombs it. Panting slightly from my efforts, I knock off the big chunks of earth clinging to it and stare at what I've found. My little pink baby carriage, one wheel missing, squashed completely flat. I stare a little longer, waiting. I want so much for this to be my Proust's Madeleine, the token that unleashes a torrent of memories.

Nothing.

"Audge? What's the big deal? What is that?" Ty's voice comes to me from a million miles away.

I remember pushing the carriage. I remember endless loops. I remember my mother's voice.

That's it. Movie over.

Jill has returned to the office and I need Ty's help to move a large bookcase that's blocking my access to a crawlspace under the eaves. God knows what's in there—probably squirrel shit and dried up hornet's nests—but even though I know my father's not a saver, the possibility that something valuable might be waiting behind that blocked door pushes me forward..

"Ty!" I shout. "Ty, come up here for a minute and help me, will you?"

No answer. Him and that damn iPod. I pull out my phone and text him. Stare at the phone and wait for a reply. Nothing.

I head for the stairs. Out in the hall, a big window overlooks the street. I see a shiny black Hummer parked at the curb. Ty stands next to it, talking with a man.

I step to the side of the window and look out from behind the drapes.

The other man is also African American, a little shorter than Ty, but broader. He seems to be doing all the talking, while Ty stands silently with his hands shoved in the pockets of his hoodie. Then the man pulls something from his pocket and shows it to Ty. Ty nods.

I don't like the looks of this. Who is this guy? If he's just a friend from the neighborhood, why did Ty ignore my text? God knows, he answers texts constantly when I'm talking to him.

The man turns away and steps off the curb. I see Ty's mouth move. The guy pivots in a flash, pushes his face right up to Ty's, says something else, and pushes Ty out of his way.

What happens next makes my stomach lurch.

The man heads for his car. Ty lets him go. No challenge, no fighting back. Ty was disrespected and he did nothing.

This can't be good.

I'm standing in the foyer when Ty re-enters the house.

"What was that all about?" I ask.

"What? Nothin'—jus' hadda give my friend something."

"He didn't look like a friend to me."

Ty brushes past me and heads to the kitchen. "Don't worry about it, Audge. I got it under control."

I trot after him, addressing his strong, sinewy back. "Ty, if you're in some kind of trouble, I want you to know you can tell me about it. I'll help you. If you need a lawyer—"

Ty spins around. "This ain't work for no damn *lawyer*."

There's anger in his eyes, but bigger than anger, there's fear. My heart sinks.

"Ty, what does Mondel Johnson want with you?" I dredged the name out of my memory of the conversation with Coughlin. It sails through the air and hits Ty like an arrow through the heart. Anger disappears; fear consumes him.

"How d'you know that name?" His voice is a hoarse whisper, as if Johnson were in the next room.

"That cop, Coughlin, told me. He thinks you're selling drugs for the guy Johnson works for."

"Me!" Ty's voice comes out like a cartoon character's squeak. "I ain't sellin' drugs. Audge, c'mon—you know I don't mess with that shit."

"Well then, what's going on? Why were you talking to him? Why have you been so jumpy and secretive?"

Ty backs away from me, shaking his head. "This ain't nothin' that concerns you."

"Nothing that concerns me? It concerns me if the guy I saw pushing you around is the same guy who cracked my head like an egg." The words fly out of my mouth before I think about their effect.

Ty seems to get bigger before my eyes. He pounds his chest with his thumb. "You think I'm responsible for you gettin' hurt? You think I let them mess with you insteada me?"

"Coughlin thinks you owe them money. That they took it from me when they couldn't get it from you."

"This don't have nuthin' to do with money. This is bigger than money."

"What could be bigger than money to a drug dealer?"

Ty's face becomes a block of stone. "Audge, what you don't know won't hurt you. Or me."

"But it is hurting me, Ty. The police aren't looking for the man who really attacked me because they think you did it. Coughlin is following you. He sees you talking to that Mondel guy."

A crease of worry appears on Ty's forehead. I'm getting through to him at last.

"I thought that big cop was off your case. What happened to the skinny guy with the brown hair?"

"Detective Farrand is still investigating my assault. I don't know if he's getting anywhere or not." I look down. It's hard for me to say this. I'm supposed to be the boss, the grown-up. "I'm scared Ty. Creepy things keep happening to me. I feel like someone's watching me, like whoever attacked me isn't quite done."

"What you mean?" Ty's shoulders go back and his chin juts forward. This is the Ty I know, always ready to protect his turf.

So I tell Ty that someone was in my condo going through the trunk of jewelry, about the person I thought followed me from Dad's house, and the missing yearbook.

Ty looks at me quizzically. "I don't know, Audge. If Mondel's crew found that jewelry at your place, they woulda took it, know what I'm sayin'?"

I do know what he's saying, which is why all of this continues to make no sense. "What about those pills we found in the kitchen, Ty? Did Mondel take them back? Does he think we kept some of them or something?"

"Them pills don't belong to Mondel. Guy he works for deals strictly in weed and blow. Stuff that gets smuggled in through Mexico."

"So who did they belong to?"

Ty shrugs. "Some white dude, probably. That's who mostly sells pills."

Ty says this so matter-of-factly that I assume it's true, but really, how can I be sure? Coughlin would know. I'm right back where I started, wondering if I should confide in Coughlin or not.

"Ty, I never told the police that it was you who found the Ecstasy in Mrs. Szabo's house, and that you immediately turned it over to me. If I told that to Coughlin now, I think it would take some of the suspicion off you. After all, if you needed money to pay off Mondel, you could've kept that Ecstasy, but you didn't. So I think I should tell him, OK?"

Ty snorts. "Tell him. Don't tell him. Won't make no difference. That cop got it in for me. Even after I get clear of Mondel, Coughlin still be watchin' me."

I look into Ty's big brown eyes. "Are you going to get clear of Mondel?"

"This weekend, Audge. Everything be straight then."

I'd love to believe him, but something tells me Ty is playing with fire, a fire he can't control. "Look, Ty, let's tell Coughlin everything. About the Ecstasy, about your problem with Mondel. Let the police figure it out. That would be the safest option."

Ty looks weary, like he's lived as long as the folks at Manor View. "You know the problem with you, Audge? You too nice. An' then you think everybody else as nice as you. World don't work that way."

Chapter 38

I've been driving around for two days with the crushed baby doll carriage in the trunk of my car. Why was it flattened? Why was it buried? If it was broken or I lost interest in it, why didn't Dad or my grandparents just throw it away? Every time I open the trunk, I ask those questions. I'm not sure why this toy has such a powerful hold on me. I can't bring myself to throw it out. And I'm certainly not going to bring the filthy, broken thing into my condo. So it stays in the trunk, going everywhere I go. Finally, after about the tenth time I'm startled by it lying there, I realize where I need to take it.

Mrs. Olsen puts a plate of cookies and a pot of tea on the table between us. "You went through a phase," she says, "when you were obsessed with burials."

"I did? Why?"

"When you got old enough to understand about funerals and cemeteries, you started asking to visit your mother's grave. Your grandparents had insisted on having a marker for Charlotte at St. Paul's cemetery, but of course, there're was no one buried there because your mother's body was never recovered. Your father never believed in sugar-coating things for you, and he told you the truth when you asked if your mom was in there. This was when you were about six or seven, I guess, and you had seen some elaborate burial on a TV show. So, you started wanting to give everything a funeral. You buried your goldfish when it died, and Melanie's gerbil got a state funeral. You buried Barbie dolls with missing limbs and ripped stuffed animals. So it doesn't surprise me that you'd want to bury a broken doll carriage."

Why is this all a blank to me? I can recall things that happened in first grade; why can't I find a memory of digging little graves and interring dolls and pets?

"You don't remember this?" Mrs. Olsen asks.

I shake my head as I focus on the crinkle of smile lines radiating from my friend's brown eyes and the soft, pillowy expanse of her bosom. I want to lay my head there, but I hold myself back somehow. "It's kind of morbid, Mrs. O. Didn't anyone try to stop me?"

"I think it upset your grandmother a bit. But I felt we should let you do what you needed to do. You were obviously working through some issues. Eventually you stopped. The funerals weren't necessary anymore. You moved on."

Yeah, right.

"Thanks for telling me this. There was something about that carriage, some memory floating around the edge of my brain, that I couldn't quite grab hold of."

"Maybe now you can throw the silly thing away."

"Yeah." I pick up another cookie. I'm not hungry, but I'm not ready to leave. There's more I need to ask. "Mrs. Olsen, did my mother ever talk to you about her work? Mention who her clients were, what projects she was working on?"

She shrugs. "Not so much. I was a little touchy about having given up my career for the kids, so Charlotte avoided the subject of her work. Why?"

When I don't answer, Mrs. Olsen takes my hand in hers and simply holds it. The gentle reassurance of her gesture melts something deep inside me. Soon, the words are tumbling out. I tell her all my suspicions: that my mother ran off with another man, gave birth to a child who's my half-sibling, is out there still.

When I've talked myself dry, she continues to sit there, never letting go of my hand. "What are you thinking?" I finally ask.

"She wouldn't have abandoned you, Audrey. I'm sure of that."

I slip my hand out of her grasp and stand to go. Does Mrs. Olsen really know what my mother would have done? Maybe all my old friend knows is that *she* would never have abandoned *her* child, and she can't imagine a mother who would.

"Thanks for the cookies," I say.

"Visit me any time." Mrs. Olsen walks with me to the front door, bending to pick up a pile of mail the mailman stuffed through the slot while we talked. "Nothing but junk to recycle," she complains.

"Once the election's over, there will be less," I say, as I watch her sorting through all the political flyers.

"Thank goodness." She laughs and holds up a blue pamphlet plastered with Spencer's smiling face. "Hey, here's someone your mother used to work for. I do remember that she came up with the slogan for his campaign, and he was crazy about it. 'Spencer Finneran for Congress. *Honestly.*' Kind of a play on words, because he was the long-shot underdog and his opponent was a real crook. Get it?"

Too stunned to answer, I just nod.

I get it.

Chapter 39

Palmer County weather for this Halloween—bee-yoo-ti ful. Tell mom no heavy coat over the costumes, 'cause there's zero chance of rain and the low is a balmy 60. And there's going to be a FULL moon, so watch out. Now, back to the music...

Damn! I totally forgot today is Halloween. After leaving Mrs. Olsen's house I feel like driving directly to the Finnerans, pounding on the door and demanding to know why Spencer lied about knowing my mother. But Spencer, Anne and Cal are on the road campaigning today, wearing silly Democratic donkey-ear hats and handing out candy and blue Finneran buttons.

I make a sharp right into the ShopRite parking lot—may as well buy a few bags of candy right now. I used to get only a few trick-or-treaters, toddlers of the young couples who live in the condo development. But two years ago, word went out on the teen grapevine that working the condos is a great way to score a lot of candy with very little walking. Now, the doorbell rings nonstop for three hours, and woe be the person who comes up short on candy—eggs on the front door, shaving cream on the windows.

When I finish my run to the supermarket and make it home, I see my neighbor, Marge, by the mailboxes. "All ready for tonight?" I ask.

"I've got five bags of Skittles," Marge folds her arms across her chest. "When that runs out, I'm turning out my lights and locking my doors. And if my bell rings after nine o'clock, I'm calling the cops."

I'm not as crabby as my neighbor, but frankly, I'm happy to have Marge take a hard line on late-night revelers. Although I try to hide it, I'm still plenty jumpy around strangers at night. At least I have Ethel to protect me.

At home, I click on the front porch light and sit back to wait. At first, Ethel barks frantically each time the doorbell rings, but she soon realizes that the intruders aren't coming onto her turf, so she settles down in the foyer and keeps a watchful eye on the proceedings. The little princesses and pirates are done by seven, the hippies and ninjas peter out by eight-thirty. There's a lull, then the bell rings insistently. I open the door and a crowd of kids, dressed as sullen teenagers, thrust their bags at me silently. I dole out one candy bar apiece and shout "you're welcome" to their retreating backs. No sooner do I sit down than the bell rings again. This crowd is also uncostumed, although one kid has made an effort by wearing a "scream" mask. They have the decency to look sheepish demanding their loot, and they chorus "thank you" as they leave. I hope Marge takes note of that.

Outside, the shouts of kids grow fainter and fainter. The evening seems to be winding down. Ethel and I are absorbed in the final minutes of "When Good Dogs Go Bad" on Animal Planet, when the doorbell rings again. I hesitate, but it's under Marge's deadline, so I open the door.

A strangled shriek springs from my throat and the basket of candy hits the floor.

On the stoop stand four men dressed all in black. They leer at me through pantyhose that flatten their noses and distort their lips. Ethel's hackles rise and she barks harsh, staccato notes.

One drops to his knees. Why is he trying to crawl into my

house? Frantically I move to shut the door. Ethel lunges at him.

Too late I realize they're laughing. The one on his knees is trying to scoop up the fallen candy. Ethel is having none of this. She nips his hand.

"Ow! What the fuck!"

They turn and run off.

"I'm sorry!" I shout after them. "You shouldn't have scared me like that."

Kicking aside the candy, I slam the door. My hands are shaking so badly I have trouble turning off the porch light. I slide into a heap on the floor and rest my head on Ethel's back.

I'm done with Halloween.

An hour, some deep breathing exercises, and a cup of green tea later, I've returned to my logical self. I'm sitting at the dining room table working on my accounts payable when I realize I've left an entire folder of invoices back at the office. Go get it or leave it until tomorrow? I really want to get these bills postmarked by November 1, and tomorrow is already jam-packed with appointments. With all the adrenaline circulating in my system from my scare, I'm feeling wide awake. Might as well go and get this project finished up.

"Ethel, want to go for a ride in the car?"

But Ethel is snoring on the sofa and doesn't even hear the magical "c" word. Fine, I'll go solo.

The folder was just where I left it, and I'm back home within a half hour. Turning the key in the lock, I use my hip to push open the door, then brace for the Ethel onslaught. It doesn't come.

She must be sulking because I went out without her. I drop the folder on the table in the dark hall and sniff. What's that smell? Has the dog gotten into something?

"Eth—"

Something wraps around my neck, cutting off my voice. Ridiculously, my immediate impulse is to scream.

Nothing. Screaming requires air and I have none.

The smell is stronger. Warmth. Dampness. Hair.

My senses sort it out. A human arm is wrapped around my neck. The rest of the human is behind me, breathing in my ear.

"Me and you need to have a little talk," the voice says. I don't recognize it except in a generic way: male, Jersey, white. His grip tightens around my neck and I feel my feet leave the floor. Instinctively, I claw at the arm. It's like scratching at a metal pipe. "A quiet talk. Understand?"

I try to nod. The arm loosens a bit. My feet come back down to earth. There's a steel-toe boot under my sneaker. I can swallow, but my heart is pounding so hard it's still hard to breathe. The smell catches in the back of my throat. Sweat, covered by too much strong, musky cologne.

"You don't learn, do you? You and the kid got some customers for my product, that's fine. But you two work for me, not on your own." He shakes me. "Understand?"

The kid? What the hell is he talking about? He thinks Ty and I are both selling his pills? But Ty doesn't know this guy....I don't understand. Not at all. But I'm afraid to say anything. All I can think of is the sound of my skull cracking the last time that boot connected with my head. I don't want that pain again. I don't want to be in the hospital. I don't want to die.

"Please..." I whisper.

"And now you got Mondel Johnson sniffing around you. What's up with that? Huh?"

"I don't know him. He—"

· The arm crushes my neck. "You lie! I've seen him watching your office. You think you're some kinda player. We all got our turf. You don't mess with that, hear?"

He stays behind me. I can't see his face, but I can smell his breath. Cigarettes. Beer. Onions. And that awful cologne. Repulsive—I twist my head to keep my face as far away from his as I can. It's so dark in the hall, I can't even see the color of the skin of his arm. If only I can get him to understand that I didn't take his drugs. That I'm not trying to pull something over on him. "Please," I gasp. "Let me talk."

I hear whining and scratching. Ethel. I'd forgotten about her. It sounds like she's in the powder room. He must've shut her in there when he broke in. Now that she's heard my voice, she's flinging herself against the door, desperate to get out. Once. Twice. I know what's coming. Ethel can open the lever handle of that door if she hits it just right.

Boom. The door flies open and hits the wall. In three seconds, Ethel is in the front hall. She leaps on my attacker, tail wagging, tongue slobbering.

"What the fuck!" With one swing of the guy's arm, Ethel is airborne and I'm out of his grasp. She crashes against the wall, and crumples in a heap.

I shriek. And then I kick the guy. "You didn't have to hurt her. She's just an innocent dog."

Bad move. He picks me up and pins me against the wall. A nylon stocking covers his head, distorting his features, and gloves hide his hands. It's dark, but now that my eyes have adjusted, I can see his neck and his arms. He's white. His hair is brown and there's lots of it. Holding his face inches from mine, he exhales his putrid breath with every word.

"I run a simple business," he says. "Killing people's not my style. But I might make an exception for you, stupid bitch." He slaps me across the face. The sound of the blow shocks me as much as the pain. "Now, you and boy wonder-- Augh!"

Suddenly, I'm free.

"Ow! Get off of me. Fuckin' dog's biting me!"

Fur swishes by my face. Nails scrabble on the floor. I mostly see outlines, but I know what's going on. Ethel has sunk her teeth into him and she's not letting go.

He shakes his leg, and Ethel rises up into the air with it. Her jaw is locked on his calf, and I can see the white flash of her bared teeth.

For a moment I'm paralyzed, not sure what to do. Then reason kicks in. I reach for my cell phone and dial 911.

"Palmyrton Police. What is your emergency?" The voice is calm, bland, unflappable.

"There's a man in my house. He's trying to kill me and my dog. Send someone fast. 419 Bishop."

He's trying to pull Ethel off now, but that just makes her clamp down harder. He swings his free leg back to kick her, but she dodges the blow. All the while he's screaming, "fuck, fuck, fuck" at the top of his voice.

"Can I verify your address, M'am?" The dispatcher sounds bored out of her mind.

"419 Bishop," I yell into the phone. Then I stuff it into my pocket without hanging up and turn my attention to the fight. I've never seen Ethel like this. Her courage gives me courage. I look around for something I can use to defend myself. I've had enough of this crap. Enough of being a victim. Enough of not knowing who's after me or why. Ethel and I are keeping this guy here until the cops come. I switch on the overhead light and grab the heavy ginger jar lamp from the hall table.

"Call off your damn dog! Make her let me go!" I hear fear in his voice, the panic of someone who's lost control.

And no wonder. Ethel's no longer a house pet; she's a rabid wolf. Her big canine incisors, stained red with her victim's blood, are sunk into the flesh of his calf. Ears flat against her head, eyes bulging, she looks like a creature at the top of the food chain. Weird guttural whines rumble from somewhere deep inside her. She's scaring me. I'm not sure I could call her off even if I wanted to.

My hand tightens on the lamp. Am I brave enough to swing this thing like a bat right into his head? Am I brutal enough to crack his head the way he cracked mine? I lift the lamp up, but my arm trembles.

Then I see a metallic flash. A knife. His right arm comes up, ready to plunge the blade into Ethel's neck. I swing! The lamp crashes against his head and shatters in a million pieces.

He staggers. The knife falls beside him. But the shower of ceramic shards has distracted Ethel. She loosens her grip and my attacker shakes free of her. In the distance, I hear sirens. I search for another weapon, but the foyer doesn't have much to offer. "Get him again Ethel!" I shout.

She springs, but just misses him. He grabs his knife and charges out the door with Ethel on his heels.

Leaping down the stairs to the sidewalk three at a time, he opens a lead between him and the dog. I'm running after both of them, screaming like a crazy woman. But it's Halloween—my neighbors have tuned out the noise and turned off their lights.

I keep running, not to catch him, but to keep him in sight until the cops come. The moon, so brilliant just half an hour ago, has slipped behind a bank of clouds. Now my condo development is full of shadows and inky recesses. Ahead of me, Ethel and my attacker disappear into the next cul de sac.

Chapter 40

I turn the corner.

Four parked cars. Two fluttering witch flags. One smashed Snickers.

"Ethel?"

Silence. A sputtering jack-o-lantern winks at me from a doorstep. Nothing stirs.

I spin around. "Ethel? Ethel!"

The sirens are drawing closer. I race out of the cul de sac and dart into the street. "Ethel!" Where is she? I picture the knife in that goon's hand. What if Ethel caught up to him and he stabbed her?

"Eth-hel!" my voice is shrill with panic and fear. She won't come to me if she hears that. She'll think she's in trouble and keep running.

If she's able.

I take a breath and try to steady my voice. "Ethel, here girl. Come, Ethel. Come get a treat." I produce a linty snack from my coat pocket. "Eth—hel, look what I've got. Come!"

Through the trees, I can see the flashing red and blue lights as squad cars pull up to my door. I want to run over to them, but not without Ethel.

I keep circling the complex, calling until my voice is hoarse. As I head into the last cul de sac, I hear footsteps behind me.

A cop shines a bright flashlight beam into my face. What does he see? A crazed woman with a tearstained face, uncombed hair and a crumbling Milk-Bone in her hand.

"Have you been drinking, ma'am?"

"No! I'm the one who called…the man was in my condo…my dog chased him out here…now she's lost."

"Let's calm down ma'am. Let's go back to your condo and sort this out." He reaches for my elbow, but I shake him off.

"I have to find my dog. She's lost out here. Ethel!"

The cop shines his flashlight into the underbrush. Two eyes glow.

"Ethel!"

A fat raccoon waddles out, looks at us with contempt, and slithers into a storm drain. Hot tears well in my eyes. Ethel is out here somewhere, with wild animals. She doesn't know how to protect herself. She doesn't know how to find food. She'll see a chipmunk and chase it right into the path of a speeding car, I know she will. Oh, Ethel!

"Call animal control in the morning," the cop says. "Put up a few flyers. I'm sure she'll turn up." He takes my arm firmly and reports via radio that he's found me.

The thought of Ethel's smiling face on a Lost Dog poster completely unhinges me. No one ever looks for the dogs on those things. Ethel will wander onto Route 80 and be flattened by a semi. She'll starve and her collar will fall off and she'll wind up in the pound and they'll send her to the gas chamber. I'll never find her.

"Ma'am, let's—"

"No!" I start running, calling frantically for Ethel. Up ahead, three men are coming toward me. One is very big. I stop, too frightened to go forward, too panicked to go back. I put my arms over my head and sink to the ground.

Moments later, a hand is pulling me up and a familiar voice speaks. "Are you all right, Ms. Nealon? We need you to come inside so we can get your statement."

I open my eyes. It's Detective Farrand. The big guy with him is Coughlin. "My dog…"

"The patrolmen will look for Ethel, Audrey," Coughlin pulls out his phone. "I'm calling the animal control officer myself, right now."

I listen as Coughlin reports Ethel missing, then numbly, I let them guide me back home. The entire Palmyrton police department and ambulance squad is in my condo filling every square inch with squawking radios, crime scene paraphernalia and first aid tool boxes. I'm pushed along like a can on the conveyer belt at the supermarket. First the EMT examines me, then Farrand questions me, then someone takes my fingerprints, then Coughlin questions me. I keep asking each one if he knows who this drug dealer is, but none of them will give me a straight answer. Through it all, my front door opens and shuts, admitting more cops. Each time my head springs up, hoping someone is bringing Ethel home. Each time I'm disappointed.

I see Coughlin and Farrand talking to each other, then Farrand shrugs and Coughlin wags his finger, and they both come to talk to me again.

Coughlin leads off. "Audrey, there's no sign of forced entry anywhere in the apartment. Your windows are all locked; you've got deadbolts on both doors."

I spring up from my chair. "What are you saying? You think I let this guy in? That it's someone I know and I'm lying to you?"

Farrand ignores this outburst and gestures me back into my seat. "Tell me again about the trick-or-treaters. Did you lock the front door after each visit?"

"No, I was answering the door pretty steadily there for a while. I shut it, but left it unlocked."

"So someone could have slipped in between kids and hidden in the front closet," Farrand says.

"No, Ethel would've barked." Then I run my fingers through my hair. "Well, maybe—she was barking off and on all night. But if he was in the closet all along, why did he wait until I went out and came back to attack me?"

Coughlin looks pointedly at Farrand, as if that's the point he's been trying to make all along. "Audrey, I think this guy may have the key to your condo. Did you change your locks after the first attack?"

"No, but he didn't take my keys. They were in my pocket, and at the hospital, they gave them to you, right?"

Coughlin nods. "They were in an evidence locker until I returned them to you when you left the hospital. Who else has a key to your place?"

"Jill, because she watches Ethel for me if I'm away. And my dad."

"Griggs could've gotten access to the key though Jill." Coughlin says this as a statement, not a question.

I'm tired of arguing on this point. Who the hell knows—maybe Coughlin is right. "Yes."

"Your father is in a nursing home, correct?" Farrand says.

"Yes. He doesn't have my key with him there. It's at his house. He keeps it—"

I picture it clearly. My key is attached to a red plastic keychain, the kind you can label. My father has written "Audrey's Condo" on the tab in his perfect printing. It hangs on a hook in the mudroom.

"—keeps it on a hook by the back door. With my name on it. I don't know if it's still there."

Coughlin leans forward. "Who has access to his house?"

I tick off the names on my fingers. "Ty, Jill, Isabelle Trent, the real estate agent, and maybe a guy named Brian Bascomb who visits my father at the nursing home. "And," I look at Farrand, "whoever broke into my dad's house and took the yearbook and the file folder."

The EMT returns, demanding to take my blood pressure one more time, while Coughlin and Farrand retreat to the front hall for more talk.

"Coming back to normal," the EMT says, "but you really shouldn't be alone. Is there someone you can call to come stay with you?"

Is there? I can't very well call Lydia at 2AM and ask her to leave her baby to come tend to me. I guess I could call Jill, but she's so jumpy and excitable that we'd both be awake all night long. And I'd have to tell her about Ethel. I can't face that. I shake my head.

"A guy friend," the EMT persists. "You know, so you'd feel a little safer."

Cal. Could I call Cal in the middle of the night to say I need him? Can I wake Cal up and say I know you're tired from campaigning all day but can you drop everything and come and protect me?

No.

"I don't want to bother anyone," I say, but I'm terrified. I can't stay here if this creep has my key.

Eventually the EMT finishes and a few more cops filter out with him. That leaves Coughlin and two other cops, huddled in my livingroom.

All I want to do is have a stiff drink and take hot shower to finally scrub away the smell of sweat and cigarettes and overpowering cologne that still clings to me.

"I'm going to take a shower," I announce. When I come out of the bathroom, Coughlin is sitting on my sofa.

"Thanks for waiting. Maybe I should stay at a hotel tonight, until I can get the locks changed."

He doesn't move.

"You can't sit here all night."

Coughlin glances my way, as if he's barely aware that I've spoken.

Outside, a car door slams. I jump and clutch my chest like an actor in a spaghetti western who's milking his big death scene. Coughlin says nothing, just extends his hand.

Suddenly the fight goes out of me. I'm tired and scared and lonely and heartbroken. I sink onto the sofa, horrified to feel hot tears welling in my eyes. I rest my head on his massive chest. He smells plain and clean: Tide, Dial, Colgate. Under his shirt his heart gives powerful, slow beats. I let my breathing synchronize with his.

I'll just rest for a minute.

When my eyes next open, sun is streaming through my livingroom window and the scent of fresh coffee hangs in the air. I rotate my stiff neck. Why did I sleep on the sofa? I catch sight of the clock on the cable box: 8:30. Ethel will be—

Ethel.

Despair rushes back to claim me. But maybe she came back during the night. Maybe she's on the front porch, waiting to come in.

Staggering up from the sofa, I notice a crushed cushion on the chair next to me. I see the full coffeepot on the kitchen island. Coughlin stayed here all night? I can't believe it. I open my mouth to call out, but suddenly I'm shy. What do I call a man who held me when I was frightened, who spent the night watching over me in an uncomfortable chair, who made me coffee?

Detective? Sean?

I run to the door to look for Ethel. Instead, I see Coughlin unlocking his car. He looks up and offers a mock salute, then gets in his car and drives off.

Last night's clouds have blown away, and every tree and bush and car is outlined in the bright, hard sunlight. The street is empty. Ethel is gone.

I cry and cry. No one hears.

Chapter 41

Anne steps over the huge retriever sprawled across the threshold to the kitchen. Bix opens one eye, just like Ethel does. It takes every ounce of self-control to keep from collapsing on top of the dog and burying my head in his shaggy, honey-colored fur.

"Have you had lunch, Audrey? I have more food than I know what to do with after Nora and Jim's anniversary party."

There's always some kind of Finneran family get-together to keep that hulking stainless steel fridge stuffed, but I'm too keyed up to consider eating. "No thank you. I really appreciate your seeing me on such short notice." As soon as Detective Coughlin left this morning, I called the locksmith. Then I called Anne. Didn't even think it through, just dialed, blurted out that I knew my mother had worked directly with Spencer, and said I needed to talk to her. Any tact that I ever possessed has been driven away by this second attack and the loss of Ethel. To her credit, Anne didn't try to bullshit me-- she told me to come on over.

Anne smiles and her laugh lines crease, but her eyes have a distant look. "No trouble at all dear. I've been looking forward to your visit." She extends her arm. "Come on in here where no one will bother us."

I follow her through a door off the kitchen that I never noticed before. Behind it is a cozy little office/sitting room with two shabby chintz easy chairs and a desk overflowing with piles of paper. Framed photos cover the walls—not pictures of Anne and Spencer with presidents and senators and rock stars, but candid snapshots of kids and grandkids at the beach, on skis, in class plays, Spencer at the helm of a sailboat, Anne decorating a Christmas tree. Sun streams through the window, illuminating a big vase of fresh flowers. They have to be from a florist since nothing's blooming locally now, but somehow Anne's arranged them in a loose, tumbling way that makes it seem like she just picked them in her back yard.

"What a great room," I say.

"Thank you. It used to be a maid's room, back in the days when the maid had to wake up early to light the coal stove." Anne makes a wry little face. "Most days I feel like it's still the maid's room." She waves me into one chair and sits herself in the other.

For a moment there's an awkward silence as we gaze at each other, uncertain where to begin. Then Anne plunges in. All these years as a politician's wife have taught her how to manage any type of conversation, even one about how she and Spencer lied about knowing my mother.

"So, you want to know about your mother, and the work she did for Spencer's campaign. Well, you've seen her pictures so you know she was beautiful, but photos really don't do her justice. She was—how can I express it?—simply vibrant." Anne reaches over and pats my hand. "I don't mean this unkindly dear, because in many ways I feel you and I are very much alike, but your mother could command attention in a way that women like us will never be able to fathom. She didn't do it with sexy clothing or provocative behavior. It was something much more subtle—and powerful—than that." Anne shakes her head and pauses.

"I guess she was born with it," I say, "and it skipped a generation in me."

Anne's eyes meet mine. "She was born with it, but just as one cultivates an inherent talent for art or music, your mother worked hard to develop her gift."

I squirm under her gaze. "Sounds like you knew my mother pretty well. When did you first meet her?"

"Oh, I only talked to her a few times, but she made quite an impression." Anne curls up in her chair, her eyes focused on a point over the desk. I know she's looking back to a time before I was born. "Spencer and I lived in DC when we first married. He had a job on Capitol Hill." The silence stretches on until I can't bear it any more.

"But then something brought you to New Jersey," I prompt.

Anne jumps a little, as if she's forgotten I'm there. "Yes, Spencer decided he wanted to run for elective office. We moved back to Palmyrton so he could make a run for Congress."

"Back to Palmyrton?"

Anne arches her eyebrows ever so slightly. "My family has always lived here."

Always. I think about the oil portraits in the upstairs hall, the Duncan Phyfe chairs. The Piersons have been here since the Revolution. "Your family connections would help him win." I say it as a statement, not a question.

Anne offers a shallow smile. "My father persuaded the Palmer County Democratic party machine that Spencer was their best hope against an entrenched Republican. He raised a small fortune to finance that campaign. And it was all lost, because of her..." Even after thirty-five years the bitterness in her voice is unmistakable.

"Because of my mother? Why?"

"It was a razor thin race. Spencer was a dark horse. No one thought he stood a chance, but slowly he started creeping up in the polls. He needed the very best campaign team to keep the momentum going. Charlotte started out doing brilliant work for the campaign. Writing speeches, coming up with slogans, managing events. Whenever I crossed her path, she was at the center of a whirlwind of activity."

It hits me hard that Anne must have never liked my mother, even before she supposedly cost Spencer the race. "So what changed?" I ask.

"All those long hours away from her husband and child, in the company of journalists and politicians and PR men..." Anne arches her eyebrows. "She fell in love with one of them. Fell hard. Suddenly her work went out the window. She started missing ad deadlines, forgetting important appointments, scheduling Spencer to be in two places at the same time. The kicker came when she arranged for Spencer to be interviewed on the Today show as part of a profile on up and coming young politicians. Charlotte got the day wrong and the reporter kept looking at the empty chair on the stage and commenting on Spencer's absence. Her antics cost Spencer the election."

I watch Anne's mouth harden into a thin line. Something about this doesn't seem right. After all, Spencer went on to have great political success. Why is Anne still so angry at my mother? "There's something more, isn't there, Anne? Something personal."

Anne's fingers dig into the dainty needlepoint pillow on her chair, and she continues. "You have to understand the times your mother and I were living in. On TV and in magazines, Gloria Steinem and Betty Friedan were telling us we could be anything we wanted to be, that we didn't have to be confined to the roles of wife and mother. That we could enjoy sex wherever we found it, just as men have always done." Anne stretches out her legs and studies the gold buckles on her proper black flats. "They were the generals in the Pentagon. As in every war, the reality on the ground was quite different."

Anne looks directly into my eyes. "I had just about convinced my parents and Spencer that it would be a great idea for me to go back to law school. Then your mother came along—the living embodiment of every anti-feminist stereotype. Women are a distraction in the workplace. Women are too emotional to be trusted with important work. Working women destroy their families."

I feel an irrational need to defend my mother, the adulteress. "You're blaming my mother because you didn't get to become a lawyer?"

"That's an oversimplification. Of course I could have dug in my heels and fought for what I wanted. But what happened to Charlotte made me question whether I really did want that career."

"What happened between the election and Christmas Eve?" I ask. "Who was this mystery lover?"

I watch Anne closely. Of course it's dawned on me that the other man could've been Spencer. I know she'll never admit to me that her husband ever had an affair—not now, just days before the election. But I should be able to tell, shouldn't I, if I've brushed too close to the truth?

Anne shrugs. When she speaks, he voice is no more anxious than when she's puzzling over menu choices with her caterer. "No one was sure; so many men were besotted with her, it was rather difficult to tell. And she must've been discreet about the actual...er...assignations. But the rumor was he also was married."

"Why didn't Mr. Van Houten tell me any of this?"

Anne smiles. "Even Reid Van Houten wasn't immune to her charms."

"You think Mr. Van Houten was her lover?"

"No, but he probably knew who was. However, Reid was the consummate gentleman, then and now. He protected Charlotte when Spencer and my father wanted her fired. After the election was lost, my father was so furious he threatened to blackball Reid from the entire Palmyrton business community if he didn't get rid of Charlotte." Anne leans forward and takes my hand. "So you can understand why Spencer and I felt it was easier to tell a little white lie at dinner and say we barely knew her. Why rake up all this past unpleasantness when Spencer and I both think of you as such a wonderful match for our dear Cal."

I try to smile; I'm sure Anne notices it's a little stiff. Sliding my hand out of her grasp I ask, "So, did Reid fire her?"

"He decided Charlotte had better start looking for a new job. From what Spencer told me, the plan was to break the news to her right after the holidays."

"But—"

Anne shrugs. "Maybe she suspected something. Maybe she called her lover on Christmas Eve. Maybe things were said. The holidays are a difficult time to be the other woman. Or so I've been told."

"You think she—" I can't bring myself to say "killed herself."

Anne simply spreads her hands. Anything is possible, she implies. Anything is possible when you've betrayed your husband and someone else's husband has betrayed you. You kill yourself and the baby you no longer want and leave your daughter motherless.

My trembling hands rest in my lap. I realize I've been twisting my mother's ring around and around as I try to process what Anne is telling me. Was my saintly mother really a sexually liberated temptress? My aloof, logical father a wronged husband? The dignified Mr. VanHouten a lovestruck fool? Who are these people? I feel like I'm watching a soap opera in which the lead characters are suddenly being played by new actors, with no explanation made to the loyal viewers.

If my mother killed herself, how did the ring get in Mrs. Szabo's attic? And why was my father so surprised to see it?

The cheery melody of my cellphone's ring breaks the heavy silence. Normally I'd switch it off with an apology, but I'm grateful for the interruption. I want to get out of here. I glance at the caller ID, prepared to tell Anne it's an important call no matter who's calling. Palmyrton PD flashes on the screen. No need to lie; it *is* an important call.

"It's the police," I say. "I'd better answer."

Anne nods, watching me as I listen to Detective Farrand. When I hang up, I feel a smile spreading across my face. I want to share my good news. "They've caught the guy who broke into my apartment."

"Thank God! Who is it?"

"They wouldn't tell me his name yet, but he's a drug dealer with a record. They found him because he went to the emergency room to have his dog bite treated."

"And do they think he's the same man who beat and robbed you in the parking garage?"

"I don't know." Unexpectedly, I feel tears pricking my eyelids. "I hope so. I really need this to be over. Detective Farrand says they're interrogating him now."

Anne tugs me out of my chair and wraps her arms around me. "I'm sure the police will get to the bottom of it. Then you can finally sleep easy."

Chapter 42

Telling Jill about Ethel's disappearance is the second worst thing I've ever had to do. We spend a good fifteen minutes crying in each other's arms, then Jill pulls herself together and, mustering her formidable artistic talents, creates the most compelling lost dog flyer I've ever seen.

Ethel stares out at the world, her eyebrows arched, her tail held high. In the photo, her mouth is slightly open and Jill has created a cartoon bubble that says, "Bring me home. My mom needs me." We hang these all over Palmyrton, especially in Ethel's favorite haunts: the bagel shop, the park, and the neighborhoods around the office and home. Everywhere we go, we look for her, call for her, but the streets are depressingly devoid of unsupervised dogs. Finally, with 200 flyers taped to poles and pinned to bulletin boards, we head back to the office. Jill and Ty head off to our newest job, but I'm too distracted to work.

For the fourth time today, I check in with Animal Control. No Ethel. Don't call us, we'll call you. Maybe Detective Farrand will be a little more willing to talk. I call for an update on the man they arrested. I want to know where he ran after he left my house; how far Ethel followed him. But after four rings, I'm sent to voicemail.

Taking a deep breath, I dial Coughlin. Same deal—leave a message after the beep. I could call Cal, but my fingers stubbornly refuse to dial. The break-in at my condo has been reported on the local news, and Anne has certainly told Spencer about my visit. Surely, Cal should call me. I put my phone in my pocket.

Cal. A guy hasn't done this big a number on my head since my totally unrequited crush on Billy Bednarchuk in tenth grade. As a sophomore, I risked suspension to let Billy copy all my answers during Calculus, just to keep him smiling at me all semester. And once he got his A, he never even nodded to me in the halls. Seventeen years later, have I wised up any? I study the ring on my finger. Cal and I are linked by this ring. Somewhere along the line, his aunt came into contact with my mother. He claims he barely knew his great-aunt, but is that true? He said he'd ask his mother about Agnes's past, but did he? He arranged to get Coughlin taken off my case, and Farrand put on, but who's the better cop? Yet I continue to lie for Cal. Even as terrified as I was last night, I still didn't tell Coughlin or Farrand about the trunk of jewelry or who really found the Ecstasy. The detectives have made me realize there are only a few degrees of separation between my condo keys and just about anyone in the state of New Jersey. That puts the search of the trunk while it was in my closet in a new light. Someone had to be looking for the one thing that was missing from the trunk.

I hold up my hand. This ring.

My dad knew I had the ring, but didn't know the trunk was in my condo. Cal, Jill and Ty knew I had the trunk, but at the time the trunk was searched, didn't know I had taken the ring. My head starts to throb the way it did when I first got out of the hospital. I feel like I used to feel in AP English Lit, the only class I ever got a C in. Making sense of the ring, Cal, my mother and father is like spotting the metaphors in poetry, a task in which it seemed to me there was never a definite right answer, only plenty of wrong ones.

Now what?

Shakily, I stand up and reach for my car keys. Until either

Coughlin or Farrand calls me back, there's not much I can do. Not much except something even more awful than telling Jill about Ethel: tell my father.

Dad makes it easy for me. When I show up in his room, he lurches out of his chair, nearly falling into my arms. "Wha' happen? You hur'?"

I'm surprised he even knows about the break-in. He never watches TV, and the incident happened too late last night to make this morning's *Daily Record*.

I ease him back into a chair. "I'm okay…I guess." I tell him the good news first. "The police called this morning. They caught the guy."

Dad's face lights up. "Goo'! Who? How?"

Now the bad news. I start with Ethel's heroic defense, and end with the Lost Dog flyers. As I speak, Dad's gaze shifts away from my face. By the time I finish, he's looking out the window. Once again, I've let him down. Lost the one thing about me of which he approved.

He sits silently for a moment, then pushes himself out of his chair. "Less go."

"Go where?"

"My house. I show you whatta kee' Everthin' else, go."

I'm about to protest—not today-- but then I figure, why not? I can't concentrate on work. This will keep me occupied.

In silence, we drive to the house. An empty Dumpster occupies the flat area outside the garage waiting for whatever junk we won't be able to sell, so I have to park behind it, on the incline. This could make getting Dad out of the car tricky.

"Wait here while I get your walker out of the trunk," I tell him, then open my door. Immediately Dad gets flustered, searching for something on the console between the driver's and passenger's seat.

"What's the matter? Did you drop something?"

"Bray! Mersunsee bray!"

"What?"

Dad slaps the dashboard in frustration. I take a deep breath and try to remember what his therapist told me to do in these situations. Sound out each syllable of what he's said to try to make sense of it. E-mer-sun-see-bray. Emergency brake. "You want me to put the emergency brake on? It's over here on the floor." I set the brake and he relaxes.

"Alway set bray on hill," he scolds. I remember now that he was sort of fanatical about that when I was learning to drive. Not that he ever took me out to practice—that job fell to Pop.

I get the walker out of the trunk, where it nestles next to my crushed doll carriage, but by the time I arrive at the passenger side of the car, Dad has already opened the door and is struggling to get out.

"Take it easy, Dad. Let me help you," I say as I place the walker in front of him and reach for his elbow. He shrugs off my guiding hand and pushes himself up. For a moment he teeters on the uneven ground, then steadies himself and starts purposefully for the back door. I have to trot to get ahead of him. When I get into the mudroom, I check the row of hooks with keys. My condo key isn't there.

Inside the house, Dad moves through the rooms, passing judgment like a Roman emperor. He wants his books and CDs, and a painting done by a fellow professor. Everything else—dishes, furniture, rugs, lamps—gets the thumbs-down. "I buy new," he says blithely every time I hold something up for consideration. With every item he condemns, his mood brightens.

I'm stunned. He's barely bought one new thing in thirty years, and now suddenly he's up for a total overhaul. Even things I considered heirlooms—the Oriental rug my grandparents gave him and my mother as a wedding gift, the wedding china and crystal—all go on the sell list. I notice he doesn't offer them to me. Of course I manage to be wounded, but really, what would I do with a Royal Doulton service for twelve? The same thing he's done with it for the past thirty years—let it sit and collect dust.

He pauses in front of his easy chair—saggy, overstuffed, shiny with wear. He's spent almost every night of his adult life there, reading and listening to music. Surely that will go with him to the new apartment. But he shakes his head and grins. "Sit in tha' now, I never ge' ow. New chair!"

I hope he realizes the implication of all this discarding—acquiring replacements. Dad's never been one to embrace the retail experience. "You're going to have a lot of shopping to do," I warn.

"Okay. You come with me."

Suddenly, I'm entering into the spirit of this purge. Maybe by getting rid of every vestige of our life in this house, we'll get rid of the silence and chill between us. "I need some new furniture for my place. This will get me motivated."

"Together, make decisions fas'." Dad snaps his fingers.

"What about upstairs?" I ask. "Do you want your bedroom furniture?"

"Ge' rid of it. Keep desk and c'puter."

"Do you want to go up there?" I ask.

He looks at the steep stairs and shakes his head. "No. You tay care." He turns toward the front door and makes his way over to it. Maybe he wants to look at the front yard one last time. I open the heavy oak door to reveal the small front porch and winding flagstone walk. Dad lurches to a stop, leaning heavily on the walker.

"Wha' happen to holly?"

Two miniature spruces don't begin to fill the cavernous space occupied by the hollies. "The real estate agent said they were too overgrown. We had to put in something with more curb appeal."

He backs away from the door, his upbeat mood vaporized.

Why would he care so much about those shrubs? He's never shown the slightest interest in gardening. "I'm sorry about the hollies, Dad. I guess I should have asked you first."

He shakes his head, whether at my intransigence or to dismiss the need for an apology, I'm not sure. The possibility of that father-daughter shopping trip seems to have dissolved in an instant.

Desperate to recapture our earlier mood, I say, "Guess what I found out there when Ty dug out the old bushes? A little baby carriage of mine."

His hands turn white gripping the walker. I feel compelled to go on, although I'm sinking deeper in quicksand with every word I utter.

"Mrs. Olsen says I went through a phase of burying things. I don't even remember that, do you?"

He shakes his head, more in the manner of someone trying to rid himself of a pesky fly than someone saying no. Without glancing at me, he starts shuffling toward the kitchen.

"Dad, wait." I position myself in front of him. Things start clicking together in my mind and I feel like I do when I've suddenly seen my way clear to solve a really hard quintic equation. I don't know what the answer is. I can't explain exactly how I'm going to do it. I just know I'll get the solution. I answer my own questions almost as fast as I ask them. "The carriage—it was flattened. Did I leave it in the driveway? Did someone run over it? That's why you're so paranoid about the emergency brake, isn't it? Did I almost get run over?"

Deer in the headlights doesn't begin to describe my father's look of panic. He knows he can't outrun me. Can't ring for an aide who will chase me away. For the first time in our lives, he's entirely at my mercy. I almost feel sorry for him.

Almost.

More facts swarm my brain. I can't process the information fast enough. "I didn't bury that carriage—it was down too deep. You buried it. Right?"

He stares at me, a cobra mesmerized by the snake charmer's flute. "Yeh."

The word is so soft, I see it more than I hear it. Why is he so terrified? If he'd nearly run over me when I was a toddler, he would've been scared when it happened, but not scared thirty years later. After all, I'm alive and well.

But my mother isn't. The numbers realign. The formulas shift.

Clarity approaches.

"You killed her," I say. "You ran over her with the car." This is the truth he thinks I don't want to know.

"Not me—" His lips are positioned to form another word but no sound emerges.

I see what that next word was going to be. You.

Not me, you.

Chapter 43

Dad and I spend two hours huddled together on the couch of our family home as he chokes out the story in his stroke-ravaged voice, and I fill in the missing pieces.

My mother had been sick all of Christmas Eve day. In the late afternoon, my father finally recognized the symptoms for what they were. She was pregnant. He had known about the other man, but he loved my mother so much he hung on, hoping the affair would run its course. The baby changed everything. He left the house and drove around for hours, numb.

Meanwhile, my mother called her lover and told him that her husband knew everything. He too was married. They had been planning on telling their spouses after the holidays, but now the plan was changed. They agreed to meet.

By this time, the snow was falling. My mother put me in the car. No child safety seats back then—I was beside her in the front seat. She started to back down the driveway when she felt the car hit something. She must've gotten out of the car to look.

I was alone in the car. Three years old, curious, energetic.

By nine o'clock, my father came home. He found the car off the driveway, backed into the row of evergreens separating our house from the neighbor's. The engine was still running. The gear was in Reverse. I was asleep on the front seat.

The carriage lay crushed in the driveway.

My mother lay beside it.

My father carried me into the house and put me to bed. I never even woke up. This is where things got really strange. Sitting alone in this very room, on this very sofa, Dad decided there were only two things he could do for the woman he loved. He could protect me and he could protect Nana and Pop, because we were the people Charlotte had loved.

And so the myth was born: snow angel Charlotte, going out to buy those last few gifts, sliding into the lake.

"But where is she?" I ask my father, who lies flung back on the sofa, spent from his effort. "Did you throw her body in Heart Lake?"

Dad shakes his head. "No lake. Ocean."

The Atlantic. No wonder her body was never recovered. But how would dad have been able to dump her body in the ocean on Christmas Eve?

"How did you—"

"I couldn' do ih. He did. Had a boat."

"Who?"

Dad doesn't answer; he's too exhausted. Then I understand— who else could it be?

"Her lover got rid of the body for you?"

Dad nods. "He came here looking for her. He didn' wan' the truth to come out either. Never did tell his wife."

I look down at my mother's ring on my finger. "Then he took this off her finger, before....before he threw her body in the water. He kept the ring as a memento?"

Dad nods. "He must have."

"That's why you were so shocked when I found it. Then Mrs. Szabo must've stolen it from him. Who was he, Dad?"

He waves his hand, his eyes half shut. "Wha' matter? I should'a known."

"Known what?"

" I could'na keep a woman li' your motha."

There it is: her perfection terrified Dad as much as it's always terrified me. I could reach out to him now, tell him how I've always felt that I didn't deserve to be her daughter. Confide my switched-at-birth conviction that somewhere, some perfectly ordinary mother must have the gorgeous, accomplished daughter that should have gone to Charlotte.

But I don't tell Dad any of this. I just shake his knee, determined to knock loose the facts. This man who changed our lives needs an identity. I want to know what he did with the ring, how he's connected to Mrs. Szabo. "It was someone she worked with, right? What was his name?"

Dad says nothing. He has his eyes shut, like a child. If he can't see me, maybe I don't exist. I won't let him get away with this. I shake his knee harder. "Was he a reporter? Someone who worked at The Van Houten Group?"

Stubborn silence. I won't let up.

"Was it Spencer?"

Dad opens his eyes and shakes his head.

I'm a dog person, but my voice takes on the cajoling tone necessary to elicit cooperation from cats. "Just tell me his first name."

Dad takes a breath, then speaks. "Jude. His name wa' Jude."

The ride back to Manor View passes in silence. I feel as if a huge boil has been lanced. The pressure has been released, which brings relief from the constant throbbing. But the pain hasn't gone away; it's been replaced by the discomfort of a huge open wound. Gaping, ugly, requiring meticulous care.

Who will nurse this wound? Not Dad. He's slumped in his seat, exhausted, diminished.

Not me. Nursing requires a gentle touch and right now I feel as compassionate as a grizzly jolted from hibernation. The elation of knowing, finally knowing, has passed. Now I'm seething. He blames me.

Thirty years of frost and distance and criticism because he blames a three year old child for leaving her toy in the driveway. Blames a curious toddler for nudging that gearshift into reverse. He invented the last minute Christmas gifts story to shield me from the knowledge of what I'd done. But the story didn't offer the protection I needed most.

It didn't protect me from him, did it?

Chapter 44

Autopilot. That's the only way to get through this day, this week, perhaps the rest of my life.

I woke up this morning and experienced a moment of emotional neutrality, but by the time I sat up in bed and rubbed the sleep out of my eyes, it dissipated. The first thing I remember: Ethel is gone. Despair settles on me like a lead apron. But wait, there's something else to be miserable about. Oh, yeah…I killed my mother. And my father blames me. Now, let's go run an estate sale.

But that's what I do. The ads have been placed, the signs are up—there's really no alternative but to open the doors of the Siverson house and start selling. So with one section of my brain I add and subtract, make change, persuade, haggle. With the rest, I let out one long, silent howl.

The Siverson sale is busier than I anticipated. Doing it without Jill was a mistake—Ty and I have been running nonstop since the doors opened. But since Jill's and my little dust-up over the trunk of jewelry, I've been treating her with kid gloves. She clearly enjoys staging my father's house for sale, so I told her to finish that up today.

My phone chirps. I glance down—text message from Jill.

"So, twenty-five dollars for the vase, the bowl and the Dustbuster?" A woman with the hungry eyes of a hawk with a mouse in its sights refuses to be ignored.

"Thirty." I speak decisively, then look away to read Jill's text.

There's stuff here u need to see. Come by house after u r done @ sale.

The woman tosses a ten and a twenty at me with a disgusted huff, but scoops up her loot quickly. She knows she got a bargain.

There's nothing important left in my father's house—I've already been through everything twice. I text Jill back before the next customer steps up to the cash box.

Just toss it.

"There are only five of these salad plates," a perfectly coiffed woman complains, setting a stack of Portmeirion in front of me. "I need eight."

Apparently she thinks she's in Bloomingdales, not the dining room of a dead person, and that I can nip back to the stockroom for a few more. "That's all there are," I reply, keeping my voice neutral, but putting my hands on the plates as if I might repossess them. "Do you want the five?" My phone chirps again.

Don't want to. U shld decide.

Damn Jill. Why is she so indecisive? She seemed to be getting more confident, but working on my father's house has sent her back to square one. While the Portmeirion lady vacillates, I text back:

Tomorrow. Will b late here.

"I guess I'll take them." The woman slides the plates out of my grasp. "Will you call me if you find three more?"

I'm about to tell her no, when my phone chirps a third time. Geez, Jill—enough already!

Better tonite. Isabelle showing house in A.M.

"Excuse me!" someone at the end of the line shouts. "Can I leave exact change for this? I'm in a hurry."

"No, I can't call you about the plates. Yes, you can leave the money."

Chirp. *Audrey? R u coming?*
K! @ 7

It's well past seven when I pull up to the top of the driveway. I expect to see Jill's big boat. Instead, there's a smallish navy blue Mercedes. Is that Isabelle's car? Does she drive a Mercedes or a BMW? I really can't remember. I'm forced to park my Honda on the incline. I set the handbrake with a vicious yank. Wouldn't want to kill anyone else now, would I? For a moment, my vision blurs. Then I blink and sniff and move on. The downstairs windows are all dark, but I see a dim light in some upstairs windows.

I walk into the dark kitchen and, despite my exhaustion and grief, I have to smile. The place smells great! Jill has banished the musty odor of abandonment with a combination of her earth-friendly organic cleaning solution and her pomegranate scented beeswax candles. When I turn on the overhead light, I see the candles lined up on the kitchen table, their blackened wicks sprouting out of still liquid puddles of melted red wax. She must've just blown them out. I drop my purse on the table and shout.

"Jill? Isabelle? It's me, Audrey. The place looks great."

No answer. iPod, cellphone—those two are always wired to something.

I move through the dining room into the living room. Turning on the floor lamp, I see that Dad's sagging easy chair is gone, replaced by two sleek new chairs from Ikea. She's changed the art on the walls and added some throw pillows. The house seems to be on its way to a second life.

Maybe we'll sell it to a young couple just starting out, full of hope and enthusiasm. Maybe they'll have a little kid, maybe another baby on the way. They'll fill 37 Skytop with laughter and music. And probably arguments and middle of the night crying and the blare of mindless cartoons too, but even those will be the sounds of life, no? Maybe the Nealon house can be resurrected.

My phone rings. I figure it must be Jill, unaware that I'm right downstairs. But the caller ID says Palmyrton PD.

"Hello?"

"Where are you," a voice barks.

"Who is this?"

"Coughlin. Where are you?"

"At my father's house. Why?"

"Get out. Get out right now. Go someplace where there's a lot of people."

"Why? What's wrong?"

"I finally understand what's going on with Griggs and Mondel Johnson and the drugs. It's not safe for you to be alone. Go— Fuck!"

I hear a cavalcade of horns and squealing tires. "What are you doing? What's going on?"

"I'm driving. I'm chasing him."

"Who?"

"Jesus Christ, Audrey! I can't explain it now. Get out of that house. Go to WalMart or McDonalds or someplace crowded. Just trust me."

Over the phone line I hear sirens and the screech of metal scraping metal. Then the line goes dead.

Trust me. I stare at my cellphone. That's the problem. I don't trust Coughlin. Or Farrand, or anyone else on the Palmyrton Police Department. Who is Coughlin chasing? Is Ty on the other side of that crashing metal? Ty, who just left me after escorting me to the bank with no trouble. Ty, who waved a cheery goodby as he walked the few blocks home to his grandmother's place. I feel my rage at Coughlin rising again. I know Ty hasn't been totally straight with me, but Coughlin's pursuit of him has moved beyond relentless to crazed.

Who do I trust? Not my father. Not Ty, much as I want to. Jill? Maybe. Cal? Not so much.

Who does Coughlin think is going to come after me here? I glance around the living room, suddenly wary. Whose car is that outside? I'm not positive that it's Isabelle's. But it certainly doesn't belong to some street punk drug dealer. And where the hell is Jill?

I step toward the front window. Maybe I should get out of here. But what if someone's waiting for me outside? What kind of advice did Coughlin give me? Go to WalMart. Who ever heard of a cop telling a victim that?

I head into the front hall. This too is dark, and the scented candle smell has been replaced by some thing else. Something a little acrid. Uneasiness morphs into paranoia, a roadside weed choking out the flowers of rational thought. What am I doing here? Why was Jill so insistent that I come? Why did she turn out all the downstairs lights if she's still working upstairs?

My fingers tighten around my car keys as I back away from the stairs in the foyer. Time to start over, go out to my car, lock myself inside, send Jill a text. If she doesn't answer, I'm out of here.

I turn toward the kitchen. Then I hear a creak. I stop walking, stop breathing. Again it comes—the creak of old wooden joists, not merely settling, but moving under the pressure of someone's weight. Someone is in this house with me. Run or turn to look? I'm a squirrel paralyzed by indecision as the car bears down.

Run, my instinct screams. *Turn,* my intellect counters.

Intellectual curiosity trumps gut emotion. I am my father's daughter.

I turn. But I don't understand.

Chapter 45

"I'm sorry. Did I startle you?"

I know this woman, know her well, but she has nothing to do with my father, this house, estate sales. And for a moment her disconnection from this part of my life drives her name right out of my mind. I stare, silent.

"Are you all right, dear?"

Her voice restores my memory. "Anne. What are you doing here?"

She offers me a Mona Lisa-ish smile. "I thought I'd come and look around one last time. I'm glad I did. Sometimes the line between pleasure and pain is a rather fine one, wouldn't you say?"

What's gotten into her? She looks dreamy and distant, not at all the sensible, brisk Anne I've come to know.

"How did you get in?" I ask. "And where's Jill?"

"She couldn't wait. I told her I'd show you the things she was concerned about discarding."

"But how did you know I would—"

Wincing, Anne lowers herself to sit on the steps.

"What's wrong?" I ask.

"There's something I have to tell you, dear. I've been diagnosed with pancreatic cancer." Anne keeps talking over my gasp. "I've known for a while. I told the doctor I didn't want chemo—what's the point, a few lousy extra weeks of illness? I'd rather enjoy the time I've got left. I was hoping to not have to tell Spencer until after the election, but—"

"Wait! Spencer doesn't know?"

"He wouldn't have run for governor if he had known, so I decided not to tell him. He's so oblivious, I doubted he'd figure it out. But last night I had to tell him. My wedding ring slid right off my finger into the spaghetti carbonara—I haven't been this thin since I finished breastfeeding Abby." She smiles slightly. "Finally a diet that works for me."

"Anne, you can't just give up without a fight!"

"Oh, I wouldn't say I've lost my will to fight. I've just redirected it."

I'm about to ask her what she means when I hear something upstairs. Not a voice, more a crackling sound. "What's that? Is someone else up there?"

"I noticed the sound myself. Perhaps you should check, dear. That's what I was doing when you got here." Anne slides over to let me climb past her.

I reach the landing, where the staircase makes a ninety degree turn. Now I can see a light haze of smoke snaking through the upstairs hall.

The candles! Jill's damn scented candles must have ignited something up here. The curtains, maybe, or a lampshade.

"It's a fire!" I shout to Anne as I race up the remaining steps. "Call 911."

Dad's room and mine are fine—the smoke is pouring out of the little office at the end of the hall. I run there to see what I can do. The cloud of smoke thickens, enveloping me. Gray, choking smoke, reeking of melted plastic, invades my eyes, my mouth, my lungs. In an instant, I'm blinded.

A hand touches my arm. I shriek.

"It's spreading."

My heart rate steadies. It's only Anne. Her voice is so calm.

"I've called the fire department," she says. "But we might be able to contain it. Throw some water on it...fill up the wastepaper can from the bathroom, maybe?"

"Good idea. I'll do it—you go down and wait for the firemen." Anne retreats to the far end of the hall while I fill the can with water. The air in the bathroom is fresher, and I take some deep breaths before crossing the hall. Maybe I shouldn't mess with this, but if the fire is small, shouldn't I try to put it out?

I step into the room with my can of water, looking for the flames. Thick and black, the smoke has erased the outlines of the desk, computer, bookcase that I know are here. The smell is strongly chemical—the plastic housing of the computer and printer melting into oblivion. I notice a few tongues of orange near the window. Can I toss the water that far? I edge closer and throw. Behind me I hear a click. I glance over my shoulder. It's too smoky to see, but I sense a presence nearby. Who's upstairs with me?

Frozen by panic, I stand there breathing in the fumes that will kill me, still clutching the can of water. Then some primal instinct kicks in and I sink to the floor.

Down here it feels cooler, the air cleaner. I take a few breaths and my mind clears. Right, you're supposed to stay low in a fire. Now I understand why. Thinking that I could extinguish this myself was crazy—I need to get out of here fast. I turn to crawl toward the door.

I can see my hands on the floor, nothing else. The panic rises again. Did I turn around when I got in here? Is the door in front of me or behind me? I feel my eyelids straining, as if by stretching my eyes open I can will them to admit light. To see. Instead, I stare into a void.

I reach out, groping for the wall. Once I find it, I can work my way along to the door. My stretched fingertips anticipate the smooth, hard surface of plaster; they encounter something warm and yielding.

I recoil with a stifled scream. Someone's in this room with me.

A hand, strong but not rough, grips my right wrist. I flounder with my left hand until I feel hair, a smooth bob. "Anne? Why did you follow me in here? We've got to get out."

I move forward, but she doesn't yield. "Anne, come on—back up! The door's right behind us." Every word costs me, smoke searing my throat.

"No, dear. We're staying right here. It's important they find our bodies together."

Find our bodies? Is that really what she said? There's no time to consider her meaning. Heat scorches my back; smoke burns me from within. Instinct drives me forward. I push away from Anne, scrabbling for the door. She's still latched on to my right wrist. Her weight pulls me down and we're rolling on the floor like puppies. She splays herself on top of me pushing what little breath I had out of my lungs.

I'm pinned, too stunned to struggle.

"That's better," she murmurs in my ear as if she's comforting a feverish grandchild. "It won't take long." Her grip on my wrist lessens.

Cancer or no cancer, Anne's a good fifty pounds heavier than I. But I'm in better shape. When I feel her relax, I tense my body and surge upward. Surprised, she rolls off me.

I lunge in what I think is the direction of the door and mercifully feel its raised panels. I drag myself up, groping for the doorknob. Anne grabs my ankle and pulls me down.

Dizzy, frantic, burning within and without, I kick back viciously. I hear her sharp cry of pain and I'm free, tumbling through the door into the blessed coolness of the hall.

My relief is so great, I take a huge gulp of air, then collapse coughing. Everything is relative. The air out here is clearer, but still plenty smoky. I have to keep moving, get away. I stumble forward and crash into a wall.

Panic moves in now, displacing reason like water displaces air.

Think, think.

If the office is on the right hand side of the hall then I must have to turn left to get to the stairs. Despite the headache lacerating my brain, I pivot and stride forward. Right into Anne's arms.

Locked together, we sway like inept ballroom dancers.

"Anne, please—we've got to get out of here." I still can't get my head around the idea that she means to harm me.

"You're just like your mother," Anne wheezes in my ear. "She never knew when to stop, never could leave well enough alone." She pushes me a step closer to the burning room. "Had to destroy my family. Now you...just the same."

"What are you talking about?" Although our arms are locked together, I succeed in bringing my knee up between us to push her back toward the stairs. Stalemate. "I don't want to hurt anyone."

"Dylan. I won't let you ruin his life." The words seem to give her superhuman strength. She kicks my leg and I crumple, pulling her down on top of me. "Family," she whispers. "Family is everything."

She places her forearm across my neck and leans forward with all her weight. I buck and kick, dig my fingernails into her arm. Anything to get the weight to lift, get the air back in my lungs.

Her lips are moving. She's saying something; I'm not sure what.

"Just like your mother."

Chapter 46

White bursts of light explode inside my head. Anne's voice disappears into a roar in my ears. I feel myself slipping.

I hear a pop, followed by the tinkle of shattered glass. The windows are exploding. As oxygen feeds the fire, there's a rush of unendurable heat. The pressure on my neck lifts. The stars dissolve, replaced by orange flames. Instinctively I roll away and discover I'm free. I can move.

Flames pour out of the office, consuming everything behind me. I inhale, but nothing enters my lungs. Scuttling like a crab, I follow the runner of carpet on the hall floor, willing my hands and knees to go on even though my lungs have let them down. Anne has left my mind—all I can think of is oxygen. One more step, one more. I'm outside my body, cheering it on. I reach out my hand to feel the next stretch of carpet, but touch only air. Too late to warn the knees. I've found the stairs, and I'm tumbling down them.

Smooth, cool fingers stroke my hand. I snatch it away.

My eyelids feel as big as donuts and all I can see are two thin slivers of light. "Anne? Where's Anne?" The words croak out of my swollen lips.

A familiar voice speaks. "Ssshh. It's all right baby. You don't have to talk until you're ready."

My brain works to process these words. "Cal?"

"Yes, baby, it's me." My hand is picked up again. "How do you feel? Is it hard to talk?"

"Where's Anne?" My voice is so hoarse that the words seem to come from another source.

Long silence. "Audrey, honey, uh, I'm afraid…afraid she didn't make it. But don't bla—"

"She tried to kill me."

He stops stroking my hand. "Baby, baby—the fire was an accident."

"She set it and she tried to trap me in the house with her."

I hear Cal stand up. "Look, honey—you're injured, you're on painkillers, there's no need to talk about this now. Just rest. "

I feel him leaning over me. His lips graze the top of my head. I turn away.

"I'll see you tomorrow…" His footsteps click away.

"I'm glad she's dead," I whisper to the wall.

The next time I wake up, my eyelids have shrunk to the size of ravioli and I can detect motion as well as light through the marginally bigger slit. Once again, someone's got my hand. Once again, I pull it away.

"Sorry. How ya doin'?"

My hand retains the impression of the fingers that touched it. Big. Calloused. Coughlin.

"Not too good." My throat is raw. Every word I speak costs me dearly. "Guess I should've listened to you."

"I knew you wouldn't. That's why I sent a patrol car over there as soon as I could. Guys broke down the front door when they saw the flames. Found you at the bottom of the stairs and pulled you out. A minute later the upstairs caved in. No one could've saved Anne Finneran."

"She tried to kill me."

Unlike Cal, Coughlin accepts this news without comment. I sense his bulk in the chair beside my bed, waiting, attuned.

But I want to know one thing before I tell him my story. "Who were you chasing? Ty or Mondel Johnson?"

"Neither. Mondel Johnson has nothing to do with what happened to you. I was after Dylan Finneran, although I didn't know it at the time. The guy who attacked you was his supplier, a pill dealer named Frank Zegna. He rolled on the kid, but he just knew him by a street name. Dylan was quite the little entrepreneur--half the teenagers in Palmyrton were his customers. Kept 'em juiced on E, painkillers, Adderall."

"But not weed or coke."

Coughlin shakes his head. "No one-stop shopping. That corner of the market is controlled by Mondel Johnson, and his boss, Nichols."

"So the pills in Mrs. Szabo's kitchen belonged to Dylan?"

Coughlin raises his eyebrows. "Farrand told me Tremaine found those pills before you ever came on the scene. Why did you feel you had to lie about that?"

I smile weakly. "Complicated. I promise I'll tell you everything. But finish telling me about Dylan first."

"The Ecstasy must've belonged to Dylan. I think he tried to double-cross Zegna by telling him you took the E, which is why Zegna came after you in the parking garage and at your condo. Not that Dylan's admitting any of this. He's got the best defense team since OJ Simpson. But we had enough on him to search his room and seize his computer. One thing it shows was he was monitoring estate sales. I figure he used different empty houses to hide his product. The average dumb kid keeps it in his sock drawer until mom goes on a cleaning binge and he's busted."

"Finneran grandchildren are all above average." I turn my head toward Coughlin but the tube pumping oxygen into my lungs restricts my movement. All I can glimpse is a field of blue, the shirt covering his massive chest. "Anne thought I wanted to harm Dylan, destroy her family. I—" I start to cough, can't go on.

"We have a lot of work to do to build our case. We may never get forensic evidence to prove Anne set the fire and tried to trap you, but your testimony will be vital to prosecute Dylan, Audrey. You discovered the pills. You told Tremaine about them. You got attacked by Zegna. You're the one who links Dylan Finneran to a violent drug dealer. Without your testimony, they could get this hushed up as a youthful indiscretion."

I think of all the other things Anne knew that linked me to Dylan, things that Cal told her about. How I found him smoking weed the night of the birthday party, how I caught him shoplifting at the Reicker sale. He must've been collecting another one of his hidden stashes that day. I'll tell all this to Coughlin, but not right now. I don't have the strength. But I understand now what Anne meant when she told me she hadn't given up but was just redirecting her fight. She was dying anyway, and if she could save Spencer's election and keep Dylan out of jail by going a few months early, and taking me with her…. But she failed. I'm alive.

"I'll testify," I whisper to Coughlin.

"Good. Even the next governor of New Jersey could have a hard time covering up two counts of attempted murder."

I've lost track of what day it is. "The election?" I ask.

"Finneran won."

I close my eyes and take as deep a breath as my damaged lungs will hold. All Cal's hard work has paid off. Spencer Finneran is the new governor of New Jersey and Call will be his chief of staff. At least someone's fondest wish has come true. I'm happy for Cal, even if he doesn't believe Anne tried to kill me. It would be nice to congratulate him.

"So listen, Audrey," Coughlin starts up again. "The press is all over this. There are reporters camped outside the hospital. But you need to keep quiet until we get our ducks in a row, all right? No talking to reporters, or to anyone in the Finneran family…or their representatives."

"What's that supposed to mean?

"Tremaine. Keep your distance."

I struggle to sit up straight so I feel more in control. The tube forcing oxygen in my nose slips out, and Coughlin leans over to readjust it.

"Easy, there."

His hands are surprisingly gentle, but I bat them away. "You're telling me I can't talk to my— Can't talk to Cal?"

A ripple of emotion passes across his normally implacable face. "I'm telling you the hospital's the safest place for you. Turn away all visitors. I'll post an officer at your door."

"I hate the hospital, I wanna go home." Coughlin's commanding tone instantly gets my hackles up. Physically, he couldn't be less like my father: hulking not wiry, fair not dark, blue-eyed not brown. But somehow Coughlin manages to push exactly the same buttons as dear old Dad. There's the same insistence that he knows best; the same infuriating refusal to trust my judgment. "You have no right to imprison me here, or dictate who I can and can't see."

"I'm just telling you, Tremaine is loyal to one person, and that's Spencer Finneran. Watch your back."

"You're just—" I was about to say jealous, but I bite the word back. This has nothing to do with sex, and everything to do with control. I try to put some calm authority into my wheezing voice. "You were wrong about Ty and you're wrong about Cal."

We glare at each other until Coughlin lifts his hands in surrender and stands to go.

Strangely, I feel a stab of remorse. I'm being petulant. Coughlin acts like a hovering helicopter mom; I act like a defiant brat. "Sean, wait—," I say as he reaches the door. But my voice is too weak. He heads off down the hall.

Chapter 47

Coughlin's dream of keeping me locked up in the hospital is defeated by my insurance carrier. They're not paying for another night, so the morning after Coughlin's visit, the nurses disconnect my oxygen supply, hand me some antibiotics, and cut me loose. I was kind of hoping Cal might appear to take me home. Instead, Jill arrives promptly at nine. I hate having to rely on her to look after me. Still, the warm rush of her chatter comforts me.

"Ohmygod Audrey I can't believe you're in the hospital again and I totally missed the whole thing because I agreed to drive up to Albany with my friend Gabby to help her move into the dorm because she got into graduate school for microbiology did I tell you that? And anyway she needed help with her stuff so when I got up there I realized I didn't have my cell phone and I was totally out of touch for the whole weekend and it was killing me and then I got back and Ty told me what happened and ohmygod Audrey I just can't believe it."

"Yeah, it sucks," I say as I settle into a wheelchair for the ride down to the lobby. Apart from the fact that my hair is singed on the side of my head that was closest to the doorway when the fireball erupted, I'm in good shape. But my lungs were damaged from the smoke and the doctor says I can expect to be short of breath for months. Eager to conserve oxygen, I let Jill do all the talking.

"And when I got home from Albany I searched everywhere for my cell phone and I couldn't find it. So now I think I must've lost it at your dad's house so it's definitely gone for good and I had to buy a new one and re-enter my whole address book and that was such a pain but I like the new phone and I finally feel whole again you know what I mean because you just feel lost when you don't have your phone."

Jill's words wash over me like elevator music. I'm eager to get to the office. My mind ticks with things I need to do, calls I need to make. With Ethel gone, there's no need to go home first. My eyes well with tears when I think of the welcome home that I would have received from Ethel. I turn my head, hoping Jill won't see as she leans over me to press the DOWN button on the elevator.

"So Audrey I'm still so confused about what happened. The paper said something about the fire starting from a candle. Why did you light them? Why was Anne Finneran there? Audrey?"

"Huh?" I make an effort to process Jill's stream of monologue. "The candles? No, I didn't light them. I thought—" Wait a minute. Something's not adding up here. "When did you leave for Albany?"

"Four o'clock. Remember I told you I was going to finish at your dad's house and then take off?"

I don't remember, but that's because I often listen to Jill with only half an ear. "Did you text me late in the afternoon and ask me to meet you at the house so you could show me some stuff before you got rid of it?"

"No, why would I do that? You and your Dad already said you didn't want to keep anything but the books and CDs and the computer."

The elevator doors open. We roll out into the hustle bustle of the hospital lobby. Jill pushes me toward the exit and a tall, lean man holds the door for us. The next thing I know, he's loped around us and is blocking our path on the sidewalk.

"Evan Shapiro, New York Times." He thrusts his hand out. "I have a few questions for you, Ms. Nealon."

I dodge his hand. Coughlin was right about one thing--the press is after me. I'm not ready for this. "No comment. Keep going, Jill."

Shapiro trots after us. "Why was Mrs. Finneran in the house? Did you invite her there? What were you discussing?"

I practically dive into Jill's car and slam the door in the reporter's face.

"How well did you know Anne Finneran?" he shouts as Jill pulls away from the curb.

"Not well enough." I mutter.

"What did you say?"

I look over at Jill. "You didn't lose your phone. Anne, or more likely, Dylan, stole it and used it to send me a message that would lure me to the house."

Jill's mouth forms a perfect "O" of surprise. "I had all the windows and doors open to air the house out. I was going in and out all day, tossing stuff in the Dumpster. Someone could've slipped in the front door while I was out in the back. But why did Anne Finneran want to meet you at your dad's house?"

"I'll explain it to you on the way to the office."

Jill responds to my story with a rising crescendo of "Get out!"s and "No way!"s. By the time we pull up to the office, she's finally stopped chattering. She helps me out of her car, then glances at the AMT van parked behind it. "Ty must be back from delivering those antique chairs to Gerald," she says. "Hey, now that they've arrested Dylan, does that mean the big red-haired cop will stop harassing Ty?"

"I hope so," I answer aloud, but in my head I'm thinking, but he'll still be pursuing him about his relationship with Mondel Johnson.

We walk into the office and find Ty packing boxes for a UPS shipment. He drops his tape gun and opens his arms wide.

"Hey, Audge! How you doin'?"

"I'm great!" I lie, then sway and crash dizzily into my desk chair.

"What you bring her here for?" Ty scolds Jill. "Shouldn't she be home in bed or something?"

"No really, I'd rather be here with you guys than home alone anyway." I see a quick glance pass between them.

"Think I'll go to the bank," Jill says, snatching a pile of checks from her desk.

I know she's just as distraught over Ethel's disappearance as I am. The only way we can hold ourselves together is to studiously avoid mentioning the dog in each other's presence. "Good idea," I tell her. I'd like a few minutes alone with Ty anyway.

When she's gone, Ty goes back to wrapping boxes, and for several minutes the only sound is the zipping of tape.

I gather up my courage. "Ty—"

"Look, Audge—"

"You first," I say.

Ty drops into a chair. "Look, Audge, I know I been actin' kinda crazy. But now that you know that shit in old lady Szabo's house wasn't mine, that I didn't have no part in what happened to you—"

"I never thought you did, Ty," I interrupt. "It's just…that Mondel Johnson person—I mean, something's going on, right?"

"Was going on. Now it's all settled."

I straighten up and start talking. My brush with death has given me courage. I'm surprised at how authoritative I sound. "Look, Ty, I *have* to know what was going on. I can't accept 'it's all settled.' You need to tell me the truth right now if you want to keep working for me."

Ty gives me that awful prison stare he's got down cold. I stare back. I'm pretty sure he's going to stalk out and I'll never see him again. It's not what I want, but it may be what I have to accept.

Then suddenly he drops his gaze. His shoulders slump and his big foot jiggles. "I had to help my cousin Marcus," he says.

"Marcus? Isn't he the one who graduated from Rutgers and got a job at Citibank?"

Ty rolls his eyes. "That's him. Our family's big success story. My whole life that's all I hear from our Grams, 'Why can't you be more like Marcus? He's so good in school. He's never hangin' on the street.'"

"Little bitter?"

"Listen, Marcus is book smart, but he got no street smarts, know what I'm sayin'? He had a full academic scholarship, but what they don't tell you is it don't cover books, and computer, and food and shit. So he had this job in the library workin' twenty-five hours a week and he still can't pay for everything. Thought he was going to hafta drop out. That starts our Grandma cryin' her eyes out, 'cause all she wants is for one of us kids to turn out right. So Marcus gets the idea he could sell a little weed on campus to pay his bills. Our other cousin Jimmy sets him up with Nichols. Now Marcus himself don't ever mess with drugs, not even weed. But he figures he could sell to a few friends. Before long, he got a real nice business goin'. And because Marcus is good with numbers and not messed up on usin' the product, Nichols likes workin' with him. Keeps pressuring him to expand."

Ty takes a deep breath. "Then in the spring, Marcus graduates. Gets a job offer from Citibank. Goin' to have a fancy office in a skyscraper and wear a suit every day. Grams about to explode, she's so happy. Tellin' everybody she knows about Marcus. This is where Marcus is so damn dumb. He thinks he can quit workin' for Nichols, the way you quit a job at Wal-Mart. No way Nichols goin' to walk away from the bizness Marcus built up. And Nichols knows Marcus can't snitch without gettin' himself busted. So now Marcus got two jobs—working for the bank all day and sellin' on campus at night."

"And that's where you came in—helping Marcus with his night job?"

Ty jumps up. "No way! I did not sell no drugs, Audge. I told Marcus I ain't touchin' nothing that gets me sent back to jail. But Nichols was threatening him, and he couldn't go to the police without getting in trouble himself and losing his job and that would kill my Grams. So I helped him for her sake, know what I'm sayin'?"

"What exactly did you do, Ty? Why was that Mondel person following you around?"

"I had to get someone else to take over Marcus's business. The first guy Marcus found didn't work out so good. Couldn't keep his accounts straight. That's when Nichols sent Mondel around, to collect the money he was owed. Marcus don't know nothin' about dealin' with people like that. I had to step in and work it out. Set up Nichols with a guy I knew from inside."

"So you're telling me you're an executive recruiter for a drug dealer."

"Look, there's always going to be weed on a college campus, right? If my man don't sell it for Nichols, someone else will."

"What kind of crazy rationale is that?" I feel a real rant building. "There's always going to be kiddie porn, too. And car-jackers, and slave traffickers, and, and... Should we just turn our--"

Ty looks me straight in the eye. "I couldn't let Nichols kill my cousin."

There it is: the blood is thicker than water bottom line. I put my head down on my desk and speak without looking up. "Fine. Just tell me it's over. Promise me you and Marcus are both completely out of Nichols's business."

"It's over. New guy I found is doin' great. Marcus doin' great. Everybody happy."

I keep my head down until I hear the reassuring zip of Ty's tape gun. I'll never be able to explain this to Coughlin, but I imagine he'll give up on Ty when he realizes Mondel Johnson isn't hanging around anymore. And curtailing the flow of weed onto the Rutgers campus is some other cop's problem.

Finally I lift my head up and start going through the messages that have piled up. Five from Evan Shapiro. Two from Walt Anthony of the Newark *Star Ledger*. Two from News 12 New Jersey. One from some dope at the *Daily Wretched*. I've got to talk to someone about how to handle all this. Cal would be the logical choice, but he's been completely out of touch. I hate when he makes me feel like a teenager, reluctant to make the first call.

"I'll deliver this stuff over to UPS, and when I get back I'll drive you home, okay." Ty says this as a statement, not a question.

"No, no," I object. "I can drive myself in the van."

"You still dizzy. You gonna crash. I'll drive."

"Well, if you're sure you don't mind. I'll pay you overtime."

Ty pauses with his hand on the doorknob and looks back at me though narrowed eyes. "I don't want no overtime. Why would I *mind* to drive a friend home? Sometimes I think there's somethin' wrong with your head, Audge."

I shuffle papers on my desk until he's safely out the door. Why did I insult him like that? Why can't I accept a simple gesture of kindness? I feel the tears pricking my eyes again. How I long for Ethel. The sweet furrow between her brows. The forgiving wag of her tail. I rein myself in. If I give in to this now, I'll never stop crying.

Purposefully, I sort the mail: junk, bills, payments, info for Jill to file. At the bottom of the pile lies a rectangular, flat cardboard mailer. I glance at the return address: Yearbooks.com. This is the replacement I ordered for Dad's lost Princeton yearbook. Now that I know Dylan or his supplier were behind all the break-ins, the theft of the yearbook seems even more puzzling. I leaf through the pages until I find Dad's senior picture. He stares off the page: lean, dark-haired, serious. Not quite handsome, but definitely attractive.

Intense.

Where else would his picture be? Not in football or basketball—I skim through Sports until I reach cross-country. There he is, thin but muscular. What else? Certainly I won't find him in these candid party shots, but maybe in something geeky like Chess Club or Latin Forum. I page through, reading the captions, smiling at the shaggy hair and wide sideburns of the late Sixties. I laugh at the Young Republicans and the Young Democrats, pictured on facing pages. The Republicans are dressed in sports coats or polo shirts; the Democrats in torn jeans and tie-dyed tee-shirts. I bet Cal must've been in the Young Democrats at Brown. I glance at the candids taken at some rally for George McGovern. A beautiful face leaps out at me. I pull the book closer. Sure enough, it's my mother. I'd heard from Nana how my parents met. Mom was an English major who'd put off taking her math requirement. Dad met her weeping over her calculus book in the library and tutored her through her final. A knight with a shining calculator.

She was a year behind Dad, so she would have been a junior in this picture. Not surprisingly, a handsome guy has his arm around her, and another guy, his face turned slightly away, is holding a big McGovern sign up in front of the three of them. I read the caption: *Charlotte Perry, Spencer Finneran and Roger Nealon leading the charge for George McGovern.*

I stare at the caption as if I'm deciphering a sentence in a foreign language, translating each word but still unable to grasp the total meaning. The man in the picture is Spencer, younger, thinner, with dark hair, but definitely *the* Spencer Finneran, governor-elect of New Jersey. Spencer knew my parents, both of them, long before any of them came to Palmyrton.

Another lie.

Why?

I slap the book shut. My father would know. I suppose I'll have to go and visit him. I dread making the trip, and without Ethel as a buffer, it will be even worse. Tomorrow, I'll deal with Dad tomorrow.

Chapter 48

Despite my heartfelt desire to avoid my empty condo, I have no choice but to allow Ty to deliver me here. The place has never looked more barren. We're perfectly matched, this condo and I—empty, impersonal, stripped of everything that has ever mattered. The featureless beige walls taunt me. There's nothing to distract you here, they seem to say. Now you have to think about your mother, your father, the fire, Anne, Ethel.

Outside, a car door slams.

Looking out the window, I see Cal emerge from his BMW.

About time he shows up. Even though I defended Cal to Coughlin, I feel a blossom of rage unfolding within me. I've barely heard from him since Halloween, apart from that one blurry visit when I was in the hospital. Sure, everything that happened to me was right before and during the election, but still, doesn't even a low maintenance hook-up like me deserve a little more attention than this? That damn Coughlin's probably right—I shouldn't even open the door.

I watch as he struggles to pull something out of the passenger side of his car. Probably some ginormous bouquet of flowers—he figures he can solve everything with his AmEx card and speed-dial to the florist. Well, forget that—the novelty's worn off. I turn away from the window. Although making him stand on the front stoop begging for admission does hold some appeal, there's a part of me that worries he might say, "OK, never mind," and leave. And I have a few things to say to Cal Tremaine.

When I hear his footsteps on the stoop, I fling open the door.

Cal stands there, arms stretched out before him, carrying something wrapped in a lime green beach towel.

"What in the –"

The beach towel moves. A flash of fluffy brown appears.

"Ethel!"

I'm out the door so fast I feel like I'm levitating. I rip the towel back and Ethel struggles to lift her head. She looks puzzled, as if she doesn't know how she got into this mess but she's counting on me to get her out.

I gather her into my arms. "How? Where?"

"Let's get her inside," Cal says. "She's really weak. I tried to feed her something but she wouldn't take it from me. I figured it was best to get her straight to you."

Ethel has been missing for five days. Her fur is matted, there's a nasty cut on her front right paw, and she looks about ten pounds thinner. Her eyes are glazed and her nose is dry.

"I think she's dehydrated. It hasn't rained all week. She probably couldn't even find a puddle to drink from."

Sure enough, when I hold her in my lap with a bowl of water in front of her, she laps it all up.

"How did you find her?" I ask.

"This past week has been so crazy. The election…the fire… you in the hospital…everything. I felt so out of control. And this morning I woke up and said to myself, "I want to make one thing right, one thing. And I realized," Cal traces my jaw with his index finger, "I realized, I want to make something right for Audrey."

The anger drains out of me. Cal has spent the day, not with Spencer, not with his high-priced clients, but looking for my little lost mutt.

Cal jumps up and starts pacing. "I know I didn't offer much support when Ethel got lost—too concerned with my own problems. But today I sat myself down and tried to think like a dog. When I was a kid, our dog got lost and he turned up a week later all the way across town at the nature trail where my parents used to walk with him. The vet said dogs return to a place that smells familiar.

"I knew you took Ethel to visit your dad at his nursing home. So I thought, maybe she's there, maybe that's a place that would smell familiar to her. I went out there and walked around the grounds. One old guy told me he'd seen a dog running around a few days before. So I kept searching, and I found her curled up under some branches." Cal leans over and strokes Ethel's head. "She'd just about given up, huh girl?"

Ethel sighs and closes her eyes.

I look at Cal's perfectly manicured hand on Ethel's matted fur and all my doubts and insecurities melt away. He found Ethel. No one has ever done anything kinder for me in all my life.

Cal and I spend the early evening at the vet's where Ethel is cleaned up, patched up and dosed with antibiotics. He doesn't even suggest we go out to dinner, just meekly calls in my order for Thai carry-out and runs to fetch it after carrying Ethel back into the house and settling her on the sofa. When he returns I'm sitting on the floor, my head buried in Ethel's neck, breathing in her sweet, musty dogginess. Cal slides down next to me and pulls me into his arms, kissing my tear-stained cheeks, my singed hair, my canine medicine-coated fingers. We make love while the Thai basil chicken cools on the counter. Later Cal runs me a bubble bath and sets me to soak while he dishes up the food. We eat, sharing bites with Ethel.

After dinner we snuggle in bed watching Seinfeld re-runs. I stroke Ethel's head; Cal strokes mine. I have peace. I have Ethel, and Cal, and sex, and affection and food, and rest. Don't I deserve this? Can't I simply enjoy it for a few hours? Is that so much to ask?

And yet, and yet.... Other thoughts, awful thoughts, push insistently into my head. Now that the extent of Dylan's drug-dealing is known, does Cal still think Anne only wanted to talk to me...that the fire was an accident? How will he react when I tell him I plan to testify against Dylan? And does Cal realize that Spencer knew both my parents in college, long before my mother worked on Spencer's first campaign?

"Cal?"

"Hmm." His eyes are riveted to the antics of George and Kramer on the screen as his fingers idly brush my bangs off my forehead.

"Cal, we need to talk about Anne and the fire and ...things."

Cal throws his head back on the pillows and closes his eyes. "I know, baby, but this has all been so overwhelming for me too. I can barely get my head around it."

I sit up. "So you believe me when I say that Anne started the fire and tried to trap me in the house."

Cal's eyes are open, but he's looking up at the ceiling, not at me. "I believe you, yes, but...but, there's just got to be some explanation. I mean, I'm mourning the Anne I knew—the kind, generous friend—at the same time that I'm coming to grips with the idea that she nearly killed the woman I—" He looks me in the eye. "The woman I love."

Ah, geez, I wasn't expecting that. Speechlessly, I let him kiss me. For a while, his lips, gentle yet demanding, drive all rational thought from my mind. But as his hand slides under my t-shirt, I come to my senses.

"Cal, did you know that Spencer knew both my parents at Princeton? He and Anne lied to me about that—why?"

Cal pulls back as if I'd slapped him. "Really? They lied?"

"Anne specifically told me that Spencer first met my mother when she was working on his first campaign. But I found a picture in the Princeton yearbook that shows Spencer and my parents together in 1968."

Cal massages his temples. "I don't know, Audrey. I don't understand anything anymore. I tried to talk to Spencer yesterday, but he's in shock. The police, the press, Dylan's lawyers, all his kids—they all want a piece of him. And without Anne, he doesn't know how to manage it. He begged me to give him a little space. Of course I said yes."

"Reporters have been calling me too." I take Cal's hand. "I understand. You've given so much of yourself to this campaign, and you won, and you should be celebrating, but instead—"

Cal sits up in bed and faces me. "A man who's been my idol is suddenly a stranger to me."

The stress and confusion of the past week have actually altered his appearance. The perfect regularity of his features has been disrupted. Cal looks rumpled—not his clothes, because he's only wearing boxers—but his very being. And I'm glad. His uncertainty draws us closer. For the first time since I've met him, I don't feel intimidated.

I open my arms and Cal curls into my embrace. I twine my fingers through his and gently kiss his eyelids. He moans and pulls me on top of him. Soon, tee shirts are flying, legs are thrashing and Ethel, grumbling, abandons the bed.

I awake to a sunny bedroom, a whining dog and a ringing phone. 9AM—my God, I slept like a rock. No wonder poor Ethel's crying.

"Okay, Eth—we'll go outside in a minute. Let me see who's calling."

The caller ID says Manor View. Probably more planning for Dad's discharge. That can wait until after Ethel's walk. I'm not ready to deal with anything concerning my father yet. As I swing out of bed, I notice a note on the pillow next to mine.

Thanks for making everything better. Talk to you later today.

Love,

Cal

While I get dressed for our walk, I switch on the TV news.

"...*we're seeing the coolest temps in Connecticut and Long Island, slightly warmer in the city.*"

"*Thanks, Al. I'll tell you where it's really hot—New Jersey, where controversy continues to swirl around governor-elect, Spencer Finneran.*"

Despite Ethel's frantic scratching at the front door, I sink down before the TV, one sneaker on, one off.

The camera zooms in on the anchorwoman. I watch her lips moving and her eyebrows bobbing under her helmet of stiff hair as she tells me that there's no official word on what Anne Finneran was doing in the house on Skytop Drive that burned to the ground. But sources who refuse to be named hint that her presence there may be linked to the arrest of her grandson, Dylan Finneran, on drug possession charges. And then a picture of my own condo appears on the screen as the newsreader tells the world that the woman who lives here escaped the fire that killed the governor-elect's wife.

I keep watching, waiting to hear if they'll report that Anne set the house on fire, that Anne tried to kill Audrey Nealon. But the anchor woman moves on to reports of suspected terrorists, impending hurricanes and Wall Street shenanigans. I take Ethel's leash and head out the door. Across the street, twenty people mill around three vans sprouting antennae and satellite dishes. The reporters surge forward. I pull Ethel back inside and slam the door. Now what? The poor dog's gotta go. I look out my back window to the grassy courtyard shared by four of the condo development's units. There's a path between the buildings that will eventually get us out to the street behind the buildings. No reporters lurking there, so we make our escape.

How good it feels to be walking Ethel, following behind the familiar plume of her tail! Waiting while she sniffs her way through each pile of leaves on the curb, I vow I'll never yank her leash again. With Ethel back in my life, everything seems manageable. Even my dad. Even Cal. Even those reporters. I keep glancing over my shoulder. When I see two people approaching from far down the street, I decide it's best for us to get back inside.

As Ethel settles herself on the sofa, I remember the call I declined to answer this morning. I press the play button and listen to my message:

"Ms. Nealon? This is Manor View Nursing Home calling. I'm afraid we have some upsetting news. Your father has had a second stroke. He's at Palmyrton Memorial right now."

Chapter 49

The reporters follow my car to the hospital and descend on me as I cross the parking lot to the front door. I keep my head down, ignoring everything they say, a hapless middle-schooler hounded by bullies, until I reach the sanctuary of the lobby and the security guard chases them away.

This freaking hospital is starting to feel like my second home. The smell of institutional food mixed with decay and death, the constant squawk of doctors being paged, the blank, hopeless faces of the patients and their visitors. How can people work here? I'd sooner be a coal miner.

A bored nurse buzzes me in to the ICU, then returns to tending the machinery of impending death while pointing me to Dad's bed. He lies there slack and empty, tubes running into and out of him. Beeping, blinking machines insist that he's alive, but I have my doubts.

"Dr. Morganthal is making his rounds," the nurse says. "He'll be right over to talk to you."

I sink into the chair beside his bed. Dad's pathetic condition should soften my heart, but it doesn't. Instead, the rage I've kept boxed up surges forward. I want to scream at him, demand answers. But the rage has no place to go. He can't hear me, can't see me, can't answer.

Once again, my father has evaded me.

His right hand lies on top of the white blankets. A good daughter would hold it, murmur words of reassurance. I stand like a soldier. "Get better," I say. "We're not done."

A tall bald guy in a white coat strides up and yanks out the clipboard from the foot of the bed. "You the daughter?" he asks without even making eye contact.

A prick this arrogant could only be a brain surgeon.

"Yes. How bad is it? Does he need surgery?"

"Surgery? That won't help."

The doctor might as well have added, "you moron" to the end of his sentence. "He had surgery after his first stroke," I remind him.

"I looked at his MRI—there's no new damage to his brain. No stroke, no heart attack." He continues scribbling on Dad's chart.

"What is it then?"

"I have to run some more bloodwork, but it looks like he ODed on sleeping meds. Probably hoarded several day's worth and took them all at once."

"Huh? You mean—"

The doctor snaps his clipboard shut. "Suicide attempt."

I stagger out of the hospital in a daze. The reporters, held in check by a burly guard, shout their questions, but I have more pressing ones of my own. Why did he do this now, when he was getting so much better? Why now, when the secret he'd been trying to keep from me was finally out? We could have started over. Why is it that with every step I take toward my father, he runs a mile back? I stumble down the rows of parked cars, barely aware of what I'm looking for.

The doctor said he'd been hoarding his medication, planning this. Was he angry that I finally made him tell me the truth about my mother? How could he have done this, done it *to me*? Because that's what this suicide is—the ultimate act of one-upmanship, the final fuck you. My knees buckle and I sag against a shiny red minivan for support. Where the hell is my car? I'm so disoriented I have to press the panic button on my remote and follow the hoot of my horn two rows over. When I finally collapse into my Honda and turn my cellphone back on, I see that I've missed two calls from Cal.

"Where are you?" he asks as soon we connect. "Are you okay? Is the press after you?"

"At the hospital. My father--" I can't say the words. My heart is pounding and I can't catch my breath. "He's sick. They're not sure if—"

"My God, Audrey—why didn't you call me? You shouldn't be there alone."

"Sorry. I didn't think…" I haven't really gotten used to this concept that I have a boyfriend who loves me. That boyfriends are people you call to report big events in your life. Maybe I'll get the hang of it eventually.

"I'll be right over," Cal says. "We can have lunch."

"No!" I can't cope with Cal right now. This is too big, too raw. "I…I think I need to lie down. I'm going to go home and rest."

"Are you sure? I could bring you something. Soup?"

I smile at the phone. Cal's offer, the fact that he was worried, is enough for me. I don't need his actual presence.

"I'm OK, really. Maybe tonight?"

"Definitely. I'll call you later. Get some rest."

When I was outside, all I wanted was to get back to my bed and Ethel. But now that I'm lying here, sleep won't come. My breathing has returned to normal, but my brain is churning. I see my father's suicide attempt like a hologram—one image and then another depending on the angle of the light. Anger has morphed to guilt. Telling me about the night of my mother's death was traumatic for him. Did I comfort him, reassure him? No, I interrogated him, gave him the silent treatment, and dumped him back at the nursing home.

I killed my mother, and now it seems I've killed my father too. I twist the covers over my head, ashamed for even Ethel to see my miserable black soul.

Then anger reasserts itself, slithering out of the cracks of my conscience, a snake relentlessly seeking heat. I'm giving myself way too much credit. My father would never kill himself because I, of all people, hurt his feelings. No, he did this to regain the upper hand, I'm sure of it.

I can't take this anymore! Flinging back the covers, I leap out of bed. Ethel looks hopefully at her leash, but the vultures are still posted outside my door and I don't have the strength to run that gauntlet right now. I click on the TV, but what old sit-com or preposterous advice show could possibly hold my attention today? Reading is equally hopeless and working on my accounts makes my head throb. I'm like a tiger in one of those supposedly enlightened zoos with the "natural" habitats—my surroundings are pleasant but the bars are no less real.

I need a project, some mindless yet absorbing task to keep my thoughts at bay. The hall closet is open and I catch sight of the trunk of jewelry from Mrs. Szabo's attic. Now that the election is over, I guess we can give it to Sister Alice. I'll ask Cal tonight. In the meantime, I might as well go through it and get a rough estimate of what the stuff is worth. I haul it into the middle of the living room and dump it out.

The cascade of gold and gemstones takes me back to a day that now seems like eons ago. So much has happened since this jewelry tumbled out of Mrs. Szabo's attic, yet nothing's been resolved. I still don't know how my mother's ring got into this trunk, and I don't know who else did just what I'm doing now—upended the trunk here in my condo to search through it.

Empty, the trunk itself holds more interest for me. Although the outside is dusty and scratched, the inside striped silk lining is pristine. I've seen trunks like this before—they were popular at the beginning of the 20th century. With a little clean-up, I could probably get two hundred bucks for this, but only if the inside partitions are sturdy. Sitting cross-legged on the floor, I run my hands along the inside walls. Shit—the lining is loose on one side. Water damage? Bugs? Gently, I tug at the lining and it peels away from the side wall of the trunk. Behind it are some papers: Mr. Szabo's discharge papers from the army at the end of World War II, the Szabos' wedding certificate, the title to a 1952 DeSoto, and an envelope that looks less yellowed with age than the other items. The glue has dissolved over time. I unseal it and remove a single sheet of paper.

The gasp of air I draw in burns my wounded lungs. I know this handwriting. The long loops of the "g"s and "p"s, the dramatic swirls of the capital S and B. This is the handwriting on the Christmas decoration boxes of my childhood. This was written by my mother.

The paper trembles as I read:

My darling,

I know you can never forgive me for what I am about to do-- I will not ask so much of you. I'm not good at keeping secrets. I feel better now that the truth is out. Believe me when I say that if I thought there were a chance that any of us could achieve happiness by following some other path, I would take it. I cannot keep going over the rational reasons for staying; I must follow the <u>true</u> reasons for leaving. I will not separate you from Audrey. I know how much you love her. I love her too (that's why I cannot continue to poison her with my misery). It's best for me to leave right now--I'm sure Audrey won't wake before you return.

All I ask is that someday you will understand.

C

I read the letter a second time, then a third. Ethel approaches and lays her head on my knee. I let the letter slip to the floor, and speak out loud to the empty room. "Goddamn it to hell. She was going to leave me behind."

Chapter 50

Am I shocked? I poke and prod and decide this new wound looks a lot worse than it feels. The letter confirms what I've suspected, deep in my heart, since childhood: my mother chose to leave me.

Then my heart rate kicks up as the hologram dissolves to yet another image of my father's suicide. Guilt. If my mother left this letter for my dad, then I was never in the car with her that night. I didn't run her over.

I push myself to my feet, pace to the window and back. He killed her. He must have. And when I got close to the truth, he told me this terrible, terrible lie. And felt so guilty he killed himself. I snatch up the phone and dial the hospital. The doctor is gone, but the nurse tells me there's no change. My father is still unconscious, but stable.

I sit on the floor stroking Ethel's head as the daylight slowly slips away. Who knows how much time passes as I twist and turn the pieces of the puzzle, looking for the pattern to emerge?

I've been assuming Mrs. Szabo acquired my mother's ring the same way she got all the other deposits in her larcenous 401k. But the presence of the ring *and* the letter in this trunk changes that key variable in the equation. She didn't steal my mother's ring by chance, when an opportunity presented itself. She had both items for a reason, and cleverly hid like items with like items: the ring among her stolen jewels and the letter among her own valuable papers. Someone gave them to her. Maybe that's why she was so anxious to get to the trunk in her attic. She wasn't worried about the stolen jewelry being found; she was worried about this.

Why?

Whoever broke into my apartment to search this trunk was looking for the letter, because he knew the ring had been found.

Who?

I can't get all the pieces to fit together; some are missing, for sure. But of one thing I'm sure: Agnes Szabo knew someone in my mother's love triangle.

I have to find out the identity of this other man. Jude, my father said his name was. Is it too late to call the Van Houten Group and demand a search of their personnel files? Or at least talk to Reid himself and twist his arm? I dial 411, but as the computerized voice demands, "City and state" my gaze rests on the Princeton yearbook on the table. Spencer, Roger and Charlotte were friends in 1968.

The phone slips from my fingers. *Jude...Judas*. A rare burst of metaphor from the mathematician. Dad was betrayed by his friend.

Spencer *was* my mother's lover, yet my father lied about this too. Why?

I can't talk to my father, but I sure as hell can talk to Spencer. I reach for the phone again. Then drop it again. What the hell am I thinking? Spencer's not an ordinary citizen. He's walled off behind a cordon of reporters, security guards and lawyers. And Coughlin has specifically forbidden me to talk to any Finnerans.

Not that I ever listen to Coughlin.

I have to talk to Cal about this. There's no other way. He'll help me get in touch with Spencer. He has to—he knows how much this means to me. I have to know, once and for all, what really happened that night. Once I know, I can let it go. I can.

I think.

I leave an incoherent message on Cal's voicemail, talking so fast I know I must sound like Jill on meth. I babble on about the letter and the trunk and Agnes and Spencer and my dad, and when the phone beeps and cuts me off, I call back and babble some more, ending with, "Call me as soon as you get this."

Then I begin to pace, Ethel right at my heels. A peek out the front window reveals the vultures still on their roost. "C'mon, baby—we'll sneak out the back again. I know it's not much of a walk, but it's the best I can offer right now."

I triple check to make sure I have my phone, then Ethel and I head out.

I'm in no mood to deal with reporters right now, so I keep a sharp eye peeled as Ethel and I step off the condo pathway onto the sidewalk. The street is empty except for one parked car. Ethel and I set off in the opposite direction. As soon as she does her business, I turn and head back. A head of me, a man steps out of the parked car and stands waiting by the pathway into my development.

I sigh. Damn reporter. At least he doesn't look too imposing, and I do have Ethel. My hand tightens on her leash as I prepare to push past him.

"I'm Brian Bascomb."

I stop and stare.

Megan the speech therapist told me Brian Bascomb was "cute." I have to question her judgment. Cute is not the adjective that leaps to mind here; awkward is more like it. A little taller than me and probably not a pound heavier, Brian wears faded jeans that cling to his skinny butt through sheer willpower. He's got a mop of unruly, dirty blond curls, deep-set brown eyes and a slightly beaky nose. Definitely not the hunky Brian Bascomb I found on Facebook. I laugh slightly.

"What's funny?"

I shake my head, thinking of my preposterous belief that Brian was my long-lost half-sibling. He's just a standard-issue math whiz, the kind of geeky boy who sat next to me in Calc III or Tensor Analysis all through college.

He shoves his hands deep in his jeans pockets and looks down at his battered running shoes. "I need to talk to you."

I can see that talking to strangers, particularly strangers who are women, is torture for the poor kid, and I take pity. "Walk along with Ethel and me."

His head jerks up. "That's Ethel? I thought she was lost. Your dad was really upset."

"She was, for five days. But my...my boyfriend found her. Out by Manor View—isn't that amazing?"

Brian shoots a quick glance at me before dropping his gaze back to the ground. He speaks in a rapid monotone. "That guy you've been dating, the one who works for Spencer Finneran, your dad doesn't like him. He's worried about you. He told me—"

I come to a quick halt, jerking poor Ethel who's trotting ahead. "Who *are* you? How is it that he tells you so much when I can't get him to tell me a freakin' thing?"

"I was his student at Rutgers and now I'm getting my PhD at Princeton. I used to come to see your dad at his office to toss ideas around for my dissertation. After he had the stroke, I came to see him at Manor View. That's when he first asked me to help him." Brian shifts from foot to foot in the freezing evening air. "It's up to me to look out for you. It's what he'd want me to do."

I look at this strange, scrawny person bobbing in front of me. What in God's name is he talking about? "My father would want *you* to look after *me*?"

Brian nods vigorously. "Ever since you found that ring he's been worried. He asked me to keep an eye on you, and to find out some things for him."

"Keep an eye on me?" I glance over his shoulder to the street and notice that his car is small and gray with a dented front bumper.

"You're the person who's been following me? You're the one who stole the yearbook I found! He sent you to spy on me because he was afraid I was going to find out the truth about my mother!"

"He wanted to protect you from knowing the truth about her accident. He only told me after you already knew."

I reel Ethel in closer to me for comfort. Grabbing Brian's arm with my other hand, I give him a little push. "Everything he told you is bullshit. I didn't kill my mother, he murdered her. And now he's tried to commit suicide because he can't face the truth coming out."

Brian shakes his head furiously, making his curls fly like a feather duster.

"I was with him when he found out about the fire. He was scared, really scared and really worried about you. He told me you were in danger. He didn't try to kill himself. I know he didn't."

"How can you be so sure?"

He holds his head up straight, his awkwardness slipping away. "Because I *know* him. He just isn't capable of that. And he sure isn't capable of murder."

I look at Brian's intense eyes. It must be nice to enjoy such certainty. Too bad I don't share his conviction. "Frankly, I have no idea what my father is or isn't capable of."

"Trust your father, Audrey. He cares about you."

I snort and pivot away from him, dragging Ethel after me. "Get away from me, Brian. Go sit by my father's bedside. And if he happens to wake up, tell him I found the letter. Tell him I know the truth."

Chapter 51

Striding away from Brian Bascomb, my heart pounds and my lungs burn as if I'd just run a four minute mile. I feel muddled and unsteady. My poor brain, simultaneously deprived of oxygen and overloaded with information, is barely able to command my legs to walk. As Ethel pulls me across the courtyard toward home, my cellphone rings. Cal, at last!

"I need to talk to Spencer," I say as soon as I answer. "You need to set it up."

"I've talked to Spencer, Audrey. He can't see you, not with Dylan under arrest and the media watching us all like hawks. But he and I talked. I told him your happiness depends on getting all this resolved. So I want you to come here to my place and I'll explain everything."

I hesitate. This is what I wanted, and yet-- I wish I hadn't blabbed everything about finding the letter. If Spencer knows—

"Audrey? What's wrong? If you're worried about Ethel, bring her along. I don't mind."

I smile. "No. she'll be okay by herself for a while. I'll be right over."

"Pull directly into the parking garage of my building. I'll give you the code. That way you won't have to deal with the reporters."

I've never been to Cal's place. He moved into the penthouse apartment just a month before we met. The building is brand-new and largely unoccupied, the developer having over-estimated Palmyrton's desire for downtown luxury dwellings. But Cal seems confident he made a good deal and that the market will catch up to him.

I press a few buttons and glide into the garage, leaving the rabble of reporters outside gnashing their teeth. I'm on P1, which is entirely empty. Cal's car must be on the next level. I park near the elevator and take a deep breath to steady my nerves.

As I glide up ten floors to Cal's place, I compose my questions. After thirty years, I'm within striking distance of the truth.

I ring the bell. Seconds later I'm enveloped in Cal's arms. I bury my head in his shoulder and inhale his subtle scent. Jesus, everything they say about pheromones is true. My attraction to him is primal. Even with everything I'm desperate to know, there's a part of me that wants nothing more than to lie wordlessly in his arms. Finally I pull away and look around.

What a man cave! Across a polished expanse of hardwood, two buttery chocolate brown sofas flank a gleaming glass and metal coffee table. Floor-to-ceiling windows dominate one wall, framing the bright bustle of downtown. The lighting is low; soft jazz purrs in the background.

I slip my fleece jacket off. "Very nice, Cal."

"It's a little impersonal. The decorator chose that painting to color-coordinate with the sofa. You could help me pick something better."

I smile, but I didn't come here to talk art. I march to the sofa and sit down. Cal drops beside me. I keep a little distance between us so I can focus on the matter at hand.

"Spencer was my mother's lover." I say it without the rising lilt of a question.

"Yes."

Even though I came here knowing this fact, Cal's unvarnished confirmation sends a shiver across the back of my neck. This is it. I've been climbing, climbing, climbing to the crest of the roller coaster. Now the car is about to drop.

"How long have you known?"

"Just since you left me that message, baby. Honestly." Cal's eyes--anxious, pleading—seek mine "I finally got Spencer alone this afternoon. I made him tell me everything. He agreed to let me tell you—he knows he owes you the truth."

I nod, and Cal begins to talk. "When your parents moved to Palmyrton, they renewed their friendship with Spencer and they met Anne. Spencer recommended Charlotte for the job at the PR agency. As it turns out, that was a big mistake."

A mistake that cost my mother her life. The story of Anne and Spencer and Charlotte and Roger seems at once very distant and terribly close. I'm watching a movie, only this movie is the prequel to my own life.

"Spencer and your mother worked together long hours on his campaign," Cal continues, sliding his arm around me. I hold myself stiffly, but I don't push him away. "He's not proud of what he did, Audrey, but they were both young and a little reckless. The whole thing might have blown over if it hadn't been for your father." Cal pauses and squeezes my shoulder. "He told you that you killed your mother, that you accidentally ran her over with the car—right?"

I nod.

"That's what he told Spencer too, when he showed up that night. But Audrey, Spencer saw her body. The car ran over her torso, but her neck was bruised. Your father strangled her, Audrey. Strangled her in a rage of jealousy, then ran her over with the car to cover up his crime. Spencer accused him of that, but he insisted you'd done it."

My fingers dig into Cal's hand. What kind of father comes up with an alibi like that? How could my father have told anyone, let alone me, such an awful thing? But my father has always applied the absolute certainty of a mathematician to every aspect of his life. Whenever he made a decision—yes to math camp, no to after-prom party--his decree was absolutely non-negotiable. I can imagine him analyzing the results of the one time in his life that he acted with irrational passion. His wife was dead, his child motherless—nothing could change that. So he came up with the one alibi that could keep him out of prison and me from becoming an orphan. He moved forward and never wavered. I'm sure it must've seemed perfectly logical to him. We sit quietly for a moment, Cal stroking my hand, as I absorb the enormity of it. But when the wave of emotion passes, my rational mind clicks back into gear.

"But if Spencer thought my father killed Charlotte, then why did he help him get rid of the body?"

"He could see his crazy story about you running her over would never hold up. Once the police realized he'd killed her, they'd want to know why. Spencer's affair with Charlotte would have certainly come out. He couldn't let that happen. He had to think of his family. He did it for Anne."

I snort. "Oh, come on, Cal—even you must see he did it for his career."

Cal holds out his hands. "Of course, that was a consideration. But Audrey, you must believe me. Spencer loved Anne. And he cared about your mother, too. That's why he kept her ring and entrusted it to Agnes. That night… that night was the worst night of his life."

"Yeah, tell me about Agnes, why don't you? How does she fit into all this? You've always known that Spencer knew your aunt, right?"

Cal bites his lip. "It's complicated. Agnes worked for Anne and Spencer for nearly ten years when their kids were young. When they didn't need a nanny anymore, they found her a new position. They always provided her with glowing references. She was devoted to them."

"And that's how you met Spencer—through Agnes, not through an ex-girlfriend?"

Cal nods. "Agnes loved knowing a famous politician. Spencer helped my Uncle Jack get a liquor license for his restaurant and recommended my cousin for the Naval Academy. I've known him since I was a kid. After my parents divorced, he reached out to me…got me summer jobs, made sure I stayed on track for college. Once I came back to Palmyrton after law school, I started working on his campaigns."

Cal gazes out the window to the lights of Palmyrton below. "At first it was just a game to me. I did it for the adrenaline rush of the competition." He shakes his head. "But this campaign. This is different. This one matters."

I pull myself into the corner of the sofa. I remember that night on our second date when he told me so smoothly, so effortlessly, how he met Spencer. And it was all untrue. "So why did you lie about that to me?"

"Why did you lie to me at first about taking your mother's ring out of the trunk?"

I finger the ring protectively. "It was mine. I didn't know how it got in your aunt's trunk, but I knew that ring belonged to me."

Cal sighs and continues. "When you discovered the trunk of jewelry, I knew immediately that Agnes must've stolen it. I told Spencer right away—I wanted his advice on how to handle it. That's when he asked me not to mention his connection to Agnes—he didn't want any hint of scandal during the campaign. It seemed like a harmless white lie."

"But it wasn't!" I hear an unfamiliar edge of hysteria in my own voice. "You kept lying to me, even after—" *Even after you said you loved me.*

Cal looks a little queasy. He knows better than to try to touch me right now. "Spencer told me today that he was stunned when you showed up wearing your mother's ring. He had told Agnes years ago to get rid of it, but for some reason, she never did. But I didn't know that, Audrey, you have to believe me. I thought Agnes stole your mother's ring just as she stole the other jewelry.

"As I got to know you better, and saw how important it was to you to figure out what happened to your mother, I brought it up to Spencer again. Since he'd given Agnes references, I figured he must know whom she'd worked for. By that time, he'd met you and liked you. Spencer promised me that after the election, he'd dig though his files and help you find the other families Agnes worked for." Cal extends his hands, palms up. "I believed him."

Cal's explanation is making me more agitated, not less. I lean forward, searching his face for signs of distress and coming up empty. "But he lied to you too. He saw me wearing the ring, but didn't explain to you what that meant. Doesn't that bother you?"

Cal rolls his eyes. "C'mon, Audrey. This was intensely personal. He didn't want to admit to me that he'd had an affair. He knew I looked up to him. He knew I loved Anne. He wanted the past to stay buried. Surely you can understand that?"

"What did he think was going to happen after the election? Sooner or later I would have figured it out."

"Politics is a game that's played minute-by-minute, baby. As soon as you map out a strategy, you can be sure it'll be upended by events you can't control."

Cal stands before me in his gray flannel slacks and crisp oxford shirt, but I see Cal the runner, winning the race by putting his head down and focusing on the stretch of road directly beneath his feet. He honestly doesn't see a problem with this approach. "I'm sorry—I just can't believe that Spencer thought this deception was a viable option."

"I'm sure he figured he'd cross that bridge when he came to it."

I jump up. "Welcome to the middle of the freakin' bridge, Cal!"

Cal steps towards me, takes my shoulders in his hands. His eyes are shining, locked on mine with such intensity that I feel I couldn't look away if I tried. "Spencer has spent every day since the night your mother died trying to atone for what he did. Everything he's fought for as a state representative, as a senator…everything he hopes to do as governor has been because of that terrible night. He can't bring Charlotte back, but if he can do some good in this world—enact education reforms so that poor kids in Newark have the same opportunities as rich kids in Mountain Lakes, restructure our tax system so that everyone pays a fair share—"

"Oh, please Cal! Spare me the damn stump speech. You're not the guest speaker at some rubber chicken dinner. This is my life we're talking about here."

Cal pulls me down next to him on the sofa. "That's just it, Audrey. It's not only *your* life. This is bigger than one person's needs and desires. This is about the future of our state. Of this country."

I narrow my eyes. "Spencer wants to run for president?"

"In four years he'll be sixty-nine. It's then or never." Cal grabs my hands. "Spencer would make the ideal Democratic candidate. Socially liberal, fiscally moderate. Smarter and more experienced than anyone else on the horizon. Why should some indiscretion that happened thirty years ago derail that?"

I yank my hands away. "Indiscretion?" Cal's capacity for understatement blows me away.

"Franklin Roosevelt, John Kennedy, even Martin Luther King— they all had affairs, but they led their country, they changed the world for the better." Cal's face is lit up like a Times Square billboard. "Yes, they were flawed, but they were still great men."

"Flawed? *Flawed?* My mother was murdered and Spencer helped dispose of the body. And let's not forget that his wife tried to kill me. We're not talking personality quirks here."

Cal takes a deep breath. "Spencer wants you to know how truly sorry he is for all that's happened. Anne….well, Anne wasn't in her right mind, you've got to see that. The cancer, the pain, the drugs she was on—she just wasn't herself."

"I was there with her, Cal. She was very much herself. Her smart, commanding, determined Anne Finneran self. She wanted to kill me. And I'm beginning to think it wasn't just to protect Dylan.

How much did Anne know about the ring and the trunk?"

A furrow of confusion appears on Cal's forehead. "Anne? Anne never knew about the ring. I told you, Spencer was trying to shield her from the affair."

"Are you positive, Cal? Spencer relied on Anne's advice for everything. Why not this?"

Cal shakes himself the way Ethel does when a pesky fly lands on her head. "Anne knew nothing about the ring. What happened during the fire….she didn't mean to do it."

Didn't mean to do it? That's what you say when your baseball breaks a neighbor's window, not when you try to pin someone down in a burning building. I'm stunned into silence.

Cal's face is so close to mine I can smell his spearminty breath. He cradles my cheeks in his hands. "Baby, you must see that no good can come from revealing all this to the media. Anne did so much good in her life. Spencer has so much still to offer the world. It would be best if we kept the affair and the circumstances of the fire within the family." He kisses me. "Do it for me."

I jerk away as if I've been slapped. The sound of my own breathing roars in my ears. *Keep your friends close and your enemies closer.* That's it. Of course it is. Coughlin warned me that all Cal's loyalties lay with Spencer. I should have listened.

"Spencer assigned you to keep an eye on me and bring me into the Finneran fold, didn't he?" My voice ascends the scale. "The romantic dinners, the flowers, the sex—all in a day's work for you, wasn't it?"

Cal reaches for me. "No, it wasn't like that!"

But his protest comes a split second too late. I see the shadow of guilt pass over his face. I've nailed it. Deep in my heart I've always known the truth—a man like Cal would never be interested in me.

I spring up just as my phone starts to trill. If it's another reporter, this time I'm taking the call. I lift the phone to my ear. In one swift lunge, Cal grabs my phone and hurls it across the room. It crashes against a wall and breaks apart. He latches onto my arm and jerks me around to face him. Any pretense of affection has dissolved. I see a fierce passion there that has nothing to do with me. "Grow up, Audrey. You think you were the only person in the world with an unhappy childhood? That everyone's family was perfect except yours? My father dumped my mother for a woman ten years older than me. Anne's mother had a nervous breakdown, Spencer's father was an unemployed drunk. Shit happens. Get over it."

I break free and run for the powder room, slamming the door in Cal's face and locking it.

He pounds hard enough to make the wood vibrate. "Audrey, come out of there. We're not done."

Oh, but we are. We're so done.

Soon he stops hammering. A minute passes and his voice softens. "Baby, I'm sorry. I overreacted. It's true that Spencer asked me to…get to know you. But Audrey, that was just at the beginning. I really did fall for you. Let's talk, baby—we can work this out."

"Shut up! I'll come out of here when I'm good and damn ready. And stop calling me baby." I sit on the edge of the toilet and run my fingers through my hair. Hunched and trembling, too numb to cry, I pick up each betrayal and caress it, admiring the artistry that went into its creation. I'm outclassed here—a Play-Doh sculptor at the Louvre.

I get up and walk to the polished marble sink. Trying not to look at myself in the mirror, I splash cold water on my face. My breaths come in short, hard bursts. I have to get more oxygen to my brain. I can't think.

I can't trust Cal, that much is obvious. His belief in Spencer goes way past loyalty. It's more like a fundamentalist religion that causes its followers to speak in tongues. Cal has given me lots of information, but how can I tease out what's true and what's false?

My mind makes a sudden leap back to my college days, tutoring non-math majors in calculus. One girl used to hyperventilate every time she saw the sea of numbers and letters and symbols staring up at her from her text book. The answer is right in there, I would tell her.

Relax and you'll see it.

That should work here, but it doesn't. Because a calculus textbook isn't filled with false information masquerading as fact. I could solve this equation any number of ways, but I still won't be sure I have the right answer. Garbage in, garbage out as the computer science majors used to say.

Reason, Audrey. Start with what you know is true. No doubt Spencer dumped my mother's body, kept her ring, and gave it to Agnes to keep. There can be no other explanation for how it came to be in that trunk. But what about the letter? Cal and I argued before he even attempted to explain that. Why would Spencer have taken the letter? And why leave it with Agnes? A letter to another man is hardly a sentimental memento.

Another thing is certain. I blew off Brian Bascomb and my father too soon. I'm ashamed by how unquestioningly I accepted Cal's explanation that my father killed my mother. Maybe he did...but isn't it just as plausible that Spencer killed her? I need to hear his version of events, if he's able, or willing, to tell me. Has he regained consciousness? It's too late to visit the hospital now, but I can call when I get home.

I lean against the cool tile wall and close my eyes. I want nothing more than to be held. Instead, I have to go out there and face Cal. I have to face that I'm totally alone. I will not cry. I will not.

Opening the bathroom door, I poke my head into the hall. The apartment is dark and silent; could Cal have gone out?

I slip toward the front door. I want out of here, away from the Finnerans and everyone connected to them. Their house, their family, their life was a sham. I'm ashamed for ever being attracted to it.

"You were in there for a long time." The voice--calm, quiet--floats to me in the darkness.

My heart pounds. "I was thinking."

Neither of us speaks. We don't need to. Despite all the deception, we have built a bond, we two, over this past month. He knows that to me, empirical truth is paramount. I know that to him, everything is relative. It hardly matters who actually snuffed out my mother's last breath. The result is the same: the end of Spencer's career.

"The world is not black and white, Audrey." Cal's disembodied voice, low and even, caresses me like warm seawater. "Your mother's dead; Anne's dead—nothing's going to change that. Your father and Spencer did what they had to do to protect the people they loved. What good can come of telling the media this old story? More people will be hurt. And none of it will bring your mother back."

So intense, so pragmatic. Cal the horsetrader; give a little to get a little. That always works with constituents and donors. He doesn't understand he's not offering me the right deal.

It's not my mother I want back. It's my father.

Chapter 52

I open the door of the apartment and walk out. No good-bye, no slam—I'm done with drama.

On the elevator ride down I plan what to do first. Call Coughlin, the New York Times, the hospital? Everything will have to wait until I get home to my landline.

On the lobby level the door slides open and a tall man in a stocking cap and a canvas coat faces me.

Figuring he intends to go up, I warn him, "This is going down to the parking garage."

He nods and steps in. The door slides shut and we're alone together.

I feel my heart rate quicken. This is ridiculous—I have to get over my fear of elevators. Keeping my eyes focused forward, I edge away from my fellow passenger. Silently, we descend two more levels. When the door opens on P1, he stands aside to let me exit first.

Whew! Gripping my keys in my coat pocket, I set off toward my car. My footsteps echo in the empty, cavernous space. I don't notice another car. I wonder what that guy—

A footstep. A swish of air. The cold grit of concrete against my cheek. I'm down so fast I don't have time to utter a sound. There's a knee in my back and fingers laced through my hair. He yanks my head back to slam it into the concrete.

I manage to get my arms up to block the impact. He shifts his grip for better leverage. I twist around to look at him.

He knocks me back down. Now we're face-to-face as he puts his hands around my neck.

The face is familiar, yet strange. The head is bald, the teeth are crooked, the eyes are brown.

But the lips, the chin, the cheekbones are ones I know well. They belong to Spencer Finneran.

My eyes widen and he grins.

"Good disguise, huh? I never wanted to be one of those politicians whose fame puts him in a bubble. I use this to get out among the people, hear what they really think. Amazing how when you change your most distinguishing characteristics, no one recognizes you."

His hands tighten. I stare straight into his creepy, brown contact lens-shrouded eyes. It takes a long time to strangle someone to death. I'm not going to make it easy for him.

"Is this how you killed my mother?" I whisper.

The pressure increases. He shakes his head. "Shut up, Audrey."

Shut up. That's what Cal wanted me to do, but I wouldn't agree. Cal. He set me up for this. I should have known he wouldn't let me walk away and destroy everything the two of them have worked for.

Starbursts of white light explode before my eyes. Spencer's BlackBerry chirps the arrival of a text. I stop struggling, shut my eyes, and go limp.

The pressure lessens. It's enough. Rage propels me out of Spencer's grasp. Keys in hand, I slash at Spencer's eye. He screams and touches the damage. His hand comes away bloody. Through it all, his phone keeps chirping.

I'm up on my feet and racing for my car. Almost there. Then I feel my leg yanked out from under me. I'm airborne, my head bouncing off a concrete column. Dazed, I can't fight back when Spencer gets his hands around my neck again. He won't fall for the going limp trick a second time. Game over.

The exploding lights appear again…fade to gray…black is next…

"Stop!"

Spencer flinches and oxygen rushes back into my lungs. Another man appears above us.

"Jesus Christ, Spencer, what are you doing? You said you wanted to talk to her. You can't *kill* her!"

Spencer looks up at Cal. "You had your chance. You told me you could make her listen. Clearly, you were wrong." Spencer's hands resume their work. "This will look like Dylan's drug-dealing friends did it. Get out of here if you're too squeamish to watch."

Cal pulls Spencer off me. They stagger, grappling for the upper hand. Cal is younger but Spencer is taller. Neither one is a street fighter. Cal breaks away and takes a swing, but lands only a glancing blow to Spencer's shoulder. I struggle to push myself to my feet. Instinctively, I reach for my phone, but it's lying shattered upstairs.

"Get in the car, Audrey," Cal yells. "Go for help."

Just then, Spencer delivers a punch to Cal's head and he reels. I scream and stumble toward them.

Cal regains his footing. "Go, Audrey!"

He's right. I'm too weak to be of any use. The car is the best solution. As I fall into the driver's seat and start the engine, I hear a terrible scream. Looking around, I see Cal slump down along the length of a column. A bright blossom of blood marks the spot where Spencer slammed Cal's head against the concrete.

Even after all that's happened, my instinct is to run to him, comfort him.

Then, in my headlights, I see Spencer Finneran sprinting up the exit ramp. In a moment he'll be out on the street, out of his disguise, out from everything he's done to Cal…my mother…my father…me.

I accelerate.

Chapter 53

Eight hours after Spencer Finneran is admitted to Palmyrton Memorial Hospital for trauma surgery, my father is released, the overdose of medications flushed from his system. The police are searching for a newly hired Manor View aide who stopped coming to work after my father was poisoned. Maybe Spencer promised her a green card for her husband or a civil service job for her son.

We are sitting together in the solarium at Manor View, preparing to solve the biggest problem of our lives. The Hodge Conjecture and the Reimann Hypothesis pale in comparison to the complexity of the Nealon Quagmire. Sharpened pencils with good erasers and a high-end graphing calculator won't help us here. This is mental math gone wild.

I speak calmly. "Tell me again exactly what you remember about that night."

His voice is steady even though his speech is still a little slurred. His eyes never blink. "When I ga home aroun' nine, your mutha was already dead."

"Who was there?"

"Spencer in the driveway, crying. You asleep in the fron' seat of the car. Charlotte under it. "

"Did you understand right away what had happened?"

Dad shakes his head. "Too much to absorb. Charlotte dead. Spencer there. The snow, so much snow."

"Who said that I must've put the car in gear?"

"Spencer. He foun' the crush doll carriage after I arrived. Saw how you were slumped over the gear shift."

"And you believed him?"

Dad nods. "Spencer so distraught. He loved your mutha too… I thought . And, and…he had been my friend."

Betrayed. I know how that feels. I touch his hand lightly. He doesn't pull away. "Look." I hand him the letter. "Have you ever seen this?"

I watch his face crumple as he reads it. Thirty years later the shock and pain are still raw. My father's no Robert De Niro—this is the first time he's read that letter.

"My mother meant to leave me behind, Dad. She took off while I was asleep in my bed. I was never in the car with her."

Our eyes meet. "My God," he whispers.

For thirty years my father has resented me for what he thought I did that night. Now I've proved my innocence. What should I be feeling here—relief? Triumph? Anger? I try each emotion on and reject it. Instead, I'm stunned to discover a little flicker of sympathy. My father's response to my three year old self was totally unjust, totally irrational. For the first time in our lives, he seems fully human to me.

Not that we're about to throw our arms around each other in an orgy of tears and apologies. We are Nealons, after all.

When I speak again, my voice is steady. "Did you ever see her neck?"

"No, wearing a scarf." He looks at me. "Car didna kill her?'

I shake my head. "Strangled, I think. Tell me what happened next."

"Spencer and I argued, but worked ou' a plan. What to do with the car. Putting toys he bought for his kids in the trunk. What to do with body." Dad stares at the hospital ID bracelet still on his wrist as if he wouldn't know who he was if it weren't printed right there.

"Where was I?"

"I carried you in house. Put you in bed. I hadda leave you alone for a while, when I took car to the lake with Spencer. Didna' like it, but no other way. You slept righ' through."

"And Spencer took care of the rest," I say. " Drove to the shore. Put Charlotte's body in his boat and took her out to sea. But when it came time to throw her in the water, he slipped her ring off. Wanted that one little memento."

"Spencer tol' me wait 'til mornin' to call police. By then, the body would be in ocean and he back home."

I get up and pace around the overheated room. A huge geranium drips brilliant red petals on the floor. Outside, the world is black and gray and brown. "But what about the letter? Why did he save that? The ring might be a memento, but the letter was written to another man. It incriminated him. Why wouldn't he have destroyed it?"

Dad shakes his head.

I experience a moment of great clarity, as I do when I can see five moves ahead to how I'm going to win a chess game. I look at my father.

"I remember the cops being there when I woke up on Christmas morning. What time was that, Dad?"

He shrugs. "Eight or nine."

"Do the math, Dad," I say softly. "I slept more than twelve hours straight. I slept alone in the car. I slept when you carried me through the snowstorm into the house. Slept while you and Spencer argued about your plan. Slept when you left me to dump the car. Slept long past the time most little kids are up to see what Santa has brought."

"Drugged." Dad breathes the word out. "I remember you had an empty sippy cup in your hand. You loved juice. Spencer must've given you somethin' before I go' there."

I hold up my hand. "Not Spencer. Anne." *Anne with her handy Benadryl for crying babies. Good mother Anne, ever ready with cups of juice and bags of snacks.* "Cal told me Spencer helped you cover up my mother's murder to spare Anne from knowing about the affair. But that can't be true. She must've known right from the start. Spencer was out all night long on Christmas Eve getting rid of the body. How could he possibly have explained that to the mother of his children? Anne knew. Anne knew because Mom must've called and told her she was pregnant with Spencer's child. She was tired of waiting. She jump-started the action."

Dad sighs and nods. "Tha' was your mutha."

I take the letter out of Dad's lap. "Maybe that's why she said, 'I'm not good at keeping secrets.' After all, you already knew about the affair. Anne was the one who truly hated Charlotte. And I know for a fact she's strong enough, and determined enough, to kill. So as mom was running off to meet Spencer, Anne intercepted her in the driveway and strangled her. Then Anne must've realized she couldn't get rid of the body herself. She needed to call her husband for help.

"Spencer arrived and together they ran over my mother's body with our car. With the hedge along the driveway and the snow coming down so thick, the neighbors wouldn't have been able to see a thing."

Dad clenches the arms of his chair. "The crush doll carriage... perfec' prop. Charla' really did run over tha'."

I slept through this night thirty years ago, but today I see it with stunning clarity. "Then Anne came in the house to get me. Mom's letter to you was probably right on the kitchen table. She took it, but why did she keep it?" I feel I'm so close—that the answer is there for the taking.

"I thin' I unnerstan'," Dad says. "Anne very proud. Didn' wanna admit mistakes to her fatha. No' wanna risk Spencer leavin' her again. Letter was insurance."

I nod. Dad and I are on to something here. Collaborators, not adversaries for once. "She kept the letter—and the ring as well-- to hold over Spencer's head. We'll never know, but it must've been Anne who gave the stuff to Agnes for safekeeping—she would have been closer to the nanny than her husband."

"Risky."

"Not so much." I slide my chair closer to his and hold out the letter so we can both see it. "It starts 'My Darling' and it's signed 'C'. If Agnes had ever read it, which I don't think she did, she wouldn't have understood what she had. And then, somewhere along the line, Anne must've felt she no longer needed her insurance policy. She probably told Agnes to get rid of it. But by that time, the poor old soul couldn't get up into her attic to do Anne's bidding." I give a bitter little laugh as I recall how Anne was able to control her household help with a nod of her head or a lift of her eyebrow. It probably never occurred to her that Agnes wouldn't obey her.

I drop the letter in my father's lap. "This only had meaning for Spencer, Anne and you."

"An' you."

"Yeah, and me. If anyone else had found that trunk, none of this would've happened." I nudge my father's leg. "Remember when you finally accepted I was going into the estate sale business, you told me not to choose a silly name like Another Man's Treasure. If I had named my company "Nealon's Estate Sales" maybe Spencer and Anne would've encouraged Cal to choose a different firm. Like in chess, Dad. The opening gambit determines the whole course of the game. "

He sits there, rigid as the Sphinx. When he speaks again, his voice is tinged with awe. "What a marriage the Finnerans had!"

"Amazing, for sure. The murder seemed to make it stronger. Spencer saved Anne from a life in prison. Anne saved Spencer from a messy, career-ending affair. You keep my secret, I'll keep yours— that was the basis of their union."

I twist to face my father head-on. "Why were you so determined to keep it from me that Spencer was my mother's lover."

"Dangerous for you to know before election. You would

confron' him even if I tol' you no' to.'"

I narrow my eyes. Would I have? "What makes you say that?"

"You nevuh listen ta me."

"You always think you're right!"

There it is, every parent and child's lament. I wouldn't listen when he wanted me to stay in the Chess Club in high school, wouldn't listen when I chose UVA over Princeton, wouldn't listen when I started Another Man's Treasure, wouldn't listen when I hired Ty. Maybe he's right. Maybe I wouldn't have listened. But he could've tried. Instead, he did what he thought was best, always convinced he was right.

We glare at each other for a moment. Then I stretch back in my chair and gaze up at the ceiling. "Anne must've been stunned when Spencer told her about the trunk. I bet it was Anne who stole the key to my condo from your house and went through the trunk looking for that letter. I wonder—"

Dad waits for me to go on. When I don't, his expression shifts. Maybe he's noticed the tears in my eyes. He reaches for me, but I pretend I don't see and fold my arms across my chest.

"I wonder which of them persuaded Cal—" The tears are flowing now.

"Don' torture yourself, Audrey," my father says.

Oh, but I will. I can't stop thinking about how they ensnared him, controlled him, engendered such loyalty.

Cal lost his soul trying to save the Finnerans.

He lost his life saving me.

Chapter 54

"So, what are you doing for Thanksgiving," I ask Coughlin. We're walking through Jockey Hollow Park with Ethel on her long, retractable leash so she can have the illusion that she's free to chase wildlife.

He sighs and rolls his eyes. "Going to my Cousin Brendan's house."

"You don't sound too happy about it. I thought you were really into the big family get-togethers."

"I used to love Thanksgiving. It was my favorite holiday until Brendan and Adrienne—oh, excuse me Ah-dree-*enn*—hijacked it. We used to rotate between four of my aunts' houses on Thanksgiving. Fifty people crammed into a little cape cod or split, folding tables stretched from the dining room through to the sun porch. All the men gathered around a Motorola TV in the rec room to watch the game. A thirty pound Butterball, sweet potatoes with marshmallows and canned green beans with the dried onions on top. It was fun, know what I mean? Then Brendan hit it rich trading derivatives or credit default swaps or whatever the fuck he does— sorry. He bought this house with a *great room* and a *media center"*— Coughlin makes air quotes when he says these words— and Adrienne has dinner catered by some freakin' frog restaurant. Last year when Aunt Gert brought a big casserole of her sweet potatoes, Adrienne wouldn't even put them on the table."

"She sounds awful." I keep my eyes trained on Ethel, who's doing her best to intimidate a chipmunk chattering at her from just beyond the leash's reach. "But at least you're all together."

"A turkey on rye from Sol's sounds like a good alternative to me. Maybe I'll join you and your dad."

I fixate on reeling Ethel in. "Thanks for the offer, Sean. But your nieces and nephews need you. You've gotta organize the touch football."

Coughlin looks down and scuffs the ground with one enormous hoof. "Yeah, right. It's nice to be needed."

I look away. I'm not going there now.

He scrambles to cover the awkwardness. "Looks like your dad will only get probation for his part in helping dispose of your mom's body. The DA's got bigger fish to fry. Finneran's getting out of the hospital tomorrow. They'll move him straight to the prison in Trenton. Got a special wing there for disgraced New Jersey politicians."

"Really?"

"Joke, Audrey."

"Well, if they don't, they ought to. What I can't understand is how Spencer thought he'd get away with it," I say. "He should have realized that if I turned up dead, you'd never let up on the investigation."

"Oh, I'm just a dumb clod, right? Easy to dupe--no match for the likes of Spencer Finneran."

There's a jab in there for me too. "I'm sorry, Sean. I should have trusted you when you warned me to stay away from them. I was blinded, crazed. This thing with my parents—it consumed me."

He brushes my hand with his. Forgiven.

But I can't let go of the arrogance of Spencer's crime. "Spencer took such a risk. How could he have believed he wouldn't get caught?"

"I guess these guys reach a certain level of power and they think they're untouchable. How else can you explain Elliott Spitzer meeting hookers in midtown hotels? Jim McGreevey chasing guys when he was married to a woman? John Edwards denying paternity of his girlfriend's baby when a simple DNA test would expose him?"

"Maybe I'm not so shocked he was willing to risk killing me. But I still can't believe he would turn on—" Ethel bounds up. My mind flashes to Cal carrying her home to me. A lump rises in my throat. I can't go on.

The tendons in Coughlin's neck tighten. "Why are you wasting your tears on him, Audrey? He used you. He set you up to be killed."

"No! You weren't there. He didn't realize what Spencer was planning. Cal saved my life. He died for me. He threw his life away on Spencer Finneran. How can I not cry over that?"

"He made his choices. He chose wrong. He doesn't deserve your tears."

"Shut up!" I punch his arm. It's like punching one of the oaks lining the trail.

He grabs my clenched fist. "I won't apologize, Audrey. It would be a lie. Tremaine hurt you. That's the bottom line for me."

His protectiveness is endearing. Still, I resent the way he tries to dictate my emotions. "Give up, Sean. You'll never get me to deny the good in Cal."

"Better off without—" he mutters, looking away into the woods.

"Stop! You're like my father. You think you know everything."

"And you're like my mother—stubborn and starry-eyed."

We stand there glaring at each other. Then at the same moment, crack up.

"Why do we always argue like this?" I ask.

He reaches out and tugs my hair gently. "Why do boys pull girls' pigtails?"

Coughlin's body hulks there beside me, vulnerable as a fawn.

My smile fades. "I'm not ready for this, Sean, not ready to move on."

The sentence lands like a shotput between us. Coughlin steps away. "Understood. You don't have to tell me twice." His long stride pushes him ahead of me on the path.

"Sean, wait!"

He stops but doesn't turn. I touch his arm. The hairs on his wrist are downy and golden. "In a while…maybe…."

He hunches his shoulders against the breeze and keeps his eyes on the horizon. "I can live with maybe."

Chapter 55

The sound of pleading reaches me before I open the door. "What do you mean? Not even to wash pots?" Jill's voice escalates toward desperation. "C'mon, you have to let us come! Okay. Yeah, I understand. So maybe next year..." The receiver slips from her fingers as her head plops down on the desk. Her shoulders shake. I realize she's crying so hard she can't even catch her breath to wail.

"Jill, honey, what's the matter?"

"The Soup Kitchen wo-wo-n't let my mom and me work," she pauses to smear tears across her face with the back of her hand, "there on Thanksgiving."

"So?"

"Now we have to go to Uncle Ph-i-i-il's."

"Wait, you wanted to volunteer at the soup kitchen to get out of going to your Uncle Phil's house?"

"In Staten Island. It's awful. They make fun of mom and me. Try to trick us into eating meat. Snicker at my mom's Brussels sprouts. Ask stupid football questions they know we can't answer. It's ghastly. I can't go there again."

"So why don't you just stay home and have Thanksgiving at your house?" I ask.

"All alone? Just the two-o-o of us?" Jill keens like a coyote. "That's not what Thanksgiving is about."

Tell me about it. But if Jill and her mother are also lost souls on T-giving, maybe we can join forces. Trouble is, I can't cook and Jill and her mom live in a funky bungalow that's long on cats and short on conventional furniture. I wouldn't mind going there, but I don't really see Dad curling up on a Peruvian hammock as he tucks into his Tofurky, edamame and Brussels sprouts. And whither I go, Dad goest.

Ty comes in. He looks from Jill's tear-stained face to my grim one and back again. "I only been gone a half hour. Who's dead now?"

"No one. Jill's feeling down in the dumps about Thanksgiving."

"Really? This the first year in a long time I'm lookin' forward to it."

"How come this year is different?" Jill asks.

"'Cause last year I was in jail eatin' turkey slop off a foam tray with a spork. An' most years before that, my grandma didn't have enough money to buy all the food for a nice meal."

Ty drops into his favorite chair. "These white church ladies always comin' to our house to give us stuff. Dusty old cans from their kitchens that they didn't want no more. Pickled beets. Saurkraut. Chick peas. One year we got something called hearts of palm. My grandma opened it up just to see what was inside. Looked like soggy white sticks in water. Nasty."

One big basketball shoe swings as he warms to his story. "Worst thing about it, my grandma always hadda say, 'Oh, thank you very much.' Act all grateful an' shit. This year I told her, those ladies come knockin', you tell'em we don' need their damn hand-outs. I took my grandma to Shoprite yesterday. Told her to buy everything she needs. I paid for it all. She's startin' on the pies today—pumpkin and apple."

At the mention of pies, Jill's head drops on to her desk and she starts sobbing again.

Ty springs up. "What? What'd I say?"

"It's not you, Ty," I explain. "Jill's feeling like she and her mom don't have anyone they actually like to spend Thanksgiving with."

"Hell, ain't no use to cry over that. Come have Thanksgiving with us."

The switch controlling Jill's tears clicks off. "Really? We could come to Grandma Betty's house?"

"Sure. You know she likes you."

Jill immediately starts dialing. "Wait'll I tell my mom! No Uncle Phil for us."

Great. I've succeeded in finding a date for my date.

"How about you, Audge? What you doin' on Thursday?" Ty asks.

"Me? Oh, I think I'll just take my dad to a restaurant for dinner."

Ty looks like a freshman calculating a differential equation. "Restaurant? On Thanksgiving? Why don't you come to my Grandma's house too? You know she l-o-o-ves you."

"Oh, no…I couldn't. It would be too many people for your grandma to feed…with my dad and all…an imposition."

"You an your old man don't eat that much, Audge. This is one big-ass turkey." Ty picks up the sports section of the *Times* and points to me with it. "You comin'."

The turkey in question does, in fact, have a really big ass. So big that Grandma Betty can't get it into her apartment oven. Which is why, at six AM Thanksgiving morning, the party is moved to my place. Now my condo is stuffed fuller than the fowl who's given his life for our eating pleasure. Folding tables normally used for estate sales stretch all the way across my living room. Borrowing a variety of mismatched china and silverware from the Sister Alice cache, Jill has set the table for eighteen. As the smell of roasting turkey fills the air, Jill and Ty's Aunt Vonda discuss the pros and cons of African braiding, while Jill's mom and Marcus debate sustainable agriculture.

Vonda's husband, Wesley, works the room dispensing beverages. Ty and his cousins watch the football game. The youngest and oldest persons in the room are together: Dad is teaching six year old Kyle to play chess. Their heads, one grey, one dark, nearly touch over the board.

"Audrey," Grandma Betty yells, "you stirrin' that gravy like I said?"

I dash back into the kitchen. As a private in Betty's culinary army, I've learned it's not wise to leave my post. "How much longer 'til showtime?" I ask.

"Five minutes. You start bringing out those vegetables. Vonda, get the potatoes workin'."

In a final surge of energy from the cook, the food emerges from the kitchen. Bowls and platters cover the table from end to end and everyone gathers around. There's a moment of quiet as we admire the feast.

"Let's eat!" Kyle shouts.

I'm about to agree, when Betty takes Kyle's hand, then Ty's. "Not so fast, young man. First, we got to give thanks to the Lord for this fine day and all He has provided."

Uh-oh, I forgot about the whole saying grace aspect of Thanksgiving. I watch Dad closely as hands begin to link around the table. Will he go along?

Kyle snatches Dad's left hand. I exhale in relief as he doesn't pull away, and I pick up his right. When the circle is fully linked, Betty begins.

"Dear Lord, we just want to thank you for the glory and power of your amazing works in bringing us such a *magnificent* dinner this year….."

"Uh-huh." Vonda and Wesley murmur an affirmation.

I should have known this wouldn't be the quick and tidy Episcopal grace of my grandmother's table. I cast a furtive glance from under my bangs. How's Dad holding up? Everyone else is looking down, but Dad is studying Betty intently.

"...and Lord, we want to offer up praise for gathering in so many of your lambs that we thought might be lost, but they ain't lost no more..."

"Praise Jesus!" Vonda shouts.

Ty and Marcus manage to look both embarrassed and grateful. Dad's gaze hasn't left Betty's face.

I'm hoping Betty might be winding down, but she seems to be gathering more steam.

"...and Lord we want to shout our praise for sending us the gift of a woman who opened up her home to us today and who gave our Ty a second chance and that would be your sweet child, Audrey..."

"Shout it out!' Vonda calls.

"Uh-huh," the rest of the guests murmur. Dad is silent. I feel his fingers twitch in my hand.

Poor little Kyle is ready to face-plant into the mashed potatoes as Betty takes yet another breath.

"Lord, ain't none of us know what tomorrow will bring. Might be joy, might be pain. We try to walk on a righteous path, Lord, but let's face it, we all sinners and we probably gonna stray. But we know you gonna forgive us. That's what keeps us goin'. Brothers and sisters, believe the good news—we are forgiven!"

Silence shimmers and twists before us. I can't look up.

"Amen." A piping little whisper. Kyle.

"Amen," a ragged chorus as we break our chain. Kyle is watching Dad, noticing his lips aren't moving. He elbows my father sharply.

Dad turns to face me.

"Amen."

ABOUT THE AUTHOR

S.W. Hubbard's most recent novel is *Another Man's Treasure*. She is also is the author of three mystery novels set in the Adirondack Mountains: *Take the Bait, Swallow the Hook,* and *Blood Knot.* Her short stories have appeared in *Alfred Hitchcock's Mystery Magazine* and the anthologies *Crimes by Moonlight, Adirondack Mysteries,* and the upcoming *Mystery Box.* She lives in Morristown, NJ, where she teaches creative writing to enthusiastic teens and adults, and expository writing to reluctant college freshmen.

Visit her at www.swhubbard.net.

Made in the USA
Lexington, KY
29 September 2019